APHRODITE

D.G. Rampton

Front cover image: detail from *Portrait of a Woman* by Jean Marc Nattier

Cover design: Dan Kenny Design

www.dgrampton.com

Acknowledgements

To my extraordinary editor Ingrid Ronga, I couldn't have done this without you. Two novels together and counting! I am in awe of your meticulous brain and your generosity, you lift me up with your words.

To the multi-talented Claudia Neal-Shaw, thank you for offering me your insightful perspective. You're a force of nature and I treasure your input in work and life.

And the biggest thank you of all must go to my husband who has had to put up with all sorts of deprivations in the name of my art, and yet is always ready to offer love, support and much-needed shoulder rubs.

This book is dedicated
to all the feisty and wise women in my life.

The Regency Goddesses Series

The novels in the Regency Goddesses series are standalone and can be enjoyed in any order. They share only one minor character (have you spotted them yet?).

Chronological order:

Artemisia – Book 1 (1812)
Aphrodite – Book 2 (1820)
Aurora – Book 3 (1821)

"Delightful, funny and filled with clever conversation. Two thumbs up!"
A. Sockwell

"There are so few Regency novels that are this well-written, with such strong characters, a good plot and sexy, but clean relationships."
C. Sparks

"An enthralling Regency romp full of endearing and meddlesome characters, a stubborn hero and heroine, and hilariously entertaining mix-ups and tangles!"
Austenesque Reviews

"Truly witty, delightful characters …. the author has mastered the art of satire with a heart."
Dragonlady

Love is ageless and we are ageless in love.

One

Baroness Hartwood, a widow of two years standing, looked across at the gentleman seated beside her on the settee in her drawing room and asked: 'Albert, you have given your nephew a hint not to stare at April, have you not?'

'I've had no opportunity to do so as yet,' replied The Right Honourable the Viscount Paisley, a genial man on the shady side of fifty and with a decided trend towards corpulence. 'Hugh wouldn't do so, in any case. He's never been one to be enslaved by a pretty face – quite the opposite actually!'

Lady Hartwood's large blue eyes regarded him with a good deal of uncertainty.

'No doubt you know best, dearest. . . only, it *would* be unfortunate if he were to do so. You know how April dislikes to be stared at. And not for the world would I want to see my daughter give a relative of yours a sharp set-down, as I fear she is entirely capable of doing!' she admitted, wringing her hands.

Lord Paisley, who considered himself fortunate to have secured her ladyship's acceptance to enter the married state a second time, took hold of her dainty fingers in a comforting grip.

'Don't let it worry you, my love. I'd like to see April – or anyone else, for that matter – give Hugh a set-down. The shoe is firmly on the other foot,' he chuckled.

Lady Hartwood was a little daunted by this not entirely favourable description of Mr Hugh Royce. From all she had previously heard of him, he was a well-liked man of good character and with an outlandish fortune to his name, and he was one day to inherit the Marquisate of Talbott from a great-uncle who still clung tenaciously to life.

'Is he not an amiable person?' she asked anxiously.

'Oh, he's perfectly amiable when it suits him! But he's not one to suffer fools or sycophants gladly. And why should he? He's had enough to try his patience these last few years. Ever since he inherited that obscene fortune from his miser of a father, everyone remotely related to him has been coming out of the woodwork to claim kinship and milk his generosity.'

'Oh dear, that *would* try one's amiability, to be sure.'

'Not to mention all the matchmaking mothers who make a beeline for him whenever he strays into their vicinity. I'm half inclined to think he only offered for the Starling girl to take himself off the marriage-mart. That's certainly the only explanation I can think of as to why he's decided to leg-shackle himself to such a strait-laced prude. Had she been born a man, she'd have made an excellent vicar! All propriety and sobriety.'

'There is still time for them to realise their mistake,' said Lady Hartwood with her customary optimism. 'It is clear they are sadly ill-matched. . . not that I know the circumstances *personally*, of course,' she hastened to add. 'I have simply gathered as much from all you have said on the matter.'

'Well, it's true,' he sighed. 'I can't say I like to see Hugh throwing himself away on her, but it's none of my business. At least she won't inflict any dramatics on him, the way my sister used to do on his father! Not wishing to speak ill of the dead but there's no denying Georgina was a terrible wife and mother. . . not much of a sister either, if I'm being honest.'

'I'm sorry to hear that, dearest,' said Lady Hartwood, giving his hand a squeeze.

'Oh, I didn't mind overly much! I was never close to either of my sisters. But Hugh. . . well, I wish I could have done more for the boy. He wasn't raised in a happy household.' Shaking off his brooding expression, he smiled and said philosophically: 'I suppose one can't blame him for preferring an insipid wife to one overflowing with sensibility and loose morals.'

Having her own particular interest in this subject, Lady Hartwood asked: 'Are you *certain* there is no love between Miss Starling and your nephew? One would not wish them to suffer if their engagement should – for some reason – come to an end.'

'Hugh keeps his cards close to his chest but, to my mind, a man in love doesn't treat his fiancée with the type of cordiality he reserves for his relations.'

Lady Hartwood digested this information with satisfaction.

'In any case, dearest,' she remarked after a few moments, 'we must do all we can to make a good impression on Mr Royce this evening.'

Correctly interpreting this gentle reminder, his lordship said reassuringly: 'I'll arrive early tonight, my love, and the moment Hugh enters the house I'll drop a word in his ear not to stare at April.'

Lady Hartwood smiled. It was a lovely, warm smile that infused her whole complexion and gave her the appearance of a woman much younger than her true age of seven and forty.

She had never been a beauty of the first order, but her sweet countenance, girlish figure and impeccable sense of style had always commanded a high degree of admiration. She had married young and had quickly produced a daughter, her only child, some twenty-eight years ago, and for a good number of those years had become used to people mistaking her for her daughter's sister.

This compliment was always graciously accepted by her. She might not be an overly vain woman, but she did possess a healthy degree of pride in her appearance, and, together with her lady's maid, worked tirelessly to always appear at her best.

As Lord Paisley held her hand and looked adoringly into her eyes, she felt herself to be the most fortunate of women to have secured the affections of a man who was so obliging as to always hold her comfort as his chief concern; a felicity she had not experienced in her first marriage.

'Thank you, dearest,' she said. 'I don't know why I should be so nervous about meeting your nephew, but so it is! I suppose I don't wish him to find anything to censure in myself or April.'

'Hugh's in no position to judge you,' said Lord Paisley firmly. 'And I'd think it a great impertinence if he did so! But I'm certain the thought would never even enter his head. He might be of the highest ton, but he isn't top-lofty.' He paused briefly, before continuing: 'That said, you may as well know, my love, he's not one to recommend himself to the ladies. Doesn't have the address for it – never did! But although he looks boorish, and may act it on occasion, he's a capital fellow when one gets to know him.'

A little unsettled by this confidence, Lady Hartwood professed that she was thankful he would be at her side to welcome his nephew that evening.

However, despite Lord Paisley's best intentions, she was not to have this comfort.

Mr Royce was shown into her drawing room and announced by her aged butler one hour earlier than he was expected.

As the visitor stood on the threshold and took in the startled expression of the youthful-looking lady who inhabited the room, he realised there had been some mistake.

'Forgive me for intruding,' he said with a bow. 'I believe your mother is expecting me?'

Lady Hartwood could only blink in astonishment at the uncommonly large male who filled her doorway.

Hugh cast a look of enquiry at the butler, but the old man simply shrugged and, eager to be off to rest his aching joints, retreated from the room and closed the door behind him.

'Oh my!' her ladyship exclaimed softly and let out a nervous laugh.

She put aside the novel she had been enjoying, while waiting for her betrothed to make an appearance, and rose to her feet.

'Welcome, Mr Royce... please, *do* come in. I... I apologise if I appear a little surprised, only, you see, your uncle informed me that you could come no earlier than eight o'clock, owing to a previous engagement.'

Hugh's harsh features relaxed into a smile.

'I *did* have a prior engagement, but I told him I would make certain to leave early and join you all at seven. It appears he didn't absorb the information.'

'I daresay he did not!' she laughed, more naturally this time. 'I have come to realise Albert does not care overly much for details.'

'Please accept my apologies. You must be wishing me to Jericho! I'll take myself off and return at eight. There's nothing more calculated to put me in your mother's black books than to arrive an hour early for dinner.'

'Oh, there is not the least need for you to be concerned! I thank you for the compliment of mistaking me for my daughter, but *I* am Lady Hartwood.' She extended a hand to him. 'How do you do?'

A flicker of surprise registered in Hugh's eyes.

'My uncle is most fortunate.' Executing a bow over her hand, he added with a grin: 'I now understand why he developed a sudden sense of familial duty and extended his stay with my Aunt Mathilda in Cornwall. As a rule, they fight like cat and dog so their visits to each other are usually brief and far-in-between.'

'Yes, Mathilda is an acquaintance of mine and has often referred to her quarrelsome scoundrel of a brother,' she said, smiling. 'But now of course I know she must have been funning. Albert is nothing of the sort! Please.' She indicated for him to be seated and sat down herself. 'They do nip at each other but nothing to signify.'

'You must be able to bring out their best behaviour, ma'am. I hope my uncle recognises his good fortune in having captured your affections.'

Lady Hartwood blushed and deflected his praise with a few incoherent murmurs.

She was rapidly amending her first impression of her guest. Initially, all she had been able to take in was the image of a tall and powerful brute of a man, negligently dressed in the clothes of a gentleman. It must have been the shock of having him arrive unexpectedly that had given her such a fanciful notion, she decided, for after spending a few minutes in his company it was clear that he was really rather good-natured.

It was a shame there was no hint of this in his outward appearance as people were bound to judge him unfairly. His swarthy countenance held little beauty and his size could not help but overwhelm. However, she of all people knew the pitfalls of judging on looks alone. Her late husband had been blessed with extraordinary beauty on the outside and little to speak of on the inside, and she had quickly learnt that one could not depend on a handsome countenance for one's happiness.

Hugh's acquaintances would have been surprised to hear the word *good-natured* used to describe him, or to see him exert himself in that direction. But it had not taken him long to realise that he was in the presence of a pure soul, and he had set out to banish the doe-like alarm in his hostess' eyes.

He was succeeding in his task to such a degree that when he asked whether she had made the acquaintance of her future father-in-law, Lady Hartwood found herself confiding in him.

'I have not as yet been introduced to the Earl of Wulfingston,' she said a little despondently. 'He never responded to Albert's letter informing him of our betrothal, and... and I cannot help but feel that he does not wish to recognise me.'

'I wouldn't let that concern you, ma'am. As head of the family the old rascal takes it upon himself to rage and disapprove of us all. It's a habit with him by now and he enjoys the sport of it so much it would be cruel to expect him to give it up. Personally, I hold him in great affection and do all I can to set up his back.'

Lady Hartwood could not help laughing but shook her head.

'I cannot believe that course of action is open to *me*.'

All at once, the drawing room door burst open, and Miss April Hartwood hurried into the room in a state of considerable disarray.

Her dark hair was partly down over her face, a dozen hairpins were jutting out of her mouth, and both her hands were busy removing the remaining pins from her coiffure.

'Quick, Mama, you must help me before Rachel sees us!' she said on a laugh, forcing the words out through the pins.

She looked surreptitiously behind her and pushed the door shut with her foot.

'Her attempts at dressing my hair are abysmal,' she continued, 'but the poor girl is taking such pains over her new duties I don't have the heart to criticise her.'

As she spoke, she ran her fingers through her hair to remove the last of the pins, then tossed back the whole glorious mass until it settled about her head like a dusky halo.

Her gaze landed on their guest...and she froze.

The smile that had been playing about Hugh's lips at the entrance of an unguarded and tousled young lady slowly faded.

Good God, he thought to himself.

He had never before encountered such a face; it really was quite extraordinary.

Her eyes alone would have earned her a place amongst the chief beauties of the day. Their colour was an astonishing cerulean blue with a pale green, almost yellow, centre. And they were large and so wide-set that they gave her an exotic, other-worldly appearance.

Her eyes, however, were not the end of it. The good-fairies that had been present at her birth had been most generous: a heart-shaped face, flawless complexion, soaring eyebrows and plump lips. He had the fanciful notion that each item had been drawn by the hand of a master for not one could be improved upon.

Had he been of a disposition to fall in love with such a blatant show of beauty he would have felt uneasy about the prospect of welcoming her into his family.

He could only be thankful that his disposition was otherwise.

Surveying her with critical interest, he hoped she would not prove to be too vain and wearisome, as past experience had taught him to expect from women of her breed.

Rising politely to his feet, he looked over at his hostess and waited for the necessary introductions.

'April-love, let me present you to Mr Royce...Albert's nephew, of course,' said Lady Hartwood agitatedly. 'Mr Royce, my daughter, Miss Hartwood...I must beg your pardon, sir, you have had a most abysmal welcome so far!'

'Not at all,' he returned. 'I can see I have put you out. Besides, we should lay the blame where it is deserved: at my uncle's door.'

Turning back to Miss Hartwood, he was amused to find her still staring at him.

It was rare for a gently bred young lady to regard him so openly. His looks alone were usually enough to subdue them into a submissiveness he found irritating. Yet Miss Hartwood was not only blatantly surveying him, but there was also an admiring quality in her gaze.

He would have had to be insensate not to respond to it on some level.

He smiled.

It slowly dawned on April that she was gawking at their guest in a truly improper manner.

And what was worse, she was doing so with a dozen hairpins sticking out of her mouth. She quickly whipped them out and hid them in her hand.

'I apologise for intruding before I was expected, Miss Hartwood,' Hugh addressed her in an easy manner.

This won him a look of approval from Lady Hartwood, who was relieved to see he appeared perfectly capable of retaining his wits when faced with her daughter's beauty.

'We are delighted to welcome you,' replied April, making an effort to smile. 'You are almost family, Mr Royce, and one does not stand on ceremony with family.'

She stepped forward and held out her hand... then quickly withdrew it. The hairpins landed softly on the rug by her feet and the hand was once more extended out to him.

Hugh gave no indication of having noticed the small interruption and clasped her hand in his own large one.

A sudden jolt of sensation surged through them both, and each caught the look of surprise in the other's eyes.

'Call me Hugh.'

'Thank you... and you too.'

Amusement crinkled his eyes.

'I don't believe it would be proper for me to call you *Hugh*, Miss Hartwood.'

'Oh, I... I did not mean...' She paused, frustrated by her own gaucheness. 'I would be pleased if you would call me April.'

'April.' He turned the name over on his tongue, not quite ready to let it go.

'Odd, is it not? To be named after a month? I suppose I should be thankful Mama did not take a fancy to December!'

'I like it. It suits you.'

April smiled.

And this time it was not her society smile that made an appearance but an entirely natural, spontaneous one that only those close to her knew well.

Hugh was unaccountably shaken to see the fierceness of her beauty was softened by the charm of that smile, and one endearingly crooked front tooth. It transformed her from a lofty goddess of perfection, into a warm and altogether too-enticing creature.

It was in that moment that he sensed danger.

Lady Hartwood watched their exchange with great interest and thought to herself that her betrothed had seriously misled her when he had said his nephew did not possess the type of address that recommended him to the female sex.

Evidently, Albert knew nothing about the female sex!

She had never before seen her daughter so affected by a man, and it was all she could do to suppress a smile. Clearing her throat delicately, she broke the silence that had engulfed the room.

'It is a shame your fiancée could not join us this evening, Mr Royce,' she remarked. 'I hope we will have an opportunity to become acquainted with her shortly?'

April snatched her hand out of Hugh's grip (where it had inexplicably remained all this time).

'I shall be certain to introduce Miss Starling to you at the earliest opportunity,' replied Hugh, regaining his smile.

The butler's heavy, shuffling gait was heard out in the corridor and, in the next instant, he entered the room and announced Lord Paisley.

'What the devil are you doing here?' boomed his lordship on catching sight of his nephew. 'Don't you know not to intrude on your hostess before the agreed time?'

'Dearest, I forbid you to scold Mr Royce,' said Lady Hartwood. 'It was your own fault he thought he was expected at seven.'

'I don't know why the deuced fellow thought *that!* But if you forbid me to scold, my love, I shall oblige you,' he replied, raising her hand to his lips.

He immediately perceived some tension in her and looked up to scan the other occupants of the room.

His nephew returned his scrutiny with unruffled composure. However, April was looking flushed and ill-at-ease and he wondered as to the cause. He would have understood a show of displeasure from her, if Hugh had been so mutton-headed as to forget his manners over her pretty face, but that did not appear to be the case.

'Good evening, my dear,' he addressed her in his paternal way. 'Have you done something new with your hair? I can't profess to be a connoisseur of such things but it looks different to me. Most fetching, in fact.'

April laughed and walked over to plant a fond kiss on his cheek.

'Albert, how can you give me such an absurd compliment? I must look a fright! Mama, gentlemen, please excuse me while I make myself presentable.'

Once she had left the room, Lord Paisley looked across at his nephew.

'If you've done something to upset her, Hugh, I'll have your hide for it!'

'Really, Albert, he has done no such thing!' insisted Lady Hartwood. 'April simply needed my assistance with her coiffeur and was a little disconcerted when she realised Mr Royce was also in the room.'

Hugh returned his uncle's critical look with a wry smile and did not defend himself. He was hard-pressed to understand, let alone explain, what had just occurred between April and himself.

The girl was ravishing without question, but he had never been even mildly interested in the society beauties that had been thrust his way over the years. And although his fiancée was considered to be a pretty young woman, he had chosen her for her sweet disposition and strict morality, rather than any superficial physical attributes.

If anything, April's looks did her a disservice in his eyes... so he was damned if he knew why he felt as if fate had just thrown a punch at him.

April entered her bedchamber and immediately made her way to her mirror. It confirmed what she already suspected: her cheeks were flushed, and her hair was in a state of tousled abandon. She looked positively wild.

She groaned and, walking over to her dressing table, began to quickly pin up her hair into some semblance of order.

What in heaven's name was wrong with her, she wondered. One would have thought that she of all people would know better than to be dazzled by physical appearance!

What did it matter that the man had such a handsome countenance?

Or an engaging sparkle in his eyes, for that matter?

Or that he was modeled along Olympian lines and looked as if he could lift her above his head with the greatest of ease? What an utterly stupid attribute to possess, after all! It served no practical purpose whatsoever to be able to lift a woman above your head.

The image that this absurd scenario conjured up drew a smile from her.

'You are a silly creature,' she told her reflection. 'He may be the incarnate of some girlish ideal but that does not excuse your conduct. You are eight and twenty and not some schoolroom miss addicted to novels. And if that salutary note is not enough to subdue you, then the fact that he is an engaged man must do so!'

After talking to herself in this bracing manner for a few minutes, and resolving to treat Hugh as if he were a cousin she had known from birth, she smoothed out her skirts, unconsciously wetted her lips, and returned downstairs.

Two

One brief glance at Hugh as she entered the room was enough to convince April that the intensity of her reaction to him was not dulled by being relived a second time.

Pushing this appalling realisation out of her mind, she went to sit beside Lord Paisley and drew him into conversation, leaving her mother to entertain their other guest without her assistance.

Lady Hartwood was in the midst of sharing with Hugh her conviction that poor Queen Caroline's recent death was no doubt precipitated by the mortification of her husband refusing her admittance into Westminster Abbey for his coronation, when a casual glance at her daughter startled her sufficiently to make her lose her train of thought.

April's hair had been pinned up high on her head into something that could only be described as resembling a bird's nest; one that looked to be in imminent danger of toppling over.

Lady Hartwood attempted to catch her daughter's eye and bring this problem to her attention, but her subtlety went unheeded. And as Hugh was patiently waiting for her to continue her story, she had to abandon her attempts and console herself with the reflection that the gentlemen at least did not appear to notice anything amiss.

And in this she was correct. Lord Paisley was not one to disassemble the overall effect of a lady's appearance, while his nephew barely glanced in April's direction.

When dinner was announced, some minutes later, Hugh was the first to stand and offer his arm to Lady Hartwood.

His uncle, however, had other ideas and shooed him away without any compunction, claiming a greater priority. Then, taking his betrothed's hand into the crook of his arm, led her out of the room.

Unable to do anything else, Hugh offered April the same courtesy he had extended to her mother, but in a manner so curt and reserved that her sense of humour rather perversely reared its head.

'You quite terrify me with such formal manners!' she remarked. 'There's not the least need for you to offer me your arm, Cousin Hugh. We agreed to not stand on ceremony with each other, did we not?'

'So, we did... *Cousin* April,' he replied, smiling at her usage of such a familial term.

April's amusement faltered. She felt perfectly capable of handling the aloof version of the man before her, but when he smiled at her she had the strangest sensation that her legs could no longer adequately support her weight.

Hugh, in turn, had just discovered that he had been unfair to label April's lips as merely plump. At this close distance he could see the exquisite undulating curve of the top lip and the opulent swell of the bottom one. Their crimson colour gave her the appearance of having just eaten cherries and he felt a sudden urge to kiss away the cherry stain.

He looked away, frowning.

Freed from his gaze, April headed for the door and, as they passed out of the room, tried to think of a subject with which to begin a conversation.

Finally, and rather desperately, she blurted out: 'Albert told us you were in the war!'

Hugh looked down at her with faint surprise and she winced inwardly.

'I hope you don't mind that he discussed the matter with us?' she said, forcing herself to continue more naturally. 'He is very proud of you. I understand your career was most distinguished.'

'That is taking it to a grander level than it deserves.'

'You were at Waterloo, were you not? And were awarded a medal of some sort – I'm sorry, I forget the name?'

'It's of no consequence,' he replied in a detached way. 'I was merely following orders and keeping myself alive long enough to fulfil those orders. And as all this occurred over five years ago – when I was still too foolish to know any better – any expectations of heroism from me are bound to be disappointed.'

'Surely you are being too harsh on yourself?'

'Not at all. Watching your friends die while you survive has a way of focusing the mind on what is important and what is not. And the battle-crazed exploits of my youth don't deserve admiration.'

April risked a sideward glance at him.

She did not know what she was trying to uncover in his uncompromising profile and suddenly felt as if she was encroaching on his privacy and looked away. She could understand why he did not want to benefit from a war that had brought so much loss to so many.

Judging that her sympathy would only be rebuffed if she tried to articulate it, she decided instead to lighten the mood.

'Well, no one could accuse you of pumping up your own achievements, but you need not fear allowing me to judge for myself. I will not be inclined to think your actions deserving of praise beyond their true merit, and if I find them unworthy, I shall be certain to tell you so!'

'Now you alarm me.'

He stepped to the side to allow her to pass into the dining room before him.

'There is not the least need for alarm,' she laughed over her shoulder. 'I always play fair.'

A smile was won from him.

Following her to the table, he waved aside the footman who was waiting to pull out her chair and performed the task himself. April was uncertain what to make of this gallantry, for he appeared to offer it absentmindedly and did not even glance at her when she thanked him.

Taking his seat beside her, Hugh kept his attention fixed on Lady Hartwood and his uncle across the dinner table. Lord Paisley was in the act of kissing her ladyship's hand and looking upon her with great tenderness, and it struck Hugh that he had never before seen his uncle, a confirmed bachelor until now, so besotted.

'Have you decided on a date for the wedding ceremony?' he asked them.

'No, not as yet,' replied Lord Paisley. 'I would marry Eleanor tomorrow if she would let me, but she favours a long engagement – don't you, my love? But perhaps early in the new year?'

He regarded her so eagerly as he said this that Lady Hartwood felt obliged to nod.

'Yes... I... I hope so, dearest,' she answered with a noticeable lack of conviction.

Reaching for the glass of wine her butler had just poured for her, she raised it to her lips and turned her large, expressive eyes to her daughter, pleading for support.

April offered her a reassuring smile and said: 'My mother is yet to meet your family and friends, Albert, and she feels that a long engagement would be best as it would allow them time to become acquainted with her.'

'Yes, that is what I feel!' agreed Lady Hartwood.

'I don't care in the slightest what my family or friends think of you!' insisted Lord Paisley. 'Not that anyone could think of you as anything less than perfection, my love. Nevertheless, if it is your wish, I'm content to wait and allow you time to adjust to the notion of becoming my wife.'

'Oh, *Albert*,' sighed Lady Hartwood, much moved. 'I don't need time to adjust to the notion of becoming your wife. I would happily marry you tomorrow!'

'Then why don't we do just that? Maybe not tomorrow, but I could get my hands on a special license by the end of the week.'

Her ladyship, recollecting the obstacles to be overcome, was at a loss for words.

'Yes... um... we could, of course, dearest... but... that would surely be improper... and people would say it was all rushed for some horrid reason... and... and...' She turned to April for assistance once more.

But this time her daughter withheld her support. She would be only too happy to see Albert overcome her mother's scruples, which to her mind were quite absurd.

'But, my love,' said Lord Paisley, 'if two people of our mature years want to marry, surely what other's think can be of little consequence?'

Lady Hartwood nodded mutely, feeling cornered.

It was impossible for her to confess the real reason for her procrastination... her mother.

A mother who was in fact *not* deceased, as she had led her betrothed to believe, and who was withholding her permission for her daughter to marry until such a time as April found a husband.

Lady Hartwood shuddered as she remembered the awful scene that had followed her mother's announcement of this condition. April had argued with her grandmother in a manner that had quite overset her ladyship's nerves; and when that line of attack had failed to produce results, she had turned her attention on an easier target and had begged her mother to marry Albert *immediately*, parental consent be damned.

Lady Hartwood, however, had lived her whole life under the heavy-handed influence of her formidable parent and found it impossible to disobey her; and particularly since that parent was always willing to help her out of the monetary embarrassments she found herself in all too frequently.

But most importantly of all, Lady Hartwood would not go against her mother's wishes because, on this occasion, she was in complete agreement with them. It was time for April to marry.

To her mind, the only opportunity a woman had of finding happiness was to start a family. And if a little good-intentioned blackmail was needed to secure this opportunity for April, then she saw it as her duty to reconcile herself to this necessary evil.

With the weight of her companions' gazes bearing down on her, she twisted the napkin in her lap with nervous hands, until she could bear it no longer and burst out: 'I have vowed to not remarry until my daughter is wed!'

A stunned silence followed this pronouncement.

Three pairs of eyes turned to look at April; one pair begging for forgiveness.

April was not easily brought to blush but for the second time that evening a warm glow infused her complexion.

'I am sorry, Albert,' she said with commendable composure. 'I have repeatedly attempted to convince my mother that I am content with my spinsterhood, but she won't be satisfied until I am ensconced in the married state. . . and I have finally been brought around to her way of thinking.'

'I did not know you'd met a young man, my dear?' said Lord Paisley, looking bewildered.

'Oh, I haven't!' she replied, eyes twinkling at the absurdity of it. 'But you will be happy to know that I am on the lookout for him and am not in the least fussy. Anyone will do really, as long as they are unmarried and male.'

'April-love, must you?' Lady Hartwood admonished weakly. 'Hugh does not yet understand the levity of your character and may mistake your jokes for the truth.'

'Well, he would be a simpleton to do so, and I don't think he is that – are you, Cousin Hugh?'

'Not to my knowledge,' he replied equably.

'No, I have decided that you are not. In fact, I suspect you of being a good judge of character. You may even be useful in my search for a husband.'

'I admit to knowing several unmarried males. Are there any further criteria you require in a partner for life?'

She felt a twinge of vexation that she could not tell if he was teasing or mocking her. She speared some asparagus with her fork and took a bite, appearing to consider his question.

'I would prefer if he were not a hunchback,' she mused. 'One has to consider the children, after all. And it would be nice if he had all his own teeth, although that is not a necessity. Even intelligence is negotiable. I have often observed that the most intelligent of men tend to be the most conceited and critical.'

'Must he be able to incite affection and esteem, or are they also negotiable?' asked Hugh as he studied her, giving nothing away.

She grew uncomfortably warm under his look, and was then angry with herself for caring what he thought of her. It was none of his business if she had decided to contract a marriage of convenience.

Not that she had decided anything of the sort. She was simply *pretending* to acquiesce to her grandmother's wishes.

'And what of fortune?' continued Hugh. 'A consideration, surely?'

April no longer doubted that he was mocking her, and her smile glinted dangerously.

'Why, of course!' she replied with a toss of her head that caused the unstable mass of hair on top to wobble precariously. 'I can think of nothing I want more than to marry a fortune.'

Lady Hartwood stared at her with dismay and felt driven to exclaim: 'I beg you stop your teasing, love! What must our guest think of you?'

'He is free to think whatever he wishes,' responded her daughter, a martial light in her eyes.

'Eleanor, you can't be serious in wanting to wait until April is married?' Lord Paisley spoke up, steering the conversation back to its original purpose.

'But I *am* serious, dearest,' said Lady Hartwood, relieved that a part-truth had escaped her lips rather than an outright lie, for she could now defend it with conviction. 'I cannot reconcile it with my conscience to be blissfully happy as your wife when my child will be all alone in the world.'

'But, my love, she will not be alone! April, I thought I did not need to say, you are very welcome to live with your mother and me? In fact, I depend on you to do so! I have become attached to your company and would miss you greatly if you did not.'

'Albert, I thank you with all my heart,' she replied through the lump in her throat. 'I would love it above all things to call you Father. You have been kinder and more caring towards me than my own ever was. And you have my promise that I will invade your house for months at a time without the least invitation! But I cannot and will not become your dependent – I hope you can understand?'

'Well, I shan't press you now, my dear,' said Lord Paisley gruffly. 'We will speak of this again another time.'

With his companions temporarily overcome with emotion, it was left to Hugh to revive the conversation.

'Have you visited London before, Lady Hartwood, or is this your first trip to the capital?'

'Oh, yes, we have visited before,' she replied, offering him a grateful look. 'But only twice. And we did not go into Society. . . my late husband was not fond of public life.'

'Mama, you wrong him,' said April. 'He simply refused to go to the expense of hiring a house for the Season. The most we could hope for was one or two weeks in a *respectable* hotel. Nothing modish or indecently priced, you understand. . . certainly no Grillon's or the Pulteney.'

'I take it you didn't agree with his economy?' asked Hugh.

A footman was serving between them in that moment and she found it perfectly natural to avoid meeting his gaze.

'How could I? What young girl wants to consider economy when her life's ambition is centred around going to balls and parties? Poor Papa! To have sired such a frivolous daughter. But I have since come to understand his penny-pinching. The estate could not have supported such an expense.'

'You were never frivolous, love, and I defy anyone to say so!' said Lady Hartwood loyally. 'I will always be grateful to your father for having the good sense to leave the management of the St Mawes estate to you. If you hadn't taken over the reins when you did, the creditors would have left us penniless.'

'Ah, but that was pure necessity,' replied April. 'It does not negate the frivolity of my nature.'

'But it does show you capable of overcoming it,' Hugh put in.

She looked across at him with surprise, and the sharp movement caused her already lopsided mass of hair to slip further down her head, until it sat at a peculiar angle over her right ear.

April registered none of this as she returned Hugh's gaze. She was still smarting from his earlier remarks and was unwilling to accept approval from him. However, his dark eyes were cool and reserved, certainly not approving.

'At all events, Mama,' she continued, looking away, 'you would not have been left without an income.'

'Oh, yes – something about contracts protecting part of my dowry? My mother's doing, of course! She has always been. . . ' Lady Hartwood hesitated, looking self-conscious, '. . . she *was* always so clever with money. And I have found it such a comfort to know that, had we lost St Mawes, we could have lived on the proceeds of my dowry quite happily in a quaint little cottage somewhere.'

April had to stifle a laugh at the absurdity of her mother living in a cottage.

Having acquired the habit of commanding the luxuries of life from infancy, Lady Hartwood was incapable of economising. As the much-loved natural daughter and only child of an earl who had never married, Lady

Hartwood had resided in his wealthy household along with her mother. And when her parents had arranged an advantageous marriage for her with a distant relative of her father's, she had swapped the luxuries of an earldom in Dorset for those of an affluent barony in Cornwall.

It was therefore unsurprising that when a run of disastrous investments decimated her husband's fortune, it was rather late in the day for Lady Hartwood to master the principles of economy.

Her expensive habits had been the cause of much aggravation in her married life. Her husband had not been a man who excited – or had much use for – such tender concepts as love and affection, and whatever attraction had driven him to marry, it had not lasted long enough to oil the cogs of married life.

From an early age April had learnt to manage her father's hard character and had enjoyed his respect, if not his affection, but Lady Hartwood was made from a gentler mould and had suffered greatly. April had always resented her father's uncompromising manner towards her mother and had tried her best to shield her from it, but when he had fallen ill and she had assumed the running of the estate, she had discovered the extent of her mother's debts and had had to own that (in this at least) his provocation had been great.

'Speaking of contracts,' Lord Paisley addressed April, breaking in on her thoughts. 'Did my secretary visit you today with the rental documents for this house?'

'He did, poor man,' she replied, smiling. 'I kept him here for over two hours and had him explaining every clause in painstaking detail. He was terribly kind and patient. Thank you for sending him to me.'

'No, no, you need not thank me. I only wish you had allowed me to settle it all for you.'

'Had I allowed you to bamboozle me into such a thing you would have found a way to saddle yourself with the rental costs. And I, for one, can see no reason why I should burden you with my expenses. And, besides, you have already done me a great service by engaging all the necessary staff before our arrival and sparing me the pain of interviewing the applicants.'

'Do you like the house?' Hugh asked.

'It is difficult not to! I had not thought my resources could stretch to such a grand property as this, and, from what I have learnt, in one of the best addresses to be had in town. I don't know how you managed to find it for us, Albert?'

Lord Paisley smiled conspiratorially at his nephew.

'Well, if you must know, my dear, I'm on friendly terms with the landlord.'

April turned startled eyes to Hugh and said in a manner that sounded suspiciously like an accusation: 'This is *your* house?'

Three

Hugh took a leisurely drink of his wine, his gaze remaining on her over the rim of his glass.

'My house is in St James's Square,' he said. 'This particular property is an investment, one of several I own in London.'

April pursed her lips in annoyance. It was intolerable to be indebted to someone whom she suspected disapproved of her.

'And may I know what rent you customarily charge?' she asked.

'I never recall such inconsequential information.'

'Then perhaps I should apply to your man-of-business for an answer?'

'If you wish. Although, he has an erratic memory and is unlikely to remember.'

'It is a wonder then that he is still in your employ! I would have thought a poor memory would be something of a handicap in a man-of-business?'

'It is. Thankfully, he does not have a poor memory. He is perfectly capable of retaining information I wish him to remember.'

His inference was perfectly clear, but for some reason she was amused rather than offended and had to press her lips together to contain her smile.

After a moment of inner struggle, she managed to muster her displeasure once more.

'I had a feeling the rental price was ridiculously low. Albert, why did you not tell me? I . . . *we* refuse to become a charity case.'

'There's no need to reproach my uncle,' said Hugh. 'The house can command a high price during the Season, but we are now almost in November and it is worth a great deal less than in, say, March or April.'

This consideration had not occurred to her, and she was bound to admit it had merit.

'But if you feel you are not paying enough for the property," he went on, "I'll speak to my man-of-business and find out why he did not think to exploit your generous expectations.'

Lady Hartwood had been listening to their exchange with growing apprehension and at this last comment, which she feared was bound to antagonise her daughter, she mumbled 'Oh dear' and reached for her wine glass.

Her fears were misplaced, however, for April's displeasure had evaporated.

'You would charge me more?' she asked, no longer able to contain her smile.

'If you are determined to be fleeced, why not?' replied Hugh, smiling in turn.

Her laugh rang out and she shook her head at him.

'You have overplayed your hand. You should have ended with that perfectly plausible explanation that rents are higher during the Season.'

'Perhaps. I appear to have underestimated my opponent.'

'I owe you an apology,' she said ruefully, her gaze taking in both Hugh and Lord Paisley. 'I did not mean to sound churlish and ungrateful, only it was a shock to discover I had cause to be so *very* grateful. I don't like to be beholden.'

'So I gather,' Hugh observed. 'From my perspective, I don't particularly wish to be known for turning a profit at the expense of members of my own family. My first inclination was to offer the property to you free of charge, but it was made clear to me that you wouldn't countenance such an arrangement.'

'No, certainly not! You would have lost income.'

'If that is your only concern then allow me put your mind at ease. The house is rarely let during this time of year and had in fact been sitting empty for several months prior to your arrival.'

April attempted to read the truth in his eyes.

Hugh saw her hesitation and, sensing victory, turned to her ladyship to press his advantage.

'Lady Hartwood, I hope you'll forgive me for not bringing you an engagement gift tonight. I first wanted to make your acquaintance before deciding on something that would be to your liking, and now I believe I know what that might be. With your permission, I would like to tear up the rental contract and offer this house to you without charge for as long as you may require it.'

Lady Hartwood did not share April's scruples when it came to extravagant gifts (especially from one's family!) and promptly and graciously accepted Hugh's offer, before her daughter could complicate what seemed to her to be a perfectly proper arrangement.

'You have left me with little to say on the matter,' April told Hugh, her eyes conveying a mixture of emotions, of which gratitude was only part. 'But – and I am certain my mother will agree with me – we can only accept your kindness until March, at which point, by your own admission, you would be able to achieve the full rental on the house.'

Lady Hartwood felt obliged to concur; Lord Paisley, desirous of a wife before March, was perfectly content with this arrangement; and Hugh gave the appearance of accepting her condition without ever actually saying so.

The rest of their meal passed without any further incident to mar the harmony that had been achieved, and after dinner Hugh unbent sufficiently to entertain them with a few of the more comical mishaps that had befallen him while serving under the Duke of Wellington.

This put April so in charity with him that by the time he and his uncle said their goodbyes at the end of the evening, she was wishing he would do something to alienate her growing regard for him.

It was almost midnight when Lady Hartwood knocked on the door of her daughter's room and entered. As she had expected, April was soaking in a copper bath that had been set up in front of the fireplace; a nightly ritual she had loved since she was a little girl, and one she needed as much for its mental soothing as for the more practical purpose of removing the dirt of the day.

April was staring absentmindedly into the flames of the fire but at Lady Hartwood's entrance she turned her head and smiled.

She took in her mother's freshly-washed complexion, her long silver and gold hair, which had been brushed until it shone, and the white silk robe trimmed with lace around her slender figure. No one could possibly have a mother as lovely as her mother, she thought to herself.

'What a fetching negligee! Is it new?' she asked.

'I thought that perhaps I should begin to prepare my wedding trousseau,' said Lady Hartwood, through habit looking self-conscious and feeling a need to defend herself. 'And it *is* quite lovely, isn't it? Although, at first, it was so extravagantly priced – *fifteen* pounds, if you can believe! – that I was determined not to allow myself to be swayed. You would have been proud of me, love. But then, imagine my surprise when the shop assistant informed me that since I was buying several other items, I could have it for only *ten* pounds. Such a bargain! It would have been a shame to refuse. And I do think it suits me,' she finished, endowing this statement with an enquiring quality.

April laughed lightly and said: 'It looks ravishing on you, Mama! Albert will definitely approve of this particular bargain.'

It would have been useless to attempt to explain to her mother that ten pounds was an extortionate price to pay. Or that, however unfair she thought it, her present income could not stretch to accommodate her shopping habit. April had tried many times to explain this unpalatable reality to her, but Lady Hartwood possessed a flexible reasoning and could twist hard facts into unrecognisable alternatives.

April could only be deeply thankful that, after an embarrassingly frank conversation, Lord Paisley had confirmed his fortune was large enough to cover the difference between her mother's income and her expenditure. If he had not come along when he had, April suspected she would have had to contract a highly mercenary marriage to keep her mother out of a debtor's prison.

Pleased to know that her purchase had her daughter's approval, Lady Hartwood sat herself in a wing chair beside the fire, rearranged the silk robe around her legs and turned her mind to the reason for her visit.

Before she could speak, April said playfully: 'You know, Mama, I have a bone to pick with you! How could you have allowed me to sit through the whole of this evening with my hair in a fine mess and hanging over my ear? I was never more mortified than when I saw my reflection a few minutes ago!'

'Oh, but I *did* try to bring it to your attention! And when you failed to perceive my signals, I thought it best not to make a fuss in front of the gentlemen. They did not appear to notice, in any case – you know how men are! They probably thought it was a new hair style.'

'*Cheveux de bird nest* perhaps?' April giggled and sunk lower into her bath.

'Speaking of Hugh. . . ' said her ladyship with studied casualness.

'We were not speaking of Hugh,' April pointed out, instantly on her guard.

'Well, we *referred* to him, and it brings to mind that I wanted to tell you how delighted I was to make his acquaintance. He was not at all what I expected. I had of course heard high praise of him from your. . . from *various quarters*. But I was pleasantly surprised to find that he has a great deal of kindness in him. . . some might even say *charm*. What was your impression, love?'

28

'He certainly has engaging manners when it comes to *you*,' April said teasingly. 'But it's impossible to know if he is truly amiable or putting on a performance for his uncle's benefit – one can see that he holds him in great affection. Personally, I thought I could detect a certain cynicism in his conversation, especially over dinner, that was not to my taste.'

Having given her mother this little criticism to absorb with the aim of throwing her off the scent, she then felt able to state the obvious.

'But one cannot deny he has a compelling air about him, and is exceedingly handsome besides! I found it impossible not to stare when I first laid eyes on him.'

Lady Hartwood regarded her with a good deal of surprise.

'Would you call him handsome? He is well-looking enough for a man, but it's his kind nature and...'

'Well-looking enough? Oh come, Mama! Don't dissemble. He is a veritable Adonis!'

Lady Hartwood was rendered momentarily speechless.

To think she would see the day her daughter finally lost her head over a man!

'Love, you are blinded!' she laughed. 'But I don't mean to try and change your mind. Hugh would make the perfect husband for... someone.'

'Whatever can you mean? Of course, I did not mean I had developed a *tendre* for him...after only a handful of hours?'

'Hours, weeks, months – what does it matter?'

'It matters a great deal, one would suppose. The difference between a fool and a person of sense. But that's beside the point. I can assure you, I have no feelings of *that* kind towards Mr Royce... and he certainly has none for me! At dinner his disapproval was perfectly clear.'

'I think *disapproval* is too strong a word, love. If you *would* say such outrageous things – as you know very well you did! – in the company of someone who does not yet understand your character, then you cannot be surprised if he reached certain conclusions. In my opinion, he acted with wonderful restraint. And did you notice how little your looks meant to him? Not for one moment did he regard you with unbecoming warmth or fascination. That must have pleased you, surely?'

As Hugh's polite and indifferent manner towards her had pleased her very little, and as her own reaction to this fact annoyed her considerably, she was hard-pressed to know how to reply.

Lady Hartwood perceived April's confusion and smiled to herself. She had been a little worried that she was being too precipitate in planting a seed in her daughter's mind, but overall she was pleased with how matters were progressing.

'He is engaged,' April muttered.

'Yes, he is. . . at present.' Feeling she had said quite enough for one evening, Lady Hartwood yawned delicately behind her hand and rose to her feet. 'Oh my, how tired I am! I really must go to bed. Albert is to take me to Kew Gardens tomorrow and he has a thoroughly *exhausting* walk planned for us. Sleep well, love.'

She placed a kiss on her daughter's forehead and walked out of the room, leaving April to stare after her, a look of consternation on her face.

How was one expected to sleep well after such a conversation!

Four

'Mrs Delamer is here to see you, Miss April,' announced the butler, entering the parlour where April was busy writing to her steward. 'Are you free to receive...'

A veiled figure pushed past him and entered the room, the stiff silk of her amethyst morning-dress rustling against her resolute stride.

'That will do, Layton, that will do,' the woman informed him peremptorily.

April put down her pen and, with an inward sigh, rose from the escritoire.

'Good afternoon, Grandmama. What a pleasant surprise!'

Mrs Delamer lifted her veil and revealed an intelligent and still beautiful countenance, which was lined far less than one would have thought possible in a woman approaching her seventieth year.

She was dressed, as always, in the French style. The exuberant use of lace that she favoured might have appeared overly fussy on another woman, but on her tall, graceful frame, topped with an abundance of artfully pinned white hair, it looked both dashing and elegant.

'If I had known we were to expect you today,' continued April, 'I would have asked Mrs Plum to prepare a hot posset for you.'

'I have no idea who Mrs Plum might be, and I have no need of a posset from her or anyone else!'

'She is both our cook and housekeeper while we are residing here, and a most capable woman,' April replied, undaunted. 'I hope the drive to London did not fatigue you? It is shockingly cold today.'

'I did not make the journey from Richmond to exchange pleasantries with you, child,' said Mrs Delamer, eyeing her critically.

'I did not suppose it. No doubt you will appraise me of your reason soon enough, when you are more comfortable. Come, let us go to the drawing room and we can sit by the fire and warm ourselves.'

Her grandmother relented a little under this solicitude and allowed herself to be led down the hall to the drawing room. While she was settling herself into a chair beside the flames in the marble hearth, April drew Layton a little to the side.

'Please have the tea tray sent up, as well as the macaroons that were delivered yesterday from Gunther's. Preferably the chocolate ones, they're her favourite. And if my mother and Lord Paisley should return from their outing, for goodness sake, do not show them in here! Mama is likely to swoon if she is forced to witness another altercation between her mother and her fiancé.'

'You need not fear Lord Paisley's conduct,' replied Layton, in the forthright manner of an old retainer.

'It's not *his* conduct I fear. Lord Paisley's manners are beyond reproach but, you know as well as I do, that would only set him at a disadvantage. He should be given a medal for the restraint he has shown so far in dealing with a belligerent woman he has been told is merely an old friend of the family.'

Layton chuckled, perfectly cognisant of the hazards to be avoided. He had been present in the dining room at St Mawes Castle several weeks ago when Mrs Delamer had subjected Lord Paisley to a thorough interrogation, and, apart from other gross impertinences, had demanded if he could afford to keep a wife whose expenditure exceeded eight thousand a year.

As Layton shuffled out of the room to carry out his orders, April returned to her grandmother.

Mrs Delamer had taken off her gloves and was warming her slightly arthritic fingers before the fire. However, as soon as April took a seat opposite her she once again put on the soft kid leather. She was not a woman to place herself at a disadvantage, even with family.

'I take it my daughter is not at home,' she said, without the least attempt to cloak the statement as a question.

April wondered, not for the first time, who out of their small household was pocketing her grandmother's bribes to spy on them.

'Mama and Lord Paisley left some time ago. I believe they plan to visit Kew Gardens – but perhaps your information is more accurate?' she asked with amusement.

'I am here to talk about our plans to find you a husband,' said Mrs Delamer, ignoring the pointed remark. 'Is that silly daughter of mine still determined on marrying her equally dim-witted fiancé?'

'Neither Mama nor Viscount Paisley are deserving of the names you have assigned them,' April replied equably, accustomed to her grandmother's sharp tongue.

'*Viscount* Paisley – ha! Nothing more than a courtesy title! He won't gain a proper title until he inherits the Earldom from his father.'

'That makes no difference to either of them, for they share a deep love that is not bound by such considerations. And they *will* be married.'

'They will if I will it! If you would only allow me to find you a husband without insisting I pander to your mother's ridiculous infatuation, I wouldn't be in the position of having to accept a *Paisley* as a son-in-law,' said Mrs Delamer with loathing. 'The Lord only knows why she chose to complicate matters by fixing on *him* of all people! She knows perfectly well I have plans for his n...' She stopped abruptly, seeming to regret her words, then continued in a guarded manner: 'I don't even have the satisfaction of knowing she has set her sights on one day becoming a countess, for I know this one advantage of the match has never even entered her head.'

'I had not realised your objection to Albert is that he is a Paisley,' April said with surprise. 'I thought the family were considered perfectly respectable?'

'Barnaby Paisley respectable?' Her grandmother snorted indelicately. 'That would be a day to see hell freeze over!'

'But who is Barnaby Paisley?' asked April, perplexed.

'The current Earl, of course.'

'You mean Albert's father? The Earl of Wulfingston? But why should you... *oh*...' April bit her lip to stop a smile forming. 'Don't tell me he was one of your protectors?'

As her grandmother had earned for herself the stellar reputation of being one of the greatest courtesans in Paris some fifty years previously, this question was not without merit.

'I wouldn't have accepted him if he were the last man alive!' retorted Mrs Delamer. 'He may have been devastatingly handsome, but he was also a self-important reprobate. The stories I could tell you if I wished to soil your ears!'

'*I* have no objection to you soiling my ears,' April informed her, a twinkle in her eyes.

'I wouldn't demean myself.'

April smiled and asked: 'But surely there can be no objection to Lord Wulfingston now?'

'From what I hear, time has done little to improve his character. He's still a reprobate, and a cantankerous old tyrant besides! I count myself fortunate I had the resolution to resist him.'

'Oh dear, it sounds like you knew each other very well. Is there a danger he may recognise you?'

'After the passage of so many years, highly unlikely. Although if he does, it will be all your mother's fault!'

'You are being unreasonable, Grandmama. How could she have known your history? And besides, you cannot hold Albert's father against him. How unjust the world would be if we were all held accountable for the actions of our family.'

'If you mean to put me in my place by alluding to the fact that you disapprove of my past career, you need not veil your insults. I like a direct opponent.'

'I hope I am never so conceited as to judge you in such a way! I am perfectly aware you did what had to be done in order to survive.'

'You forget I enjoyed it, I was good at it, and I earned a lot of money out of it. Does that make your forbearance more difficult to sustain?'

'I can only be happy that you managed to find enjoyment in a profession you were driven to by the improvidence of your parents,' April returned with spirit. 'I was simply suggesting that just as my character cannot be judged on the actions of anyone in my family, so too Albert's cannot be judged on the actions of his.'

'But you *will* be judged on my actions should anyone ever discover my past – don't forget that! Which is why the fewer people who know we're related the better.'

'I admit I don't understand why you believe you can continue to conceal our kinship, especially now that we are in London. Surely your acquaintances will recognise Mama from when she lived with you in Dorset?'

'After all the precautions we went to, I should hope they would do no such thing!' declared Mrs Delamer. She did not immediately continue, but when her granddaughter remained silent, she smiled lightly and said: 'You want to know more, do you? Well, I suppose it can do no harm.'

Five

Mrs Delamer took a moment to adjust her position so that her face was angled away from the heat of fire.

'When I returned from Paris with your grandfather, and went to live with him at Windermere, I did so as Mrs Delamer, the widow of a wealthy landowner. And although it was known that I was your grandfather's mistress it was, in its way, a respectable connection. But I wanted more for your mother than to be forever known as a child born out of wedlock. And so she was reared in a limited society and as soon as she was of age we married her to your father. From the moment she left Dorset and went to live in Cornwall as Baroness Hartwood, your grandfather and I ceased to be her parents and, as you know, became simply friends of her husband. . . it was not in her best interest to have a mother such as I.'

Catching the sympathetic look in April's eyes, she said brusquely: 'That's the way of the world and there is no point regretting what cannot be changed. I've never allowed a few obstacles to sway me from my course – there are always ways to achieve what one sets one's mind to, remember that! Now, child, are you ready to begin our marriage campaign?'

It took April a moment to adjust to the abrupt change in subject. She knew she had to tread carefully if she was to convince her grandmother that she was willing to take part in this absurd plan of hers.

'Yes, I am ready. But, you will remember, Grandmama, that I have stipulations. For one, the man must be good-natured.'

'Most men can be good-natured if they get their own way! The trick is to make them believe they *are* getting it.'

'He must also be a gentleman.'

'I know how to value your charms, even if you do not. I aim no lower than a duke for you!'

Ignoring this rather surprising piece of information for the moment, April went on: 'And I have another stipulation.'

'I hope you don't mean to be difficult?' muttered Mrs Delamer.

'I only ask that you give your blessing to Mama's marriage to Albert.'

'I have already agreed not to oppose the marriage, if you allow me to find you a husband – what more do you want from me?'

'That's not the same as giving your blessing. You must know how happy it would make Mama to know you approve of her choice?' April said coaxingly.

'Bah! I did the best I could with her when I found her a Baron for her first marriage. Her beauty was never of a type to match ours, but she had the charm of youth to recommend her, and was biddable besides. Your father had no cause for complaint. But she has improved with age, and, if I were inclined to it, I could make her an even more advantageous *second* marriage.'

'I hope you'll not be so inclined!' exclaimed April. 'In fact, I will go so far as to say, if you show any such inclination I will run off with the first merchant to cross my path and ruin all your ambitions for me. I do *not* admire your ability to choose husbands for my mother! And you are quite right, my father certainly had no reason for complaint. Unfortunately, his nature was of a type that could not recognise his good fortune. *He* was not worthy of *her*. His abuse of her may not have been physical in nature but there are other ways to bruise so sweet and gentle a character as she possesses. If you only knew how she suffered from his abrasive temperament you would not be so quick to congratulate yourself!'

'Calm yourself, child – there is no need to get worked up over less than nothing. I said *if* I were inclined, which I'm not. I have bigger fish to catch with you than I ever could with your mother. I have no further ambitions for her.'

April regarded her grandmother suspiciously as she brought herself back under control.

'If that is the case, then do I have your word you will give Mama your blessing?'

'Yes, yes, she is welcome to her viscount, I care not! Now, let us return to more important matters. I have been in correspondence with a friend regarding your introduction into society and she has agreed to sponsor you. Amelia Jameson – a grand old bird! Fat as a sow but not a bad bone in that hefty frame of hers. You'll like her.'

'Was she a colleague of yours?' asked April, allowing herself to be distracted by this disclosure.

'She certainly could have been,' her grandmother chuckled. 'Amelia has the heart and soul of a courtesan. But the poor creature was born into a shockingly respectable and well-to-do family, and marriage was her only possible career. Fortunately her husband had the good sense to die young, so she never suffered from much restraint.'

'Then how did your paths cross?'

'She attended the house parties your grandfather and I held at Windermere. Actors, politicians, poets – even the king's brothers! – they all used to vie for an invitation, but few ladies of quality would demean themselves by attending a gathering presided over by a mistress. Amelia, however, never cared a jot! And she never once made me feel I had no right to call Windermere my home... as some others saw fit to do.'

A faraway look came into Mrs Delamer's eyes, and when she presently returned her attention to April she was frowning.

'I heard the nincompoop who inherited from your grandfather has completely overhauled the place. All the furnishings I had sent over from Paris, gone! All the furniture...!' She flung out a disdainful hand.

April's countenance hardened at the mention of this relative.

When her grandfather, the fifth Earl of Windermere, had died several years back without producing a male heir, the whole of the entailed Windermere estate in Dorset, along with his title, had passed to his nephew.

Regrettably, the sixth Earl had proven himself to be a man of puritanical leanings. He had not even waited until after the funeral before ordering Mrs Delamer from the house and banning her from ever returning. April had been little more than a child at the time, but she still seethed with indignation when she thought of the injustice of it.

'At least you had the foresight to remove the more valuable items to your house in Richmond,' she said with relish. 'And you have the satisfaction of knowing that the current earl knows you did so!'

'He certainly suspects,' agreed Mrs Delamer, a roguish glint lighting her eyes. 'He came to Windermere before your grandfather passed away and tried to bamboozle us into believing it was to pay his respects. We knew well enough it was to familiarise himself with his inheritance. He saw the Rembrandt and the Rubens. And I myself showed him the Michelangelo! I should invite him to Richmond so that he can view them again.' She laughed and sank for a moment into pleasant reflections. 'But enough wool-gathering,' she said suddenly, rousing herself. 'I want to talk about Amelia's *soirée*. It's little more than a week away and there is much to be done...'

She paused as a maid entered the room, carrying the tea tray, and helped herself to a chocolate macaroon as the girl passed her.

The moment they were alone again she continued as if no interruption had occurred: '. . . I have every hope that Amelia can entice a certain gentleman I have my eye on for you to attend her party.'

'I take it from your earlier remark that he is blessed with being a duke?' April said dryly, beginning to pour the tea.

'Yes, he's a duke. But what there is in that to sneer at I'm at a loss to understand?'

'Why, nothing! Only, I cannot help but hope he is blessed with other qualities I might find endearing for a lifetime.'

'I trust you will manage to suppress your unbecoming pertness in front of His Grace?'

'But Grandmama, I thought you liked my pertness?' April replied with a saucy smile.

Mrs Delamer regarded her haughtily as she accepted a cup and saucer from her.

'You're not setting out to attract *me*. The Duke of Claredon does not possess the same tastes in humour as a retired courtesan. That's not to say I set him above me in anything but rank! But no one can deny that dignity and decorum have featured more widely in his life than in mine. His mother would have seen to that.'

April wisely refrained from teasing her further.

If she was to make her dear but deluded grandmother believe that she was willing to sacrifice herself on the altar of matrimony, then she would need to pretend to treat this scheme of hers with greater seriousness. . . at least, until her mother was safely married.

'How do you wish me to prepare for Mrs Jameson's *soirée*?' she asked and sipped her tea.

'First, we must agree on your age. Unmarried at eight and twenty is difficult to explain away. People will think there is something wrong with you.'

'If they met the eligible gentlemen within fifty miles of my home they would understand!' responded April, nettled. 'Reginald Poppley and William Stanton were the only ones whose attentions did not horrify me, and my father saw fit to reject their suits outright because he considered them beneath me.'

'That might be true enough but there are bound to be whispers as to why you were not brought to London for the Season. With your looks, everyone would think some acquaintance would have been willing to invest in your future, even if your family was unable to do so.'

'My father refused to be beholden to anyone!'

'You need not tell me that, I was there when he rejected my offer to pay for your coming out. I always thought it the height of hypocrisy that he never suffered from the same scruples when it came to borrowing money for his horses.'

'Did he owe you money?' April asked sharply.

She had spent the last two years devising ways to repay the most pressing of the debts she had inherited, but until the tenant farms on the estate became profitable, in a year or two with any luck, she had no way of settling the remainder, including the substantial mortgage. She could, of course, settle all the debts if she sold the entire St Mawes estate (the land alone, without the home farm and castle, would not be enough) but that was something she would never contemplate.

'Your father never liked me enough to borrow from me,' replied Mrs Delamer, then hurried on: 'As to what age we must invent for you, I believe you can pass for three and twenty. Any younger and there will be comparisons drawn with the debutantes. Any older and people will start to draw their own impertinent conclusions.'

'Is it truly necessary?' asked April, having no fondness for the idea.

'Would I suggest it if it were not? And we will tell the truth as to why you are unmarried: lack of funds, gothic father, restrictive society,' Mrs Delamer counted off on her fingers. 'And when your father passed away, you went into deep mourning for two years. . . yes, I believe that story will do nicely!'

'I cannot say I like to hear my life reduced to a melodrama,' said April, wrinkling her nose in distaste.

'Let us move on to the duke. I have a list.' Untying the strings of her beaded reticule, Mrs Delamer pulled out her spectacles and a slip of paper and began to read. 'Hair: His Grace favours a modern style, cut short and curled in the classical way. I will arrange an appointment with my hairdresser. Clothes: His Grace dislikes immodest displays of flesh, however, he is a dandy, so a fashionable mien is of great importance.'

A look of blank astonishment descended over April's features.

'Horsemanship,' continued Mrs Delamer. 'His Grace is a notable rider and his duchess must be able to join him in the saddle when the occasion arises. I know you're not partial to horses, but you must make a push to overcome your fear.'

'How did you come by such a list?' exclaimed April. 'And how can you seriously expect me to follow its dictates? You must be jesting, surely?'

Mrs Delamer took off her spectacles and regarded her with piercing blue eyes.

'One does not joke about landing one of the greatest matrimonial prizes of the decade. Do you mean to tell me you are having second thoughts?'

April sighed and reminded herself that her mother's happiness was at stake.

'You simply took me by surprise, that is all. Pray, continue.'

'Hmm,' huffed Mrs Delamer and put on her spectacles again. 'Where was I...' She studied the list in silence for some moments. 'There's only one more item here that we need to consider. We can ignore the rest. There's no point giving a man too much of what he thinks he wants – it's bound to disappoint him.'

'And what is the last item for our consideration?' April asked, resigned.

'Passion.'

Six

'*Passion?*' echoed April, thoroughly appalled. 'I cannot be expected to feel passion for a man I will barely know!'

The image of Hugh flashed through her mind, and was quickly suppressed.

'You mistake me,' said Mrs Delamer. 'His Grace disapproves of displays of passion of any kind. His duchess will be a lady of even temperament, one who has complete mastery over her emotions. In other words, child, you must rein in that temper of yours!'

'Dear Lord,' April mumbled into her teacup.

Mrs Delamer put away her spectacles and, folding the slip of paper, handed it to her.

'Here, take it. You may study it at your leisure.'

'I don't quite know how to thank you.'

'Minx! Don't think I don't know what's in that mind of yours. The duke's preferences may seem ridiculous – what man doesn't have unrealistic expectations when it comes to his wife? – but, as my mother always used to say, when you're setting a trap it doesn't hurt to grease the hinges.'

'Is that what we're doing… *greasing the hinges?*' asked April, barely holding back her laughter; she suspected it would have sounded rather hysterical.

'Certainly. No man can be expected to resist you when you look as you do *and* you conform to his nonsensical ideals of femininity.'

'You don't think very highly of men, do you, Grandmama?'

'They're all our maker has seen fit to give us so there is no point in quibbling. But if I'd had the creating of them, I'd have taken the time to fix the glaring flaws in their design.'

The idea of her grandmother instructing God on how to improve his design of man was the final straw for April's gravity.

'I don't see what there is to laugh about?' Mrs Delamer said reproachfully.

'Let us blame my odd sense of humour,' replied April, wiping away a tear.

'Do try for some control! You'll need the practise for when you meet His Grace. Now, if you have finished your tea, I am going to take you shopping. If you must be clothed demurely then we must rely on my milliner to create some hats that will endow your outfits with à la modality.'

'But what are we to do with all the dresses we ordered from your modiste last week? One can hardly call them demure.'

'We must also visit *Madame Franchot* today and ask her to amend her designs to conceal the *décolletage*.'

'When I agreed to come to London in search of a husband,' said April a little wistfully, 'I had hoped I would finally be allowed a little fun and frivolity and a wardrobe to match. Now it seems I am to be dressed like a nun while I attempt to attract a man who expects me to act like one as well. And, if all goes to plan, I am to become shackled to him for eternity! I must have lost my mind to even consider such a future.'

'You're considering it because you want me to permit your mother's marriage.'

'She's a grown woman! She doesn't need your permission!'

'But we both know she is unlikely to marry without it.'

April threw her grandmother a disgruntled look.

'Yes, that much is abysmally clear. I won't conceal from you that I wish she possessed a little more backbone. You have trained her too well.'

Mrs Delamer's countenance softened. For all her bluster she was inordinately fond of her granddaughter.

'If it will make it easier for you to reconcile yourself to your immediate future, remember that engagements can be broken.'

'But. . . I thought you expected me to marry the duke?' April said with surprise.

'I may wish it, but I will not force you. The betrothal period will allow you both the time to become better acquainted, and if you decide not to proceed with the marriage, I will extricate you without any loss to your reputation.'

'Grandmama, what are you scheming?' asked April, a shrewd look in her eyes. 'This is not about finding me a husband, is it? You have some other plan in mind. I'd lay odds on it!'

Mrs Delamer rose to her feet and began to shake out the wrinkles from the skirt of her amethyst dress. After she had completed the task to her satisfaction, she looked back at April.

'Finding you a husband is of *paramount* importance. What, pray, do you think will become of you once your mother marries?'

'Ah, I see your point! You mean to give me a hint that Mama and Albert are likely to throw me out onto the street as soon as they are married.'

'This is no time for levity! You are eight and twenty and too used to ruling over your own household. Surely you don't expect Paisley to tolerate your autocratic behaviour in his own house? You would all be miserable within a sennight! You need a home of your own in which to exert your considerable talents. . . and before you interrupt me, *no*, I most certainly do *not* think that living by yourself in Cornwall is suitable in the slightest!'

April was oddly touched that her grandmother had given such serious consideration to her future.

'I agree with you,' she said with a soft smile. 'Living alone in St Mawes holds no appeal to me. . . although I do have some hope of one day finding a husband I can love. But, be that as it may, don't think you can distract me!' she went on boldly. 'You have some plot in mind apart from finding me a husband. Has it something to do with the Duke of Claredon's family? If I knew the details, I could better assist you.'

Mrs Delamer started walking towards the door.

'I am perfectly capable of handling my own affairs. Are you coming, child, or will I have to buy your hats without you?'

April's curiosity was aroused but she knew better than to keep pressing her grandmother for information.

'I will buy my own hats,' she replied, following. 'I only agreed to allow you to buy me some new clothes as I don't want to disgrace Mama by looking like a provincial dowd.'

'You're a fool to waste every penny on your mother and leave nothing for yourself.'

'This is her first proper introduction into London Society, and I will do all I can to ensure it's a success.'

'She has already caught herself a viscount, which is more than I can say for you! It's high time you gave some thought to your own needs.'

April saw no point in attempting to explain, yet again, that her happiness did not depend on the trappings of wealth that were as intrinsic to her mother's comfort as breathing.

Unwilling to be drawn into an old argument, she said simply: 'I will go upstairs and change.'

'Make haste!' And to stress that she did not expect to be kept waiting for long, Mrs Delamer proceeded down the stairs to the entrance hall.

When April rejoined her, some fifteen minutes later, she was sitting in a porter's chair beside the front door and demanding answers from the butler as to the suitability of the house.

Layton had known Mrs Delamer for close to thirty years and was unaffected by her imperious ways. He answered her in a manner that gave the impression he was humouring a recalcitrant child, and when she asked a particularly impertinent question, he retreated behind his hearing impairment.

'You cannot fool me, you old goat,' Mrs Delamer informed him. 'I know perfectly well you're no more deaf than I am!'

Something similar to enjoyment flitted across the old man's countenance, but he preserved his silence.

Before his defiance could be further remarked on, April asked: 'Shall we go?'

Mrs Delamer cast one last fulminating glance at her old adversary, then turned an appraising eye on her granddaughter.

April had changed into her favourite walking dress, a peach-coloured muslin with long sleeves and three flounces. Her hair was tied back in a simple knot at the base of her neck and a plain but beautifully made moss green velvet hat, reminiscent of the tricorns of a previous age, sat on her head.

A short veil of silk tulle was attached to the front of the hat and partially hid her features. Whereas her grandmother wore veils to protect her complexion from the sun and weather, April used them to escape the relentless attention her looks attracted.

To guard against the cold, she had chosen a padded pelisse that was made from the same velvet as her hat. It fit snugly around her upper body and dropped elegantly to the floor. The velvet had become a little worn on the underside of the sleeves, but since only a particularly astute observer would have noticed this detail April was content with her appearance.

Mrs Delamer nodded her approval.

'Remember not to refer to me as *Grandmama* in public!' Rising to her feet, she lowered her veil and swept out the front door, held open for her by Layton.

'I expect I shall be gone for most of the afternoon,' April told the butler as she passed him.

'Shall I inform Mrs Plum that Mrs Delamer will be staying for dinner?' he asked.

'It would not do for her to undertake the journey back to Richmond at too late an hour,' April replied with a conspiratorial smile. 'I think we are safe from that pleasure for tonight.'

Seven

Despite the cold, Mrs Delamer and April relinquished the comfort of a hackney coach for the pleasure of walking in the gentle October sunshine, and headed for the shopping quarter that had blossomed around Bond Street at the end of the last century and that now almost exclusively serviced the wealthy and titled.

Compared to the long country walks they were in the habit of enjoying, they had only a short distance to cover and were soon entering the milliner's shop patronised by Mrs Delamer.

The owner of the establishment was engaged in assisting a young lady with her purchase, but the moment she saw them enter she indicated to her assistant to take her place and came over to greet Mrs Delamer with every indication of delight.

'Mrs Warrick, allow me to introduce you to Miss Hartwood, the daughter of Baron Hartwood, an old acquaintance of mine from Cornwall,' said Mrs Delamer, pumping up April's consequence and explaining their connection in one. 'She has only recently arrived in London and will be going out into Society for the first time.'

Mrs Warrick, a rotund woman of middle years, who was dressed with neatness but without any flamboyancy that might overshadow her customers, looked at April with unmistakable interest.

'This is to be her debut?' she asked.

'Exactly,' Mrs Delamer replied with a smile; the bait had been taken. 'We shall need at least ten hats.'

'Ten!' exclaimed April. 'Surely that is excessive?'

Her grandmother silenced her with a look.

'My young friend is being modest. I shan't scruple to tell you, Mrs Warrick, that it would not do for a certain duke, whose attentions have become quite marked, to see her wearing the same small collection of hats.'

April was once more subjected to a thorough perusal, and she felt driven to say: 'I think you refine too much upon the point, ma'am.'

'It is most becoming in you not to gloat over such a triumph, as most girls would be eager to do,' said Mrs Delamer approvingly.

With an effort, April kept herself from making any further comment. It was clear she would only be playing into her grandmother's hands.

Transferring her gaze to the various hats that had been put out on display, she became aware that the other customer in the shop was regarding her with patent disapproval.

April gave her a cool, challenging look. The girl had evidently overheard their conversation, however, it was one thing for *her* to disapprove of her grandmother's tactics and quite another for someone else to pass similar judgment.

The stranger was the first to turn away, and, beckoning her lady's maid who was waiting in a chair by the door, quit the shop with her head held high.

Good riddance, thought April.

After a pleasant half an hour spent trying on different hats and discussing the various styles that would suit April's purposes, the subject of cost was raised by Mrs Delamer. The milliner had always believed haggling to be below her talents and rarely made allowances for her wealthy clientele, but one did not survive in her line of work without learning to recognise an exceptional business opportunity.

She could count on one hand the number of times she had seen a face of such beauty as Miss Hartwood's enter her shop; and of those, most had belonged to customers in the theatrical world and the *demi-monde,* and they could not be counted on to thrust her into the rarefied sphere of the *haute ton,* as was her ambition. To be the milliner responsible for dressing a face that was certain to draw every eye and show every creation to advantage was too good an opportunity to be passed by.

A few minutes later, April followed her grandmother out of the shop, quite unable to believe they had managed to secure ten hats for the price of three.

'I believe I have grossly misjudged your abilities!' she laughed.

'You are not the first,' said Mrs Delamer, accepting this praise with a quirk of her lips.

'Did you make a similarly remarkable bargain with the modiste?'

'Of course.'

'I see now that I should have never resisted your attempts over the years to bring me to London! It's not at all prohibitively expensive if one has a fairy godmother at one's side.'

'Foolish girl,' said Mrs Delamer mildly.

Next, they made their way to the establishment of the exclusive French modiste they had visited the week before, and, on securing a few minutes of *Madame Franchot's* valuable time, Mrs Delamer explained the need for modesty in all the dresses that had been previously ordered.

The small Frenchwoman regarded them sceptically over the top of her gold-rimmed spectacles, not at all pleased with the idea of debasing her creations. But after sharing with them her thoughts on *les Anglais,* who according to her knew nothing of dressing to advantage (an observation Mrs Delamer agreed was all too true), she finally relented when it was pointed out to her that no other modiste could successfully create stylish gowns that preserved the wearer's modesty.

April silently lamented her capitulation, but as she did not have the funds to pay for the gowns herself, she accepted their puritanical fate with good grace.

It was only after they had left the shop and were walking away that she was overcome by an urge to rescue at least one of them. Informing her grandmother that she had forgotten her gloves, she hurried back inside.

'Excuse me, *madame,*' she said, approaching the modiste. 'I have changed my mind regarding the red velvet evening dress. Let us keep the design as we originally discussed.'

'You do not require modesty in that one, *mademoiselle?*' asked *Madame Franchot,* looking surprised.

'No. Not that one.'

Eight

'Which one did you save?' asked Mrs Delamer when April re-joined her.

April threw her an exasperated look, torn between laughter and annoyance.

'I refuse to say! It is most vexing that you always seem to know everything! I thought I gave a fine performance of needing to retrieve my gloves?'

'Perhaps. But you allowed a few too many sighs of disappointment to escape you while we discussed the changes with *Madame Franchot.*'

'How annoying! I had no awareness of doing anything of the sort... *oh, pardon!*' she exclaimed suddenly, startled to find herself almost walking into a gentleman who had appeared out of nowhere.

He was a well-dressed young man, with a cane in one hand and a tall beaver hat in the other, and he was breathing a little fast, as if he had been running.

'I beg your pardon,' he said, offering her a low, respectful bow. 'I will not be so presumptuous as to ask your name, I only hope you will allow me to tell you that you are the most exquisitely beautiful woman I have ever beheld!'

April realised she had forgotten to lower her veil and, with an inward sigh, quickly did so.

'Thank you, sir,' she said, assuming a shy demeanour and shrinking towards her grandmother.

This was the quickest way she had found to rid herself of earnest young men. She had an entirely different tactic for impertinent ones.

'May I offer you my escort to your destination?' he asked, his eyes attempting to penetrate her veil.

April lowered her chin and remained silent.

Finally comprehending that he was causing the ravishing, shy creature before him grave discomfort, and disconcerted by the mocking smile directed at him by the elderly matron at her side, the gentleman declared his admiration once more and then, reluctantly, departed.

'Less than a minute,' Mrs Delamer observed approvingly as they proceeded on their way. 'You have improved your technique. It used to take you at least ten minutes to get rid of them.'

'That was when I still had patience and took pains not to cause offence. I have since learnt that any conversation on my part is seen as encouragement and their attentions become downright insidious.'

Mrs Delamer laughed lightly.

'I sound so conceited, don't I?' sighed April. 'But it's only with *you* that I can speak so bluntly. You're the only other person I know who has suffered from an excess of male attention and can understand that their adulation is a gross imposition from sheer weight of numbers.'

'I might understand but I was never as squeamish as you when it came to using that adulation to my advantage.'

'I clearly lack your resolve,' owned April, quite cheerfully.

'No, child, what you lack is *motivation*. Whether it's provided by circumstance or by a man, you have not yet been tested. And when you are, I don't doubt your resolve will match mine.'

'Why, thank you! That must be the nicest thing you have ever said to me.'

'Sarcasm?'

'On my honour, it's no such thing!' laughed April.

Mrs Delamer smiled in response and the subject was dropped.

They passed a linen-drapers some minutes later and April stopped in front of the window to view the various fabrics on display. With a look about her to make certain no one was watching her, she lifted her veil and peered through the glass.

Seeing nothing she wished to purchase, she was on the point of moving on when a familiar gentleman came into focus inside the shop. As if feeling her eyes on him, he turned his head and met her gaze.

April quickly dropped her veil and hurried after her grandmother.

'No, no, no!' she muttered to herself.

How mortifying to be caught staring at him. Again!

'What are you mumbling about?' asked Mrs Delamer.

'Hmm? Oh. . . nothing. Nothing at all. . .'

'Cousin April,' a deep voice called out from behind them; polite, yet taunting.

April groaned.

Mrs Delamer's eyes rested briefly on her, and then she slowly turned around. Securing the veil away from her face, she regarded the interloper with a derisive expression.

'I would have expected better manners from you, Hugh Royce, than to be hollering after a lady in the street.'

If April had not been so startled to hear her grandmother address Hugh by name, she would have greatly enjoyed the expression of surprise, followed by boyish discomfit, on his countenance.

'How do you do, ma'am?' Hugh greeted Mrs Delamer, taking off his hat. 'I apologise for accosting you in such a manner.'

'I did not realise you knew each other?' exclaimed April, lifting her veil.

'Oh, we know each other very well,' said Mrs Delamer, enjoying their confusion. 'I counted Hugh's father amongst my closest friends. And sometimes, if he behaves himself, I allow him to invest in my business ventures.'

Hugh smiled and did not contradict her; although they both knew it was *he* who usually brought a promising investment to her attention.

'As for how I know Miss Hartwood,' Mrs Delamer continued, 'her father too was an old friend. . . and, yes, I'm aware that her mother is marrying your feckless uncle, who was only ever good for polishing off the food placed before him!'

April and Hugh exchanged an amused glance.

'My uncle is indeed fortunate! I saw you passing,' he addressed April, 'and wanted to convey my thanks for your hospitality last night.'

'My mother and I were pleased to offer it,' she replied. 'I hope it was not too awkward for you?'

'Should it have been?' he asked, his smile cautious.

'Well, I imagine some might feel awkward to be hosted in their own house,' she said provocatively. 'Of course, had I been aware it *was* your house, I would have made a greater effort to put you at ease. . . but, as you know, I was not aware of it.'

Hugh smiled at the small barb.

'I felt no awkwardness, Cousin April. If anything, not knowing if I was welcome or about to be shown the door added a certain. . . let us say, *spice* to the evening.'

April's lips twitched.

'There was never any danger of you being thrown out, Cousin Hugh. I was raised in the *strictest* of propriety.'

'What is this *Cousin* nonsense?' snapped Mrs Delamer, looking from one to the other with displeasure. 'You are *not* related. And though you may soon to be related through marriage, that does not count! There's no need to look at me as if I've grown horns, child. *Cousin* this, *Cousin* that – it's common! And unhealthy!'

'Unhealthy?' asked April, perplexed.

'I don't like it. You must stop it at once!'

'I'm happy to fall in with your wishes, ma'am,' Hugh conceded docilely; although the smile he directed at April invited her to share his amusement.

It was beyond her to resist, and she smiled back.

'Mr Royce, *there* you are!' a woman's bright voice suddenly intruded.

An instant later the body belonging to the voice appeared at Hugh's side and linked an arm through his.

April almost groaned as she recognised the young lady from the milliner's shop.

'I hope you don't mind me joining you?' she said to Hugh. 'I finished my shopping sooner than I expected and have sent my maid home in the carriage.'

'Of course not, my dear,' he replied, smiling down at her. 'May I introduce you to Mrs Delamer, a friend of many years standing, and Miss Hartwood. Ladies, my betrothed, Miss Starling.'

Miss Starling exchanged greetings with them in such a charming manner that if April had not seen her look of disapproval earlier, she would have thought the girl was delighted to make their acquaintance.

'Miss Hartwood, I feel as if I know you already!' declared Miss Starling. 'Lord Paisley has been entertaining us with stories of the time he spent in Cornwall this summer. It appears to have been delightfully idyllic. And how much I wish to see for myself your splendid castle! By all accounts, it could have been created within the pages of a gothic novel. Does it really have four turrets?'

'It does,' replied April. 'It was originally built as a fortress. But I'm afraid it's not at all splendid – it's horribly inconvenient, actually. Some part of it is always in need of repair. And it's full of drafts and, because of its size, impossible to heat in winter.'

'I suppose, having lived there all your life, you are bound to fail to appreciate it in the same way as a visitor seeing it for the first time,' said Miss Starling, smiling sweetly. 'Still, it must be very dear to you?'

'Yes, it certainly is that,' agreed April, matching her in amiability, although she was certain she could detect something patronising in her tone.

But in thinking that Hugh's fiancée was knowingly being condescending April wronged her. Miss Starling had been taught that good manners were the mark of a great lady, and it would not have crossed her mind to demean herself by showing April her disdain of her.

She was a young woman who knew her worth. She may have reached the age of two and twenty without attaining the sanctity of marriage, but it was not because she had never received any offers. She had received several. However, none of her suitors had possessed all three of the attributes that were key to her happiness: impeccable lineage, sufficient wealth to satisfy her mother and, of course, a title.

In Hugh she had found the first two of these attributes, and as the third would come in time she had condescended to accept him. In direct line to inherit the Marquisate of Talbott from a suitably elderly great-uncle, Hugh would one day make her the Marchioness of Talbott, which was compensation enough for the years she would only be known as Mrs Royce.

And one did not, after all, want to attain the age of *three* and twenty still unmarried.

Continuing to smile, Miss Starling set out to make herself agreeable through flattery and introduced a topic that, little though she knew it, was certain to fail in its objective.

'Excuse me for staring, Miss Hartwood, but I am quite overcome by your beauty,' she gushed, in an oddly serene way. 'My fiancé did not do you justice when he described your looks to me as *pleasant*...that was terribly misleading of you, Mr Royce! I will forgive you only because I know you meant to spare my vanity.'

April would have ordinarily turned the subject at this point, but Hugh had the look of a man who wished to have the subject turned, and the devil in her prompted her to say: 'Why, Cousin Hugh, you disappoint me – merely *pleasant?*'

A smile tugged at one corner of Hugh's mouth. He shook his head, unwilling to take the bait.

Miss Starling, not at all pleased to hear her fiancé referred to in such familiar terms, failed to catch the underlying playfulness of April's remark.

'Oh, pray don't be disappointed, Miss Hartwood,' she said at her most gracious. 'Mr Royce does not care for superficial attractions. He believes the greater the beauty of the flesh, the greater the damage to one's character.'

An uncomfortable silence filled the air.

April lifted an eyebrow at Hugh.

'I don't believe I ever expressed myself in such absolute terms,' he said. 'Although that is certainly true in some cases... and as Miss Hartwood only made her comment to mock me, I will punish her by not clarifying whether or not I think she falls into that category.'

'You are a hard man to mock,' April countered. 'And as you most certainly cannot be trusted to protect *my* vanity, I will not press you to clarify.'

It cost Miss Starling considerable effort to join in with everyone's laughter. She was miffed at her own misstep and attributed the blame for it to Hugh, who she felt should not have contradicted her.

Mrs Delamer had been closely observing the interaction between her companions and was secretly pleased on a number of counts, however, she now decided the time had come for her to enter the fray and she enquired after Miss Starling's family.

This left April at liberty to study the affianced couple; and it did not take her long to come to the conclusion that no real warmth existed between them. Miss Starling kept her hand on Hugh's arm, but there was nothing loving about the gesture, it was merely possessive; and although Hugh smiled at her with a degree of fondness, he clearly had no amorous feelings towards her.

April found their equanimity for one another highly irritating, and, realising she was frowning at them, she looked away and allowed her gaze to travel up the street.

Almost immediately she became aware of a group of men who had congregated a short distance away and were staring at her, with what could only be described as *voracious* expressions.

They appeared to be benign and smiled when she looked in their direction, nevertheless she could not shake the sense of unease that came over her.

She quickly lowered her veil.

Some part of her emotions must have shown on her face before it was concealed for she caught Hugh studying her. He looked over his shoulder and, as soon as he caught sight of the men, his expression darkened.

Having no wish to be the cause of a public brawl, April touched his arm and gave a subtle shake of her head when he glanced at her.

'I hope you will excuse me,' she said aloud for the benefit of all, 'I must be off! My mother is expecting me home. Miss Starling, it was a pleasure to meet you at last.'

Miss Starling looked faintly put out by this interruption to her conversation with Mrs Delamer, but replied pleasantly enough: 'Likewise, Miss Hartwood!'

'Have you accepted Mrs Jameson's invitation to her *soirée?*' Mrs Delamer asked Hugh.

'Yes, Miss Starling and I will attend. Do I have you to thank for it?'

'Don't flatter yourself,' she retorted with an astringency that had been known to put royal dukes in their place. 'I can't think of anything more unlikely than to be putting myself to the trouble of securing social invitations for you. I merely chanced upon Mrs Jameson the other day and she mentioned she had invited you. I might attend myself – we shall see. Miss Starling, be sure to give your grandfather my warmest regards when you next see him! He was a firm favourite of mine... and a most *stimulating* companion.'

April darted a nervous glance at her, wondering if she had heard the emphasis correctly. The naughty gleam in her grandmother's eye confirmed her suspicion.

Thankfully, no one else seemed to have noticed the carnal connotation and, after saying their goodbyes, the two groups parted ways.

Nine

As soon as Hugh and Miss Starling were out of earshot, April exclaimed: 'Good Lord, don't tell me Miss Starling's grandfather was *acquainted* with you in Paris?'

'Not in the way you mean – he couldn't have afforded me!' scoffed Mrs Delamer. But there was a secret smile on her lips, and, after a moment, she added: 'He certainly wanted us to become better *acquainted*, to use your term. And he was very persuasive.'

'Oh dear, say no more.'

'Don't be prudish.'

'I'm not prudish! Well, perhaps a little,' April owned with a laugh. 'But who would want to hear such details when they concern one's own grandparent? More importantly, how you can be so calm when you're in danger of being recognised by him?'

'I'm not the ninnyhammer you seem to think me. Delamer is not a name with which he's familiar. And I, of course, first ascertained the state of his health – weren't you listening?'

April did not reply.

A commotion up the street had claimed her attention and she was mesmerised by the extraordinary sight of Hugh grabbing the coat lapels of one of the men who had ogled her earlier, and then lifting him clear off the ground.

While the remaining group of men dispersed, Hugh appeared to have a mostly one-sided conversation with the gentleman dangling in the air.

When he was finished, he lowered the man to the ground, smoothed out his coat with a friendly pat and then strolled over to where Miss Starling was waiting, a shocked expression on her face. Placing her limp hand on his arm, he led her away as if nothing untoward had occurred.

'You're not listening again,' complained Mrs Delamer.

'I beg your pardon,' said April, returning her attention to her grandmother. 'I just witnessed the most extraordinary thing... but never mind that, what were you saying, ma'am?'

'I was saying, I have no fear that Miss Starling's grandfather will recognise me. Poor Harry apparently had a stroke a few years back and no longer leaves his estate. A great shame! He could always be counted on to brighten the dullest of gatherings. Why do you dislike Miss Starling?'

The question was asked so abruptly April found herself responding: 'She is so high and mighty... oh, I mean, I don't dislike her!'

'You could have fooled me. There's nothing the matter with Miss Starling that I can see. What has she done to warrant your censure?'

'Nothing! Although, you may not have noticed, she was in the milliner's shop earlier and was listening to our conversation. You should have seen the look she gave me!'

'Is that your only reason?'

'What other reason could there be?' April asked touchily.

'Hmm... well, if she's willing to ignore the incident, I suggest you do the same. She's not a bad girl, by all accounts. Thinks highly of herself but with good reason. With her looks and breeding she could have looked as high as she wanted for a husband if her father hadn't frittered away her dowry. She's fortunate he died before he reduced her and her mother to penury.'

'She has not done so badly for herself, so you must excuse me if I don't feel inclined to pity her. And don't you think it odd that she continues to call her fiancé *Mr Royce*, as if he were of no more importance than a passing acquaintance?'

'It's old fashioned, certainly. That would be down to her upbringing – nothing to get uppity about! There's no love between them, but if you'd known Hugh's mother you'd understand why he's used his head in choosing a wife and not his heart.'

Her curiosity aroused, April waited for her grandmother to continue.

But Mrs Delamer appeared to lose interest in the conversation and became absorbed in the various shops they passed.

April battled with herself for several minutes; but the lure was too great.

'Lord Paisley never mentions his youngest sister, so I know little about her,' she remarked casually. 'Was there something wrong with her?'

'Hmm?'

'You said *if you'd known Hugh's mother you'd understand.* What was the matter with her?'

'Well, for one, she and her husband were both in love with the same woman,' Mrs Delamer observed dryly. 'He worshipped his wife and she worshipped herself! She was one of the most beautiful coquettes of her generation – full grand passions and not an ounce of restraint! Unsurprising really, when you consider Barnaby Paisley sired her. I warned Hugh's father not to marry her. She ended up plunging him from one scandal into another, and he, poor fool, was so besotted he'd not hear a word against her. But, in time, even his forbearance reached an end, and their public quarrels became renowned. Your grandfather was dining with them on one occasion when an argument grew so heated that she threw a glass at her husband's head, and then continued to ring a peel over him as he sat bleeding over the dinner table. And when some of the guests attempted to calm her, she apparently turned on them for taking his side, burst into tears, and topped off the night's dramatics by fainting dead away.'

'Oh dear!' April exclaimed. 'It sounds like a most uncomfortable household. What happened after she fainted?'

Mrs Delamer chuckled.

'Well, as you know, your grandfather never could stand a fuss. He threw the water jug over her, told her she'd had an adverse reaction to the oysters and ordered the staff to carry her to her bed. I wish I could have been there to see it! He was never more magnificent than when he took control of a situation.'

'He was splendid, wasn't he? You know, I used to be quite terrified of him, and – I'm ashamed to say – used to dread your stays in Cornwall. Until the day he gave me a kitten for Christmas! It was very clever of him. Nothing could have been more calculated to put him in my good graces.'

'It was never his way to show excessive emotion, but he certainly adored you. . . though, if he knew how you've squandered the inheritance he left you on that pile of stones you call a home, he'd have an apoplexy!'

'I prefer to think he would recognise that I'm investing in the future of my family.'

'You should have sold it. It isn't entailed and you'd now be plump in the pocket.'

'How could I? My father saw fit to leave the estate to me so that I could make a push to reverse its fortunes. I could not reconcile it with my conscience to treat his trust so callously.'

'The real reason is, you love the place,' her grandmother retorted, not unkindly.

'Both reasons happen to be true.'

Some minutes passed in silence as they continued down the street.

Until, prompted by the feeling of camaraderie that had sprung up between them, April ventured to ask: 'Were you never tempted to marry after Grandpapa died?'

Her grandmother's gaze remained fixed ahead. She was silent for so long April thought she would not answer the question.

'We were together for close to thirty years,' she said at last. 'I may not have been a widow in the eyes of the law, but I felt like one. And afterwards, I could never find another man I wished to converse with over the breakfast table.'

After a long pause, she went on, as if the words were drawn from her: 'Your grandfather was the only one I ever wished to marry. And I had to refuse him. His father tied up his inheritance in such a way that he stood to lose everything if we married... *everything*. I could not allow that to happen. Away from the things he had been bred to – Windermere, his land, his stables – he would have been a fish out of water, and in time, undoubtedly, he would have come to resent me... *argh*, what a dismal subject!' she exclaimed dismissively. 'This is why I've no patience with reminiscing – it's a damned futile pastime!'

April linked her arm through her grandmother's, and they continued homewards in silence.

Ten

On being let into the house by Layton half an hour later, they were informed that Lady Hartwood had returned and could be found in the drawing room. . . alone.

April smiled her thanks at this piece of information, and, after handing him her hat and gloves, escorted her grandmother upstairs.

Lady Hartwood looked up from the correspondence she was reading when they entered the room and offered them her lovely smile.

'How wonderful to see you, Mother!' she cried, and, rising, came over to kiss her parent on both cheeks. 'Have you had a lovely afternoon of shopping? When Layton told me you had gone on foot in such a horrid wind – northerly, no doubt! – I was worried you'd catch a chill. Won't you come and warm yourself by the fire?'

'Don't fuss over me, Eleanor!' snapped Mrs Delamer. 'I'm not yet in my dotage.'

'Well, for myself, I admit I am feeling the cold,' said April, deftly drawing her grandmother towards the fire. 'And more than anything I would love a cup of tea.'

'Whisky for me,' said Mrs Delamer. 'I don't maudle my insides with tea all day long.'

'Of course! At once!' replied Lady Hartwood and gave Layton, who stood in the doorway, a significant look. 'Oh, how cosy it is to have the three of us together again,' she went on brightly, taking a seat. 'I hope you mean to remain for dinner, Mother?'

'Not today. However, before long, you will host a dinner party here and I'll make certain to attend on that particular occasion. We shall set a date after Amelia Jameson's *soirée*. Once April has made her *début*. Nothing too large, you understand – ten persons at most. I'll send you the invitation list shortly.'

Lady Hartwood was rather surprised by this request, but was too well-mannered to show any of this on her countenance.

'Of course, I would be delighted to hold a dinner party for your friends! Will you require me to. . . to put on any particular entertainment for them?' she asked with some trepidation.

As her mother's friends included a rather bawdy collection of aging reprobates, from all walks of life, she was more than a little daunted at the thought of what would constitute an evening's entertainment for them.

Mrs Delamer eyed her with barely contained exasperation.

'For goodness sake, Eleanor, why would I wish to foist my friends on you when I can entertain them myself in Richmond in grander style than you could ever achieve in this London rabbit warren? I am, of course, referring to inviting persons who will be of use in securing a husband for April. . . which, need I remind you, is the chief reason you came to the Capital!'

'Oh, of course,' said Lady Hartwood, looking relieved. 'How stupid of me! You may count on me to do all that I can in *that* regard.'

'The chief reason we are here,' corrected April, 'is to introduce Mama to Albert's family and friends and to launch *her* into Society.'

Mrs Delamer did not deign to reply to this. She spent the next hour discussing with her daughter their various acquaintances and how they could be put to good use on April's behalf; while the subject of their discussion reclined comfortably in her wing chair and listened to them in amused silence, unable to shake the feeling that Hugh would find their stratagems as entertaining as she did.

When Mrs Delamer's carriage arrived at the appointed hour to collect her, April and Lady Hartwood escorted her to the front door.

Turning to her daughter, Mrs Delamer gave her chin a fond pinch.

'You always were a goose, Eleanor, but you have a good heart and such pretty manners that you never gave your father or I the least cause to be ashamed of you.'

April rolled her eyes at this double-edged praise, but Lady Hartwood was quite overcome and threw her arms around her parent.

'Oh, Mother, thank you!'

Mrs Delamer, caught by surprise, looked uncomfortable at the show of affection.

'There, there. . . enough of that,' she said gruffly, patting her daughter awkwardly. 'You're a good girl.'

Lady Hartwood disengaged herself with a watery smile and took out her handkerchief to dab her eyes.

April gave her grandmother a twinkling look and kissed her cheek.

'Goodbye, Grandmama. We hope you will condescend to stay with us for a few days on your next visit?'

'We shall see,' replied Mrs Delamer grandly. 'Don't forget I will be sending my hairdresser to you. Allow him free rein! He'll know exactly what will suit you.'

April bit back a retort and reminded herself that the loss of her hair was for a good cause... her mother's happiness.

Mrs Delamer turned to Layton, who was waiting to escort her to her carriage, and, placing her hand on his arm, descended the few stone steps to the pavement.

'You make certain to take care of our girls, you ne'er-do-well,' she told him. 'They're not as seasoned as we are. I trust you know how to depress the presumptions of any jackanapes or libertines who come knocking?'

'That I do, ma'am,' he replied without hesitation. 'I've had a great deal of experience dealing with Miss April's suitors over the years.'

'You have, indeed!' she chuckled. 'I still remember the time you threw the hearth ashes out the window onto that dim-witted Mr Spingells.'

A sparkle shone in the old butler's eyes.

'I had attempted tact on several occasions, as you know, ma'am, but the young man appeared immune to reason. I don't believe he will ever again forget himself to the point of disturbing a gentleman's household with his serenading well past the bedtime hour.'

Mrs Delamer's laughter could still be heard as her carriage pulled away.

'Did you know Grandmama knew Albert's father in Paris?' April asked her mother as they made their way back upstairs.

'Lord Wulfingston? *No!*' exclaimed Lady Hartwood, looking horrified. 'Oh dear... was he... did they...?'

April laughed and shook her head.

'No, apparently not. According to Grandmama she would not have had him if he were the last man alive. She appears to hold some prejudice against him, but *what* I could not discover.'

'Oh, this is *terrible*! What are we to do? If he should recognise her... it does not bear thinking about!'

'I too was concerned at first, but then I realised how unlikely it would be considering an interval of fifty years and a different setting.'

'Let us hope you're right, love! Sometimes I cannot help wishing – I know it's *shockingly* uncivil of me – that there were no more of my mother's acquaintances left from that time. Only *then* can we be comfortable.'

'Very uncivil of you, indeed,' agreed April, a tremor in her voice. 'How could they be so disobliging as to stay alive and ruin our peace?'

'Now you are laughing at me,' said Lady Hartwood with wounded dignity. 'But you must own it *is* uncomfortable to be continually living in dread that someone will recognise her and denounce her as a fraud. Not that I worry on our account. She has shielded us well in case of just such an occurrence. But, although she is in astonishingly good health, there is no denying she is almost seventy and the shock of such a denouncement *cannot* be at all good for her!'

'Don't gift Grandmama with your sensibility.'

'But surely anyone would be distressed under such circumstances?' insisted her ladyship.

'More likely, she will simply laugh it off. She's old enough and wealthy enough to be indifferent to people's opinion of her... *tis a consummation devoutly to be wished.*'

'Really, love, if you think that spouting Shakespeare at a time like this is likely to soothe my nerves then you have done me a grave injustice!' Lady Hartwood declared with feeling. 'I have no patience with the man at the best of times! His writing is so incomprehensible and self-indulgent it never fails to give me a headache.'

Eleven

With barely two weeks having passed since their arrival in the Capital, the funds that April had brought with her from Cornwall had started to dwindle at an alarming rate.

She had hoped to stretch out the amount for at least a month before needing to replenish it, however, this was proving impossible, and she was coming to realise that she had failed to take into proper consideration the extortionate cost of food, coal, candles, and other such essentials in London.

She could only be grateful that Lord Paisley had brought them here in his travelling chaise, sparing her the cost of stabling for her own horses and carriage.

And, thanks to their landlord, they were now making a substantial saving by not paying rent; but as that arrangement had always been between their respective men-of-business, she had not taken the amount into consideration when calculating her cash reserves.

So, one windy late-autumn afternoon, April dressed in a stylish, high-necked walking dress and lovely russet-red pelisse (both delivered by the modiste only yesterday) and went to inform her mother that she had an errand to run.

She did not divulge the particulars of her errand for they would have only depressed her mother's spirits, as talk of money always seemed to do. And, in any case, her mother would not have approved of her intentions. Her ladyship shared society's view that such tasks as visiting banks were the domain of men, and no genteel lady should set foot in such a place.

It would have been pointless to debate with her the finer points of the matter; such as the fact that even though they had a man of business in Cornwall, who could perform the task for them, they could not afford a second such gentleman in London.

Dropping a kiss on her mother's cheek, April promised to return in time to dress for their theatre engagement with Lord Paisley and left her to her blissful ignorance.

Before leaving the house she went in search of Kenan, the footman she had brought with her from Cornwall; a trustworthy individual who was as handy with a gun as with his fists and could be counted on to protect them. And, to add to these merits, he had never shown the least tendency to fall in love with her.

It did not take her long to find him in the nether regions of the house and they were soon hailing a hackney coach to take them to Child & Co, her family's bank for the last hundred years.

Situated in Fleet Street, on the city side of what Lord Paisley had helpfully told her was Christopher Wren's baroque gateway, Temple Bar, the bank was no great distance away as the crow flew. But, owing to the heavy traffic they encountered on the way, it took over half an hour before they pulled up in front of this institution.

Bidding Kenan to wait for her outside, April made her way to the large oak entry doors. She passed a couple of gentlemen in the process and their conversation faltered as they looked her over with interest.

She lowered her veil with a practised hand and quickly walked into the bank to get away from their stares.

She entered in such a hurry that, before she knew it, she was halfway across the large, marbled foyer. Resisting the urge to look about her and take in the grandeur of this male bastion, like some over-awed yokel, she instead concentrated on making her way over to one of the tellers without tripping over her feet in her nervousness.

The young man behind the counter looked up from the papers in his hands and offered her a surprised smile.

'Good afternoon, ma'am.'

'Good afternoon. I would like to withdraw a sum of money.' Taking a document from her reticule, she slid it across the counter. 'My letter of introduction.'

The teller was staring at her so intently that she raised a hand to check that her veil had been lowered. She found it to be in place and could only suppose his reaction was due to the fact that she was committing a social transgression.

Tearing his gaze away from her, the young man picked up the letter, broke the seal and began to read with flustered concentration.

When he was finished, he said deferentially: 'Lady Hartwood, we are honoured to have. . . '

'Lady Hartwood is my mother,' April interrupted gently. 'The letter should refer to a Miss April Hartwood, and I am she.'

'I-I see,' he replied, disconcerted.

Bending his head, he carefully reread the letter. When he looked up again, the apologetic look in his eyes alerted her that something was wrong.

'The letter refers to a Baroness Hartwood,' he said, and, swallowing uncomfortably, began to read: '. . . *Baroness Hartwood who inherited the estate from her father the 7ᵗʰ Baron Hartwood in its entirety and all rights thereof. . .* etcetera etcetera. Under the circumstances, ma'am, I regret to say, I'm not certain we will be able to release any funds to you.'

'Oh, pray don't say such a thing! May I?'

She took back possession of the letter and read it.

'You are right,' she said, greatly vexed. 'It appears Mr Brightly, my man of business, has been premature in using the title I inherited from my father. . . and has not even seen fit to write out my name in full!'

'You inherited your father's title?' asked the clerk, forgetting himself for a moment so great was his surprise.

'Yes,' she replied absentmindedly. 'The Barony of Hartwood was created by writ, and the remainders of baronies by writ are not limited to male heirs. . . how *foolish*!'

'I-I beg pardon. I should not have presumed. . . '

'Oh, not *you*,' she said, throwing him an apologetic smile. 'Mr Brightly has been foolish. He knows very well I have not yet had a chance to claim the title.'

Or more accurately, she had refused to claim it.

It would have been a betrayal of her mother, who had more than earned the right to call herself Baroness Hartwood. April's signature might be required on all official documents to do with the estate, but she was adamant that her mother would continue to enjoy the honours of her position. Only after she married and became Viscountess Paisley would April think of formally taking up the title, and not a moment before.

'Do you have any documentation, ma'am, to prove that you are indeed the daughter of Baron Hartwood?' asked the clerk, wishing to be helpful to the ravishing creature before him, whose beauty could not be fully concealed by a short veil at such close distance.

'No,' she replied, momentarily daunted. 'I have documentation, of course, only not in London. What is to be done?'

'Perhaps if the current Baroness Hartwood could visit us and clarify a few details?'

'There is not the least likelihood of my mother visiting your bank,' she said frankly. 'And as I have no man of business to represent me in London, some solution will need to be agreed upon before I leave today. Would you be so good as to ask your manager to join us?'

Impressed by her business-like tone, the clerk took himself off at once and returned a short while later with an older man, who he introduced as Mr Wethering.

'May I be of assistance?' asked Mr Wethering, regarding April through the spectacles on the tip of his nose.

'I certainly hope so!' she replied and proceeded to explain the circumstances to him.

He was all politeness but advised that he could not release any funds without the correct documentation. He suggested, most humbly, that the young lady could ask her man of business to correct the wording on his letter of introduction.

'That's all very well,' replied April, barely containing her impatience, 'but what am I to do about my expenses while I await a reply from Cornwall?'

'I am afraid, ma'am, that I am unable to advise you on this point.'

April pressed her lips together to stop an unbecoming and, she had to own, unwarranted retort. It was not the poor man's fault she found herself in this predicament.

'Before I go to the trouble of posting a letter to Cornwall and awaiting a reply,' she said, 'perhaps it would be wise to first ascertain what exactly is required...'

'Good afternoon, Cousin April,' a familiar voice interrupted.

April turned swiftly about, a hand flying to her breast.

'Good Lord, Hugh!' she exclaimed. 'What a fright you gave me! *Must* you sneak up on people?'

She lifted her veil and frowned up at him.

'It was not my intention to alarm you,' he said, offering her a smile.

April's eyes slid away from him.

'No, of course not. I... it's of no consequence.'

'Mr Royce, a pleasure to see you again,' said Mr Wethering, coming forwards to shake hands with one of his bank's most valuable clients.

'Is there a problem here, Wethering?' asked Hugh.

'Only a slight misunderstanding, sir. I apprehend, for I could not help overhearing, that Miss Hartwood – or Baroness Hartwood, as the case may be – is the daughter of the 7ᵗʰ Baron Hartwood and your cousin?'

'That is correct,' said Hugh without hesitation.

'And, if I may be so bold, sir, can you vouch for the lady?'

'Certainly. I will also guarantee whatever money she requires to be released to her.'

'Well, then, there can be no further objections!' said the manager, wreathed in smiles. 'Miss Hartwood, please accept my apologies for detaining you. Stevens will be only too happy to assist you in completing your transaction.'

April resisted the urge to roll her eyes, and instead offered her thanks to the two men who had taken it upon themselves to settle her business for her without her input.

Twelve

In less than ten minutes, April had withdrawn a sum of money she hoped would be enough for the next couple of months, stuffed the considerable roll of notes into her reticule and was ready to leave the bank.

Hugh appeared to have finished his own business and was waiting to escort her out.

'I don't know how to thank you,' she said, smiling up at him. 'Your appearance could not have been better timed! I was beginning to fear I would have to live on credit until the matter was settled.'

'You need not fear living on credit for such a short period,' he replied. 'The *ton* live on credit for years at a time!'

'But how contemptible! Surely *you* don't withhold payment from honest tradespeople?'

'I would hardly admit to it knowing you would find me contemptible,' he said with a hint of amusement.

'I'd wager all your bills are paid in a timely manner.'

'I don't see how you can know such a thing?'

'It feels as if it would be out of character for you to do otherwise. Am I wrong? Do you not think it disgraceful to impose on those less fortunate?'

His all-too-attractive smile made an appearance and her heart performed an odd little skip.

'I do,' he admitted. 'Though I risk inflating your conceit by admitting you have read my character correctly.'

A startled laugh escaped her.

'My conceit is not inflated, I thank you! How abominable you are,' she declared and walked off towards the exit.

'I hope you didn't venture here alone?' he asked when they stood outside on the steps.

'Would it shock you if I did?' she replied, evading the question to punish him a little for his last comment.

'I wouldn't be even mildly surprised.'

'Oh? Because of a want of conduct on my part?' she asked sweetly.

'Because, as yet, you are unaccustomed to the ways of London Society. . . and there's no need for you to show your hackles when the truth of it is undeniable.'

'I am not so green as you seem to think me! If you must know, I brought my footman.'

She gestured to Kenan, a few feet away. . . and, as she did so, caught sight of the gentlemen who had looked her over earlier. They had grown in temerity and were now openly ogling her.

An angry glint entered her eyes and, turning to face them, she offered them her most dazzling smile.

'It is an exceedingly beautiful face, is it not?' she said with exaggerated amiability. 'By all means, take out your quizzing glasses and inspect it more closely if you feel it necessary. . . no? Oh well, perhaps you're right. You would not want to come across as being any more ill-mannered and vulgar than you already are!'

The gentlemen mumbled their apologies and retreated into the bank.

'A most effective strategy,' remarked Hugh, laughing.

'I may as well belong to a travelling circus!' she said hotly. 'At least then I would be paid for the ignominy of being gawked at. I'm sorry if I embarrassed you, but there was no bearing it!'

'You need not apologise to me,' he replied with a sympathetic look. 'I don't embarrass easily. Is your carriage waiting?'

'No. I did not bring my carriage to London. And now, I must bid you good day,' she said briskly, holding out her hand to him. 'Thank you, again, for your assistance. I'm very much obliged to you.'

'I'll drive you home,' said Hugh, ignoring her outstretched hand.

'Thank you but there is not the least need for you to do so. We can catch another hackney.'

'I insist.'

'I don't care if you insist! I'm quite capable of. . . '

'Yes, yes, I know you want to snub me, but you'll just have to do so on another occasion. On *this* occasion, as it would be unsafe for you to travel in a public conveyance with so much money on your person, you'll have to spare me.'

April opened her mouth to argue; then just as speedily shut it again.

She was not so plump in the pocket that she could take the risk, however small, of being robbed today.

'I was not trying to snub you,' she said, a degree of stiffness in her voice. 'But I take leave to tell you that you are in dire need of one! You are atrociously high-handed. Do you always bamboozle those around you until you get your own way?'

'Always,' he said, smiling at her in a manner she considered thoroughly inappropriate.

'Well, there is nothing in that to be pleased about! I would be ashamed to admit it!'

'Would you?'

A smile began to tug at the corner of her mouth and she had to look away before she betrayed herself.

'Your point regarding the risk of riding in a public vehicle has merit,' she owned, after a moment. 'It appears I am to be obliged to you once again.'

'Think nothing of it. I've some business to attend to in your area that I shouldn't put off any longer.'

'So I am, in fact, doing *you* a favour?'

'Yes.'

April laughed and shook her head at him.

'So untruthful, Cousin Hugh.'

'I thought we agreed to drop that familial prefix? I don't wish to incur Mrs Delamer's wrath, after all,' he said conscientiously.

'Yes, I saw how terrified you were of her! But you yourself called me Cousin April inside the bank?'

'Would it be inflating my own self-importance to admit it was purely to help you out of your dilemma?'

'It was certainly effective! And, as I was the beneficiary, my manners must keep me from teasing you over it.'

'Only manners?'

'Yes,' she replied, laughing again.

She was secretly pleased with herself for being able to maintain an unaffected style of conversation, despite his proximity. It gave her hope that before long she would be able to be in his company without the least discomfort.

'Speaking of prefixes,' said Hugh, smiling down at her, 'why did Wethering refer to you as Baroness Hartwood?'

'Oh... I suppose because I inherited the title from my father,' she replied, discomposed by a subject that always aroused feelings of guilt. 'However, for various reasons, I have not yet taken it up.'

Hugh regarded her enquiringly and she felt herself blush under his steady gaze.

Before he could ask any more questions, she turned away and called Kenan over to inform him that he need not wait as Mr Royce would see her home.

When she looked back at Hugh, she was relieved to see he appeared to have decided against pressing her for further information. He simply offered her his arm and led her over to a high-perch phaeton, parked on the side of the road. A couple of strong-willed chestnuts were harnessed to the vehicle and were doing their best to flout their groom's attempts to steady them.

April eyed her jostling nemeses with misgiving, before forcing her attention away from them and examining the phaeton.

'I have never seen the body positioned so high off the ground. Is it safe?' she asked.

'It depends on who's driving.'

Hugh climbed in and leant down to help her to mount.

As she placed her hand in his, for the second time in her life a strange jolt of sensation shot through her body.

Her self-satisfaction from moments ago died away. It seemed she was doomed to suffer discomfort in his company, after all.

As she climbed into the phaeton with Hugh's assistance, and made herself comfortable on the padded bench-seat beside him, she silently lamented the fact that her body should have chosen *him* of all males to react to in such an unnerving manner.

A faint sigh escaped her and Hugh turned to study her profile.

Looking away abruptly, he took the reins and whip his groom held up to him, exchanged a few words with the young man and then ordered him to 'let them go'.

The horses were released and surged forward.

April gave a squeal and grabbed Hugh's arm to stop herself from flying out of her seat.

After a few tense minutes, she was relieved to realise that he could handle the spirited pair and would not allow them to bolt. Her posture relaxed a little and she discreetly let go of his arm, hoping he had not noticed the intimacy.

'You may hold on to me if it will make you feel more comfortable,' he said.

'Thank you,' she replied with some embarrassment, 'I'm perfectly comfortable.'

This was, of course, untrue. However, as holding onto Hugh made her something entirely the opposite of comfortable, she was determined to choose the lesser of two evils.

They took the next corner at sufficient speed to make her sway towards the edge of the vehicle, but before she could discard her scruples and reach for Hugh's arm, his hand shot out and grabbed her elbow.

'Careful!' he warned.

'I'm not accustomed to high-perch phaetons,' she said apologetically.

'And I'm not accustomed to driving a female in one,' he admitted, letting go of her and pulling back on the reins to reduce their speed.

'Was that an apology or a dispersion on my sex?' she asked, grasping for levity. 'My response would vary depending on your intent.'

Hugh smiled, his eyes on the road.

'Let us say it was simply an observation. My curricle is a vehicle more suited to driving your sex.'

'Oh, so it *was* a dispersion! I'll have you know many of us excel at driving vehicles of all shapes and sizes. Although I freely admit I'm not one of their number. I was never blessed with a wonderful sense of balance.'

'Were you not?' he asked, looking across at her with amusement.

'Should you ever have the misfortune to dance with me you'll understand what I mean.'

'I thought girls of your age always profess to enjoy dancing?'

'Oh, I enjoy it well enough. I'm simply abysmal at it! I no longer dare to dance the quadrille – or any dance with complex figures – in case I should injure my neighbours. I restrict myself to the waltz.'

'And why the waltz?'

'Because it is the man's responsibility to hold me in the necessary position and take me along with him. All that is required of me is to relinquish control of my body and allow him to do with me as he pleases.'

Hugh stiffened beside her.

He cast her a hard, appraising look, searching for signs that she was playing the coquette.

April sensed his reaction and, turning to look at him, asked: 'Is something the matter?'

Her expression was so free of guile that he could only suppose she had spoken the double entendre in innocence. He knew he should simply be amused, but both his body and imagination were causing him discomfort.

'No,' he replied gruffly, shifting his weight.

April could tell from the tension in his countenance that something was wrong and, placing a solicitous hand on him, asked kindly: 'Are you suffering from a spasm of some sort? My mother experiences them on occasion and finds great benefit from a glass of water with a little vinegar and. . .'

'Lord spare me from female ministrations!' Hugh burst out.

'There's no need to be rude! I was only trying to help. Any fool can see you are in discomfort.'

'I neither expect nor want your help. . . and may I suggest,' he said in the tone of someone pushed beyond endurance, 'if you need to hold on to me, my arm would be of more use to you.'

He looked down pointedly.

Following his gaze, April saw her gloved hand resting on one well-muscled thigh covered in buckskin.

She snatched her hand away, blushing furiously.

She would have liked nothing better than to inform him that she had not been trying to seduce him. And that, in fact, *nothing* would be more unlikely! But as this would have entailed continuing to discuss a subject that filled her with mortification, she remained silent.

And she lowered her veil for good measure.

No further conversation was exchanged between them until the horses came to a stop in front of her residence.

'I can't let go of the reins to come around and help you to dismount,' Hugh said in a curt tone. 'But if you take my hand and step down, as you did on mounting, you'll be quite safe.'

'Thank you, but I do not require your assistance,' April replied haughtily, and began to climb down.

Unfortunately, without his hand to steady her, it was a rather awkward descent and not at all in keeping with the dignified impression she was trying to convey.

To make matters worse, partway through her petticoat became tangled underfoot and tore, and, muttering to herself with exasperation, she had to stop to free it before continuing.

After contorting herself into several unladylike shapes, her feet found the pavement at last and she stood and looked up at Hugh through her veil (she was not going to do him the courtesy of lifting it!).

'Thank you for your escort, Mr Royce,' she said coolly.

Hugh kept his unbidden smile firmly in check and politely tipped his hat at her.

April nodded, just as politely, and waited for him to drive away.

He remained where he was, watching her.

'Why are you staring at me?' she demanded.

'I'm not staring at you. And neither am I so ill-mannered as to drive off before I've seen you safely inside.'

'Oh, for goodness sake! *Now* you discover your manners?' she retorted.

Turning smartly about, she climbed the stairs and knocked on the front door, and, as soon as it was opened, whisked herself inside without a backward glance.

Thirteen

'April-love,' said Lady Hartwood, letting herself into her daughter's bedchamber on the eve of Mrs Jameson's *soirée*, 'Albert has arrived. Are you ready?'

'I cannot accustom myself to this new haircut,' April sighed, regarding herself in her mirror.

Familiarity with her own looks might have made it impossible for her to admire them, but she was not wholly devoid of vanity and wanted to look her best for her first outing amongst the *ton*.

'Mr Pigott insisted on cutting it so uncompromisingly short,' she went on, 'I feel utterly exposed!'

'Well, for my part, I think he did a splendid job! There is now nothing to distract from your lovely features.'

'So I can be stared at even more!'

'To hear you talk, love, one would think you resented being blessed with beauty?'

'Well, I'm not so eccentric as to wish to be plain. But I do feel that to be pretty rather than beautiful would be more suited to my disposition.' She smiled at her mother's baffled expression. 'Oh well, at least Rachel now finds it easier to dress my hair. And I'm only too happy to be spared her sticking hairpins into me as if I were a pin cushion!'

'I don't know why you insisted on hiring the girl?' complained Lady Hartwood. 'For *years* I begged you to hire a lady's maid for yourself but, with all the good will in the world, Rachel is not fit for the role. . . though I suppose we must now call her Browning, if you insist on keeping her.'

'You know perfectly well why I hired her, Mama.'

'Of course, I understand you felt responsible for her after you convinced her to run away from her employer. But, as I said at the time, you could have simply given her some money and sent her on her way!'

'Where could she have gone when she has no family? Don't worry, she will soon learn her role now that your talented Keighley has taken her under her wing.'

'Well, I don't want to disappoint you, love, but I must tell you that Keighley is not *entirely* reconciled to what you have asked of her. She has warned me not to expect miracles, and insists on repeating – in the most tiresome way! – that she cannot make a silk purse out of a sow's ear.'

'She may grumble but she'll do her best – which is all I ask!' When her mother did not look to be entirely convinced by this reasoning, April added gently: 'Surely you would not have wanted me to leave such an innocent girl working at that inn? With such a lecherous landlord?'

Lady Hartwood sighed in resignation.

'No, no. . . certainly not!'

'He is fortunate we did not lodge a complaint against him with the magistrate,' said April, eyes kindling. 'Only imagine what would have happened if my bed had not been so uncomfortable that I was awake to hear her protests when he forced his way into her room?'

'I don't want to imagine,' objected Lady Hartwood, shuddering delicately. 'The poor girl! I was never so incensed in my life! And although I might wish that you had not taken such an active role in the matter – for, you know, love, it was not at all lady-like to clout the man with the bedpan – I was nevertheless *delighted* when you rendered him unconscious. He will think twice before forcing his attentions on another woman. And as for his atrocious beds – *well*! I don't believe I slept a wink myself that night! I surely had the lumpiest, most ill-filled straw mattress in the entire kingdom. If it had been shaken and turned *once* in all its years of service I would count myself astonished. And the sheets were *not* aired, no matter what that horrible man said to the contrary!'

April could not help smiling. It was unclear from this speech what her mother found more shocking: their landlord's lascivious intentions or his lack of housekeeping skills.

'That whole episode is best left forgotten,' went on Lady Hartwood resolutely. 'For all our sakes! And as for your haircut, love, it looks charming on you and you have no need at all to feel self-conscious, or exposed.'

April regarded herself in the mirror again.

'I suppose I shouldn't feel exposed when this new gown covers me up so admirably.'

Lady Hartwood eyed the high-necked evening gown a little dubiously. She was not used to seeing her daughter dressed in such a concealing style.

Still, there was no denying the sky-blue silk had been expertly moulded to her shape and looked surprisingly dashing.

With its straight skirt, puff sleeves and a neckline that reached almost to the chin, *Madame Franchot* had created a gown that was stunning in its simplicity. There were no frills or lace to mar its sleek silhouette, only a row of pearl buttons that marched daintily down the bodice, over April's bosom and finished where the skirt of the dress gathered under the bust.

'I look as if I have joined a nunnery,' April remarked dispassionately.

'Nothing of the sort! No nun would allow herself to be seen in such a tight bodice, I assure you.'

April threw her mother a twinkling look.

'Then perhaps I should be concerned that I'm revealing too much?'

Lady Hartwood's brow creased as she contemplated this possibility.

'I'm only teasing, Mama!' laughed April. 'I'm certain I'll be the most soberly dressed woman there tonight! Now, let us go and join Albert before he loses all patience with us.'

A few minutes later, with their cloaks draped over their arms, the ladies walked into the parlour off the vestibule, where Layton had placed Lord Paisley and given him a glass of sherry with which to fortify himself while he waited.

Upon their entrance his lordship put aside his drink and came forward to kiss his betrothed, saying with awed appreciation that no one could hold a candle to her.

Lady Hartwood blossomed into even greater beauty under his adoring gaze.

'And you, my dear, look as pretty as a picture,' Lord Paisley told April. 'You are bound to have an offer of marriage before the end of the night.'

'Thank you for the warning!' she returned, eyes full of laughter. 'I'll make sure to be on my guard for foolish gentlemen. And may I say, Albert, you are looking very fine yourself this evening? There's something different about you, but I cannot quite put my finger on it.'

'Yes, you look very handsome, dearest,' agreed her ladyship. 'Are you wearing a new coat?'

Lord Paisley looked pleased and a little self-conscious, and, putting back his shoulders, straightened to his full height.

'Yes, the coat is new. Actually, I've had to buy several coats recently. It was easier to replace them than to have them taken in.'

'Taken in? Albert, are you by chance on a reducing diet?' Lady Hartwood asked with a good deal of surprise.

'I want to look my best for you, my love. . . ahem, well then, we'd best be off! No point in standing around when the carriage is waiting.'

'I think it suits you very well,' April told him with a smile as she passed him; then she walked on ahead to allow the affianced couple a few moments alone.

By the time Lord Paisley's coachman pulled up in front of Mrs Jameson's townhouse it had started to rain with considerable force. His lordship, fearing for his companions' satin slippers, had the happy notion of carrying them from the carriage to the glass and steel portico that extended from the house to the pavement.

'Are you certain, dearest?' asked Lady Hartwood, eyeing him with trepidation. 'Perhaps your footman could assist me? I would not wish to. . . to crumple your evening clothes.'

Her betrothed might have lost some weight but that did not blind her to his limitations. A Corinthian he was not.

'No, no, I insist, my love!' he replied. 'My fellow is already wet, and, besides, we need him to hold the umbrella.'

Lady Hartwood gave him a wan smile.

'Of course. . . if you are certain I won't be *too* heavy for you?'

Lord Paisley heaved himself out of the carriage and stretched out his arms to her. He looked so eager to prove himself that she did not have the heart to resist further. She tightened her grip on her cloak and gave a brave little nod.

His lordship then surprised them all by picking her up with great aplomb, and, looking vastly pleased with himself, carried off his fragrant bundle to the cover of the portico.

April laughed and slid across the seat to the open carriage door to shout 'bravo!' after him.

A figure appeared before her suddenly and she drew back in surprise.

Hugh offered her the smile that had intruded on her thoughts far too often over the last few days (an intrusion she could have happily done without!).

'Can I be of assistance?'

'Thank you, but no, Mr Royce. Albert will return for me shortly.'

'I see I'm still sunk below reproach if we're back to *Mr Royce*. Was my behaviour so abominable?'

'You know it was!' she retorted before she could stop herself. But she did not want to be reminded of the whole embarrassing episode in his phaeton and added quickly: 'However, I don't regard it, I assure. I have become quite used to your odd manners. Now please get out of the rain! Albert will be back for me soon.'

'I think carrying your mother has finished him off. If you don't want to end up in a heap on the ground, you'd best let me help you.'

'No, really, there is no need! Please, just see to your fiancée.'

'It was Miss Starling who sent me to you.'

April looked past him and saw her mother talking to Miss Starling on the steps of the townhouse, while Lord Paisley leant against a column and appeared to be attempting to catch his breath.

'How kind of her,' she murmured, uncertain how to feel about such magnanimity.

'Come! You'll be quite safe with me.'

Seeing no alternative, April gave her permission and averted her gaze so she would not have to look him in the eye as he drew near.

In a quick, business-like manner Hugh put an arm around her waist and another under her knees.

'Are you ready?' he asked, his breath tickling the sensitive skin below her ear, exposed by her haircut.

'Yes.' She cleared her throat. Her voice had come out a little too huskily for her liking.

After a slight hesitation, he asked: 'Do you have your reticule? We wouldn't want to send some poor servant back into this weather for it.'

She looked down at the twisted silk cord around her wrist.

'Yes, I have it.'

A pause followed.

'Perhaps we should wrap the carriage blanket around you,' he said in a gruff voice. 'Your cloak will be ruined otherwise.'

April was surprised he was taking the time to think of such details while he stood in the downpour, with only the small amount of cover provided by the umbrella Lord Paisley's footman held for him.

'That won't be necessary,' she replied, daring to look at him. 'A little water won't hurt it.'

His countenance was unnervingly close to her own and was set in a frowning expression.

'I know, my hair is ridiculously short,' she said, feeling self-conscious all of a sudden.

'No.'

'No?'

'It isn't too short.'

A small smile turned up the corners of her mouth.

'Pray, don't overwhelm me with compliments!'

'I like it.'

'Personally, I think I look like an altar boy.'

Hugh did not immediately reply and she had ample time to feel the weight of his scrutiny, and the impropriety of their close proximity.

And to notice, despite the dim light, that his eyes were a dark stormy grey and not brown, as she had supposed.

A strange heat began to permeate through her. She knew it was in her best interests to force her gaze away from him, if only she could do it.

'Nothing about you resembles a boy,' he said in a terse voice; and then, without warning, lifted her out of the carriage and walked off with her so quickly the footman holding the umbrella had to rush to catch up.

In the space of a few seconds, April was deposited on her feet under the portico.

'Thank you,' she said briskly, shaking out the raindrops from her cloak.

Hugh nodded once and made his way up the shallow steps to Miss Starling's side, and, taking her hand, placed it in the crook of his arm.

April fixed a polite smile on her lips and followed.

'Good evening, Miss Starling. Thank you for sending Mr Royce to me.'

'And a good evening to you too, Miss Hartwood. Although it is too wet to be called such! I hope you did not mind being manhandled? It's irksome to rely on men's brute strength, but necessary on occasion.'

'I was only too happy for the assistance.'

'Of course... you are most practical, are you not?' Miss Starling said sweetly. 'I was just saying to Lady Hartwood how sorry I am that you will not have the opportunity to meet my mother this evening. She has caught a chill and must keep to her bed, but she sends her best regards and looks forward to meeting you both very soon.'

April replied with all that was necessary to convey pleasure at the prospect and quickly followed her mother into the townhouse.

They were met in the foyer by the butler. Once their damp outer garments had been handed over to this commanding individual and his minions, he led them up the stairs to the first floor and showed them into a spacious double drawing room, where Mrs Jameson herself was waiting to greet them.

April was the only one of the group who had never before met their hostess and she could not help staring.

For one thing, Mrs Jameson was built along generous lines that demanded attention (and made one wonder if she needed assistance to rise from her bed). And, for another, her hefty bulk, from the top of her head to the bottom of her feet, was dressed in a lavish shade of crimson.

On her elaborately dressed hair sat a large crimson velvet turban, with not one but three ostrich feathers; her crimson silk gown, cut in a classical style and (thankfully!) concealing a good portion of her enormous bust, was embellished with enough embroidery to do justice to a pope; and, if April's eyes were not deceiving her, the crimson slippers on her plump feet sparkled with an intensity that suggested they were embedded with diamonds.

'Eleanor, you look more beautiful each time I see you!' cried Mrs Jameson and embraced Lady Hartwood against her bosom.

Her ladyship's slight frame disappeared into a swathe of crimson and she re-emerged after a few moments looking a little dishevelled.

'You flatter me, ma'am,' she laughed and patted her hair.

'I have known you for over twenty years, my dear, I have no need to flatter you. Paisley, you have found yourself a jewel without price! I hope you're man enough to know how to treat her?'

His lordship bowed and began to assure his hostess, in some detail, how he considered himself the most fortunate of men and planned on dedicating himself to his betrothed's happiness.

'We shall see,' Mrs Jameson cut in on his eloquence. 'I'll be keeping my eye on you. How do you do, Miss Starling? I'm pleased you could join us this evening. I don't believe I have yet had a chance to offer you my felicitations? Hugh's quite a catch, isn't he? One cannot blame you for having said yes to him. If only I were thirty years younger I'd be setting myself up as your rival!'

An inappropriate wink followed this pronouncement and April had to stifle a giggle.

Miss Starling, on the other hand, was not in the least amused. She had never before been addressed by someone of Mrs Jameson's ilk and was momentarily uncertain how to proceed.

Fortunately, one of her mother's many teachings came rushing back to her: *people who do not abide by the rules of etiquette are to be tolerated with a polite smile but never encouraged with a response to their nonsense, for that would only be lowering oneself to their level.*

And so Miss Starling offered her hostess the rather patronising smile she had been taught.

'Yes, you certainly do resemble your mother,' Mrs Jameson remarked, looking kindly upon her. 'A handicap to be sure, but nothing that cannot be overcome with a little willpower!' And after delivering this outrageous statement, she turned to Hugh. 'So, young man! You're getting leg-shackled at last? About time, I suppose. What's the point of accumulating all that wealth if there is no one to share it with? How old are you now – thirty-two?'

'Thirty-four, ma'am,' he replied, a smile in his eyes. 'Have I disappointed you?'

'No, no, of course not. . . at least, not in *that*!' she said cryptically. 'Yours is a good age to be thinking of marriage. You've left your flighty years behind you and are now ready to settle down with the right woman. . . and this must be Miss Hartwood? I have heard a great deal about you, my dear, from our *mutual acquaintance*. I'm sure you know that we have had our heads together making plans for you.'

For one alarming moment April feared she was going to expand further and draw everyone's curiosity, but Miss Jameson only smiled and held her peace.

Eyes sparkling with relief and laughter, April dropped into a curtsey and said warmly: 'I'm honoured to be meeting you at last, ma'am.'

'Yes, you'll do,' Mrs Jameson said approvingly, before going on: 'Paisley, I believe your fiancée and her daughter would appreciate a glass of champagne.'

Lord Paisley accepted this hint with the utmost of good-humour and went off on his errand.

'You two love birds,' Mrs Jameson addressed Hugh and Miss Starling, 'will no doubt wish to spend some time alone in a dark corner somewhere, making eyes at one another. . . and as for you Eleanor, bring your daughter and come with me! I must introduce you to the Duke of Claredon and his mother.' And on those words she led the Hartwood ladies away with an energy that belied the fact she would never again see sixty.

'I believe we have been expertly dismissed,' Hugh observed dryly. Pulling his gaze away from April's retreating form, he found it necessary to exercise his gallantry by raising Miss Starling's hand to his lips. 'What will it be, my dear? Champagne or Madeira?'

Miss Starling gave no indication that this sign of affection was welcome to her and absentmindedly removed her hand from his.

'I suppose it never occurred to our hostess that we too might wish to be introduced to the duke and his mother,' she said with a forced laugh.

'I gather she has more in mind than a simple introduction. In which case, we would be quite superfluous.'

Miss Starling looked up at him with sudden interest.

'Do you mean to say she wishes to promote a match between Miss Hartwood and the Duke of Claredon? But how ludicrous! Miss Hartwood has beauty, certainly, but there are any number of more eligible young ladies for him to choose from. Why, she is reaching for the moon if she thinks to ensnare a duke!'

'No doubt,' he replied, his delivery so repressive that it brought about an end to the subject.

Fourteen

With a purposeful stride Mrs Jameson led mother and daughter towards a striking matron in her early fifties and two young gentlemen of fashion, who were conversing beside one of the two ornate marble fireplaces heating the room.

'Your Grace,' Mrs Jameson, addressed the woman, 'may I make you known to a dear friend? This is Baroness Hartwood...and her daughter, Miss Hartwood. You may have heard of the Hartwoods of St Mawes Castle in Cornwall? Ladies, the Duchess of Claredon.'

The duchess inclined her head and offered them a meagre smile; it was neither welcoming nor repelling, but made perfectly clear that she was reserving judgement on whether they were worthy of the introduction.

This inauspicious greeting may well have daunted a person of lesser self-possession, however, April was merely amused by such a mingling of pride and condescension, and restricted herself to a modest curtsy that in no way hinted at subservience.

She was happy to see that her mother, likewise, did not feel it necessary to drop her curtsy to the floor; although her ladyship's good nature made it impossible for her to greet the duchess with anything less than a warm smile.

'And these handsome gentlemen before us,' continued Mrs Jameson, 'are the Duke of Claredon and his cousin, Mr Kepling. They have been looking forward to meeting you and can be counted on to see to your comfort in my absence. Now, if you will all excuse me, I see the Rickmanns have arrived and I must go and greet them!'

As she waddled off in a swish of crimson silk, with her three long ostrich feathers swaying preposterously high above her head, April wondered how a woman of her size and age could exhibit such liveliness.

Bringing her attention back to her companions, April's eyes came to rest on Mr Kepling. He was a tall, young man with stylishly arranged blond hair and an open, friendly countenance, which communicated that no great disillusionment had cloaked his soul in cynicism.

She thought it a shame that he was already staring at her with an eagerness she recognised only too well, and, offering him a polite smile, she transferred her gaze to her prospective fiancé.

She had expected to dislike the duke on sight (if for nothing else than for the fact that his tastes tended towards the nunnery) but she realised it would be difficult to dislike the man before her.

A certain amount of his mother's dignity could be detected in his bearing, which was not to be wondered at, but it was countered by a playful, humorous glint in his eyes that was thoroughly engaging.

He was her own age by all accounts, with colouring that was a little darker than his cousin's and a build that was more moderate. And whereas Mr Kepling had boyish good looks, the duke had the classical beauty of a Greek marble bust, without any of its coldness.

He was clearly a lover of fashion, however, April decided her grandmother had done him an injustice by describing him as a dandy. He might be wearing a burgundy coat over black velvet knee-breeches, pale pink silk stockings stitched with gold embroidery, and black slippers tied with burgundy ribbons, but there were no intrusively large buttons on his coat, or an extravagant arrangement of muslin around his throat, or any other affectations in his dress that warranted the title of dandy.

'I am enchanted to make your acquaintance, Lady Hartwood, Miss Hartwood,' declared the duke.

He executed an elegant bow, with a flourish of both hands, and then earned April's approval by allowing his gaze to take in both herself and her mother with equal appreciation.

In contrast, Mr Kepling stood as one transfixed, his eyes riveted on April and a fatuous smile on his lips.

His Grace, noticing his cousin's lapse of manners, cleared his throat significantly, until Mr Kepling came out his trance with a start.

'Ergh. . . I-I beg pardon. . . your servant, Miss Hartwood!' he managed to utter, continuing to smile at her alone.

His Grace stepped into this breach of etiquette by begging Lady Hartwood to tell him of St Mawes castle, professing to be a great lover of history; and, at the same time, drew his mother into the conversation by declaring it was Her Grace who had fostered this love since he was in short-coats.

April silently applauded his finesse; then returned her attention to his afflicted cousin to try and cure him of his stunned state.

In her experience there was one subject that was, more often than not, likely to divert a gentleman's attention away from her looks.

'Do you follow the hunt, Mr Kepling?'

'Yes! Yes I do!' he replied eagerly, swallowing a lump in his throat. 'The Quorn... I-I have a hunting lodge in Leicestershire, near Melton Mowbray. You may have heard of it?'

'Why yes. My father was an avid disciple of the sport and I understand from him that Leicestershire offers some of the best hunting to be had in the country?'

This gentle encouragement was all that was needed to launch Mr Kepling into a description of one of his favourite pastimes. And, within a short space of time, his awkwardness had subsided and he began to converse with her more easily.

'You must forgive me!' he said all at once. 'I've been talking unceasingly about myself – a fault my mother always warned me against when... when she was alive.' His smile faltered for a moment, then was quickly reinstated. 'Do *you* hunt, Miss Hartwood?'

She could have admitted that she experienced nothing but revulsion at the thought of a defenceless creature being chased down and torn to shreds in the name of sport.

Instead, she replied: 'No. I do not ride.'

'Do not ride?' repeated Mr Kepling, clearly perplexed.

'I had a bad fall from a horse as a child,' she explained, 'and have been a little wary of them ever since. But... I am not totally averse to making an attempt to ride again... one day,' she forced out, remembering her grandmother's instructions that the duke's wife must be an able horsewoman.

'My mother used to say that fear is a natural human impulse,' said Mr Kepling, as if this was some great revelation. 'But although it should be *heeded*, it should never be allowed to *rule*.'

April bit back the sharp retort that rose to her lips since she could see he was striving to be sympathetic.

'Very true! I see your mother was a philosopher. You must miss her a great deal?' she said kindly.

'Yes,' he replied, looking suddenly forlorn. 'She had a way of clarifying the decisions one has to make in life.'

As this could apply equally well to someone who was wise or someone who liked to rule the roost, April wondered into which category Mrs Kepling had fallen.

'Perhaps you would allow me to ride with you in Hyde Park one day?' said Mr Kepling, tenaciously returning to the one subject she wished to avoid. 'I would be very happy to offer you some instruction. . . until you regain your confidence, that is.'

Before she could think of a suitably polite yet repulsive reply, the duke, having overheard his cousin, also put himself forward to instruct her.

'You could not ask for a better teacher than my son, Miss Hartwood,' the duchess counselled, joining in their conversation. 'I'm sure I need not tell you, Lady Hartwood, a lady's education cannot be deemed complete without the accomplishment of riding!'

Lady Hartwood threw a cautious glance at her daughter and murmured something unintelligible, which Her Grace chose to take as agreement.

'My mother used to say, a lady can never have too many accomplishments,' put in Mr Kepling, eager to do justice to his parent (whose voice, April was beginning to realise, still sounded persistently in his ear despite her demise).

'Yes, Alfred, your dear mother was quite correct,' said the duchess with a fond smile. 'I do not hold with this antiquated notion some people have of withholding a well-rounded education from their daughters. Why, I myself, in addition to the usual accomplishments expected of a lady, was taught Mathematics, History and Geography. . . and, of course, riding! And I am still considered a notable horsewoman. Modesty compels one to shrink from making sweeping statements about one's own ability, but my friends will tell you it is indeed the case.'

Her son, knowing where his duty lay, was quick to confirm that Her Grace's horsemanship was renowned amongst her acquaintances.

April glanced at her mother to share her amusement. But her ladyship was smiling uncritically at the duchess and was quite unconscious of any unintentional humour on that lady's part.

'Your Grace makes a compelling point,' said April. 'I would count myself fortunate to have your son and Mr Kepling as instructors. However, as the exercise is bound to sink all concerned into considerable boredom, I will refrain from taking up their kind offer.'

'No man could be bored in *your* company, Miss Hartwood,' insisted Mr Kepling.

'But I might well bore the horse!' she countered.

Even the duchess laughed at this quip, before continuing to extol the virtues of riding.

Somewhat annoyed that her hints of reticence were being ignored, April decided she would have to succumb to a short illness on the day allotted for her lesson. Better *that* than to be forced into close proximity with an animal she had avoided since the age of seven.

By this point in the evening, someone had started to play a lively piece of music on the piano in the adjoining salon and, coupled with a quick succession of new arrivals, the rooms began to fill with a cheerful hubbub.

Lord Paisley found the Hartwood ladies amongst the crowd of guests and delivered their glasses of champagne. After staying to exchange a few words with the duchess, with whom he was a little acquainted, he then whisked his betrothed away to introduce her to his friends.

Not long after, the duchess excused herself and walked off on the arm of a gentleman who showed signs (not without encouragement) of being her *gallant*. And as one gentleman after another gravitated in April's direction, she soon found herself surrounded by a circle of men, each intent on securing a moment's conversation with her.

As a result, she spent the next hour smiling and attempting to converse in an equitable manner with each newcomer presented to her; and would have been hard pressed to say what she found more tiresome: the incessant smiling that was making her jaw ache, or the constant assurances that she did not need to have her glass refilled.

Fifteen

Across the room, Hugh listened with half an ear to the conversation his fiancée was enjoying with him, while his eyes kept returning to April.

'Mr Royce, I could almost believe I do not have your attention!' said Miss Starling, smiling through her displeasure. 'Have you heard a word I have said, sir?'

Hugh flashed her a smile, which was, from guilt, a good deal warmer than she was in the habit of seeing from him.

Rather than being gratified, she found it disturbing and looked away.

'Of course, my dear,' he replied, and as he had partially heard that she wanted to go somewhere, he felt safe in adding: 'Allow me to escort you.'

'You wish to come with me to the ladies' retiring room?' she asked, incredulous.

'Only to the door,' he recovered quickly, 'to make certain you don't lose your way.'

An unwelcome suspicion blossomed in Miss Starling's mind; but it was quickly discarded as ridiculous.

'That won't be necessary,' she said. 'You must know, I am not one of those females who require a man to be constantly at their side.' Unable to resist, her eyes settled on April across the room. 'Unlike Miss Hartwood, who appears to enjoy a male *entourage*! It is a pity she does not realise how her lack of modesty will be perceived.'

Hugh remained silent, barely resisting the urge to inform her that she must be losing her sight if she thought April had the look of a woman enjoying the attentions of the men around her.

Even from this distance he could see her smile was growing more and more fixed. Nor had it escaped his notice that she had several times taken a discreet step backwards to evade her admirers' proximity.

If he had the smallest right he would liberate her, and only consideration for her reputation held him back from doing just that.

Miss Starling misread his expression as a sign that he too disapproved of April and said nobly: 'I beg you don't judge her too harshly! The men themselves are to blame for acting like fools around her. Few of my sex would be able to withstand such flattering devotion.'

'Yourself, surely?'

The satirical look in his eyes should have put her on guard, but, once again, she misread him.

'Yes, I believe I would have no difficulty in maintaining my modesty under similar circumstances. But not because I lay claim to having greater strength of character than other women. My advantage, if one can call it such, stems purely from having had the benefit of a superior moral upbringing.'

Hugh's lip curled in distaste, and he said curtly: 'The retiring room is on the second floor.'

Recalled to her purpose, Miss Starling thanked him prettily and took herself off.

Hugh's eyes followed her, a grim look settling on his countenance; until his unpleasant reverie was interrupted by the appearance of his hostess at his elbow.

'I'm not entirely certain Miss Hartwood is enjoying herself,' Mrs Jameson remarked and took a sip from her glass of champagne.

'She isn't,' he replied.

'One should go to her aid, I suppose. Although, for my part, I can only be grateful to her for enlivening my male guests! Why, Lord Thomson is acting positively giddy, and we all know the dear man has difficulty cracking a smile at the best of times!'

'I didn't think that you, ma'am, were one to sacrifice a guest for the amusement of others,' said Hugh, frowning down at her.

'Generally speaking, you are correct. However, on occasion it has proven to be rather useful! But I don't doubt that *someone* will come to the poor girl's rescue.'

'If you're hinting that I should extricate Miss Hartwood, then you can't have considered the conjectures that would follow. Or the awkwardness of the position in which I would be placing her.'

'Well, you certainly do think of all the proprieties, don't you? I would not have thought... *oh good God!*' she exclaimed suddenly, looking past him with genuine horror. 'What are the Longevilles doing here? Courtesy compelled me to invite them, of course, but what could have led them to suppose that I wanted them to attend? Oh, how tiresome! I shall now be obliged to be agreeable to them. One need never be agreeable to one's true friends but one continually finds oneself being agreeable to persons one dislikes quite excessively! Excuse me, won't you, dear boy.'

She started to walk away, then stopped and added over her shoulder: 'I believe I saw Miss Starling heading towards the ladies' retiring room. Perhaps she is in need of some assistance?'

Hugh found himself once more – and in rather more vehement terms – rejecting the notion that he would wish to breach this female bastion, until the laughter in Mrs Jameson's eyes alerted him to her true meaning.

'You, ma'am, are a rogue!' he announced with a grin.

Greatly pleased by this compliment, Mrs Jameson laughed and went off to try her hand at being agreeable.

Hugh returned his attention to April. He saw at once that the idiots around her had corralled her further into the corner and she was now standing with her back almost against the wall.

He thrust his empty glass at a passing footman and advanced on the group.

He made no effort to slow his progress when he reached the unfortunate gentlemen in his path and forced his way through them without bothering to respond to their outraged remarks.

'Miss Hartwood, I've come on behalf of Miss Starling,' he announced when he stood before her. 'She's in need of your assistance in the ladies' retiring room.'

A look of relief flared in April's eyes.

'Oh, of course! I shall come at once! Please excuse me, gentlemen, Your Grace.'

'Miss Starling's needs must take precedence over our own!' the duke said cordially, while his gaze absorbed the hostile set of Hugh's countenance with idle interest.

Hugh offered April his arm and, forcing a path through her admirers, led her out of the room.

Once in the corridor, they pulled apart as if by unspoken agreement.

'Thank goodness for Miss Starling!' declared April. 'She could not have asked for my assistance at a better time. I don't believe I have ever been required to speak so incessantly!'

'Are the men of your neighbourhood not as garrulous?' asked Hugh, smiling.

'The same, I suppose. But much fewer in number! Although, I had not considered *that* to be an advantage until now,' she laughed. 'Would you be so good as to direct me to the retiring room?'

'Miss Starling does not need you. I made it up.'

'You. . . *made it up?* But why?' she asked, taken aback.

This was certainly a pertinent question.

The only acceptable answer had to be borrowed from Miss Starling.

'It's not at all proper for you to be conversing, for the best part of an hour, with a group of gentlemen without the presence of another female.' His tone was mild but could only be interpreted as censorious. 'Your mother has never lived amongst the *ton* and cannot be aware of how strictly a young lady's reputation must be guarded, and so it's left to me to advise you.'

April's lips pressed into a thin line. She smiled, but it was not humour that made her eyes flash.

'I would not have thought the role of moral advisor would sit comfortably with you? How fortunate I am to have you exert yourself on my behalf! Nevertheless, I beg you to abstain from such exertions in future. I am old enough to know how to safeguard my own reputation.'

'At three and twenty and new to the. . . '

'I am not three. . . ' She broke off in some confusion as she remembered that her grandmother had persuaded her to assume this younger age. 'I. . . I am wiser than I seem,' she added, rather lamely.

'As I was saying, at three and twenty and new to the ways of London society you are not in a position to know the intricacies of behaviour expected of you. Your looks alone will make you more conspicuous and open to judgement, especially from your own sex. Jealousy will drive them to analyse your behaviour and magnify the smallest fault.'

Had her temper not already reared its head, she would have agreed that his insight had merit. She had never yet met a woman who was not threatened by her where a man was concerned.

The ready assumption of her sex that she was out to seduce every man in her vicinity had always grated, particularly as she had never once felt the smallest desire to seduce anyone. . . until very recently.

'Whether or not my looks are a hindrance to me is none of your business!' she retorted. 'And if the Duchess of Claredon saw fit to leave me alone with a group of gentlemen, it's not your place to object.'

'The duchess left you alone in the presence of her son and his cousin, and perhaps two or three others. She has been sitting in the adjoining room for the last hour and – fortunately for you! – she did not see the dozen other gentlemen swell the ranks around you. If she had, you can be certain she wouldn't have viewed the sight with indulgence. If you wish to ensnare the

Duke of Claredon you would do well to remember that you must first win over his mother.'

'How dare you!' she spluttered furiously. 'I'm not out to *ensnare*... I don't want to... to... oh, you are *insufferable!*'

Every feeling revolted at his scornful insinuations, only she was in no position to refute them. This was one evil of her grandmother's scheming that she had not foreseen.

At that moment, a footman, who was extravagantly liveried in the gold satin Mrs Jameson had chosen for her staff, opened the door of the salon and let himself into the corridor, bearing a tray of empty glasses.

As he unobtrusively walked off towards the servants' stairs at the back of the house, April called out 'excuse me' and flashed him an overwrought smile.

Startled to be the recipient of such notice, he came to an abrupt standstill.

'Would you be so good as to send a glass of scotch to the ladies' retiring room?' she asked him. 'I'm in need of something stronger than champagne to help me endure the present company.'

She did not deign to look at Hugh to see if this shaft had gone home. Keeping her eyes on the footman, she waited for him to respond.

Unfortunately, the young man appeared to be temporarily immobilised and regarded her in a stunned way.

She let out an audible groan of exasperation.

But before she had to exert herself to revive the most recent unfortunate to fall victim to her face, Hugh sent him on his way with a gentle 'that will be all'.

'You really shouldn't smile at every poor sod to cross your path,' he remarked, making her bristle anew. 'You'll only be encouraging them to fall in love with you.'

'It is not my fault they don't have wits enough to control themselves!'

'Now that's hardly fair. Even a most elevated mind can be struck senseless by an anomaly.'

'*An anomaly!*'

April never screeched.

She considered it unladylike.

So it was unfortunate to discover that she was actually rather good at it.

The door to the salon burst open and, along with the noise of carousing humanity that spilt out, Mrs Jameson's impressively dressed head appeared and tilted enquiringly at them, ostrich feathers bobbing.

'My apologies if I'm intruding, my dears, but I'm almost certain I heard a scream,' she said in an unperturbed way, as if this occurrence was nothing out of the ordinary.

'Mr Royce was startled by a mouse,' said April, sacrificing Hugh's pride.

'Surely it was a monstrous, rabid rat?' he protested.

'It was a mouse! And a tiny one at that!'

With one last fulminating look at him, April walked off and made her way up the grand staircase, to the sound of his laughter.

Sixteen

Lost in her furious thoughts, April entered the elegant parlour that Mrs Jameson had set aside for the use of her female guests and did not immediately notice the only other occupant of the room.

'Miss Hartwood?'

'Oh...there you are!' April greeted Miss Starling, offering her a warm smile; the least she could do was to be kind to this poor girl whose lot in life was to be saddled with a termagant of a man.

'Were you looking for me?' asked Miss Starling, turning from the mirror where she had been rearranging her curls.

'Yes, your fiancé sent me to find you,' replied April; then belatedly remembered she had been misled.

Miss Starling stiffened.

'I see. May I ask why?'

There were any number of reasons April could have given that would have painted an unfavourable picture of Hugh. But although she was sorely tempted to pay him back for his insolence, she did not have it in her to be malicious.

There was nothing wrong, however, in having a little fun at his expense and casting him in the role of the besotted lover.

'He wanted me to tell you that he misses you terribly and hopes you will return to him with all speed!'

Miss Starling's pretty features were marred by an unmistakable grimace.

'Don't you want Mr Royce to miss you?' asked April, unable to keep the surprise from her voice.

'I have been gone barely ten minutes!' Miss Starling retorted, her well-cultivated amiability perilously close to shattering.

'Perhaps it is longer than you think,' April suggested (without quite knowing why she felt the need to justify Hugh's fictitious actions).

'Even so, it is not possible for him to miss me! At least, not unless... oh, it does not bear thinking about! I certainly never gave him any cause to think I was *that* type of woman. And after all he told me of disliking excesses of emotion, and agreeing with me that ours would be a marriage based on respect, I never would have thought he would succumb to such a vulgar emotion. I have been greatly deceived!'

'To what vulgar emotion are you referring?' asked April, seriously intrigued by the nature of their relationship.

Before Miss Starling could reply, a tap on the door claimed their attention.

'For goodness sake, not now,' April grumbled under her breath. Striding to the door, she threw it open. 'Yes?'

'Y-your scotch, miss,' replied the footman from earlier.

He lifted his tray a little higher to draw attention to the heavy-bottomed crystal glass that rested on it.

'Oh, of course! Thank you. I appreciate your promptness.'

She picked up the glass and shut the door on the worshipful look that was beginning to bloom in his eyes.

'Is that strong liquor?' asked Miss Starling, watching with fascination as April took a sip.

'Whisky, actually. My grandmother taught me to enjoy it. I find it wonderfully restorative on occasion.'

'My mother does not approve of ladies drinking anything stronger than champagne.'

'Then she is fortunate I am not her daughter!'

'Although, I do feel as if I could use a restorative,' said Miss Starling. 'Would it be wrong of me to try some, Miss Hartwood?'

April's hand hovered uncertainly for a moment, before she offered up the glass; a noble gesture of sacrifice that was lost on her companion, who proceeded to take a generous gulp without preamble or appreciation.

April felt safe in assuming, from the contortions of Miss Starling's features, that she found the whisky unpalatable. Although this in no way deterred her from stiffening her resolve and downing the remainder.

'*Eww*... that was *vile*!'

'It's fortunate you did not enjoy it!' April said indignantly.

Oblivious to her companion's displeasure, Miss Starling put down the glass and returned to the subject uppermost in her thoughts.

'Oh how mortifying it is to find oneself in the position one was at great pains to avoid!'

'I take it you refer to Mr Royce?' said April, regarding her with a decided lack of sympathy.

Her earlier goodwill was somewhat dented and she wished for nothing more than to bring about an end to their *tête-à-tête* as quickly as possible. Besides, the relationship between Hugh and Miss Starling was no concern of hers.

'Of course, Mr Royce. Who else!' replied Miss Starling.

Now was the point at which she should simply turn the subject, April told herself firmly. And although no subject held greater interest for her, a well-mannered lady would resist the temptation to prod.

'Because he is displaying some vulgar emotion?' she prompted, despising her own weakness.

'Exactly!' said Miss Starling tragically. 'Mr Royce has fallen in love with me!'

A stab of pain pierced April's breast; then she came to her senses and recollected that she was yet to see Hugh act like a man in love.

'But surely you want your husband to love you?' she asked.

A pleasant, fiery glow had settled within Miss Starling, softening her hard edges, and, without quite knowing why, she confided: 'I suppose it's possible that our mutual respect may one day grow into something warmer. . . though, of course, I don't expect it! But that is entirely different to him being in love with me *now*. I'm not a doxy!'

'Come, let us sit down, and you can explain why you believe a husband and wife should not be in love,' said April wryly. 'I admit, this is a philosophy that is new to me.'

Once seated on a pretty rose velvet couch, Miss Starling launched into a warbled monologue on the goals of marriage, which, according to the precepts her mother had taught her, centred on: performing one's duty (the most noble gratification of all); nurturing the flame of mutual respect (difficult but not impossible if a wife donned the armour of a proper mind-set); and siring children (a rather unpleasant business but one that was linked to duty and therefore both unavoidable and noble).

The concept of love was summarily dismissed by Miss Starling as nothing more than a sordid emotion based on lust. It was, she said, what men felt for their numerous mistresses, and a lady had to learn to accept it without betraying that she was aware of its existence.

When at last these rather peculiar confidences were at an end, Miss Starling dabbed her eyes with her handkerchief and wailed: 'Can Mr Royce have so little respect for me that he believes himself in love with me?'

April suppressed an ignoble wish to bring about the end of Miss Starling's betrothal by agreeing with her. It was, after all, not the poor girl's fault that her head had been filled with some rather silly notions.

'What your mother has told you is not entirely correct,' she said matter-of-factly. 'Naturally, I cannot know her reasons, but it sounds to me that she may have experienced some disillusionment in her own marriage, and perhaps has found it easier to lower her expectations than to face disappointment.'

Miss Starling put down her handkerchief, her expression arrested.

She might have been kept ignorant of certain matters owing to her sex, nonetheless her mental faculties were no more diminished by her gender than a man's faculties were diminished by his.

'Actually... that does make some sense,' she said slowly. 'When my father was alive, I could not help but be aware that he kept several...'

'Please! There's no need to divulge anything of that nature,' April said quickly, recoiling from hearing any intimacies to do with Miss Starling's family. 'I only wish you to know that I have observed successful unions between men and women that were based on a deep, romantic love. And although it is true that many men enjoy the affections of women outside of wedlock, this does not preclude them from falling in love with the women they will one day marry. And neither does it preclude this love from being noble and respectful.'

'Mother says love is for the lower classes,' persevered Miss Starling, although with less certainty. 'A true lady does not look for such things in marriage.'

'Poppycock!' countered April, heartily sick of the opinions of the absent Mrs Starling. 'Your mother has picked up some very strange notions! Certainly, in the past, women of our station were often forced into marriages in which love played no part, but we now live in more enlightened times! In the year 1820 we need not fear such a fate for ourselves.'

'I don't doubt *you* need never fear such a fate,' Miss Starling said a little wistfully.

'It is true, my disposition would never allow me to accept a husband not of my own choosing.' April consoled her conscience with the thought that her current predicament was entirely different; she was not accepting a husband but a temporary fiancé. 'However, you too need have no such fear! Mr Royce appears to be all that is...'

She waved a hand in the air as she attempted to find a complimentary word to describe someone she found infuriating.

'Amiable?' Miss Starling put in helpfully.

'Why, yes. . . if you wish.'

A rather comical look of liquor-induced concentration descended over Miss Starling's features.

'He *is* amiable. . . at least, towards me. I know that is not always the case with others.'

'Surely that is to his credit? A man who shows so little discrimination as to be universally amiable would be excessively tiresome. One would never know if one were esteemed for their own worth or because of his lack of discernment.'

'Oh. . . yes, how true,' replied Miss Starling, swaying a little and rubbing her eyes as if to clear them. 'Miss Hartwood, I confess I feel a little strange.'

April rose immediately and went to pour out two glasses of water from a jug that had been left out for the guests. Returning to her inebriated companion, she instructed her to drink both.

Miss Starling complied without complaint.

When she was finished, she continued as if no interruption had occurred: 'But, although he is be amiable, one cannot deny that his appearance is *brutish*. And he makes no attempt to soften what nature has given him! Either through manners or dress. Why, he is so careless with both it makes one wonder if he has any respect at all for what he owes his station.'

April decided this uncomplimentary assessment of Hugh must be another transplanted opinion from Mrs Starling, for it was beyond her comprehension how any young woman could be blind to his many personal attractions. She herself had tried a number of times to dismiss them and had found the task insurmountable.

'Mr Royce's appearance is exactly as it should be – that of a gentleman,' she responded indignantly. 'But if his person disgusts you to such a degree then you should have refused his proposal!'

'But how can one refuse such a fortune? And, one day, a title? Mother was quite insistent. . . '

The door suddenly swung open to admit two laughing matrons and Miss Starling's words died on her lips.

The interruption served to clear the fog a little from her mind and she threw April a furtive look, fearful that she had betrayed herself.

April did her best to hide her anger but it could not be fully contained and, as she rose to her feet, she yanked Miss Starling along with her, causing her to yelp in surprise.

'It is time we returned downstairs,' April said with forced affability, keeping a firm hold on her arm.

'Ouch! You're hurting me,' Miss Starling complained under her breath.

Exchanging polite smiles with the two ladies, April propelled Miss Starling out of the room.

Once the door had closed behind them, she let go of her arm.

'I beg your pardon. I am told I have a very strong grip,' she said dispassionately and walked off.

Miss Starling threw an accusing look at her back and then followed her.

The two glasses of water she had consumed were starting to have a positive effect, and with this return of clarity came the mortifying consciousness that she had revealed a great deal more information than was prudent.

'Miss Hartwood. . .' she spoke hesitantly, breaking the silence that had descended as they made their way down the stairs. 'I trust you will pay no attention to my ramblings? I was not myself and may have expressed myself in terms that were not what. . . what they should have been.'

Having already reached the conclusion that Miss Starling was not unusual in thinking only of worldly considerations when it came to marriage, April's anger had mostly dissipated, and now, in light of the girl's evident distress, it vanished entirely.

'There is no need to say more on the subject,' she replied. 'You may not know this about me, but I despise tell-tales.'

Miss Starling had the grace to look ashamed.

'Thank you,' she murmured.

'Think nothing of it. We cannot allow the gentlemen to claim the bonds of honour for themselves alone. Are you quite recovered or shall we rest a while longer in the corridor?'

'No!' cried Miss Starling. 'I-I mean, I am perfectly recovered, thank you.'

April resisted an urge to laugh. Miss Starling clearly had no wish to continue alone in her company.

On entering the brightly lit salons, which held an even greater number of guests than before, April's eyes were immediately drawn to Hugh, in conversation with a group of men, a few feet away.

When his acquaintances began to look in her direction, he turned as well and met her gaze, before transferring his attention to his fiancée.

April had the dubious pleasure of realising their talk had had some positive effect on Miss Starling, for she offered Hugh a coquettish smile few men would have failed to find charming. April saw the moment Hugh was struck by it; a fleeting expression about the eyes that she would have missed had she not been watching him closely.

'Thank you for your message, Mr Royce!' said Miss Starling when he came to stand by her side.

A momentary stillness was all that gave away his surprise; then he turned to April and raised a sardonic eyebrow.

'Dare I ask, what message?'

'Why, that you were missing Miss Starling and awaiting her return,' replied April with wide-eyed innocence.

'Ah. . . *that* message.' The look he gave her managed to convey a promise of retribution. 'I am of course happy to have you back, my dear,' he told his fiancée.

His cavalier delivery, at odds with the ardent message he was supposed to have sent, went unnoticed by Miss Starling. Her attention was fixed on a spot beyond his shoulder; and, a moment later, the Duke of Claredon and Mr Kepling joined their group.

'Miss Hartwood,' began His Grace, 'when you re-entered the room it was as if a breath of sweetly scented air swept aside the staleness that had settled upon us.'

Even with only an hour's knowledge of the duke's character, April had surmised that he was an admirer of the poetic turn of phrase. . . which was not a quality Hugh appeared to value. She could feel the derision emanating from him.

She would have preferred the duke to direct his eloquence elsewhere, but, feeling a need to counter Hugh's scorn, she said: 'Thank you, Your Grace. I do so enjoy alliteration in a compliment! Are you and Mr Kepling already acquainted with Miss Starling and Mr Royce?'

'I have not had the pleasure,' replied His Grace. He exchanged nods with Hugh and offered Miss Starling his extravagant bow. 'Your servant, ma'am.'

Honoured by such elevated notice, Miss Starling sunk into a deep curtsey from which she did not appear to wish to rise; a circumstance that made April so inexplicably annoyed that she was tempted to pull the silly girl to her feet.

She stole a glance at Hugh.

He did not appear to have noticed his fiancée's excessive subservience, for his gaze was resting on her, his expression inscrutable. She questioned him silently with her eyes until he looked away.

Miss Starling rose at last of her own accord and allowed herself to be introduced to Mr Kepling. It could not be said that either one of them took much notice of the other. Miss Starling's gaze kept flitting over to the duke, while Mr Kepling offered her a vague smile and promptly returned his attention to April.

When the musicians in the adjoining room began to play a waltz, soon after, April was only too happy to accept the duke's invitation to dance and escape the immoderate looks being cast about.

Not to be outdone, Miss Starling smiled sweetly up at Hugh and informed him that she would be pleased to have the opportunity to dance to a piece of music that was a particular favourite of hers. And, linking her arm through his, gently propelled him to follow His Grace and April.

Seventeen

It did not take April long to realise that her partner was an exemplary dancer. He exhibited such skill and aplomb as he led her through the steps that, in his arms, she felt herself become a more graceful dancer than she knew herself to be.

Together they made a striking couple and more than one person turned to observe them as they moved across the floor; without having the least suspicion that April's attention was not centred on her partner.

Hugh, for his part, found himself preoccupied with the unnecessarily intimate manner with which His Grace was holding April; a circumstance that, for several good reasons, should not have bothered him in the slightest, and particularly not since he knew the duke's thoughts would never take the improper direction of his own.

But there was no denying it did bother him.

And his annoyance was only increased by the perversity of his mind, which insisted on returning time and again to the comment April had made in his phaeton the other day.

He sincerely pitied the poor sod who would one day call himself her husband. Whoever the man might be, he would not look favourably upon the notion of his wife relinquishing control of her body to anyone. . . not even an unexceptionable partner in a waltz.

He was even beginning to doubt she had made the comment in innocence.

The idea that April had intentionally set out to flirt with him took root in his fertile mind, already on the lookout for something to hold against her, and he could not wait for the music to finish so he could remove himself from her vicinity.

Miss Starling, however, had other ideas.

When the waltz was at an end, she steered them into the path of His Grace and April and nurtured a bout of pleasantries, until the musicians began to tune their instruments for the next set and His Grace felt obliged to ask her to dance.

After a proper amount of surprise and demurral, Miss Starling accepted, happy to have achieved her intent, and walked off on the duke's arm.

'It appears they are to play a country dance next,' remarked Hugh, keeping his gaze averted from April. 'I know you dance nothing but the waltz, so I'll refrain from asking you.'

'How thoughtful of you!' she retorted, and told herself she was relieved to be spared the necessity of his arms around her.

Neither of them saw Mrs Jameson drop a word into the ear of the lead musician, and they were both considerably surprised when the small orchestra stopped playing the beginning notes of a country dance and embarked on another waltz.

Matching looks of consternation crossed their countenances.

'It appears they have changed their mind,' Hugh muttered.

April opened her fan to cool her cheeks.

'So it would seem.'

'There are too many couples already. I can't imagine you would want to dance when there's so little room?'

'Are you asking me or dissuading me?' she replied crossly, shutting her fan with a snap. 'I assure you, you need not put yourself to the trouble of doing either!'

'I apologise if I have offended you, but I have no aptitude for dancing. You would be best served to find another partner.'

'What a convenient excuse for your rudeness! Does it usually achieve the desired result?'

'Which is?' he asked, meeting her eyes.

'Why, to extract you from an obligation to dance when you have no wish to dance with a particular lady.'

'That's incorrect. I simply have no. . .'

'Yes, yes, you have already told me! You have no aptitude for it!'

Her demeanour was so far removed from the flirtatious that Hugh could not stop a smile lifting the corners of his mouth.

'It happens to be true. . . but perhaps the fault also lies with my overly fertile imagination,' he admitted ruefully.

'I don't understand you. . . oh, don't bother explaining! It's of no consequence. And, in any case, you shouldn't draw back now. If you don't wish to dance, don't! Stay true to your conviction, however rude. At least then people will respect you, even if they cannot like you.'

'I take that to mean *you* fall into that category?'

'You can take it any way you wish! I have no objection.'

Hugh laughed.

'Coward! Now who's drawing back? If I apologise for my rudeness will you dance with me?'

April suddenly felt a little breathless.

'There is no need, I assure you! I was not trying to wheedle an invitation out of...'

'Of course she will dance with you!' Lady Hartwood's voice intruded from behind.

They turned as one to find her smiling at them.

'You danced so beautifully with the duke just now, love,' her ladyship went on, 'you need not fear you will disgrace your next partner. Don't you agree, Hugh-dear?'

'Your daughter could never disgrace me, ma'am. Or anyone else, for that matter.'

These simply uttered words had an astonishing effect on Lady Hartwood. Her bosom rose with some unidentifiable emotion and her eyes welled up.

'How *happy* I am to hear you say so,' she said tremulously. 'I may have had my doubts – at first, you know – but *now*...!'

April regarded her mother with misgiving.

'Hugh certainly knows how to turn on the flattery when the need arises, Mama, but there is nothing in that to get maudlin about.'

'You do him an injustice,' said Lady Hartwood, turning reproachful eyes on her. '*You* of all people should recognise the difference between mere flattery and words from the heart!'

Determined to get away from her mother before she could utter another unnerving sentence, April told Hugh: 'If we are to waltz, we should go at once.'

'I'm entirely at your disposal.'

She could have happily throttled him for his false docility.

She walked off without waiting to see if he followed, and only once she had found a place amongst the other couples did she turn to face him.

Hugh took hold of her hand and wrapped his other arm around her body, amusement lurking in his eyes.

'Don't you dare say a word!' she warned him. 'I don't know what you've done to bewitch my mother but clearly you can do no wrong in her eyes.'

When he did not reply, she said with exasperation: 'Well? What have you to say for yourself?'

'I thought I was not to say a word?'

'Don't be facetious – you know what I mean. And you also must know that if my mother learnt your true intent she would be terribly wounded.'

'And what do you suppose is my true intent?'

'It's hardly difficult to discern! You like nothing better than to taunt me and... *oh*...' She tripped over her feet and only Hugh's tightening grip stopped her from stumbling.

'I've got you,' he said, his calm manner only annoying her further. 'You're as rigid as a bedpost. If you would relax and allow me to lead without fighting me at every turn, we may yet get through the next few minutes unscathed.'

'I warned you I have no sense of balance.'

'And I don't have the dancing abilities of your duke, yet we can still manage better than this.'

'He is not my...' She took a deep breath. 'Think what you will, it makes no difference to me.'

He regarded her in silence for a few moments, and then found himself saying: 'I beg pardon, that was indeed a taunt.'

Her eyes met his in surprise.

'Yes, it was. And you now have me wondering as to the real reason you owned up to it?'

'A simple apology, nothing more. Have I given you so little reason to trust me?'

'It's not *that* exactly... oh, dear, I have turned into an ungracious harpy! It's now my turn to beg pardon. Perhaps it's best if we remain silent? I have no wish for us to keep antagonising one another – inadvertently or not,' she said offering him a tentative smile.

'We are in agreement on that at least.'

As her body and mind relaxed and stopped fighting him, Hugh was able to draw her into him and take control of their movement across the floor.

However, with nothing to distract them from the intimacy of their embrace, what initially began as merely functional soon transformed into something darker, more powerful.

The melding of their bodies heightened April's senses to an unbearable degree and she would have pulled away if she could. But Hugh's arms, his scent, everything about him, seemed to draw her closer, until she knew not where he ended and she began.

When the last notes of music hung in the air, they drew apart and exchanged a few words, neither of them knowing exactly what was said. Then, they walked off in opposite directions and spent the remainder of the evening avoiding one another with steadfast determination.

Eighteen

On the following day, the Hartwood ladies were looking forward to spending a quiet day at home to recuperate after their first London *soirée*, which had not broken up until after two in the morning. However, they had barely finished breakfast and made themselves comfortable in the drawing room when the door knocker sounded through the house.

Within a few minutes Layton entered, bearing a calling card on a silver salver, and announced that a Mrs Hall and her son had called and were asking if her ladyship was at home to visitors.

'I don't know a Mrs Hall,' said Lady Hartwood, accepting the card with a puzzled expression. She read the black sloping script neatly printed on the card, but it did nothing to prod her memory. 'Do you know a Mrs Hall, love?'

April looked over her shoulder at the card.

'No, I don't believe... oh... there was a *Mr* Hall introduced to me last night.'

'Ah, that would be it then,' said Lady Hartwood with cheerful resignation, well used to being visited by the mothers of the gentlemen who thought themselves in love with her daughter.

'I hope he did not misread my intentions,' said April.

'He undoubtedly did so, love. You know by now, men are sadly addle-brained in your company and even trifling signs of attentiveness on your part are misconstrued as encouragement.'

'It would be a stretch indeed to misconstrue my compassion as encouragement! Mr Hall was so anxious, and stuttered so painfully when he spoke to me, it was impossible not to feel sorry for him and try to put him at ease.'

'No doubt your behaviour was all that was proper, only... well, never mind! There's nothing for it, I suppose, but to see them. Thank you, Layton, you may show them in. And you'd best send up the tea tray. I fear this will not be a short call.'

When mother and son were shown into the room, a little while later, Mrs Hall was found to be a tall, lanky woman, with faded blue eyes and an aura of decrepitude about her. This was further accentuated by her dove-grey walking dress, which was composed of various floating layers of chiffon and gave her the appearance of a fashionable ghost.

She also looked to be a good deal embarrassed.

Mr Hall was even taller than his mother and painfully thin, with an abundance of ginger hair that stuck out from his head and only added to his excessive height. He had a pleasant countenance that was animated by the adoring look in his eyes as they settled on April.

Lady Hartwood took all this in at a glance and, her compassion stirred, greeted her visitors with perhaps greater warmth than their tentative connection deserved.

Mrs Hall explained the reason for their visit was owing to the fact that she had heard so much about her ladyship and her daughter from Mrs Jameson, and, being very sorry to have missed meeting them at last night's *soirée*, which she had been unable to attend, she had determined to pay them a call today.

This pretext must have sounded as flimsy to her own ears as it did to Lady Hartwood's, for her embarrassment only seemed to increase and she abruptly sat down in the nearest chair before her hostess had a chance to invite her to do so.

Lady Hartwood had no doubt that Mrs Hall had been coerced to pay this visit and, seating herself near her, immediately set out to put her at ease, in much the same way April had done with her son on the previous evening.

Left to entertain Mr Hall alone, April indicated for him to take a seat beside her on the settee.

When he complied, she offered him the reserved smile that had dashed the hopes of many a suitor and asked him if he had enjoyed himself last night.

She was agreeably surprised to discover, when Mr Hall did not have an audience, he was able to speak sensibly and with barely a stutter.

From the topic of last night they moved onto a discussion of the weather and the various restrictions it placed on one when in town, and they were just beginning to touch on Mr Nash's architectural brilliance, seen to outstanding effect in his design of Regent Street, when the butler entered again to inform them that a Mr Kepling had called.

Lady Hartwood asked for him to be sent up and he was soon entering the room with a shy smile, as if uncertain of his welcome, and a posy of daisies clutched in his hand.

'Mr Kepling, how wonderful to see you again!' Lady Hartwood greeted him with her lovely smile.

'I hope I'm not intruding?' he asked diffidently.

'Not at all! Do you know Mrs Hall and her son?'

Mr Kepling visibly relaxed under this warm welcome and offered up a cheerful greeting to the other visitors, whom he seemed to know quite well.

Mr Hall was not at all pleased to have his private conversation with April brought to an end and made no effort to respond to his rival's friendliness, restricting himself to casting dark looks in his direction.

'These are for you, Miss Hartwood,' said Mr Kepling, holding out the daisies to April. 'I hope you like them! My mother used to like flowers and I believe you mentioned last night that you were also partial to them? I wasn't certain what colour you preferred but I thought I was safe in choosing white. . . if you object to white, I can go at once to find whatever colour you wish?'

April could not help but be charmed.

Mr Kepling reminded her of an exuberant, overgrown puppy. And his little posy of daisies, with their crooked stems and wilting heads, was quite possibly the most humble gift she had ever received from a gentleman.

'Oh, how lovely they are!' she exclaimed, taking the posy from him. 'White flowers are my favourite, thank you, indeed! Please, won't you be seated?'

As she settled herself back down on the settee, she was startled to realise that Mr Kepling had the intention of squeezing himself in beside her; effectively wedging her between her two admirers.

The settee had not been designed to allow two sizeable gentlemen and a lady to converse comfortably, and particularly not when one gentleman was showing bristle while the other was sublimely unaware and full of good cheer. April had to exercise considerable adroitness to nudge along a three-way conversation under such inauspicious circumstances.

The arrival of the tea tray was the first opportunity she had for escape and, rising quickly before her mother could do so, she declared she would pour for the party.

She was interrupted in this task, a few minutes later, by the reappearance of Layton. He was out of breath and non-too pleased to have been made to climb the stairs yet again, still he managed to announce three new gentlemen callers in a voice almost devoid of irritation.

Lady Hartwood was just welcoming the new arrivals, of which the Duke of Claredon was one, when the door knocker echoed up the stairs once again.

Layton forgot himself sufficiently to groan; April met her mother's eyes across the room with a laughing look of dismay; while Lady Hartwood allowed herself a triumphant smile, and when her drawing room was full to bursting with eligible gentlemen soon after, she could not have been more pleased on her daughter's behalf.

'I see I am not the only one pleased to have found you at home today,' said His Grace, approaching April as she poured the tea for the newcomers. 'And I'm not in the least surprised! You will be the reigning belle of next year's Season.'

He spoke in a manner calculated to please but April thought he was out of spirits. There was a certain reserve about him that had not been present last night.

'You are being absurd,' she laughed lightly.

'Of course! How could I suppose such a thing when you are so *thin* of company this morning? Must I apologise?'

'Certainly you must, for you assume I wish to become a reigning belle! I don't, you know, so please don't think you are gratifying me by saying so. And besides, for all we know, at this very moment any number of ladies are finding their drawing rooms invaded by gentlemen of fashion eager for a diversion before their clubs open their doors.'

The duke laughed.

'You wrong us, Miss Hartwood! Our clubs are already open. And besides, not all of us are such frippery fellows.'

Remembering her role, April lowered her eyelids and said coyly: 'Certainly not *you*, Your Grace. I count myself honoured to have secured a visit from you today.'

'You're not honoured in the least,' he announced with the same easy camaraderie of last night. 'I'm fast coming to suspect my title does not weigh with you at all. I suppose I should act the duke and put you in your place, but the truth is, I'm delighted! You can have no notion of how many ladies have made really quite spirited attempts to become the next Duchess of Claredon. It has been utterly exhausting to endure it! I am quite in awe of their determination, of course, but must they be so *de trop?* If only they knew how they repulsed me!' He shuddered delicately.

'I won't scruple to tell you that I too know something of being overwhelmed with attention by the opposite sex. I suppose you cannot have failed to notice my face?'

She put on a superior expression and turned her head one way and then the other.

'No, indeed! Quite exceptional,' he replied. 'It must be a source of great comfort to you?'

'Oh, it is! I like nothing better than to be left alone in front of a mirror to admire it.' A giggle erupted, and, conscience-stricken, she added: 'We'd best stop before we're overheard and suspected of truthfulness. But I will say this: of the two of us, you are more to be pitied. My looks will fade and I shall be made unremarkable by age. But you and your title will remain forever a prize.'

'How appallingly true!' he laughed, grimacing. 'This is a delightfully improper conversation. I'm almost in charity with my mother for pressing me to call on you.'

'She pressed you?' asked April, surprised.

'She's taken it into her head that we might suit,' he replied with a pained expression. 'She is growing more and more desperate in her attempts to marry me off to someone... *anyone*.'

'Why, thank you! Has no one ever told you that you should never admit to pursuing a woman out of desperation, even if it is not your own?'

'I shall certainly keep it in mind, should I ever wish to pursue one. However, you can't fool me! You have no wish for me to court you. I can see it in your eyes. They lack that certain sparkle of ambition I have come to recognise so well in your sex.'

She looked away, conscience-stricken.

Their conversation was becoming too honest. The more time she spent in the duke's company, the more she realised she liked him too well to deceive him and play with his affections.

Not that he appeared to suffer from those sorts of affections, in any case. Never before had she met a man so wholly unaffected by her.

'I wish you would call me Eustace,' he said, breaking in on her thoughts. 'All my friends do... particularly those who are as passionate about Keats as I am, and mourn his passing.'

'I see I was too exuberant with my admiration of his poetry last night,' she replied playfully.

'You are certainly the only person I know, apart from myself, of course, who can recite the whole of *Ode to a Nightingale* verbatim.'

She laughed and admitted: 'It is a favourite of mine.'

'Good Lord,' he exclaimed quietly, looking past her, 'here comes the next line of attack!'

Turning in the direction of his gaze, she saw two newly-arrived gentlemen and a determined looking Mr Hall advancing towards them.

'No doubt they want their tea,' said His Grace dryly, 'never mind that they would never be seen dead drinking the stuff ordinarily. I am not brave enough to face such resolve. *Adieu, mon amie*, I depart the field of combat!'

'Don't you dare leave me, you wretch! You can make yourself useful and serve. Here...'

And she thrust two teacups into his hands.

Nineteen

A week later, after the first quiet dinner *en famille* that the Hartwood ladies had enjoyed at home for some days, they retired to the pretty blue parlour at the back of the house that they had discovered to be cosier than the drawing room, and, on a chilly late-November night, a good deal easier to heat.

Making themselves comfortable by the crackling fire, they began the respective tasks they had assigned themselves for the evening: Lady Hartwood, to read through her neat pile of correspondence, and April, to pick up her needle and sew some recently purchased lace onto the *décolleté* of an old chemise, in the hope of imbuing it with a more modish appearance.

After a long, contented silence, Lady Hartwood looked up from her reading and remarked: 'Mother has sent through the list she promised.'

'What list?' April asked absentmindedly, her concentration on her needlework.

'For the dinner party we are to host. Remember, love, she wishes us to invite some people who will be useful in launching you into society?'

'You mean, useful in securing me a husband,' April remarked sharply.

'That too, of course... you do not mind, do you? I would never wish to force you into anything you do not like, but I know you understand the benefit of marrying an eligible, sweet-tempered man who can give you a comfortable home and children.'

'Yes, certainly I want a comfortable home and children,' replied April; but for some reason she could not agree to wanting the sweet-tempered man.

It occurred to her that this was a rather strange reticence on her part.

Her needle paused in mid-air as she considered the reason for it... and, with an unwelcome jolt of insight, realised it might have to do with the fact that she could not picture a certain Mr Hugh Royce described in such terms.

'Why are you frowning, love?' asked Lady Hartwood. 'Frowning is *lethal* for a lady's complexion! So aging!'

April smoothed out her features and smiled.

'I was just wool-gathering. Tell me, who does Grandmama wish us to invite?'

'Let me see... apart from Mother, Albert and the two of us, she has also included Mrs Jameson, the Duke of Claredon and his mother, Mrs Beechcroft and her daughter... oh, and of course, dear Hugh.'

April could not imagine why her mother had fallen into the habit of saying *dear Hugh.* It was most irritating. There was nothing in his conduct that she could discern to warrant such an endearment.

'The Beechcrofts are unknown to me,' she remarked.

'I was introduced to them at Mrs Jameson's *soirée,*' said Lady Hartwood. 'The daughter is really quite lovely! And, I suppose, they could be called *pleasant* company... but, you know how it is, we had little opportunity to converse properly. However, according to Mother,' she pointed to a place in the letter she held, 'they come from an old Somerset family. And Mrs Beechcroft is a friend of the duchess, so I assume she means us to invite them on her account.'

'And why does she make no mention of Miss Starling?' asked April. 'Hugh is bound to take offence.'

'Oh? Do you think he would?' said Lady Hartwood airily. 'I don't see why he should.'

'But of course he would! She is his fiancée.'

'Well, perhaps your grandmother simply forgot about her.'

'I doubt it. Her memory is better than mine! I fear she has excluded poor Miss Starling on purpose.'

Lady Hartwood looked away self-consciously and fidgeted with the fringe of the paisley shawl around her shoulders.

'Oh well, she has her reasons, no doubt!' Rising to her feet all of a sudden, she went on: 'I should begin the invitations tonight. The date set is a little more than a week away and I am not at all certain we will be able to secure everyone's attendance at such short notice.'

'I would not be overly concerned,' said April, smiling, 'Grandmama will have somehow discovered everyone's commitments through her network of spies and picked the date accordingly. She never leaves anything to chance.'

It appeared that this prediction may have had some truth to it as the replies that arrived over the next few days were all in the affirmative.

April viewed everyone's acceptance with mixed feelings. On the one hand, she was pleased on her mother's account, for it was a triumph of sorts for her; but, on the other, she was conscious that she was being asked to feed several illustrious persons who were used to only the best of culinary excellence, and she was not at all confident that her hired cook-housekeeper or her purse were up to the task.

Thankfully, her fears were soon put to rest by the arrival of a note from her grandmother, informing her to expect the celebrated individual who graced the Delamer kitchens in Richmond, together with some supplies, within the next few days.

April might make it a rule never to accept money from her grandmother, but she was not one to look a gift horse in the mouth when it came in the shape of the talented *Monsieur Balzac*.

And certainly not when her mother's reputation was at stake.

Lord Paisley might belittle the importance of the opinion of others when it came to his betrothal, however, April knew that her mother's life would be a great deal easier if she was accepted by her peers from the start.

Monsieur Balzac arrived late one morning the following week in Mrs Delamer's carriage, and was followed by a retinue of three other vehicles.

It seemed to April that he had brought half the Delamer household with him: two kitchen underlings and three footmen; a full Limoges dinner service; five large chests of crystal and silverware packed in individual velvet-covered casings; six heavy-bottomed gilt candelabras; a generous supply of beeswax candles that prompted April to exclaim they would need to shield their eyes over dinner; the carcasses of six partridges, one wild boar and two turtles; and, a large straw basket full of bound, but very much alive, lobsters.

Somewhat startled by such a grand cavalcade, April quickly sent for Mrs Plum, whose assistance she had previously requested in greeting *Monsieur*; a diplomatic manoeuvre she hoped would better dispose the woman to having her domain besieged by an outsider.

But she need not have worried.

The moment Mrs Plum was introduced to her usurper, she dropped into a curtsy and said exultantly: '*Monsieur Balzac*, it's an honour to be making your acquaintance! Your treatise on French sauces commands pride of place in my kitchen!'

Monsieur, who had greeted April with familiar but strict courtesy, broke into a winning smile at this confession and, taking hold of Mrs Plum's hand, helped her to rise.

'*Non, non. Viens!* I cannot allow a beautiful woman to bow at my feet!'

Mrs Plum's eyes widened in surprise, and, for the first time, took note of *Monsieur's* attractive countenance and surprisingly trim physique for a man in his middle years. She had always received her fair share of male attention with her well-rounded curves, but, having given her whole heart to her profession, had attained her fiftieth year without seriously considering the marriage offers that had come her way (her self-allocated title conferring a certain formal status rather than proclaiming her marital state).

She liked to think of herself as a pragmatic woman and had not been brought to blush for many a year, yet she now found her cheeks heated with pleasure and embarrassment, and her tongue strangely tied.

'*Dîtes-moi, madame*, what do you think of the chapter on the *béchamel* sauce?' *Monsieur* asked her.

Mrs Plum looked away uncomfortably and appeared uncertain how to reply.

'Please, there is no need for diplomacy!' said *Monsieur*. 'I am interested to know your true opinion.'

'I have always thought the last paragraph finishes a little abruptly,' Mrs Plum admitted. 'But perhaps you wished to withhold one or two ingredients from publication, which is understandable! Every chef is entitled to their secrets.'

Monsieur laughed and seemed pleased by her response.

'Yes, they are! But in this case, it was a simple printing mistake on the part of the publisher. Never was an omission more keenly felt! A whole section on the importance of nutmeg.'

Mrs Plum's face lit up.

'Nutmeg? Oh, I wouldn't have thought to add it to a béchamel!'

'Together we shall replicate my original recipe and I look forward to hearing your opinion on the complexity of taste that can be achieved.'

Mrs Plum looked ready to burst with joy and April could not help but be impressed with *Monsieur's* handling of a potentially awkward situation.

'And now, if it would please you, *madame*,' he went on, 'I would be honoured if you would show me your kitchens?'

Mrs Plum agreed at once and they disappeared into the nether regions of the house, leaving behind *Monsieur's* underlings to oversee the unloading of the vehicles.

April remained in the entry hall to direct the footmen as they carried in the silverware and other items not destined for the kitchens.

After a few minutes, sensing a presence behind her, she turned to find Layton had appeared and was staring at the commotion with a scowl on his face.

'Never fear, the house will soon be back in order,' she told him, smiling her understanding.

'I don't want to contradict you, Miss April, but it seems to me we won't have a moment's peace until this dinner party is out of the way,' he grumbled.

'Well, Mrs Delamer does nothing by half! But you need not think your workload will increase. The extra staff she sent will prove useful.'

'I can handle the additional workload, Miss April,' he said, squaring his shoulders. 'I don't need to be mollycoddled because of my age.'

'I would not dream of it! Not when I know you could teach the younger members of our staff a thing or two about stamina! And I'm sure I need not tell you how much my mother and I depend on you? We are counting on you to make certain all goes smoothly for the dinner party.'

Layton sniffed, not ready to be mollified.

'I suppose I'll have to discuss the wine list with the Frenchie,' he muttered darkly.

This comment struck dread into April's breast and her smile wavered. Layton held certain deeply imbedded prejudices against foreigners and it only now occurred to her that he was quite capable of insulting *Monsieur*.

'Oh, I...I don't think that will be necessary,' she said, and frantically tried to think of an excuse with which to avert such a calamity.

'I'm unable to compile the wine list without knowing what peculiar dishes he plans on serving up,' insisted Layton.

'Actually, umm...the wine has already been agreed upon!' she announced. 'I forgot to mention it.'

'But, Miss April, begging pardon, that's *my* job,' he said with a hurt expression.

'Of course it is! And I would never dream of interfering in your domain, but you see the wine was offered to us as a gift and I could not refuse.'

'From whom?' he asked, creasing his already impressively wrinkled brow even further.

'Good morning!' Hugh called out, walking through the open front door and sidestepping past two footmen struggling under the weight of a large, oak chest.

'Hugh!' April exclaimed, and suddenly broke into a beatific smile.

'I appear to have called at a bad time,' he said, taking off his hat. 'Shall I come back later?'

'No, stay!' she cried.

Hugh eyed her suspiciously. Her apparent delight in seeing him was incongruous given what had passed between them at Mrs Jameson's. Moreover, her bright mood was entirely at odds with his own. He resented the necessity of the conversation he had come to have with her.

'What have I done to be in your good books?' he asked, lifting a cynical eyebrow.

'Why, I was just telling Layton how good you were to insist on making us a present of the wine for our dinner party from your own cellars. My mother and I cannot thank you enough!'

Her eyes beseeched him not to give her away.

He found his mood softening. The minx was up to something and he was curious to find out what.

Twenty

Hugh dragged out the silence that followed, enjoying the way that doubt, and then indignation, seeped into April's eyes.

Just when she was beginning to think he would betray her, he offered her a rather dry look and said: 'There's no need for thanks. As your landlord, it's my responsibility to keep your cellar well-stocked and it's sadly lacking at present.'

Layton gave Hugh a hard stare.

'That last part I believe, for it's nothing but the truth!' he said belligerently.

April threw her elderly retainer a look of reproach. He would not acknowledge it and continued to glare at Hugh.

'Mr Royce and I have some business to discuss. Please have the tea tray sent up,' she said hastily, before Layton's suspicion could bear fruit.

Without waiting for a response from either man, she started up the stairs.

'What game are you playing at?' Hugh asked when he had caught up with her.

April looked furtively over her shoulder and found Layton still standing in the same spot, watching them.

'Shhh,' she cautioned under her breath.

Only when they had entered the drawing room, and she had closed the door behind them, did she allow herself to speak.

'I must beg your pardon!' she began. 'I did not mean to impose on you in such a way! I will, of course, procure my own wine, only I cannot involve Layton in the task.'

'When I make an offer of a gift – whether in person or by proxy – I honour the commitment,' he responded in a calm way that made her feel abashed.

'I truly am sorry! I shouldn't have said anything so improper. I only did so as I could see no other way of avoiding a confrontation between Layton and *Monsieur Balzac* – and, I assure you, if Layton has an opportunity to air his views on the French in front of *Monsieur*, then there will certainly be a confrontation!'

'*Monsieur Balzac*? Mrs Delamer's chef?'

April hesitated briefly.

'Why, yes. . . she has kindly agreed to lend him to us for our dinner party. My mother and I have known *Monsieur* for several years now for, as you know, Mrs Delamer is a close. . . '

'Family friend,' he finished for her. 'Yes, you have mentioned it before.'

She regarded him warily. His countenance remained politely blank and this in itself fed her suspicion. Hugh's countenance was never blank.

'You are fortunate,' he continued. 'There are any number of persons who would like *Monsieur Balzac* to grace their kitchens. I believe several unsuccessful attempts have been made to steal him away from Mrs Delamer.'

'I have no intention of stealing him!'

'I know. You couldn't afford him. I was simply giving in to the temptation to bait you a little – a weakness of mine, as we both know.'

'I should think you would be ashamed to admit it!' April said indignantly.

'No, why should I?'

'Because. . . because you cannot go around admitting whatever outrageous things pop into your head!' she said with exasperation. 'Imagine if everyone were to do so? We would all sink into a mire of unpalatable truths and be continuously causing offence. We cannot have a civilised society if we do not learn to control the words that come out of our mouths.'

'Which is why I rarely take the opportunity to speak my mind with such freedom.'

April blinked in surprise.

'How fortunate I am to inspire you with such veracity,' she observed without appreciation.

Hugh laughed.

'No, certainly not fortunate.'

'You are a strange man. Won't you sit?'

She indicated to a chair and then sat herself down on the settee. Hugh, however, surprised her by walking over to the door.

'Are you leaving?' she asked, a wave of disappointment sweeping through her.

He opened the door without replying, and then walked back to take the chair closest to her.

'We appear to keep returning to this subject,' he said, 'but you do need to be more cognisant of your reputation when you are in London. Young, unmarried women do not entertain gentlemen alone with the door closed.'

For some reason, on this particular occasion, she was gratified that he was observing the proprieties so strictly on her behalf.

'Thank you! But I am not such a young woman as you seem to think me. Now, so that we are perfectly clear, I don't expect you to provide the wine for my dinner party.'

Hugh offered her a challenging smile.

'Don't smile at me in that fashion!' she snapped. 'I mean it! I will not accept the wine. And, if you are so ungentlemanly as to go against my wishes, I will simply refuse to accept the delivery. For all I care it can sit on the street to be stolen.'

'If that is how you wish to distribute your gift, so be it.'

April's agitation grew. It was unconscionable that she had put Hugh in the position of having to offer up such an extravagant gift.

Before she could think of a suitably final rejoinder, however, her mother entered the room.

'Hugh-dear, how delightful to find you here!' said Lady Hartwood. 'I hope you are well?'

Hugh stood at once and her ladyship gave him both her hands and a cheek to kiss.

'I am always well, ma'am,' he replied. 'May I ask, what or who has put that high-bloom in your complexion?'

'I was just out driving with your uncle! What a shame you missed each other. He would have certainly come up had he known you were here. And to what do we owe the pleasure of your company today?'

Hugh waited for her to be seated, before once more sitting down himself.

'I have two reasons for visiting. Firstly, I wanted to confirm the arrangements for the wine I am to provide for Friday. From my own cellars, of course.'

'Oh? Are you providing the wine? I had not realised,' said Lady Hartwood, looking across at April.

'No, Mr Royce is most certainly *not* providing the wine,' April informed her. 'He wishes to make us a present of it but I . . .'

'A small gift for *you*, Lady Hartwood,' interrupted Hugh. 'I hope you will not deny me the enjoyment of it? And especially since it is my fault your cellars here are so badly stocked.'

'Oh, how thoughtful of you!' exclaimed her ladyship, leaning over to squeeze his hand. 'What can I say but thank you! I would be delighted to accept! I understand from your uncle that your cellars are *quite* exceptional.'

April knew her mother had little idea the 'small gift' would end up costing more than an expensive piece of jewellery. April had few illusions that Hugh would provide them with anything less than the best.

Oddly, this altruism only annoyed her.

'Mama, we are perfectly capable of buying our own wine,' she said firmly.

'Why, of course we are, love! But that does not mean we are so graceless as to reject a gift based on such reasoning.'

April was silenced.

Thoroughly annoyed by Hugh's unscrupulous tactics, she was also mortified that her own actions had led them to this point.

'And what is the second reason for your visit, Hugh-dear?' asked Lady Hartwood.

Hugh found himself momentarily at a loss as to how to proceed.

He had expected to have this particular conversation with April, and had no compunction about bringing up the matter with *her*. However, he found himself reluctant to bring it up with Lady Hartwood, for the simple reason that he wanted to spare her any embarrassment.

He relaxed back into his chair and offered her ladyship an apologetic smile.

'Actually, ma'am, I wanted to broach the subject of my fiancée and her mother with you. It appears they never received an invitation to your dinner party. I suspect it stemmed from the fact that you believed Mrs Starling's indisposition still continued, and I told them as much. Miss Starling wanted me to let you know that her mother is now fully recovered.'

'Oh... that is *wonderful*, to be sure,' said Lady Hartwood uneasily; and proceeded to lose herself in a string of half-finished sentences: 'I did wonder if perhaps... if it might be inopportune... but of course... without question... I thought we had sent... but perhaps not...'

April had always thought that Miss Starling should be invited and was not at all surprised that Hugh felt the need to redress this omission. Although it occurred to her, by gifting the wine he had purposefully made it impossible for them to say no to him.

This type of calculated manoeuvre disgusted her and she was more disappointed than she cared to admit.

'Please tell the Starlings their invitation must have been misplaced,' she said, lying with a proficiency her mother lacked. 'We did think it a little strange not to have received their reply, but that is now explained! We hope they will be able to join us?'

Hugh had not wanted to come fishing for an invitation but, as Miss Starling had pointed out to him in her sweet-tempered way, the oversight could be viewed as a slight towards herself and her mother, and it would not be in anyone's interest if such malicious gossip began to take root. And so Hugh had felt honour-bound to do her bidding.

'Thank you,' he said in his curt way, although he knew very well there was no misplaced invitation.

'Not at all – a simple misunderstanding,' replied April. And, before she could think better of it, she added: 'No inducement was necessary.'

A flicker of something dangerous lived in Hugh's eyes for an instant.

'Then it's fortunate no inducement was offered,' he drawled.

'No?' asked April, an eyebrow rising in challenge.

'No.'

'What inducement?' asked Lady Hartwood, looking from one to the other, confusion in her large blue eyes.

April tore her gaze away from Hugh.

'Nothing, Mama! Simply another misunderstanding. On my part, this time, it would seem.'

She then turned the conversation by telling her mother that they would need to speak to *Monsieur Balzac* about the menu as soon as possible, and advise Hugh so that he could match the wine accordingly.

This subject distracted Lady Hartwood for a few minutes, until Hugh excused himself with the claim of another engagement and, saying he would show himself out, took his leave of them.

On his way down the stairs he passed a footman, carrying the tea tray, followed by the butler.

'I'm bringing the tea,' said Layton, a note of accusation in his voice.

'You'll have to excuse me, I can't stay to enjoy it. I will organise for the wine to be delivered to you on Thursday. I trust it will meet with your approval, but if you have a particular vintage in mind that has not been included you have only to send word to me.'

'I don't yet know why an engaged man has taken it upon himself to provide the wine for another lady's establishment,' Layton said pugnaciously, 'but let me warn you, young man, I'm watching you!'

Hugh smiled and put a reassuring hand on the old man's shoulder.

'So you should! But you have my word, you have nothing to fear from me. We both want only the best for your mistress.'

'Which one?'

'Lady Hartwood, of course,' replied Hugh, and continued down the stairs.

'It's not her ladyship I fear for!'

Twenty-One

A few minutes before eight o'clock, on the evening of the dinner party, Lord Paisley showed himself into the Hartwood ladies' drawing room; illuminated for the occasion with dozens of candles, placed in candelabras collected from every corner and dusty cupboard in the house and polished into brilliance.

'Good evening, my love! April!' he greeted them in a hearty voice.

Lady Hartwood peered behind him as he leant in to kiss her cheek.

'Where is Layton, dearest?' she asked. 'Why did he not announce you?'

'You must not blame your man. I told him there was no need for him to accompany me upstairs when his time would be better spent greeting the other guests. He does not appear to be faring well with the steep stairs in this house.'

'Oh Albert, how like you to think of others! Poor Layton! I should have pensioned him off long ago, but every time I make even the *smallest* hint that he may be more comfortable enjoying his remaining years in retirement, he asks me if I am unhappy with his service. And with *such* a wounded expression! I never know what to say except to assure him that no other butler could ever be his equal in our esteem. Which is indeed *true*. Only, there is no denying, someone younger would be more suited to the role.'

'He has served our family a long time,' said April. 'I don't believe he can imagine any other life. It would be cruel to take his duties away from him, but we do try to ease them. Unfortunately, that's not so easily done in London.'

'I don't imagine it is!' said Lord Paisley, grinning slyly at her. 'The poor man must be answering the door morning, noon, and night!'

'There are certainly more people in London than in St Mawes, so it is only natural we should have more visitors,' April replied, refusing to take the bait.

'Suitors is what I'm referring to, not visitors! How many marriage proposals have you earned for yourself so far? Three? Four?'

'Really, Albert! A lady does not discuss such things.'

'Well, let me tell you, my dear, your suitors don't have the same scruples. They seem to view me as the closest thing to a father to you and I've been accosted twice already this week by striplings eager to declare themselves.'

'Oh, never say so!' she cried, greatly vexed. 'I'm sorry you were imposed upon! Was it Mr Hall and Lord Windham? I shall certainly give them a piece of my mind when I next see them.'

'No need to get worked up, my dear,' chuckled Lord Paisley. 'Can't blame the boys for trying. It would certainly have been preferable if young Hall hadn't cornered me at White's before I'd even sat down to my dinner, but there was no harm done. And Windham was good enough to make an appointment to see me.' He laughed again at her look of consternation. 'In case you're wondering, I told them you were of age and mistress of your own destiny, and that they must pay their addresses directly to you.'

'Thank you,' she said tightly. 'I promise you, I haven't given them the least indication that I would welcome their declarations.'

'Of course you haven't, love,' said Lady Hartwood. 'But you know theirs won't be the last marriage proposals you receive while in town. You shouldn't allow yourself to be so angered by them. Back home you had a wonderful way of declining offers without causing the least offence!'

April was surprised to realise her mother was correct.

She did feel angered.

And with unwelcome clarity she recognised the reason for it: every marriage proposal she would receive from now on would be tainted by the one that would never come.

Determined to change the subject, she exclaimed: 'Why, Albert, I have never seen you look more dashing! That coat fits you to perfection.'

'Yes, you are looking very fine, dearest,' agreed Lady Hartwood. 'But. . . am I mistaken or have you lost more weight?' she asked with a worried frown.

'A little,' he replied sheepishly. 'Does it please you?'

'Oh, Albert, I hope you know I do not expect you to alter yourself in *any* way? None at all!'

'I know that, my love. But there's no denying it was high time I looked to my health! I want to live a great many more years now I am to have you as my wife.'

Lady Hartwood was not immune to this reasoning, so highly flattering to herself, and allowed him to draw her into his arms and kiss her in a way that made her tremble inside.

April discreetly looked away and turned her attention to smoothing out the skirt of her dress.

Out of the several new outfits at her disposal, she had chosen a sleeveless, midnight-blue silk underdress, over which she wore a close-fitting, silver net dress that was gathered in attractive ruffles around the neck and wrists, and embroidered with small, silver flecks.

The effect was enchanting, and when coupled with her striking looks it was unsurprising that when Hugh and the Starlings were shown into the room, a few minutes later, their eyes were inclined to linger on her.

Hugh was the first to look away and proceeded to introduce Mrs Starling to her ladyship.

'Mrs Starling, I am delighted to be finally making your acquaintance!' declared Lady Hartwood, giving not the slightest indication that this particular guest had been thrust upon her.

Offering her hostess a thin smile and her gloved fingers to shake, Mrs Starling said in a lifeless voice: 'Likewise. Enchanted. So good of you to invite me to your lovely home.'

She was a small-boned woman with a pale, withered kind of beauty, and her impassive demeanour, which she equated with good breeding, was the work of many years training.

Returning her gaze to April, she continued placidly: 'I can see the reports of your daughter's beauty were not exaggerated. Most unusual. Exquisite, in fact.'

April correctly took this as a greeting of sorts and dropped into a curtsy.

'How kind of you to say so!' said Lady Hartwood. 'I count myself amazingly fortunate to have such a daughter. Her good-humour and kindness are the *greatest* comfort to me.'

April smiled her thanks. Her mother was always the first to draw people's attention away from her looks and to her other qualities.

'I too am fortunate in my daughter,' declared Mrs Starling. 'I cannot tell you the number of times others have praised her sweetness of disposition and loveliness to me. She is to be married soon, as you know...' she paused to allow her hostess to feel the weight of this superior trait, '...and I do not know how I am to part with her.'

'We can only hope you will not be called on to part with her *too* soon,' remarked Lady Hartwood. Then, feeling the need to atone for succumbing to her inner devil, she went on quickly: 'I am so happy to see you are fully recovered from your indisposition and could join us this evening.'

'Thank you but my recovery is not complete. It will always be my burden to not enjoy good health.'

'Why, you are the picture of health!'

'An illusion,' responded Mrs Starling, rejecting such an optimistic view. 'I did not feel at all strong enough to leave the house tonight, and in such a horrible, chilling wind. But as a mother, you will understand, we must exert ourselves for the good of our children, even if we know with a certainty it will be detrimental to our constitution.'

'Oh... I am sorry to hear that,' said her ladyship, daunted at last. 'Won't you come and sit by the fire? I can have a posset brewed for you if it will make you more comfortable? Is there a particular recipe you prefer?'

'Perhaps a few moments by the fire will revive me. But there is no need at all to go to the trouble of brewing a posset, I assure you. I do not wish to be a bother. A warm glass of negus is all I require. I have found it suits me best. But if it is too great an imposition, pray do not trouble yourself. I will be perfectly content with any other beverage.'

Her ladyship assured her it was no trouble at all; and, after throwing Lord Paisley a pleading look to see to ordering this concoction of heated port, sugar, and spices, she escorted the steadfast invalid to a chair by the fire.

April saw exasperation in Hugh's countenance and struggled to suppress her smile. It was hard to imagine a man of his temperament with such a mother-in-law.

Catching her twinkling gaze on him, Hugh turned away before he could validate her amusement with his own smile.

'As you can see, Miss Hartwood, my mother does not enjoy the best of health,' said Miss Starling, some natural embarrassment creeping into her voice. 'However, she would not allow her frailty to deter her from coming tonight.'

'We are most obliged to her,' replied April, suitably straight-faced.

The next group to arrive, soon after, consisted of the Duke of Claredon, his mother and Mrs and Miss Beechcroft.

Lady Hartwood had previously met the Beechcrofts at Mrs Jameson's *soirée* but April had been elsewhere in the room at the time and was meeting them now for the first time.

As her mother had suggested, Miss Beechcroft was a diamond of the first water. Whereas April was dark-haired and the sum of her features was striking, almost exotic, Miss Beechcroft was a fair beauty and her lovely plump countenance was quintessentially English.

Both her liveliness and her ample assets were on display for the evening, and she showed herself to be most ready to enjoy herself, while leaving one with the impression that she was used to finding herself in grander company.

Mrs Beechcroft, in marked contrast to her daughter, was a plain and lacklustre woman, and her unmistakably costly attire in no way hinted that she was blessed with good taste. And it was soon discovered that her personality did nothing to ameliorate these disadvantages.

The forceful way in which she set out to question April and Lady Hartwood on their family pedigree, while drawing the duke's and duchess' attention to any perceived discrepancies, soon alienated at least half of her audience.

Had Lord Paisley been near enough to overhear he would have put a stop to her impudence, however, after the initial greetings had been exchanged, he had felt duty-bound to take up the position Lady Hartwood had vacated beside Mrs Starling and engage the woman in conversation while she drank her negus.

'It appears we are unable to convince you!' April declared after enduring several minutes of Mrs Beechcroft's inquisition. 'Nonetheless, it is a fact easily checked that the Barony of Hartwood did not die out with my father. It was created by writ, and the remainders of baronies by writ are not limited to male heirs.'

She had not meant to reveal as much but the woman had to be silenced.

'That is indeed true,' declared the duchess grandly, looking around the assembled group. 'My own dear friend, the Baroness of Highcliff came into the title when there were no male heirs left to inherit. It too had been created by writ. I believe it is a most sensible solution to a problem that could otherwise decimate the ranks of the nobility.'

'How right you are, Your Grace!' enthused Miss Starling.

'Personally,' said Miss Beechcroft, her smile fixed on the duke, 'I would not know what to do with a title in my own right! My delicate shoulders could not bear the weight of all those responsibilities. A man is better suited to such a task, wouldn't you agree, Your Grace?'

'On occasion, perhaps,' he replied diplomatically. 'However, I do not believe there is anything in the female temperament to preclude a woman from succeeding in such a duty. I have little doubt Miss Hartwood will rise to the occasion.'

'A baroness in your own right!' Mrs Beechcroft addressed April in an accusing tone, clearly affronted by the thought. 'But then why continue to call yourself Miss Hartwood?'

'I have not yet claimed the title,' April replied, the muscles around her mouth straining to maintain her smile.

'Mrs Beechcroft, you are still without a refreshment,' Hugh interjected. 'Allow me to recommend the Madeira, it's a particularly fine vintage. Or perhaps a glass of ratafia?'

This flattering attention to her comfort, by one of the *ton's* wealthiest members, greatly pleased Mrs Beechcroft's sense of entitlement.

'Why, thank you, Mr Royce! I will try a little of the Madeira, since it comes with your recommendation.'

Her Grace also acknowledged herself happy to partake of the Madeira, and once the drinks had been procured Hugh steered both matrons to take up seats beside Mrs Starling and Lord Paisley.

While Hugh was engaged in removing Mrs Beechcroft from April's vicinity, Miss Beechcroft took the opportunity to turn her vivacity on Lady Hartwood.

'What a cosy drawing room you have here, your ladyship!' she announced. 'Charming beyond words! I have heard frightful complaints about London houses for hire, but no one could ever call such pleasant furnishings *shabby*. And the curtains so remind me of my childhood! We had very similar curtains at Chattley, oh, a dozen or so years ago, when that style of brocade was quite the height of fashion. You must be delighted to have secured such homely accommodation?'

'Oh, we are indeed!' agreed Lady Hartwood, unable to recognise the subtle condescension. 'And we have Mr Royce to thank! This house is one of his properties, you know, and we consider ourselves *most* fortunate to be staying here.' She offered Hugh a grateful smile as he re-joined their group.

Miss Beechcroft was momentarily thrown off course and laughed a little uncertainly.

'Oh? This is *your* house, Mr Royce? I did not realise!'

'Why should you?' Hugh replied sardonically, well acquainted with persons of her type. Turning to Lady Hartwood, he said: 'You have done an excellent job, ma'am, in turning the house into a home. It is now filled with a warmth and beauty it lacked before.'

'Thank you, but I cannot allow you to think I had anything to do in the matter,' she replied, looking over at April with pride. 'My daughter knew exactly how she wanted to decorate the rooms with flowers and candles. Why, she must have bought all the stock at Covent Garden this morning! The hackney coach that brought her home was full to bursting.'

She gestured around the room, and everyone turned to admire the dozens of flower arrangements that had been placed about in crystal containers of every shape and size.

'And the chandler was so pleased with the order she placed,' continued her ladyship, laughing, 'he arrived on our doorstep with a posy of violets and *insisted* on giving it to her in person.'

April was uncomfortably aware that it had been herself and not her order that had inspired the chandler.

'Mama, surely the minutiae of my day can be of no interest to our guests?' she said lightly.

'You undertook to visit the Covent Garden market *yourself?*' asked Miss Beechcroft, eyebrows rising half-way up her forehead to convey her excessive surprise.

'Yes,' replied April. 'And, what is more, I enjoyed myself immensely.'

'How. . . peculiar,' said Miss Beechcroft.

'It is perfectly respectable for a lady accompanied by her footman to venture out to Covent Garden during the day,' Hugh remarked.

His casual defence of her brought a blush to April's cheeks, as Miss Beechcroft's barbs had been quite unable to do.

'I consider myself something of a connoisseur of flower arrangements,' said the duke, smoothly moving on the conversation, 'and yours, Miss Hartwood, are particularly well done. It is evident you have an artistic flair that you have been hiding from us.'

'How right you are, Your Grace,' agreed Miss Starling.

'Thank you both!' April laughed. 'But I doubt my small efforts warrant such high praise.'

'You are being too modest,' said His Grace. Then, casting a sly glance at Hugh, he went on: 'But even without these efforts, Mr Royce's sentiment holds true: your warmth and beauty pervade your home!'

As Hugh had meant nothing of the sort, he regarded the young duke with marked displeasure.

April was irritated by the comment as well, and feared Miss Starling was bound to have taken offence.

This was proven to be not the case, however, for in the next moment she gushed: 'Oh, yes indeed, Your Grace! Such warmth and beauty!'

April had to resist the urge to roll her eyes.

Twenty-Two

A short while later, a commotion out in the corridor caught everyone's attention and all turned to see a tall and elegantly dressed elder gentleman throw open the door to the drawing room and enter.

There was a determined glint in his hawkish eyes and the way he held his silver topped walking stick gave one the impression that this item was used as a weapon rather than a walking aide.

'You may announce me,' the gentleman snapped at Layton, who shuffled into the room after him, looking as harassed as April had ever seen him.

'Excuse the intrusion, your ladyship,' said the butler, eyeing up the intruder with disgust. 'This *person* would not believe me when I informed him you were not receiving visitors.'

'Father!' expostulated Lord Paisley and shot up out of his seat beside Mrs Starling.

'Ah! It appears I have the right house after all,' remarked the gentleman, flicking a contemptuous glance at Layton. 'This nincompoop wouldn't tell me if you were here or not, Albert, even though it was your own butler who gave me your direction. Well then! Is *this* the charmer you want to marry without my approval?'

He walked over to where Mrs Starling was sitting and scrutinised her in a manner that could not be construed as complimentary.

Pinning a mocking gaze on his son, he lifted his dark, bushy eyebrows and asked: 'Really, Albert? Not in your usual style, is she?'

Lord Paisley, his equilibrium quite shattered, stuttered: 'F-Father, I-I don't know what you... this is not...'

'Well, don't just stand there gabbing! Present me!'

'Yes, yes of course... at once... Mrs Starling, may I present my father, the Earl of Wulfingston.'

Mrs Starling looked very much like a rabbit startled by a hunter as she uttered a colourless 'charmed' and reluctantly extended her hand, as if fearing it would not be returned to her.

Lord Wulfingston chose to ignore the offered limb and executed the briefest of bows.

Dismissing her from his notice, he addressed his son with malicious amusement: 'The name Starling rings a bell, but not in connection with yourself. Unless my memory fails me – and it never does! – you have gotten yourself engaged to a Baroness *Hartwood*. Playing fast and loose with her already, are you? Ha! Never believed all that mawkish rubbish you wrote about being ready to settle down.'

'S-sir! Nothing of the sort, I promise you!' spluttered Lord Paisley. 'Mrs Starling is simply a guest of my betrothed.'

'And my future mother-in-law,' interjected Hugh, drawing Lord Wulfingston's eyes on himself, 'which is why the name will be familiar to you. Good evening, Grandfather. You will no doubt also wish to be introduced to my fiancée, Miss Starling, who as yet has not had the pleasure of meeting you.'

Hugh beckoned Miss Starling with a smile and she moved to stand beside him (although much against her will, for she would have preferred not to be brought to the attention of such an unpredictable character when their audience consisted of persons she was at pains to impress).

Lord Wulfingston, however, paid her as little attention as she could have hoped for, only saying cryptically: 'I knew your grandfather. You come from good stock.' Then, turning to scan the other guests in the room, he demanded of no one in particular: 'Well then... where is the woman who aspires to be the future Viscountess Paisley?'

Hugh walked over to Lady Hartwood and gently took her hand, stiff with shock, and placed it in the crook of his arm.

She looked up at him with wide, aghast eyes.

He gave her an encouraging wink and led her towards Lord Wulfingston.

April quickly followed and took up position on her mother's other side, in silent support.

'Baroness Hartwood, and her daughter, Miss Hartwood,' Hugh told his grandfather, his eyes warning him to behave himself. 'I know you will wish to beg their pardon for invading their drawing room in this haphazard manner.'

The Earl's eyes skimmed over April and landed on Lady Hartwood.

'Hmm... better, in all events,' he muttered. 'For which, I suppose, I must be grateful! Your servant.'

He bowed to both mother and daughter.

Looking back at his grandson, he said severely: 'You think you're in a position to remind me of my manners, do you? You might be my heir but I won't stand for your impudence, you good-for-nothing scoundrel!'

Being used to a great deal worse, Hugh considered this a light, affectionate trimming and accepted it with a smile.

He did not even attempt to point out that he was not his progenitor's legal heir; his uncle, beside him, being very much alive and still holding that dubious pleasure. The comment had undoubtedly been intended to put Lord Paisley in his place, and it would have done little good to thwart his grandfather's enjoyment of venting his spleen.

Hugh may not have taken offence at his grandfather's words but Lady Hartwood most certainly had, on his behalf.

Her protective instincts were roused and, whereas she could never have come to her own defence if such remarks had been levelled at her, she now straightened to her full height and said sternly: 'I take leave to tell you, Lord Wulfingston, that I will *not* have your grandson abused in my house! If you wish to continue in that insulting vein I suggest you take yourself off!'

Her sentinels, barely containing their surprise, drew closer to her, bound by a common wish to protect her from Lord Wulfingston's anger.

The earl had stiffened and a slight twitch of his left eye signalled to Hugh that an eruption was imminent.

Seeing that she had rendered his lordship speechless, Lady Hartwood added in a conciliatory tone: 'That is not to say you are not welcome, sir. You are *most* welcome, I assure you! But I am honour-bound to make certain that Hugh suffers no ill-treatment under my roof. And although I would not for the world wish to cause offence, I hope you understand why I have had to be a little firm with you?'

Lord Wulfingston's craggy features relaxed.

He liked to think he was well acquainted with the finer points of honour and chose to find it amusing that the dainty female before him was lecturing him on the subject.

'Most welcome, am I?' he said after a long pause. 'Whether that's the truth, or some pretty talking to turn me up sweet, we shall find out soon enough.' He raised his gold filigree quizzing glass and studied her through it. 'I was told you were nothing but a pretty widgeon. But I'll say this for you, you've got fire!'

'I might well be a widgeon, sir, but there is *nothing* I would not do for those dearest to me,' said her ladyship, taking no offence at this back-handed compliment.

'Mrs Delamer and Mrs Jameson,' Layton's voice suddenly boomed across the room, startling the silent observers of the unfolding drama.

'Wulfingston, I see the years have done little to soften your famed charm,' Mrs Delamer declared scornfully as she walked into the room, looking magnificent in gold satin and black lace.

'Who the devil are you?' he demanded, scowling at her.

'Father, your language! There are ladies present,' beseeched Lord Paisley; only to be ignored.

Mrs Delamer directed a taunting smile at the earl.

'You may not know me,' she replied, 'but I am well acquainted with your reputation.'

'Have we met before?' asked Lord Wulfingston, moving closer to her.

'Your lordship, allow me to introduce you to Mrs Delamer,' April responded hastily, before her grandmother could antagonise him further. 'Mrs Delamer and her late husband were neighbours of ours in Cornwall.'

'Mrs Delamer? Never heard the name! And I've never been to Cornwall!' Lord Wulfingston said dismissively; but he continued to scrutinise Mrs Delamer closely, and, after a moment, added: 'There is *something* familiar about you. . . I suppose it's possible we could have met in London?'

'No,' replied Mrs Delamer, beginning to look bored.

'Some country estate, then?'

'I abhor house parties unless I am the one hosting them.'

'The Continent?'

'I never travel beyond the borders of England.'

A puzzled frown settled on Lord Wulfingston's countenance as he studied her, and the fingers of one hand drummed a steady rhythm against the silver head of his cane.

April offered up a silent prayer that he would not be able to connect her grandmother to the courtesan he had known in his youth. The intervening fifty years had done much to keep her secret, but if she continued to play this game of cat and mouse she was bound to prod his memory.

A short silence followed; until Lady Hartwood came out of the stupefaction into which she had sunk on her mother's dramatic entrance and commenced to introduce the newcomers to the other guests. As she went to introduce Mrs Jameson to Lord Wulfingston, however, Mrs Jameson interrupted her.

'No need for introductions, Eleanor!' she said with hearty good humour. 'His lordship and I are acquainted. How are you, Barnaby? Good to see you've found your way back to town. It must be at least five years since your last visit?'

'Seven. And if I had only my wishes to consider it would have been longer,' he replied, flinging a reproachful glance at Lord Paisley. Turning back to Mrs Jameson, he raised his quizzing glass and studied her through it. 'Good god, Amelia! What are you wearing? Your husband would turn in his grave to see you decked out like a Christmas tree!'

Mrs Jameson laughed and looked down at her buttercup-yellow costume (which consisted of too many feathers and sparkling embellishments to warrant the name *gown*).

'Why, Barnaby, I think I look dazzling!'

Lady Hartwood, appalled at Lord Wulfingston's remarks, cried: 'And so you do, ma'am! A veritable jewel amongst us! Can I offer you a refreshment? And you, Mrs Delamer?'

'I did not know you were invited this evening,' Mrs Delamer addressed Lord Wulfingston, ignoring her daughter.

'I was not,' he said, unabashed. 'I came to find my son.'

'Good! Then you won't be staying for dinner.'

He threw her a challenging look, then slid his gaze across to Lady Hartwood.

Her ladyship's eyes darted helplessly from Lord Paisley to her mother, before her ingrained good manners compelled her to say: 'We would be delighted if you could join us for dinner, Lord Wulfingston. . . but perhaps you have a previous engagement?' she asked with faint hope.

'I don't. I believe I will stay for dinner,' he replied, gifting Mrs Delamer a valedictory look.

Twenty-Three

The seating plan for dinner had been devised by Mrs Delamer some days previously, with strict instructions that it was not to be altered. It had baffled April, for it appeared to follow no accepted rules, and, once her grandmother had accounted for the addition of the Starlings, it was also absurdly imbalanced, with only three gentlemen amongst nine ladies.

And now, it was to be corrupted again.

Layton naturally objected when April shared the news with him, and she had to spend some time coaxing him out of his sullens by reminding him that, for her mother's sake, it was imperative they made a good impression on Lord Wulfingston.

He agreed at last and thereafter offered up no more than a dozen or so grumblings on the ill-omen of having thirteen sit down to dinner.

They decided to put Lord Wulfingston at the foot of the table, in the spot that had been assigned to his son. This had the dual advantages of recognising his status within the extended family and, at the same time, placing him as far away from Lady Hartwood, seated at the table's head, as was possible.

April gave Lord Paisley her own seat beside Hugh, and had an extra place set for herself on Lord Wulfingston's right.

She hoped this sacrifice on her part would shield the other guests from the earl's temperament (as well as remove her from Hugh's vicinity).

Some fifteen minutes later, as the guests entered the dining room and began to seat themselves, April's sacrifice was dealt a death-blow by her grandmother.

Mrs Delamer took in the changes at a glance, and, dropping a word in Lord Paisley's ear, gave up her place to him and sat herself in the chair intended for April, beside Lord Wulfingston.

April was annoyed to see the upshot of this manoeuvring was that she once more found herself seated beside Hugh.

If her grandmother was not so adamant that she secure the duke's affections, she would have had little choice at this point but to indulge in some rather absurd suspicions.

Although it did occur to her that her relative might simply wish to sit beside Lord Wulfingston and continue to taunt him.

That, however, did not explain why the dear, contrary woman had placed the duke on the opposite side of the table, between Miss Starling and Miss Beechcroft.

She was suddenly pulled out of her thoughts by the awareness that Hugh and herself were the only ones still standing. . . and that he was holding out her chair and waiting, his amused eyes resting on her.

She quickly walked over to him.

'Thank you,' she murmured.

Brushing past him in her hurry, she caught a faint trace of his scent. It was not the first time she had inhaled it but for some reason, tonight, she found it extraordinarily intoxicating.

Mingled with the earthy tones of male there was an elusive note of something else. . . something she could not quite place.

'Have you lost your balance?' he asked, putting a hand on her elbow.

She was startled to realise she had come to a standstill and was leaning into him.

'Umm. . . yes. That must be it,' she replied, colouring.

Dear God, what was wrong with her?

One did not go about sniffing one's guests! It must surely be a rule in one of those absurd instructional tomes for ladies. And if it wasn't, then it should be!

Sitting down abruptly, she gave her attention to Mrs Jameson, on her right, and remained talking to her for a good half hour before she dared to take a peek in Hugh's direction.

He was looking decidedly bored as he listened to his future mother-in-law give her opinion on the perceived transgression of her servants, and it struck April how unhappily he was placed.

What had her grandmother been thinking to put Mrs Starling beside him? Anyone with a few minutes acquaintance of their characters would have realised the two of them should never be placed together for any appreciable amount of time.

But what was worse, in April's opinion, Hugh had an unobstructed view, directly opposite him, of his fiancée's attempts to hold the duke's attention. The smiles Miss Starling offered His Grace were a little too sparkling, and the way she thanked him for passing the creamed peas a little too excessive, to appeal to a man of Hugh's temperament.

However, to do Miss Starling justice, her efforts paled when compared to those of Miss Beechcroft.

This young lady had clearly warmed to her role as a reigning beauty and had studied the art of flirtation. She grazed against the duke's arm when she spoke to him, thrust her impressive bosom forward when his eyes were on her, laughed at every mildly humorous remark he uttered and teased him in an overly familiar manner that proclaimed their close acquaintance.

Placed as he was between these two determined ladies, one brimming with amiability and the other confident and coquettish, the besieged duke was given little opportunity to eat his dinner.

April found the whole performance absurd and had to bite on her bottom lip to hold in her laughter.

'Laugh all you want,' Hugh said quietly. 'No one is watching you.'

She looked across at him a little guiltily.

'I had not realised I was so transparent?'

'You're not.'

'I must be! You read me easily enough.'

'I was watching for your reaction.'

'You mean, you were waiting for me to slip up,' she said, throwing him an amused glance. 'And now you have discovered my secret: I can be downright ill-mannered when something pricks my sense of humour.'

'I won't betray you.'

The look in his eyes as he smiled held her mesmerised.

'Frankincense!' she burst out all of a sudden, startling them both.

'Pardon?' he asked, puzzled.

April looked away in confusion and shook her head; part denial, part apology.

She cut a piece of the partridge on her plate and hurriedly put it into her mouth.

Hugh did not press her, much to her relief, although he did continue to watch her while she ate; until Miss Beechcroft's laughter rang out once more and diverted his attention.

'She's untiring,' he observed blandly.

'She is also very beautiful,' said April, happy to speak on a different subject. 'And undoubtedly used to being the centre of attention.'

'So are you, but I'm yet to see you behave in such a manner.'

The compliment flustered her and she found herself admitting: 'I do not like to be the centre of attention. If I did, I might be tempted to make the most of people's ridiculous reactions to me.'

'Don't you enjoy being beautiful?' he asked with genuine interest.

'I rarely think of my looks. . . that is, until people begin to act strangely around me.'

'I take it they act *strangely* rather often?' he said with a quirk of his lips.

'Too often,' she sighed. 'Beauty is absurdly prized in our society but I have rarely found it to be an advantage. All it has ever done for me is to place a barrier between myself and others. And few have bothered to look beyond to the person underneath.'

Hugh remained silent; his gaze fixed on her as if he were trying to see into her very soul.

Both ill at ease and exhilarated by his scrutiny, and not at all certain as to why she had chosen to confide in him on such a personal matter, she said offhandedly: 'I know I probably sound ridiculous.'

Hugh looked down at his glass of burgundy as he played with the stem of the finely shaped crystal.

'No, you don't,' he said after a moment. 'I simply have never considered the matter from such a perspective.'

'I do not suppose you've had cause to,' she remarked and took a sip of wine.

Hugh looked up with a quick smile.

'I've never been hampered by good looks but it's hardly polite of you to point it out.'

April choked a little on her wine.

'I did *not* mean that!' she informed him indignantly when she could speak. 'You know I did not!'

'Do I?'

'Oh, do not pretend! You are fishing for compliments by forcing me to say it. . . you must know perfectly well how attractive you are.'

Disappointment flared in Hugh's eyes.

He suspected her of flattering him, and experience had taught him to be wary of women who offered him compliments. More often than not they wanted something from him.

But then he noticed the tell-tale signs of annoyance and embarrassment on her countenance and realised, with some surprise, that she was in earnest.

'I seem to have fallen into the habit of making easy assumptions,' he remarked. 'My apologies.'

He would have said more had not Mrs Starling captured his attention at this point with a light, persistent tug on his sleeve.

He tore his gaze away from April, telling himself it was for the best, and she was left to wonder over the strangeness of his reply.

Once the superb dinner that *Monsieur Balzac* and his team had worked tirelessly to prepare was at an end, the ladies retired to the drawing room and left the men to enjoy their port at the dinner table.

This time-honoured segregation was not allowed to last long, however, for Lord Paisley had been given strict instructions by his betrothed, and, within half an hour, was shepherding His Grace, Lord Wulfingston and Hugh out of the dining room and down the corridor to the drawing room.

When everyone was together once more, Lady Hartwood organised for the tea tray to be placed beside the drinks trolley, dismissed her staff from the room and tasked April and Hugh with serving the refreshments.

Next, she charmingly flattered Miss Starling and Miss Beechcroft into taking turns to play the piano and sing; and informed His Grace that it would be his pleasure to turn the pages for their lovely entertainers.

She then paired Mrs Starling with Lord Paisley and the duchess with her friend Mrs Beechcroft, and settled the four of them at the card table in the corner to play whist.

Her duties finished for the moment, she joined her mother, Lord Wulfingston and Mrs Jameson on the arrangement of seats near the fire (to where Mrs Delamer had ushered her companions while her daughter was following through with her instructions).

As Lady Hartwood sat down beside her, Mrs Delamer retired from the enjoyable task of provoking Lord Wulfingston and left Mrs Jameson to hold his attention with a ribald story about a mutual acquaintance.

'They are avoiding one another,' she told her daughter in a quiet voice. 'And they are both pig-headed enough to continue to do so until it is too late!'

Lady Hartwood nodded in agreement and said unhappily: 'I know – utterly vexing!'

Together they watched April and Hugh as they moved around the room serving the guests. They appeared to be performing some strange dance that ensured they never came within ten feet of one another.

'Albert told me yesterday that the wedding is now fixed for the last Saturday in January,' said Lady Hartwood. 'I had hoped it would not come to this but, as we are running out of time, do you think we should force the issue?'

'No. At least, not yet. They still believe it is mere attraction between them. And where there is honour attraction can be held at bay. If we are to be successful we must wait until they realise they are in love.'

'I cannot help but feel they are more than half in love already! If only they would open their eyes!'

'I have every intention of opening their eyes,' said Mrs Delamer. 'All that is required is a little resolution to create the opportunities that will throw them together and bind them inexorably.'

April appeared at her mother's elbow just then and handed her a cup of tea.

'And who are these poor creatures you have decided must be inexorably bound together?' she asked playfully.

'Lower your voice!' admonished Mrs Delamer, and rolled her eyes in the direction of Mrs Jameson and Lord Wulfingston.

'Really? I find that hard to believe,' April responded with a droll look. 'I have my suspicions you are planning to take His Grace away from me by pairing him with Miss Beechcroft.'

'Or Miss Starling,' said her grandmother, watching her closely.

April's smile faltered and she said sharply: 'Miss Starling is betrothed to Mr Royce.'

'What has that to do with anything? Betrothals are broken all the time.'

'Do not even think it!'

'And why not? Think of the advantages.'

'Advantages for whom?'

'For Hugh, certainly,' retorted Mrs Delamer.

'But also for Miss Starling, love,' Lady Hartwood offered up in a more conciliatory tone. 'When one thinks on it a little, it becomes clear she would be better off with some mild-tempered young man who dotes on her. . . and I believe we can all agree, dear Hugh is not that man.'

'You both seem to forget they are attached to one another,' said April, showing greater certainty than she felt on the subject.

'Fiddlesticks!' snapped Mrs Delamer. 'You have strayed into a world of make-believe if that is what you believe. There's more attachment between myself and my coachman than there is between those two!'

April felt torn between a sense of jubilation that this sentiment was likely to be true and a wish to argue against it.

She ignored both impulses.

'We must remember they are both of age,' she said, her expression stern, 'and perfectly capable of handling their own affairs.'

'Clearly not,' Mrs Delamer responded derisively. 'If they were, they'd never have gotten themselves into this mess!'

April threw her grandmother an exasperated look and walked off to continue her duties.

Twenty-Four

It was well known amongst her intimates that April was a keen, if somewhat frustrated, lover of art, with little scope to indulge her passion in Cornwall.

So a passing remark to Lord Paisley about wishing to visit the latest Royal Academy of Arts exhibition, had resulted in him gamely swallowing his aversion to public viewings and offering to escort her and her mother to Somerset House.

On the day agreed for the outing, the Hartwood ladies had no expectation of setting out until the afternoon as they knew from Lord Paisley's stay with them in Cornwall that he was not an early riser. They were therefore at home to a long succession of morning callers, which had become a regular occurrence since Mrs Jameson's *soirée*.

As was to be expected, many of the gentlemen were there to compete for April's attention. However, Lady Hartwood also had her share of visitors, who came to further their acquaintance with the charming woman who had tamed one of the ton's longest standing bachelors.

By the time Lord Paisley made an appearance, around one o'clock, most of the visitors had left and only two remaining young gentlemen showed a tendency to linger. His lordship soon sent them about their business with a pointed remark that his carriage was taking a turnabout the square and would be at the door in five minutes.

'Those poor boys!' Lady Hartwood laughed. 'You made them feel as if they had outstayed their welcome, dearest.'

'And so they had,' declared Lord Paisley. 'Don't tell me they hadn't been here a good while already trying to beguile you into a flirtation?'

'Oh Albert, as if they would do any such thing! I must be a good twenty years older than them! You know perfectly well they were here for April.'

'I know no such thing! Those young jackanapeses are not so foolish that they don't know how to value the charms of a more seasoned beauty.'

'Oh hush!' chided Lady Hartwood, blushing prettily.

Lord Paisley winked at April, making her laugh, and said: 'I shall be the most envied man alive when I step out with two such ravishing creatures on my arm. Shall we?'

Within twenty minutes, Lord Paisley's carriage had deposited the three of them outside Somerset House.

The Royal Academy picture gallery was housed in a chamber at the top of the building, to take advantage of the light pouring down from an immense skylight, and could only be reached by a steep elliptical staircase that had daunted many a lady.

It did nothing to deter April, however, and, lifting her skirts by a few decorous inches, she ascended eagerly, leaving her mother and Lord Paisley to follow at a more sedate pace.

Arriving at the top of the staircase, she entered the gallery and took a moment to admire its grand proportions. The room was some fifty feet by forty feet, with thirty feet high walls that gently curved inwards towards the central skylight. She could understand why Lord Paisley had praised it as the finest gallery for displaying pictures so far built.

The pictures themselves (surely upwards of a thousand!) were hung so closely together, from floor to ceiling, that their frames almost touched.

There were no crowds to contend with today, only a handful of perfectly respectable-looking visitors, so when her mother and Lord Paisley joined her, knowing their interest in the exhibition was only mild at best, she had no compunction about excusing herself and going off alone to begin a circumnavigation of the room.

Some half an hour later, having admired most of the pictures at eye-level, she turned her attention to the tier above.

Taking a few steps backwards, to find a position that did not require her to crane her neck, she suddenly collided with a hard body.

'Oh, I beg your pardon!' she exclaimed, turning quickly around.

Hugh stood a mere hand-span away from her and, greatly startled, she recoiled. . . and somehow managed to trip over her feet in the process.

She would have certainly fallen to the floor if Hugh's hands had not shot out and grabbed the tops of her arms.

April blinked up at him.

'I thought we'd lost you for sure,' he said with gruff amusement.

'Y-you startled me.'

'I gathered.'

He let go of her.

The excess of freedom was jarring and she almost wished to be constrained again.

Such a ridiculous thought! Where had her wits gone?

She stepped away from him and, with an agitated hand, adjusted her new and rather dashing rose-silk lined bonnet.

'Thank you. I'm afraid I wasn't looking where I was going.' She cleared her throat. 'I did not know you were to join us today. Is... is Miss Starling with you?'

'No. It was Mrs Delamer who solicited my escort.'

'Oh... why?' she asked with surprise, her eyes crossing the room to find her grandmother conversing with her mother and Lord Paisley.

'Not everyone is averse to my company, April.'

She knew he was teasing her, but her name on his lips sounded so much like a caress that her whole body reacted to it.

In that moment she would have liked nothing better than to be taken into his arms and...

'I seem to have rendered you speechless,' remarked Hugh, plucking her out of her outrageous reverie. 'I can only assume you don't agree with me?'

'Err... no... I mean, yes! I am perfectly able to believe Mrs Delamer enjoys your company. Still, I would have thought the drive from Richmond, in this cold weather, would have been too arduous for her to undertake simply for a visit to an exhibition.'

'We had some business to transact this morning. Does that satisfy your curiosity?'

'Are you suggesting I am being nosy?'

'I wouldn't dare accuse you of it!' And before she could object to this impudence, he added: 'Not when it's only natural you should have some concern for her health... being so close a family friend.'

His expression gave nothing away, but she could not help wondering if he had guessed the truth.

She quickly dismissed the thought. Neither she nor her mother had inherited any of her grandmother's distinctive features.

'Yes, she was a dear friend of my father's,' she told him airily, 'and both my mother and I are very attached to her. I suppose she sent you to fetch me? Well then, let us not keep her waiting! You must know, she is not known for her patience.'

Hugh started to say something as she set off, but, thinking better of it, followed her across the room.

'Good day to you, ma'am,' said April, walking up to Mrs Delamer and placing a kiss on her cheek. 'You take the shine out of all of us with such a stylish outfit!'

Her appreciative gaze took in her grandmother's dove-coloured silk walking dress, with its froth of white lace at the throat, and her stunning blush-pink pelisse that could only have come from Paris.

'Save your flattery for those who expect it,' said Mrs Delamer.

'My perversity does not allow me to offer flattery when it is expected,' replied April.

Mrs Delamer chuckled.

'You always did have a saucy tongue! Now run along and admire the pictures with Hugh – I don't know why you came hurrying over when you saw me? You know perfectly well I don't expect you to dance attendance on me.'

April flicked a surprised glance at Hugh.

Why had he allowed her to suppose that Mrs Delamer had sent him to fetch her?

'What an uncivil creature you must think me, ma'am, to believe I could ignore you,' she told her grandmother. 'My mother did not raise me to have such shoddy manners.'

'Well, now you've done the pretty by me, you may be off. I want Hugh to show you the William Etty painting I've a mind to purchase.'

'Perhaps Miss Hartwood has had enough of admiring the art,' suggested Hugh.

'I'm certain she'll oblige me, for I would be glad of her opinion,' said Mrs Delamer.

'Of course!' April responded. 'I'll be happy to offer it.'

'Good girl. Now go! You are both very much in the way here. I have something particular I wish to say to your mother and Lord Paisley... in private.'

April's curiosity was aroused at this provocative announcement and she wondered if her grandmother (in the role of an old family friend) was about to give her blessing to her daughter's marriage.

'We shall take ourselves off at once!' she said, and, linking her arm through Hugh's, led him away. 'Oh, I hope her resolve doesn't fail!' she murmured to herself.

'I don't think we need fear *that*,' Hugh replied affably. 'It almost never does. She's quite famous for it! And even if it did, I don't believe the repercussions would be all that grave.'

April's shocked gaze flew to his.

For a moment she thought he had read her mind. But then she realised he knew nothing of the context and was simply teasing her.

'Absurd man! You cannot have the smallest notion to what I'm referring.'

'No,' he agreed. 'But I wouldn't want you to think I'm not holding up my part of the conversation.'

'Ah, I see! But how was I to know to expect such fine manners from you?'

'You wound me!' he laughed. 'Tell me, to what *were* you referring?'

It suddenly struck April that, for some odd reason, she was holding onto his arm and she instantly let go.

'Nothing you would find of interest,' she replied. 'Are you taking me to the painting Mrs Delamer wishes to acquire?'

'There is no need to hedge. You're free to tell me to mind my own business.'

'I know,' she replied sweetly, giving him a sidelong glance. 'And I did. . . in a far more delicate manner than you suggest.'

Amusement animated his dark eyes as he regarded her in an assessing way.

'You know, you would be quite wasted on Claredon. You should choose another victim.'

Her good humour evaporated.

'I'll have you know the Duke of Claredon does not consider himself a *victim*,' she said crossly. 'He is most appreciative of me!'

'Perhaps. But he's not up to your weight.'

'Is that some vulgar cant to do with riding? If it is, it is quite lost on me! I do not ride.'

'Boxing, actually. And if I had meant to be vulgar I would have pointed out that he is likely to shy away from the marriage bed. . . which, you must own, I showed great restraint in not saying.'

'How dare you! That's a disgracefully inappropriate subject to raise with me!'

He watched outrage dance across her countenance and his own was softened by a half-smile.

'You're right, it is. I only wanted to put you on your guard, but perhaps it was not well done of me.'

'It was *certainly* not well done of you.' She looked down and began to fidget with the tiny buttons on her glove. 'It is no concern of mine if His Grace is not. . . does not. . . oh you know!'

Hugh's eyebrows drew together as he studied the top of her downturned head.

'I would have thought it would be of paramount concern to you,' he said.

She threw him an irritated look and remained silent.

'Why don't you ride?' he asked, turning the conversation to oblige her.

'When I was young, my father placed me on one of his stallions and I was tossed and trampled, and subsequently developed a fear of horses,' she recited in an expressionless voice. Her hand unconsciously came to rest on top of the scar on her thigh. 'You probably think I should have overcome my fear years ago. But there is no point in telling me I *should* have done so when I *did not*. . . nor do I have the least desire to try!'

Hugh looked at her with faint surprise.

'My dear girl, you needn't think I disapprove.'

'Well, not *disapprove* perhaps,' she said, thinking it best to ignore his careless term of endearment. 'But you no doubt believe I need only to place myself in the hands of an expert and apply myself and all will be overcome.'

'Speaking from experience? Your various, overly eager swain, I suppose? Too flash and foolish by half! But what difference, do you suppose, it could possibly make to me if you ride or not?'

As this was unanswerable she turned her attention to the paintings in front of them.

'Is this Mrs Delamer's painting?' she asked, pointing to a lovely still life of a vase of roses.

Hugh shook his head and she had the oddest sensation that he was holding back his laughter.

He led her on a few more paces, until they were standing in front of an intoxicating riot of colour. And an abundance of flesh.

An uncomfortable heat crept up her neck and she did not know where to rest her gaze; there were naked bodies everywhere.

She had already admired this painting a little while ago without the least embarrassment, however, she now discovered that to be standing beside Hugh while they studied it together was quite another matter.

She wondered if this was the reason he had allowed her to think Mrs Delamer had sent him to fetch her; she could certainly understand a reluctance on his part to suggest viewing this painting.

'*The Triumph of Cleopatra*,' he informed her. 'Mrs Delamer is rather enamoured with it.'

'She would be!' muttered April.

'The sense of perspective is well done, wouldn't you say?'

'Yes,' she agreed woodenly.

'But I think the inclusion of mythological beings, in what is essentially a historical scene, only undermines the impact of the composition.'

'You mean the cupids? I suppose they're out of place... but then, the whole scene appears to be a flight of male fancy and not in the least historical!'

'You are too severe. It is actually based on Shakespeare's Antony and Cleopatra: the scene where Cleopatra, as queen of Egypt, travels to Tarsus on board an extravagant ship of gold and silver to cement an alliance with Rome's Mark Antony.'

'Oh, I did not realise,' she said, thawing a little. 'I have never read Antony and Cleopatra. One day I plan to enlarge the library at St Mawes and purchase all of Shakespeare's works. Do you recommend it?'

'It is not my favourite of his plays but worth your time. I'll lend you a copy.'

'I should like that, thank you! I promise to take good care of it. Books are so shockingly expensive, aren't they?' she observed with a guileless look.

'They can be, especially the early editions. But you need not be concerned. If it is damaged for any reason I will buy another.'

'I would never allow you to do so! It would be up to me to make any reparations, and – now that I think of it – I suspect you *would* have an early edition. In which case, I thank you for your offer but, no, I cannot accept responsibility for so costly an item.'

'Are you always so full of scruples?' he asked, smiling at her.

'*Someone* in my family has to be.' Between them, her mother, father, and grandmother had discarded all the scruples one could possibly claim. But she regretted her comment and added quickly: 'That is to say, I am the only one who is thrifty by nature.'

'There's no need to wrap it up in clean linen.'

There was such an understanding look in his eye, not without sympathy, that she wondered if it was possible he knew more about her family than she had supposed.

'I don't know what you have heard,' she said in a stiff manner, 'but my family is no better or worse than the majority of the *ton*.'

'You need not think I care either way,' he replied. 'I try not to set myself up as a judge in such matters. It tends to lead to hypocrisy.'

A laugh escaped her.

'Well, you're right, of course! But you are quite unusual. I have never before met someone who was self-aware enough not to fall into judgment of their fellow men and women.'

'I'm perfectly capable of falling into judgment when it suits me. I'm no saint!'

'No, indeed,' she said demurely, a twinkle in her eyes. 'No one could ever accuse you of it.'

Hugh smiled, acknowledging a hit.

'Have we admired *The Triumph of Cleopatra* enough, do you think?' he asked. 'There are other works that deserve our attention and our relatives still look to be in deep conversation.'

'Yes, let us move on, since we are at leisure to entertain one another.'

Something sparked in Hugh's eyes. . . a sort of searing awareness that was difficult for her to define, yet impossible to misinterpret.

'I meant, *ourselves!*' she said in a rush. 'We are at leisure to entertain *ourselves.*'

After the briefest of pauses, Hugh responded: 'I know what you meant.'

Twenty-Five

April walked off in a hurry towards another painting and briefly closed her eyes in an agony of mortification.

'I simply adore pastoral scenes,' she said, forcing out the words. 'This one for example by... by a Mr Turner. The undulating hills and verdant setting are so... charming...'

She petered out as Hugh came to stand beside her.

An unfamiliar heat radiated from him and her body, awakening from hibernation, welcomed wave after heady wave.

The minutes passed in silence as they remained side by side; by all appearance, in deep contemplation of the painting before them.

But beneath the veneer of respectability seethed powerful currents, and the barrier of morals and breeding that stood between them as a solid thing grew weaker.

April realised with horrifying certainty that if Hugh made even the smallest gesture towards her, the last remnants of her self-control would desert her and she would...

She would *what?*

The shock of this unfinished thought brought back some measure of sanity.

'I think it is time to return to the others,' she spoke quietly.

She could feel Hugh's scrutiny and slowly, almost against her will, turned her head to meet his gaze.

What she saw there tugged at her very soul. A scorching emotion that took her breath away and held her captive... and then Hugh's eyes shuttered and she told herself she must have been mistaken.

Bewilderment, desire, and regret warred with each other within her. It was too much emotion for her to contain and tears gathered in her eyes.

'Don't!' Hugh said roughly. 'That's the worst punishment you can offer me.'

'Then allow me to apologise!' she retorted, stung by his tone. She searched in her reticule for a handkerchief. 'I know men dislike it when women cry, but, really, your reaction is rather excessive! I was simply overcome by the beauty of the painting.' She dabbed her eyes. 'Also, I may be more tired than I realised. It was gone three by the time I found my bed last night.'

'I suppose you've had few opportunities to stay up until the early hours of the morning,' he said in a guarded manner.

'None at all!' she replied and summoned up a determined smile.

As they walked back to the others, the pain in her chest refused to ease but at least it was easier to gather her armour around her when she was not looking into Hugh's eyes. And, by the time Mrs Delamer asked for her opinion on the Etty painting, she was able to answer in a perfectly rational way.

Her mother, however, was not fooled. She read the strain on her face and decided she had been challenged enough for one day.

'Albert, I believe it is time we left,' she said, at the first opportunity offered. 'April and I have an appointment at the glove-makers at four.'

'It's not yet three, my love,' replied Lord Paisley, consulting his watch.

'Oh, did I say four? I meant three! I do hope we shall not be too late! Good-bye Mo...ma'am,' she corrected herself, smiling sweetly at her mother. 'I hope you will do us the honour of visiting us soon?'

For those who knew Mrs Delamer well, the stiffening about her jaw was a sure sign that she was not in the least impressed by her daughter's slip.

'Good-bye, Eleanor,' she said, rather sternly. 'If I don't make it to London again this year, I shall expect to see you in Richmond for Christmas.'

April looked across at her with surprise.

'Are we to spend Christmas with you, ma'am?'

'So it has been agreed. I am holding a house-party over the festive season. Nothing too large, just a few old friends, and some young ones as well to keep the place lively. The last thing I want is a house full of my decrepit contemporaries boring on and on about their various aches and pains! Hugh, you will receive an invitation, if you haven't already. I trust you'll make the time to join us. Miss Starling and her mother are invited, of course.'

'I regret I am engaged elsewhere and must decline your invitation,' he replied.

April exhaled the breath she had been holding, greatly relieved. The idea of attending a house party with Hugh in attendance was frankly appalling. His presence would constantly be torturing her with thoughts of impropriety.

But then she perceived a gleam in her grandmother's eyes and groaned inwardly. Her unscrupulous relative was about to play her trump card.

'My dear boy,' said Mrs Delamer, 'I believe I have given you an incorrect impression. Mrs Starling has already written to accept my invitation. And although I have a certain fondness for you, it is not so excessive that it will allow me to entertain the Starlings without your assistance.'

'I was not aware you knew the Starlings well enough to warrant inviting them?' he countered. 'Or for them to accept your invitation?'

Mrs Delamer refrained from telling him that she had dangled a carrot, in the form of the Duke of Claredon, to secure their attendance.

'One is always expanding one's circle of friends,' she replied. 'You need not stay above a day or two if the company proves too tiresome.'

A frown etched itself on Hugh's countenance.

'I would count it as a personal favour,' she went on with deceptive mildness, 'if you would condescend to visit me. But, of course, it is entirely up to you!'

It was a bold manoeuvre and would have cornered a lesser man, but Hugh had never been one to bow down to pressure. There were any number of ways he could have extricated himself had he wanted to. However, a stray glance at April dispelled all such thoughts.

He did not know if she even realised it but her whole body had tensed in anticipation of the insult she clearly expected him to offer her relative.

And there was no doubt left in his mind that Mrs Delamer was April's relative. Her grandmother, to be precise, judging from the slip Lady Hartwood had made moments ago.

He had suspected almost from the start that they shared the same blood; although there was no similarity of features between them, an ephemeral likeness presented itself in certain expressions and gestures.

It was unclear to him why they wanted to keep their connection a secret, but then, it was none of his business.

His gaze sought April's anxious countenance once more, before returning to Mrs Delamer.

'To please you, ma'am,' he said, 'I will find the time to visit.' A sardonic note crept into his voice as he went on: 'And I count myself honoured that you would wish for my company to such a degree that you would inconvenience yourself by inviting Mrs Starling.'

'Oh, I have no expectation of allowing myself to be inconvenienced!' she said, looking well satisfied with the turn of events. 'Ah, I see you are eager to be off, Eleanor... yes, yes, go! Your daughter does not look well. Perhaps some time for quiet reflection might cure her of whatever ails her.'

'Nothing ails me!' said April, a little too quickly, and leant in to kiss her grandmother's cheek. 'Good-bye, ma'am.'

'I have also invited the Duke of Claredon,' Mrs Delamer said quietly into her ear. 'I am depending on you to ensure his attendance.'

April threw her a surprised look, but there was no opportunity to ask how she was to accomplish such a feat.

Twenty-Six

Several days later, a note from the Duke of Claredon was brought to the door of the Hartwood residence, confirming that he and Mr Kepling would arrive to collect April for her riding lesson at ten o'clock the following morning.

The arrangement had been made the previous week, when the gentlemen had visited April in Lord Paisley's box at the Opera, and she had had every intention of inventing an excuse and cancelling before the appointed day. Unfortunately, it had slipped her mind.

The duke's note would have served to remind her had she received it, however, due to a chain of minor household calamities, which had begun with April's lady's maid burning a hole in one of her new gowns while ironing it, and culminated in the butler taking to his bed due to a flare up of his arthritis, the note never reached her.

So when the gentlemen rode up to the house on the following day with a gentle mare that was to be her training mount, April was blissfully unaware of the treat in store for her.

She was deliberating over a letter from her bailiff in the small parlour she had appropriated as her office, when Kenan, having temporarily taken over Layton's duties, knocked on the door.

'The Duke of Claredon and Mr Kepling are here to see you, Miss April,' he told her with his pleasing Cornish inflection, which always reminded her of home.

April looked across at the clock on the mantle.

'It is only just ten,' she said, mildly surprised. 'I wonder why they have chosen to visit so early.'

'Shall I let them come in?'

'Come in? Do you mean to say you left them waiting outside on the steps?' she asked with amused dismay.

'Yes, miss. Should I have shown them up directly?'

'No, you were quite right to seek me out first,' she replied, smiling to make light of the blunder. 'Only, perhaps next time you could ask them to wait *inside* while you ascertain if I am home to visitors.'

She could hardly blame him for his ignorance. He had never before travelled beyond the borders of Cornwall and was ill equipped to take on the duties of a town butler.

She put aside her correspondence, happy to be temporarily freed from her obligations, and rose to her feet. She was looking forward to seeing her visitors. They had been in each other's company a good deal over the last few weeks, often attending the same events, and had reached such a comfortable understanding that she counted them her only true friends in London.

'Please show them to the drawing room,' she told Kenan. 'I'll await them there.'

Had Layton been on duty he would have offered up the information that the gentlemen wore riding clothes, so theirs was unlikely to be a morning call. No rider worth his salt would think to leave his high-bred mount waiting outside in the middle of December for more than a handful of minutes.

Regrettably, such a detail did not occur to Kenan, and when he showed the gentlemen into the drawing room April greeted them with pleasure and without the least suspicion of the true purpose of their visit.

Mr Kepling was the first to step forwards and bow over her hand; his boyish smile holding admiration but, thankfully, no longer the fatuous worship he had directed at her in the beginning of their acquaintance.

'I beg you excuse us for descending on you at this infernally early time,' he said. 'Eustace would have it that you'd not care a jot, and would, in fact, prefer not to have too many people about.'

'He is certainly correct in thinking you are both welcome to visit me at any time,' she replied, smiling.

'I knew you could be counted on to justify my faith in you!' said His Grace, performing an elaborate bow. 'And may I say, it gladdens my heart to simply look upon you this morning? You are an exquisite rose amongst us thorns! A goddess come to earth! Beauty, grace, and wit personified!'

'Oh, for goodness sake, Eustace, if you do not keep your flummery within the bounds of reason I'll reciprocate by going into raptures over your title,' she teased. Turning to Mr Kepling, she asked: 'Alfie, can you do nothing to keep him from making such extravagant compliments? He is your cousin, after all.'

'Only a very distant cousin, upon my word!' he replied with an apologetic grin. 'Through an obscure branch of the family tree, besides! And although I wish I could tell you I've some sway over the fellow, despite having lived with him almost my entire life, I've found it dashed impossible to rein in his flights of verbal dexterity.'

'I only exert myself when I am inspired,' said His Grace. 'And, in this case, just as Aphrodite cannot help but enslave us with her beauty, we cannot help but be enslaved.'

'Oh, I cannot presume to the heights of Aphrodite,' she laughed. 'A lesser goddess perhaps, but certainly not the Goddess of Love! For one, I cannot swim – was she not born out of the sea?'

'Yes, but that challenge can be easily surmounted. If there is no convenient giant shell at hand, every man in the vicinity would dive in to save you. I cannot countenance a lesser goddess for you, Aphrodite it must be.'

'If I cannot dissuade you from your foolishness,' she said, shaking her head at him, 'then, tell me, to what do I owe the pleasure of your company?'

'Why, your riding lesson, of course!' Mr Kepling responded first. 'You can't have forgotten?'

April's face fell dramatically as she looked from one to the other.

'Oh... but... I *had* forgotten.'

'My dear, what a shocking memory you have,' remarked His Grace. 'I sent a note to confirm the time only yesterday. I see I should have sent a second one at the crack of dawn today.'

'Oh, Eustace, I'm sorry!' she exclaimed, her panic rising. 'I never received it!'

'Did you not? Then I perfectly understand your reaction. There is nothing more vexing than to be obliged to be sociable without prior notice.'

She smiled despite herself.

'I am not vexed, only a little surprised.'

'Would it comfort you to know that I've brought the gentlest mare in my stable for you. You need not fear she will prove difficult.'

'How terribly kind... but... but... *oh*, how silly of me not to have remembered earlier!' she said with sudden relief. 'I have no riding habit! So it would be really quite impossible for me to join you today.'

Lady Hartwood came into the room just then (with what her daughter considered to be a deplorable sense of timing) and breezily dealt with this impediment.

'Oh, never fear, April-love! I have a habit you can wear. Good morning, Your Grace, Mr Kepling.'

The gentlemen greeted her warmly and voiced their appreciation of her solution.

'Yes, of course she must go with you,' said Lady Hartwood. 'It has been too long since she has shown any inclination to be on a horse and I'm delighted you have managed to convince her to try again. Go upstairs, love, and ask Keighley for the green velvet. It's too loose on me and I have not yet had the opportunity to have it altered. Can I offer you some refreshments, gentlemen?'

While Lady Hartwood played the hostess, April tried to catch her eye and convey her aversion to the scheme.

But when her mother did finally look in her direction it was to offer her a surprised expression and say: 'Why are you still here, love? Go dress! You do not want to keep your friends waiting.'

And with those words her ladyship effectively sealed her daughter's fate.

Within the space of an hour April found herself strolling through the gates of Hyde Park, in the company of the Duke of Claredon, Mr Kepling, their respective grooms, two high-bred stallions and an ominously docile mare.

Having kept a careful eye on the mare for the duration of their walk, April had no compunction in stigmatising her as concealing a twitchy personality behind her placid demeanour, and no amount of logic could dispel the alarming notion that the mare was only waiting for the opportunity to bolt with her.

By the time the gentlemen had led their procession to a quiet spot in the park, April had broken out in a cold sweat and a knot of dread had settled within her. She gave no outward sign of her turmoil, however, for she had learnt long ago to hide her fear. It only made others uncomfortable.

'Have you ever been taught how to mount?' asked His Grace, leading the mare over to her.

April fought the urge to lift her skirts and run away.

'Yes. I believe I remember the basic principles.'

'Allow me,' said Mr Kepling, coming forwards and making a cradle with his hands for her foot.

April's limbs felt rigid and unyielding, yet she somehow managed to move them in Mr Kepling's direction; and, in the next moment, she was being lifted up and had little choice but to haul herself onto the side-saddle and hook her leg around the pommel.

Once she was properly seated, Mr Kepling placed her foot into the stirrup, while she arranged the long, asymmetrical skirt of her habit about her legs.

It was all done so quickly and gracefully that the gentlemen applauded her efforts and accused her of misleading them into thinking she was an unskilled horsewoman.

April could only offer them a stiff smile; her teeth clamped together with the force of her fear.

The cousins then mounted their own horses and they all set off for a gentle amble around the park, with one groom leading April's mare and the other walking beside her.

Five minutes passed.

Then ten.

Her friends, most helpfully, offered her instruction and encouragement, and shared several anecdotes with her of their own early attempts at riding.

April only heard one word out of ten, although she managed to contribute sufficiently to the conversation to maintain the appearance of sanity. She almost laughed out loud at this testament to her acting abilities, for she had never been closer to hysteria.

She was in the grip of a primal, uncivilised emotion that made it difficult to breathe let alone think. There was a dull ache in her jaw from holding her terror at bay, and the large scar across her thigh seemed to burn with the memory of its inception.

Twenty-Seven

Hugh arrived at the Hartwood residence half an hour after the riding party had departed.

He had made a prodigious effort to avoid April since their encounter at the Royal Academy, to the point of turning down several invitations that he suspected had also been sent to her, and he was now none too pleased to find himself forced into the position of seeking an audience with her.

A sealed letter had arrived for him yesterday along with a note from Mrs Delamer, asking for his indulgence in personally delivering the letter into April's hands.

Mrs Delamer's note had gone on to explain that she had discovered some vitally important information that would be of interest to both April and him, and that the letter should be read while they were together.

Hugh suspected her of having some greater purpose but he could not deny her.

His errand, however, did not sit well with him and when Layton opened the door it was to find Hugh towering over him with a scowling look on his face.

The butler was not one to be easily cowed, and had not reached his seventieth decade without attaining a thorough disregard for the upper classes and their odd tempers.

Added to this natural apathy towards his betters was the circumstance that his knee was paining him terribly. He had stubbornly dragged himself out of his bed to take up his duties with the assistance of a walking stick, and he was in no mood for hot-tempered young bucks, who should know better than to present themselves at a lady's household in a black mood.

'What can I do for you?' he asked snappily, returning Hugh's scowl.

Hugh's smile made a brief appearance at this dubious welcome.

'Good day, Layton. Is Miss Hartwood at home?'

'I cannot say that she is.'

'Does that mean she isn't or that you don't intend to tell me if she is?'

'Miss Hartwood has gone out,' replied Layton, on his dignity.

'When is she expected to return?'

'That I could not say.'

'Surely you must have some knowledge of when she is to return?' Hugh asked impatiently.

'There's no *surely* about it. I do not know.'

'Can you at least tell me where she has gone?'

'I don't know what sort of butler you take me for, young man, but, I assure you, I am not in the habit of revealing my mistress' whereabouts to every gentleman who comes knocking on her door!'

Hugh's scowl returned.

'You need not fear I have any amorous intentions. It's hardly my wish to go traipsing after your mistress! I have an important letter to deliver into her hands, and I intend to do so, with or without your co-operation!'

Layton was enjoying himself immensely and experienced some difficulty in maintaining his glower. He grunted and appeared to consider the request.

After dragging out the moment, he said: 'She went riding in Hyde Park.'

'Riding? I thought she didn't. . . ' Hugh cut himself off. 'Thank you.'

'I take leave to tell you,' said Layton, raising his walking stick and pointing it at Hugh's chest for emphasis, 'if you wish to gain admittance into this household in future, you would do well to remember to bring your manners with you and leave your scowling looks at home!'

And on that parting shot, he closed the door in Hugh's face with a bang.

If his mood had not been soured by the casual way Layton had grouped him together with April's numerous suitors, Hugh might have been amused to find himself so expertly dismissed from his own property.

Striding down the shallow steps to the pavement, he threw a coin at the link boy he had engaged to hold the reins of his horse, and within a few minutes was riding into Hyde Park.

It did not take him long to find his quarry. And to realise she was in the company of the Duke of Claredon.

Irritation flared within him, as intense as it was unwelcome. He had not considered April to be mercenary, or on the hunt for a title, yet her obvious pursuit of the duke's company appeared to indicate the contrary.

He was inclined to ride away, but, after a moment's consideration, discarded this course as ridiculous. The sooner he discharged his errand, the sooner he could dismiss her from his thoughts.

Mr Kepling was the first to perceive him and, raising a hand, hailed him with every semblance of pleasure.

'We are teaching Miss Hartwood to ride,' His Grace informed him as he rode up. 'But, as you can see, her seat is excellent and our instructions are quite unnecessary!'

Hugh offered them both a civil inclination of the head, then turned to greet April. . . and caught his first proper look at her face.

He swore roundly.

Ignoring Mr Kepling's startled exclamation against the use of such language in the presence of a lady, he dismounted and thrust his reins into the hands of one of the grooms.

Striding over to April, he took hold of her waist and said gently: 'Come! I've got you.'

April's eyes clung to him as she unhooked her leg from the pommel and grabbed hold of his shoulders in a claw-like grip.

Hugh lifted her from the saddle and carried her a few paces away from the horses, before lowering her to the ground.

'You're safe,' he told her, his hands remaining on her waist in a comforting hold.

Finally freed from the constraint of her willpower, her breath came in fast, shallow bursts.

'Is there a problem?' asked Mr Kepling. 'Is Miss Hartwood unwell?'

He manoeuvred his horse closer and a whimper rose from the back of April's throat.

'Stay back, you fool!' Hugh ordered him roughly. 'She has a fear of horses!'

'She does?' replied Mr Kepling, greatly disconcerted. 'I. . . I didn't know. Forgive me!'

'A phobia, you mean?' asked His Grace, his mobile countenance looking grave for once.

'It would appear so,' replied Hugh.

'Ah, that would explain it. I am ashamed to say, although we knew Miss Hartwood had taken a toss when she was younger, we assumed it was nothing more than a natural wariness that kept her from riding. And it never occurred to us to doubt that assumption after we saw her mount so beautifully and without the least hesitation.'

'The motivation was no doubt difficult to resist!' observed Hugh, unable to keep an edge of bitterness from his voice.

'I suppose I did employ some persuasion,' said His Grace, misunderstanding him. 'April, my dear, I hope you can forgive us for failing to comprehend the extent of your aversion?'

'Not... your fault, Eustace,' she replied haltingly, her eyes remaining fixed on Hugh.

'Is there anything we can do to make you more comfortable?' asked Mr Kepling, eager to be of help. 'A glass of water perhaps?'

'A hackney-cab to convey her home would be more easily found and of greater use,' said Hugh. 'There's a hackney stand not far from here.'

'I know it!' His Grace spoke up. 'I will be back as quickly as I can.'

Wheeling his horse around with great aplomb, he galloped away (startling a couple of elderly matrons in the process, as he passed their landau, and making them wonder what could have prompted the impeccably mannered duke to ride at such an indecorous pace through the Park).

'Kepling, I believe Miss Hartwood would benefit from some hartshorn,' Hugh told him. 'I take it you know where to procure some?'

Mr Kepling acquiesced at once to this rather odd request, and, offering up the information that he would seek out the closest apothecary, he too rode off.

Hugh got rid of the remaining two onlookers by directing the grooms to walk the horses, and only once they had left did he return his attention to April.

'How do you feel?' he asked, his concern making him appear rather stern.

Her hands were still clutching his shoulders and her gaze, which had remained riveted to his face throughout, retained the glassy remnants of panic.

'Better,' she said slowly.

Hugh removed the pins that held her fashionably tall riding-hat in place, then threw pins and hat onto the grass.

Carefully removing her rigid fingers from his shoulders, he tucked her hands against his chest and enveloped her in an embrace, applying a gentle pressure to the back of her head until her cheek was resting against him.

'You foolish girl, why ever did you do it?'

April closed her eyes and relaxed against him.

She had the strangest sense of being safe and cherished, and although she knew this must be imaginary she remained as still as possible for fear the feeling would evaporate.

The silence stretched out, leading Hugh to think his question would remain unanswered. Which was just as well, for he already knew the duke was the reason for her folly and had no wish to hear her admit it.

'I never meant to go,' she said at last, surprising him. 'I intended to make an excuse and cancel...' her voice muffled against his coat as she instinctively burrowed closer, '...but events conspired against me. And then...well, I thought it was time to try and cure myself. I do not like to be held prisoner by my own irrationality.'

Unable to stop himself, Hugh lowered his head and brushed his lips against the strands of her hair.

'And wanting to humour Claredon had nothing to do with your decision?'

The accusation in his voice was restrained, but it was there nonetheless

April's temper ignited, and, forgetting her weakened state, she broke free of his arms and took a step back to glare at him.

'I suppose you think I only agreed to ride because I want to become the next Duchess of Claredon?'

'The thought did cross my mind.'

'Well it can *un*-cross your mind! I have no wish to become a duchess! Although, if I did,' she said, stabbing a finger into his chest, 'it would be a perfectly sensible ambition and nothing to be sneered at! Why shouldn't I wish to become a duchess? *Anyone* in their right mind would be delighted to be one!'

'Forgive me for contradicting you, but the gentlemen of my acquaintance rarely show an interest in becoming a duchess,' he teased, relieved to see her colour had returned, along with her spark of fire.

'You know perfectly well I am referring to my sex and not yours! There are so few ambitions permitted us, why not the role of duchess?'

'I thought you said you had no intention of becoming one?'

'I don't! But God-knows I just might to spite you, you horrible man!'

She blinked furiously to hold back her tears.

An unguarded tenderness came into Hugh's eyes and he found himself reaching for her.

'No!' she cried, throwing up a hand to stop him. 'I do not need to be comforted by you...or anyone! I am perfectly capable of taking care of myself.'

She gave her riding jacket a fierce tug to straighten it, gathered up the long train of her skirt and, with a self-assured nod, set off in the direction of the horses.

Hugh ignored the clear signs of a dramatic exit and, picking up her hat and pins, caught up with her.

'Why are you following me?' she asked, casting him a baleful look.

'I'm not following you. I'm walking towards my horse. And even you have to admit that I must retrieve it before I can continue on my way to the devil. . . which is no doubt where you wish me to go.'

'Don't think I'll forgive you just because you try your hand at being witty for a change!' she said, coming to a standstill.

'And there I was thinking my wit was always in evidence. I'm devastated to discover it's otherwise!'

He handed her the hat and pins, and offered her such a disarming smile that she could not help smiling back a little, although much against her will.

'You don't look to be devastated in the least!' she said. 'I'm not ready to let go of my anger, and it is unchivalrous of you to try and make me.'

'Would it help if I apologise?' he asked.

'It would certainly be a start.'

'In that case, allow me to say how sorry I am that I led you to believe your desire to be a duchess is anything but a perfectly acceptable ambition.'

April's self-control disintegrated and she whacked him with her hat.

'I don't desire to be a duchess, *you big lummox*!' she cried, and then whacked him again for good measure; leaving her beautifully crafted hat decidedly worse for wear.

Her eyes suddenly widened.

'Oh, I beg your pardon! I did not mean to hit you. . . at least, I did not *know* I meant to hit you, it just happened!' She raised a hand to her brow and, closing her eyes, said with dismay: 'I have never before hit anyone – what is the matter with me?'

Hugh's gaze was full of amusement; and something else that would have startled her had she been looking at him.

'Think nothing of it,' he advised. 'I often inspire people with the wish to hit me.'

'How can you say such a thing when it was so very wrong of me?'

'If you wish to fall into an indulgence of remorse then, by all means, go ahead. It's not my place to deprive you of it.'

April's hand fell away from her eyes and she glared up at him again.

'*Indulgence*? I am not indulging in anything, you. . .' She bit off the end of her remark.

'Lummox?' he supplied helpfully.

'*Devil* would be more appropriate.' She reined in her temper with an effort, and, after a moment, said reproachfully: 'You are baiting me on purpose, but you will not succeed on this occasion. You have my gratitude for coming to my aid earlier and I will not – I refuse! – to take offence.'

'I should hope not!' he returned with a cavalier disregard for her magnanimity. 'It has never been my intention to cause you offence, so why you would think otherwise is beyond me.'

Annoyance and amusement both stirred in April's breast.

'Surely I am not the first person to suggest that the unique manner with which you choose to express yourself might, on occasion, cause offence?'

'There may have been others, Miss Impudence,' he replied, his tone making her smile. 'I have no patience for peppering my conversation with meaningless niceties. Nor can I stand the airs some people put on to satisfy their vanity. But I am perfectly capable of exerting myself to be agreeable – you of all people should know that!'

April smiled at this absurd statement, thinking he was indulging in some irony.

However, his expression remained serious and she realised he was in earnest.

'Are you... *can* you be telling me that your conduct towards me thus far is your way of exerting yourself to be agreeable?' she asked, incredulous.

'Of course,' he replied, looking put out by the question.

April's hand rose to her mouth to stop a giggle escaping. It could not be contained.

Another followed.

And another; until she was bent over in helpless convulsions of laughter.

Hugh stood watching her, a reluctant smile spreading across his lips.

He took out his handkerchief and handed it to her.

'Oh, forgive me!' she gasped, wiping away her tears. 'But you must see how ridiculous it is?'

His expression gave no indication that he did see, being once more serious.

'My mistake, clearly you don't! Let us say no more, or I will go into woops again and you will be quite justified in thinking me abominable.'

'We both know that is not how I think of you.'

He retrieved his handkerchief and, taking hold of her chin, dabbed at a tear she had missed on her cheek.

Then he dabbed at another... imaginary this time.

April held her breath and studied him as he concentrated on his task. She had never before allowed her gaze to wander in such an intimate manner over the planes of his face; a blush bloomed at the audacity of it.

'What are you doing to me?' he asked softly, meeting her eyes.

Some enigmatic emotion vibrated between them and the filaments of the connection that bound them together strengthened, drawing them closer.

They abruptly looked away from each other, and moved several feet apart.

April was appalled at how easily her self-control deserted her in his presence, and, desperate to put some distance between them, she set off in the direction of the horses.

'Where are you going?' he asked. 'You can't be thinking of riding home?'

She came to a standstill and silently damned him for being right.

But then, before she could succumb to self-pity, he continued in a voice devoid of appreciation: 'Ah, it seems that Claredon has saved the day.'

April turned and saw the duke riding along the vehicular road, closely followed by a hackney coach.

Before long, the two groups had met and Hugh was handing April into the hired vehicle.

'You need not fear to leave Miss Hartwood in my care,' His Grace informed Hugh, covertly taking in his strained expression and the way April avoided looking in his direction. 'Although, you are welcome to join us, of course, if that is your preference?'

After a short struggle between his inclination and his common sense, Hugh said tersely: 'Your escort is sufficient.'

'How good of you to say so! In that case, sir, would you do me the favour of taking my horse to my grooms and informing them they are at liberty to return to the mews?'

Hugh agreed with a nod, and accepted the reins held out to him.

Unable to resist, His Grace then took the liberty of amusing himself at Hugh's expense by engaging him in a rather one-sided, trivial conversation, until Hugh was goaded into informing him that he should be seeing Miss Hartwood home and not wasting time with idle chatter.

Having milked what reaction he could from his taciturn companion, the duke expressed his gratitude at being recalled to his sense of duty and entered the hackney.

As Hugh walked off with the ducal mount, both the occupants of the carriage stared after him.

'I must remember to ask him if he's a member of Jackson's,' said His Grace pensively. 'One presumes so, judging by his uncommonly fine shoulders.'

Miffed at having received only a curt nod in farewell from the owner of the fine shoulders, April said tartly: 'That might be, but his manners leave much to be desired!'

'Oh, rough manners do not bother me,' said His Grace with a flowing gesture of one beautifully gloved hand. 'However, that intense way he has of looking at *you*, fair Aphrodite, is enough to bring me to blush. I do not know how you manage not to swoon!'

'Nothing about Mr Royce would ever make me want to swoon. . . unless it was from the shock of seeing him exert himself to be amiable! Which, no matter what he says, I am yet to witness!'

His Grace laughed lightly and watched her as she watched Hugh's retreating form.

She caught his appraising look and a blush threatened to rise. She managed to turn it aside with a grimace.

'I would be eternally grateful if you would take me home now. My mother's riding habit may be too large for *her*, but it's uncompromisingly small for me. I'm certain at least two of my ribs are cracked from the lacing her maid inflicted on me!'

'Then let us go at once! On no account must you sustain an injury while under my protection. In his present, unfulfilled state Mr Royce is likely to seek my blood as retribution.'

'I wish you would not talk in that nonsensical way!' April informed him crossly.

Twenty-Eight

The following morning, April received three uncommonly early calls in quick succession.

Mr Kepling was the first to sound the knocker and to be ushered into the entrance hall by Layton, just as April was coming down the stairs on her way to meet with Mrs Plum.

'I am so glad to see you, Alfie!' she greeted him warmly. 'I owe you an apology for ruining what should have been a perfectly pleasant ride yesterday.'

'Not at all!' he replied quickly. 'It is I who must beg your forgiveness for being such an insensitive clod-head! I wouldn't have blamed you if you had refused to see me today, but I wanted to find out if you were recovered.'

'Perfectly! My indisposition, for want of a better word, is only ever of a temporary nature – usually when my person happens to find itself on the back of some poor equine creature! I'm sorry if I was the cause of any anxiety.'

'No, no, the blame lies squarely with us for being blind to your distress.'

'I chose not to let you see, so the fault remains with me,' she replied, already bored by his gallantry. 'I hope you did not mind that we left the park without you? Eustace was kind enough to procure a carriage and escort me home.'

'Yes, he told me, and I didn't mind in the least, I assure you. . . ah, before I forget. . . ' He removed a small glass vial from his breast pocket and triumphantly held it out to her. 'I found some!'

'What is it?' she asked, taking the bottle from him.

'The hartshorn.'

'*Hartshorn?*'

Having no recollection of what had passed between the gentlemen yesterday, she stared at the bottle in distaste. She had always felt a certain disdain for women who relied on hartshorn and the like, and assumed feeble constitutions in an effort to make themselves interesting.

'Mr Royce suggested I procure some for you,' he explained, a little crest-fallen at her reaction. 'Only, it took me a dashed long time to find it. First, I tried an aunt of mine, thinking it'd be quicker than going to an apothecary. But she *would* have it that I sit down to breakfast with her. And by the time she let me get a word in edgewise it was near enough midday! Not that she had any, as it turned out. Apparently never touches the stuff! Seems strange to me, thought it'd be just the thing she *would* use, for she's forever complaining about her nerves failing her, so it stands to reason. In the end, I had to go to the apothecary after all. But, by then, I suspected you were already home and didn't want to disturb you in case you were indisposed. And I thought Lady Hartwood would probably have some to give you. But, the thing is, *I've* no use for it – not since my mother died – so it's yours if you want it. But, if you don't...'

'Oh, how thoughtful of you, Alfie!' she put in quickly, moved by this tangled speech. 'Thank you for going to so much trouble on my behalf. A little hartshorn is just the thing to revive me!'

Mr Kepling instantly brightened... and waited.

Too late did April realise her mistake.

'Oh, I did not mean *now*. I meant...' She faltered under the weight of the earnestness of his expression.

He appeared inordinately eager to witness her availing herself of the beneficial effects of his gift and she realised with a sinking heart that, although he hid it better, his infatuation with her still continued.

She removed the stopper and slowly raised the small bottle to her nose.

Regrettably, it was at this point that the second caller of the day made free use of the door knocker.

The noise so startled April that she inadvertently drew in a sharp breath and the noxious fumes burnt their way up her nose and into her lungs.

She instantly fell into a fit of coughing; from which she only recovered once Layton had hastily procured a glass of water for her.

Mr Kepling was all solicitude and hovered about her, until his attentions became so oppressive she snapped: 'Please don't fuss over me!'

She could see she had hurt his feelings and had to stop herself from softening her rejection. The sooner he was brought to realise that she was not the woman for him, the happier he would be.

'You know, Alfie,' she went on, when she could breathe easily again, 'I'm not at all the type of female who enjoys having a knight in shining armour at my beck and call. But don't lose hope, my dear. Somewhere out there, the perfect girl is waiting for your chivalry.'

Her expression held a wealth of meaning that made it impossible for Mr Kepling to misunderstand her. He coloured and looked away sheepishly.

Having made her point, April turned to Layton and said: 'The door, if you please. I am recovered.'

The butler cast Mr Kepling a dark look and, muttering to himself in a way that left no doubt as to where he lay the blame for his mistress' short-lived affliction, he shuffled to the front door.

'I heard you the first time!' he snapped as he opened the door and glared at the unsuspecting visitor.

It was doubtful whether the Duke of Claredon had ever been greeted in such a way before and he stood for some moments uncharacteristically lost for words.

'Layton, do let His Grace come in!' April instructed. 'My apologies for keeping you waiting, Eustace! I was temporarily indisposed.'

The butler grumbled under his breath, but stood aside and allowed the duke to enter.

'Thank you, Layton,' said April, laying a gentle hand on his shoulder. 'Could you please ask one of the maids to bring up the tea tray, and also the Madeira cake that was baked this morning. Then I would greatly appreciate it if you would sit down with Mrs Plum and finalise the menus for the coming week on my behalf. I have no time myself and I know she hoped to finish her shopping list this morning. And afterwards, perhaps you could compile a list of wines we should purchase for the coming months? I know I can count on you to know just what we like!'

'We still have several dozen bottles from the lot Mr Royce sent round,' Layton said crustily, none too pleased by this fact.

April saw His Grace's eyebrows rise slightly and felt compelled to explain: 'Mr Royce believes it is his responsibility as our landlord to stock our cellar.'

'Of course,' agreed His Grace; but there was something in his eyes that filled April with a strong desire to correct his evident misinterpretation.

'The wine provided by Mr Royce belongs to the house and must remain here,' she told Layton, 'which is why I would like us to buy our own stock. It will likely take several hours for you to compile the list, so I suggest you find somewhere quiet to undertake the task - your room, perhaps - and allow Kenan to take care of any callers.'

As soon as Layton had left to carry out his orders, His Grace said with a wry expression: 'You know, my dear, you will soon run out of tasks that require him to be seated.'

'Poor Layton,' she sighed. 'His knee is paining him terribly and his temperament suffers as a result. I hope you were not insulted by your reception?'

'Not in the least. Nothing can dent my dignity. And I rather enjoy his attempts to try and do so! If I did not fear it would kill him, I would be tempted to offer him a position myself.'

'No, don't do that!' she laughed. 'He is likely to give you a shocking set-down and put me to blush! But I know you're not here to steal my servants away from me.'

'Not on this occasion. I have come for a rather pedestrian reason: to see how you are faring after yesterday's adventure. And I see I am not the only one... Cousin, had I known you were headed here yourself I would have ventured to suggest at breakfast that we combine our resources and arrive together.'

A slight flush rose around Mr Kepling's collar at this gentle ribbing. They all knew why he had chosen to visit alone.

'Alfie, most thoughtfully, arrived early to drop off the hartshorn he purchased for me,' April said in his defence.

'Hartshorn? But I distinctly remember you telling me you cannot stand the stuff.'

'You must have misunderstood,' she replied, giving His Grace a quelling look. 'Won't you both come upstairs? I'm certain my mother will wish to thank you for all you did for me yesterday.'

The cousins showed themselves willing to follow her, and together they made their way up to the first floor and entered the drawing room.

Here they found Lady Hartwood reclining on the settee and reading a slim book of poems. It seemed unlikely that they had captured her fancy for she was frowning down at the page and moving her lips as if mulling over the words.

Upon perceiving them, she uttered an exclamation of delight, promptly dropped the book and, swinging her dainty feet to the floor, got up.

His Grace, not content with a simple salutation, glided over to her and bowed over her hand with a new flowing gesture that had cost him several days practise.

'Eustace, you put us all to shame with your execution of something as commonplace as entering a room,' teased April. 'I'd hazard a guess that your dance-master has trained you in the secrets of ballet, for you are quite exquisite!'

'Hush now, love,' her mother entreated. 'What must His Grace think of such a sally?'

'His Grace is delighted to have his efforts recognised,' he replied, smiling. 'And yes, there is a dance-master to thank – French, of course! No one embodies the maxim *truth is beauty and beauty is truth* quite like the French.'

'I have never been to France,' said April, 'so I am happy to take you at your word, my dear.'

'Never been to France!' he exclaimed. 'What a shocking waste! *You* of all people should visit. You would be worshipped as a veritable goddess!'

She smiled and said: 'Aphrodite, perhaps?'

'*Bien sûr*,' he laughed. 'Who else?'

Lady Hartwood listened to this familiar, teasing exchange and felt a stirring of alarm. From all her mother had told her of the charming duke, she had expected April to warm to him, perhaps even to befriend him, but nothing more.

However, what she was now witnessing bore all the marks of real affection. Most of the *ton* had married based on far less!

If her daughter proved to be so contrary as to take it into her head to marry the Duke of Claredon, thought her ladyship, feeling aggrieved, all the plans she and her mother had been working on for the last few months would be laid to waste.

For the hundredth time she wondered if they should have been honest with April from the start, rather than lead her to think they were hoping for a match between her and the duke. But there was no denying that matters were complicated and had to be approached with circumspection.

When her mother had first revealed her extraordinary plan, she had been adamant that a decoy was necessary to distract April from their true purpose, as it was an unfortunate part of her character that the more one tried to steer her in a particular direction the more she resisted.

And Lady Hartwood had to own, there was some truth in this rather severe interpretation of her daughter's character.

Still, it went against her nature to mislead anyone, let alone her own daughter, and had her mother not sworn her to secrecy, pointing out that their scheming was all for securing April's happiness, she would have crumbled and confessed all by now.

While her ladyship brooded over the potentially disastrous consequences of her daughter taking it into her head to marry His Grace, Layton's deputy, Kenan, entered the room and announced the third visitor of the day.

'*Mr Royce!*' he shouted, and then beat a hasty retreat, clearly uncomfortable in such elevated company.

'Where do you find such delightful servants?' His Grace murmured in April's ear. 'Am I allowed to poach *that one* from you?'

She cast him a reproving look. But her eyes did not linger on him.

Hugh entered the room and was annoyed to find that he was not the only visitor to have chosen to call at such an early hour. With all that had occurred yesterday he had forgotten to give April the correspondence Mrs Delamer had entrusted into his care and he had come today to finally do so.

At least, that was part of his reason for visiting.

The other part had a good deal to do with the unwelcome but nonetheless persistent urge to satisfy himself that April suffered no lingering ill effects.

Striding forward, he presented himself to Lady Hartwood.

'How do you do, ma'am,' he said, taking her hand and smiling down at her. 'I apologise for calling on you at such an early hour. I wanted to find out if your daughter is recovered from yesterday's excitement, before your admirers descend on you, but I see I was not early enough!'

He glanced over at the cousins in a manner that could scarcely pass as a greeting.

'It's always a pleasure to see you, Hugh-dear!' said her ladyship. 'But I shall let you address your question to my daughter. She *tells* me she is recovered but I know she would never admit to it if she were not.'

Hugh turned to study April with a deliberation she found unnerving.

'Really, Mama!' she said, laughing uncomfortably. 'I am perfectly sincere when I tell you I am myself again.'

Hugh's eyes lingered on her and April was relieved when a maid entered with the tea tray, for it afforded her the opportunity to turn away and serve.

'I hope you will excuse me,' Hugh addressed Lady Hartwood, 'but I can't stay long. My other aim in coming today was to deliver some correspondence into Miss Hartwood's hands.'

April was in the process of handing Mr Kepling a serving of cake and looked across at Hugh with a puzzled expression.

'Correspondence for *me?*' she asked.

'Yes. Mrs Delamer requested I deliver it personally. The information contained within apparently also pertains to me.'

'Oh. . . I see.'

She waited for him to hand her the letter, however, he made no move to do so.

177

'In private,' he said brusquely.

'*Oh*! Of course... I-I shall take Mr Royce to my office, Mama... unless you have some objection?' she asked, colouring.

'None at all,' returned Lady Hartwood, looking remarkably pleased.

In the last few minutes it had become clear to her that although her daughter shared an easy affection with the duke, her loss of composure in Hugh's company pointed to feelings of a depth and complexity that outweighed those of mere friendship.

'Now run along, love,' she continued, 'and have no fear that we will miss you! His Grace, Mr Kepling and I are perfectly capable of entertaining ourselves.'

'Indeed we are,' agreed His Grace. 'There is not the least need to hurry back on our account.'

'Our business will take no more than a few minutes,' said Hugh in a dampening tone; and, after waiting for April to pass out of the room before him, he followed her.

Twenty-Nine

Lady Hartwood smiled at the empty doorway through which April and Hugh had passed, lost in pleasant reflections.

She recollected herself all of sudden and turned back to her guests. She found Mr Kepling in deep admiration of his slice of cake and oblivious to the goings on around him, but His Grace's all-too-intelligent gaze rested on her and brought a slight blush to her fair cheeks.

'You may well wonder why I allowed my daughter to go off alone with Mr Royce,' she said airily. 'But, you see, we treat him almost as one of the family, and from time to time rely on his counsel.'

'I did not doubt it was something of that nature,' said His Grace. 'Let us hope you will soon have the felicity of knowing him to *be* one of the family.'

'W-whatever can you mean?' she asked nervously.

'Mr Royce is set to become your nephew through marriage, is he not?'

'Oh, *that*! Yes, certainly!' she agreed, smiling with relief.

His Grace chose to behave himself at this point and deftly turned the conversation to subjects that were calculated to put Lady Hartwood at ease again.

However, her ladyship's composure suffered a setback, some minutes later, when Kenan once more entered the room and revealed that Mrs Starling and Miss Starling had called and were asking to see her.

'Not *now*!' she exclaimed, looking so vexed as to be almost comical. Remembering the duke's presence beside her, she smiled and continued: 'A pleasure to see them, of course! Only, it is a *little* early for morning calls, so you will not wonder at my surprise.'

'I am afraid I may be the reason your visitors have decided to grant you the pleasure of their company,' he said apologetically. 'My curricle is either parked outside your door or my groom is circling the square.'

'Ah! That would certainly explain it. A shame to be sure, but although I cannot help but wish you had left your curricle elsewhere, I perfectly understand that you cannot have foreseen the evils of the situation.'

'It was most thoughtless of me,' he replied, barely a tremor in his voice. 'I hope your ladyship can forgive me?'

'Oh, there is not the least need! It is certainly a pity but you need not fear I *blame* you.' Looking over at Kenan, she told him: 'I suppose they cannot be denied.'

This sounded so perilously close to a question that the duke's lips twitched and had to be brought back under control.

Even Mr Kepling, who had finished his cake and was once more cognisant, had to smother a laugh.

While they were waiting for the Starlings to be shown up, His Grace said: 'Cousin, your enthusiastic endorsement of the Madeira cake has changed my mind. I believe I shall try some, if you would be so good as to procure a slice for me?'

Mr Kepling readily agreed to it, happy that his cousin would experience the excellence of this delicacy for himself, and, after asking Lady Hartwood if he could also bring a slice for her, which she declined, he crossed the room to the serving table.

'If you would allow me, your ladyship,' His Grace addressed her in a lowered voice, 'I feel I would be useful to you in entertaining your guests.'

'Yes, you would be,' agreed Lady Hartwood, eyeing him circumspectly. 'More than you know. But I'm not at all certain it is proper for me to accept your assistance...under the circumstances. It's something of a coil,' she sighed, momentarily dispirited by the obstacles fate had placed before her.

'I beg you do not allow the scruples of the situation to concern you,' he returned smoothly. 'I happily offer up my assistance! I may not be gifted with the intelligence of your prospective son-in-law but I pride myself on having a little finesse in delicate matters such as these.'

Lady Hartwood's eyes widened in alarm.

'Son-in-law? But you are quite mistaken! Nothing of the sort, I assure you!'

'You need not fear I will betray you. You have said nothing to me on the matter so there is nothing to betray. It is all simply wishful thinking on my part... my fanciful notions, if you will.'

Her ladyship regarded him uncertainly as she toyed with a rose petal in the flower arrangement beside her.

'I do not know what to say, Your Grace.'

'You need say nothing at all! I will simply proceed to distract Miss Starling until such a time as my exertions are no longer necessary.'

'I think your notions are fanciful indeed! And I cannot help but wonder why you would put yourself to the trouble of distracting Miss Starling?'

'Let us say – for it is quite true – I have become rather fond of your daughter.'

'Without wishing to offend you, Your Grace, is that the only reason?' she asked, showing unexpected shrewdness.

He laughed lightly.

'Perhaps it is also true that I enjoy a little comedy now and then. And there is nothing more farcical than those wishing to embark on matrimony without the benefit of love. In such situations, I am almost honour-bound to take up my bow and arrow and play cupid.'

Mr Kepling, having returned with the cake and heard this last part, said: 'It's quite true, ma'am. My cousin only last year saved our friend from contracting the most imprudent marriage. The lady was an heiress but such a shrew it was only ever going to end in disaster! Happily, the perfect girl was waiting in the wings and Eustace. . . '

'We need say no more on that, however,' His Grace told his cousin gently.

'Ah, yes, mum's the word!' Mr Kepling said readily, tapping his nose.

Kenan re-entered the room at that moment with Mrs Starling and her daughter and announced them in such an earsplitting voice that both ladies jumped in alarm.

Lady Hartwood made a mental note to remind the dear boy not to bark out the names of her guests.

Mrs Starling, feeling her nerves had been assaulted, glowered at the footman and was about to administer a tongue-lashing when she recalled she had an audience. Turning her eyes on her hostess, she gave her a thin smile.

'I hope we are not intruding, Lady Hartwood? We were passing on our way to Bond Street and my daughter had the happy notion to drop in and pay our respects.'

Lady Hartwood hid her aversion to their visit and responded with all that was proper.

'I did fear it was a little early to call on you,' went on Mrs Starling, transferring her smile to His Grace, 'but I see you are receiving visitors after all. How do you do, Your Grace?'

'Ma'am, your servant,' he replied with a graceful bow. 'And Miss Starling, a pleasure to see you again! I hope you will allow me the shocking impertinence of telling you how utterly fetching you look in that bonnet?'

This green and white confection, bought only recently, had caused some disagreement between mother and daughter; Mrs Starling labelling it as too frivolous to be becoming. So Miss Starling could be forgiven for the mild feeling of triumph that stirred in her breast.

'Thank you, Your Grace!' she replied brightly and dropped into the deep curtsy she reserved for him alone.

'It is a pretty bonnet,' said Mrs Starling. 'But there is little that does not become such a lovely face, do you not agree, Your Grace?'

'I need no encouragement to inspire my compliments of such perfection,' he returned, a guileless look masking his mockery.

'Mrs Starling, have you been introduced to my other guest, Mr Kepling?' asked her ladyship.

'*Kepling,*' murmured the matron and stared at him with sudden intensity.

'I don't believe I have had the pleasure,' Mr Kepling remarked politely. Then, turning to her daughter, he said in a friendly fashion: 'I have not seen you in the Park for some days, Miss Starling, and was afraid you might be unwell?'

'Thank you for your concern, Mr Kepling!' she replied, smiling sweetly. 'There was no need for it, however. I have simply been busy this week with my wedding preparations. If the weather holds, my friend, Miss Lumley, and I plan on being in the Park this afternoon. We hope to see you there!'

Since their first meeting at Mrs Jameson's *soirée*, some four weeks ago, Miss Starling and Mr Kepling had come across each other at various engagements, including during the promenade hour in Hyde Park. And as Mr Kepling's amiable disposition made it necessary for him to stop and talk to any passing acquaintance, Miss Starling had grown used to enjoying some conversation with him during these occasions.

However, for one reason or another, her mother had never been present to make Mr Kepling's acquaintance.

'Can it be,' Mrs Starling now addressed him with amazement, 'that you are the son of *Roberta* Kepling?'

'Why, yes,' he replied. 'Did you know my mother, ma'am?'

'Did I know your mother? Good gracious, yes!' she exclaimed in her colourless way. 'And you, Alfred George Augustus Kepling, I have known from the cradle.'

Mr Kepling's look of confusion made it perfectly clear that he had not the slightest recollection of her.

'Of course!' he announced, trying to overcome this shortcoming. 'So good to see you again!'

'You foolish boy, you were a nothing but a babe the last time I saw you,' she said indulgently. 'Your mother and I were very close at one time, but, when your father passed away, she made the decision to move north and live with his family, and so we lost touch.'

'How did you know my mother, ma'am?' he asked, his interest transforming from polite to animated.

'We attended the same ladies college in Bath. And then, of course, we came out together. She was a most excellent woman and I was grievously sorry to hear of her passing last year.'

'Thank you. . . she is still greatly missed.'

He had such a look of a lost little boy that Mrs Starling was moved to discard the decorous restraint for which she was known, and say with real compassion: 'Of course you still miss her! One cannot wonder at it! It has hardly been a year.'

'Cousin, perhaps Mrs Starling would care to sit with you and hear about your mother's life?' His Grace said helpfully; his active and fruitful mind already making plans.

'I should be delighted,' said Mrs Starling. 'That is, if Lady Hartwood has no objection? Only, it is imperative I sit by the fire, for I am most susceptible to an inflammation of the lung. And, although I do not mean to complain, I was kept waiting outside in the cold for several minutes before the door was opened to us.'

'Oh, I am sorry to hear that!' cried Lady Hartwood. 'Please *do* make yourselves comfortable by the fire. I'm certain Mr Kepling will be only too happy to sit with you while you become better acquainted.'

She threw Mr Kepling a look that was both beseeching and apologetic.

But she need not have worried he might prove reticent; he was genuinely happy to reminisce with someone who had known his mother.

'Are you partial to Madeira cake, Miss Starling?' His Grace asked, removing the plate from his cousin's hand before he moved away. 'I am told it is uncommonly good. I would be pleased to offer you my slice if you would care to join me on the settee?'

Miss Starling, feeling the weight of this honour just as she ought, thanked him prettily and allowed him to lead her away.

Some half an hour later, Hugh and April entered the room and were greeted by the unexpected sight of Mrs Starling and Mr Kepling in deep discussion on one side of the room; Miss Starling seated beside His Grace on the other; and Lady Hartwood standing a little to the side and observing the whole scene with a benevolent expression while she sipped her tea.

Miss Starling was listening with great enjoyment to His Grace, as he recounted an amusing story from Mr Kepling's youth, when she noticed the appearance of her fiancé.

'Mr Royce!' she exclaimed. 'What are you doing here?'

'I could ask you the same question,' he replied, in no mood for pleasantries and rather annoyed to see the duke had made another conquest.

Hugh had never before addressed her in such uncompromising terms and Miss Starling was pardonably ruffled.

Observing her reaction with foreboding, April waited for her mother to smooth over the awkwardness of the moment.

Her ladyship, however, made no move to do so and continued to sip her tea. His Grace also made no attempt to fill the uneasy silence. And as Mrs Starling and Mr Kepling had not yet perceived the new arrivals, no help came from that quarter.

April was labouring under a great deal of shock and vexation after her conference with Hugh and wished to remain quietly in the background.

But as the silence continued she felt obliged to say: 'Miss Starling, I hope you will forgive your fiancé if he sounds a little churlish. I have taxed his reserves of amiability with some matters of business. They must have been a great bore to him, for I know they were to me!'

This information did not appease Miss Starling but she made an effort to look gracious.

'Mr Royce, have you come in search of us?' asked Mrs Starling in a languid voice, finally becoming aware of Hugh. 'How did you know where to find us?'

'He is not here on our account, Mother,' Miss Starling said tartly through her smile. 'He has been in private discussion with Miss Hartwood.'

'I do not understand,' said Mrs Starling, surveying Hugh with a good deal of surprise. 'Gentlemen do not arrange private discussions with young, unmarried ladies.'

Hugh was on the point of explaining the circumstances to her, however, a newly-formed idea gave him pause.

When he did speak, he surprised all his listeners by addressing his future mother-in-law with formidable severity: 'What exactly are you accusing me of?'

April almost groaned at such rough handling of a delicate situation.

'Oh, my goodness...' uttered Mrs Starling in failing accents, a hand rising to her breast. 'If this is how you mean to talk to me... I can see that I have made a grave...'

'Please allow me to explain!' April interrupted her. 'It is not Mr Royce's fault that his temper is frayed. Indeed, you will not wonder at it once you know the truth.'

'For God's sake, be quiet,' Hugh told her under his breath. 'There's no need to defend me, I know what I'm about!'

April shook her head, refusing to listen.

She had hoped to keep her business private, but she could not live with herself knowing she had contributed to the breakup of Hugh's engagement; particularly since, minutes ago, he had offered to assist her, to his own financial detriment.

She might not understand why he wanted to marry a girl so wholly unsuited to him, nevertheless, she had to make a push to help him out of his current difficulty.

'You see, ma'am,' she addressed Mrs Starling, 'we have just discovered, through a series of events involving my father and one of Mr Royce's business associates, that Mr Royce is in the unenviable position of holding the mortgage on the St Mawes estate. It's a poor investment, as I have had to explain to him, and one that will likely lose him money!' she stressed, being purposefully pessimistic to arouse Mrs Starling's sympathy. 'And, what is more, I'm ashamed to say my initial reaction to the news was not constructive. So, really, it is not to be wondered at if he is not himself! A loss-making asset and an irate woman in one morning would try anyone's patience!'

'Perfectly understandable!' interjected Mr Kepling in his good-natured way (earning for himself the silent disapproval of three of the party). 'Any one of us would be out of sorts after such a trying morning. Don't you agree, ma'am?' he asked Mrs Starling.

As it turned out, neither his nor April's input was necessary to sway the matron. As soon as her first flush of indignation had died down, so too had her desire to go down a path that would scupper her daughter's betrothal.

She offered Mr Kepling a smile, happy in the knowledge that in following her ambition she would live up to his faith in her, and, turning to Hugh, said: 'How unfortunate for you, sir. I hope your financial loss is not too great?'

'Miss Hartwood has made too great a deal out of nothing,' replied Hugh. Turning his shoulder to the room, so only April could see his face, he said angrily: 'In future, I'd be obliged to you if you would keep yourself from meddling.'

'You may thank me later for saving your engagement, you ungrateful brute,' she murmured back at him.

Thirty

Leaving Hugh's side in something of a huff, April walked over to her mother.

'I do not understand, love,' said Lady Hartwood, her brow creasing. 'I distinctly remember you mentioning that a Mr Pimlico held our mortgage?'

'He did. But from what Mrs Delamer has unearthed – do not ask me how! – it appears he was recently obliged to sell it, along with some others he was holding. He approached Mr Royce and sold the whole bundle to him. I can only assume my man of business is aware of the changes and I will shortly receive correspondence from him explaining the circumstances.'

'But Hugh-dear, why did you not tell us you owned the mortgage on St Mawes?' asked Lady Hartwood, looking over her daughter's shoulder at Hugh.

'I was not aware of it until today, ma'am,' he replied. 'The mortgage does not name St Mawes. It refers only to the Blackburne estate. From what your daughter has explained to me, St Mawes is something of a colloquial term.'

'Oh, of course! I had quite forgotten the old name,' said her ladyship, happy to have that mystery explained. 'But what a wonderful turn of events! I could not have wished for anyone better to hold our mortgage! You will never dun us, will you, Hugh-dear?' she asked on a laugh.

'We must repay the mortgage at all cost!' April burst out.

'Really, love, there is no need to raise your voice. I never said we would not. Although *at all cost* does sound a little excessive, don't you think? Not that we need concern ourselves with such details at present. I'm certain all will be settled as it should.'

'In twenty years perhaps,' April remarked with ruthless pessimism, wanting to bring her mother to a proper understanding of the magnitude of the issue at hand.

Becoming aware that their guests were listening closely to their exchange, April summoned up her smile and exerted herself to turn the conversation to a subject better suited for general consumption.

Fortunately, she did not have to exert herself for long.

Hugh made his apologies to Lady Hartwood almost immediately, telling her he had an appointment in the City, and hearing this, Mrs Starling rose from her chair and elicited his escort for herself and her daughter as far as Bond Street.

Hugh gave no indication that the prospect of their company gratified him but he agreed to it.

Mr Kepling then remembered that he too had some shopping to do and invited himself to go with them, and within the space of a few minutes only His Grace remained with the Hartwood ladies.

'I can see this business has put you out,' he told April, 'and you are most likely wishing to be left alone with all speed. But before I say my good-byes, allow me the impertinence of saying that you need not be so mortified. A great many people have mortgaged estates and they go about their day without the least consciousness of it.'

'It's not the mortgage itself I find insupportable,' April replied with a sigh. 'I inherited it along with the estate and can do little about it. But the thought of being obliged to Hu. . . to Mr Royce, *that* I cannot bear!'

'Why ever not, love?' asked Lady Hartwood, regarding her daughter in a perplexed way. 'If one must have a mortgage, Hugh is the ideal person – so kind and generous as he is! – to make the whole business so much more agreeable.'

'That only makes it worse!' groaned April, running a hand over her eyes. Dropping it suddenly, she said in a vexed tone: 'Can you believe, he actually offered to tear up the mortgage? I would not let him, of course. But now we must be grateful to him for *that* as well!'

'You would not let him tear up the mortgage?' asked Lady Hartwood in a fascinated way, tinged with horror. 'But. . . but why not?'

'Mama, I know you cannot think we would accept such generosity?'

'But I *do* think it! It would have been just the thing to make our lives more comfortable! If you've told me once, you've told me a thousand times, until the mortgage is paid off we must live more simply. And although *you* might enjoy doing so, love, I think you could have considered my feelings on the matter. I assure you, I do not like to live simply!'

'But, Mama, to be beholden to him in such a way! Surely you must see it would be wholly improper?'

'I see nothing improper in a member of our own family assisting us out of a little financial difficulty.'

'He is not a member of our family,' retorted April, desperately holding on to her patience. 'And there is nothing little about the mortgage. You know it is almost to the tune of twenty thousand pounds!'

This gave Lady Hartwood pause; but only for a moment.

'Really? As much as that?' she said mildly. 'I suppose it must have slipped my mind. But then, such an amount – which seems monstrous to us, to be sure! – means very little to Hugh. We must not judge him by our own standards.'

She spoke with the conviction of someone who knew they had reason on their side and April perceived the futility of continuing the conversation.

With a sigh she signalled her resignation.

His Grace, who had been largely forgotten, and had remained a little to the side to better observe and enjoy this exchange, decided to forgo any further entertainment and make his exit.

Clearing his throat to bring their attention back to him, he said: 'If you will pardon me, your ladyship, I feel it is time I took myself off.'

'Oh, certainly, Your Grace,' said Lady Hartwood, giving him a wholly unconscious smile. 'It has been a pleasure to have you visit us.' Glancing at the clock on the mantle, she suddenly stiffened and exclaimed: '*Oh my*! Is *that* the time? I must go and change at once! Albert will be here any minute to take me to visit his father and I simply *cannot* be late. Lord Wulfingston does not strike one as a man who tolerates tardiness. Pray excuse me, Your Grace! April will see you out.' She offered him a final, lovely smile and rushed out of the room.

'You would be pardoned if you imagined yourself in a madhouse,' remarked April.

His Grace allowed himself to laugh at last.

'Not at all! Your mother is an original and so very charming I defy anyone to find fault with her. I cannot tell you how refreshing it is to visit a house so free of artifice.'

'We certainly don't appear to have the ability to pretend and deceive – even for the comfort of our own guests!' she said, leading the way out of the room.

'You need not fear your guests were made uncomfortable.'

'No? Perhaps you're right. More likely, they were entertained by the spectacle we provided and cannot wait to spread our business about.'

189

'I confess to being entertained, but, in my defence, it is so rare to find authentic, un-orchestrated entertainment I have learnt to appreciate it when it chances upon me. However, I assure you, my enjoyment was purely of the chaste and blameless variety.'

'Of course! You are a veritable saint after all,' she laughed.

'One tries! I hope I need not say, you can be assured of my discretion? And – I will make certain – of my cousin's.'

'I did not mean to imply *you* would go about spreading tales, Eustace. I was thinking only of the Starlings. How impolite you must think me! You see how my wits have been scattered by this business with Mr Royce? Thank goodness I was not included on the invitation to visit Lord Wulfingston today. I would certainly have been a liability!'

'Does he set out to terrify your mother or does she imagine his displeasure?'

'I think a little of both. But I believe today's invitation was an olive branch on his part. . . speaking of invitations, have you accepted Mrs Delamer's to stay in Richmond over Christmas? I don't mean to press you, but if you find yourself free to attend I hope you will come and keep me company. Mrs Delamer's friends are outrageous and enjoy putting me to blush, and my mother and Lord Paisley will probably go off alone together as much as possible. And if Mr Royce and Miss Starling were to do the same, I shall be left at the mercy of Mrs Starling!'

His Grace laughed.

'What an enticing picture you do paint.'

'I know, shocking, isn't it? I am a contemptible creature for wishing to inflict such an ordeal on you, but although my conscience pains me, I am self-serving enough to ignore it.'

'It need not continue to pain you. As soon as I was introduced to Mrs Delamer at your dinner party I knew she was a person worthy of further acquaintance. Which is why, fair Aphrodite, you will be happy to hear I have informed my parent I will forgo the pleasures of yet another Christmas at Claredon Manor with our too-numerous relatives, and will instead join you in Richmond.'

'Oh, thank you, Eustace! I hope you are not in your mother's black books?'

'She did initially prove reticent to give me up. But on learning you were to be one of the party, naturally all her objections fell away.' He offered her a droll look. 'I like to think my powers of persuasion had some sway over her but it is unlikely.'

'Does she still dream of a match between us? How uncomfortable for you!'

'On the contrary, it is very convenient! I quite despair when I think of the time when you shall be married and beyond my reach. I doubt I will find another woman who understands my limitations so well.'

'Will you never marry, my dear?'

'Never,' he replied cheerfully. 'I decided a long time ago that marriage was not for me. And although I believe my mother – with the intuition of all mothers – comprehends my reasons, she thinks in time they will be overborne. And as yet I have not had the heart to crush her optimism.'

'I suppose one cannot blame her for looking forward to becoming a grandmother, and securing an heir for the title.'

'I am fortunate the title already has an heir – one of whom she approves – so she cannot hold that over me.'

'Then you are released!'

'Almost. There are still grandchildren to consider. I need not scruple to tell *you*, however, that I have reached the conclusion my cousin must soon settle down. His offspring can serve as worthy substitutes.'

'Poor Alfie,' she said with feeling. 'I don't doubt you will use him shamelessly! Does he go blindly towards his fate?'

'Yes,' he admitted, laughing lightly. 'But you need not fear it will not be to his liking. Once I've placed him on his path, he will realise it's just what he wished for all along. Do you ever think of marriage and children for yourself?'

'I suppose most women do,' she replied carefully. 'But first one must have a husband and I am yet to meet someone with whom I wish to spend my life.'

'Has no one caught your interest?'

'No. . . no one suitable.'

'Perhaps he will become more suitable given a little time?'

'Oh, I was not referring to anyone in particular!' she insisted, gesturing dismissively with her hand. 'And besides, once my mother is married I will return to St Mawes. Now that matters are fixed so awkwardly, I must apply myself to making the estate profitable and will be kept too busy to think of marriage.'

'It will be as you wish, of course. However, I cannot believe Mr Royce would expect such a sacrifice. . . I would even go so far as to say, he would be against it.'

'He has no right to be against it!' she responded sharply. 'And if he tries his tricks again and attempts to make my mother a present of the mortgage, he will soon learn his error! I am my father's heir, *not* my mother.'

'I do not wish to contradict you, but have you considered that he does not need your permission to tear up the mortgage?' His Grace ventured delicately.

'He wouldn't dare!'

She looked so incensed by this suggestion that he smiled and could not help remarking: 'You appear to be inordinately determined to remain in his debt?'

Her shocked eyes met his amused ones.

'Nothing of the sort! How can you say such a thing when you know I would repay him in an instant if I could?'

'But he has already offered to forgive the debt. The need to repay him is an inconvenience of your own making.'

'It isn't an inconvenience, it's a matter of honour! And besides, he has no right to make me feel so beholden to him. It's bad enough I have to...' She halted abruptly.

'You need say no more!' said His Grace, regarding her with sympathy. 'If you allow me, I will make you a present of a little wisdom that has come my way. I have always found honesty to be overrated, apart from when dealing with oneself. Self-deception is akin to a captain steering his ship blindfolded.'

April held his gaze in silence for a few moments, then looked away with a troubled expression.

'It is not self-deception so much as self-preservation,' she muttered.

By this time they had reached the entry hall. And as there were no servants about April opened the front door herself, while His Grace picked up his beaver hat from the marble-topped table against the wall.

'Good-bye, Eustace, and thank you,' she said, embarrassment creeping into her voice. 'You are a good friend to listen to me go on and on in such an absurd way!'

'I hope to be of better service to you than that,' he responded, an enigmatic smile on his handsome face.

Bidding her farewell, he sauntered down the shallow steps to the pavement and, springing up into his curricle, waited for his groom to jump up beside him and drove away.

Thirty-One

'Albert, I hope the heavy snowfall your coachman prophesied will hold off a little longer,' said April as she looked out of the carriage window at the desolate, winter landscape through which they were travelling; made beautiful by a rapidly increasing dusting of white. 'It will be dark soon and I don't fancy being stranded in the carriage overnight in these temperatures.'

'Have no fear,' replied Lord Paisley, who was sitting across from her. 'Even if the snow were to become impassable, there are any number of respectable inns around here where we could seek shelter.'

'Oh, look! There's the river!' cried Lady Hartwood, peering out of the opposite window. 'And if I am not mistaken, I can see the gates to Ham House up ahead. This should mean we have only another mile or so until we reach Mrs Delamer's property. I wonder if any of the other guests have arrived.'

'I should think so!' said April laughingly. 'They would have, very sensibly, left London before noon.'

This gentle teasing was directed at her mother, for they had had to turn back twice to retrieve some vital item she had forgotten. Thankfully, each time they had progressed no further than the outskirts of London. Still, the delays had added two hours to their journey as, on each occasion, they had had to stop by the side of the road while her ladyship conferred with her lady's maid (travelling in a second carriage behind them, along with April's maid and Lord Paisley's valet) to determine if the item in question was packed, before a decision was made to turn around.

'Oh, I know! So *regrettable*,' agreed Lady Hartwood. 'I did not want to make a fuss and wound Keighley's feelings, but I don't know how she could have forgotten to pack my diamond tiara.'

'Perhaps she did not suppose that a simple country house party would warrant such a distinction,' suggested April.

'Keighley has been with me for over eight years, love, and she should know by now that there is nothing simple about one of Mrs Delamer's house parties! I would have felt positively *dowdy* without my tiara. Do you remember the last time dear Mrs Bolton wore her ruby and diamond set to *breakfast*...including a tiara!' she added on a victorious note.

'Yes, Mama, I do remember. But Mrs Bolton is eighty if she's a day! And, although very sweet, she is undoubtedly senile, if the outrageous things she says are anything to go by!'

'Well, perhaps she is a *little* eccentric, but that does not preclude her from being very fashionably turned out. And it is not only her! In the evenings there is so much jewellery on display, a Court presentation could not be more impressive.'

'I will accede to the necessity of us turning back for your tiara,' said April, eyes dancing, 'but was it truly necessary to return for your embroidery? You hardly ever touch it when you're at home and would never have noticed its absence.'

'But, love, it was *vitally* necessary! There is nothing like working on one's embroidery to endow one with an aura gentility. And although I admit I *detest* embroidering, I absolutely must be prepared to give Lord Wulfingston a good impression of me should he follow through with his threat...I-I mean, if he decides to grace us with his presence,' she corrected herself and bestowed an apologetic smile on her betrothed.

'No need to sugar coat it, my love,' said Lord Paisley, patting her hand. 'As it was no doubt meant as a threat, to throw us into confusion for his entertainment, we can do no less than call it such.'

'Well, if he *should* decide to drop in I'm certain he would be most welcome,' said Lady Hartwood, more hopeful than truthful.

April laughed.

'He certainly would not be!' she put in. 'Forgive me, Albert, but it cannot have escaped your notice that your father and Mrs Delamer are masterful at locking horns.'

Lord Paisley agreed to it with perfect good humour.

'I cannot speak for Mrs Delamer,' he said, 'but I have a suspicion my father has enjoyed himself in her company more than he is willing to let on. I discovered quite by chance the other day that he has been driving down to Ham House at least once a week, to visit his friend Lord Dysart.'

'Mrs Delamer's neighbour?' asked Lady Hartwood, looking dismayed.

'The same!'

'But surely, dearest, you don't mean to imply that he has been orchestrating encounters with *her*?'

Lord Paisley grinned and nodded.

'So you see, my love, if he does decide to impose himself on Mrs Delamer's hospitality, I don't believe we can flatter ourselves that it will be on *our* account.'

'Oh no, do not say such a thing!' she cried, giggling nervously. 'How awkward it would be! We must hope your suspicion is proved incorrect. I don't think she is at all inclined to think favourably of him. If she can be induced to be *civil* we must count ourselves fortunate... oh, *look*! There is the gatehouse to Marble Hill Manor! We have arrived at last!'

The carriage was soon turning off the dirt road and onto a well-kept pebble approach; and, after another few minutes, it swept around the circular drive and came to a stop outside a large Palladian villa.

The villa had been built a century earlier for the mistress of the King; a circumstance which had naturally appealed to Mrs Delamer and had made up her mind to purchase the property.

It was a beautifully proportioned building, with no wings to detract from its cubic symmetry. Each of the three main floors had large sash windows and the façade was a gleaming white, which at present blended perfectly with its snow-covered surroundings. It appeared compact when viewed from the drive, but that was deceptive. It was in fact most spacious inside.

Apart from a double reception room that looked out onto the river, a library, a music parlour, and a dining room, all on the ground floor, the house boasted ten bedchambers on the upper floors, as well as various nooks and crannies where guests could withdraw from the communal areas and snatch some private time to read or work on their correspondence.

Mrs Delamer's butler, who had been on the lookout for them all afternoon, walked out of the house at their approach, and, before Lord Paisley's footman could jump down from his place beside the coachman and open the carriage door, he had performed this service himself.

'Good day, Stevens!' April greeted him warmly as he helped her from the carriage. 'I hope you are well? I feel it has been an age since we were last here!'

The butler was one of a handful of faithful servants who had worked for the fifth Earl of Windermere and, upon his demise, had chosen to follow Mrs Delamer to Richmond rather than stay on to serve his heir. April knew the value of such loyalty and was greatly attached to him.

'I am very well, Miss April,' he replied, bowing in so stately a manner that one could be forgiven for supposing him to oversee the management of a duke's household. 'I believe it has been three years since we last had the pleasure of welcoming you to Marble Hill.'

'As long as that? Yes, I suppose you're right. The last time we visited my father was. . . still alive.'

She could say no more for a moment, suffocated by a sudden feeling of bereavement. It had been many months since such an emotion had come over her and she was surprised by it.

Stevens offered her a look of compassion. He knew most of her family's secrets, including her complicated relationship with her father.

'I'm sorry for your loss, Miss April.'

She accepted his condolences with a nod and pulled up the fur-lined hood of her cloak to ward off the cold, and his perceptive gaze.

Lord Paisley was next to alight from the carriage.

He jumped down with an energy he had not enjoyed since his youth (and which was steadily returning with every week he kept to his restricting diet) and assisted his betrothed to descend safely to the ground.

'Stevens, how *good* it is to see you again!' cried Lady Hartwood, handing her enormous chinchilla muff to her daughter and grasping his hands in her own. 'Did you say it has been three years? I cannot believe it! You have not changed in the *least.*'

Even the butler's unerring professionalism could not withstand such a greeting.

A broad smile transformed his countenance and he said with paternal fondness: 'Your ladyship, I would like to extend my own and the staff's felicitations on your recent engagement, and our very best wishes for your future happiness.'

Lady Hartwood beamed up at him through the gentle flurry of snow.

'Oh, how kind of you! Thank you! Allow me to introduce you to my betrothed, Lord Paisley. . . dearest, Stevens has been a good friend to me ever since my days in Dorset, when I was a young girl and he a junior footman in my father's household.'

'How do you do?' said Lord Paisley pleasantly. 'Dorset, did you say, my love? I thought your family was from Cornwall?'

Lady Hartwood blinked rapidly, realising her mistake.

As far as her betrothed knew, her parents had come from well-to-do Cornish families and had been neighbours of her husband.

'Ah. . . yes. . . they *were* from Cornwall.'

'They owned a second home in Dorset,' April clarified, coming to her mother's aid.

This was true enough; there was no need to explain that the Dorset estate had been her grandparents' principal residence and the Cornish house had only been purchased so they could be near to her and her mother for some of the year.

'Yes, it was their *second* home,' Lady Hartwood agreed happily. 'And I was so attached to the Dorset property as a child those memories take precedence. . . sometimes to the exclusion of all else!'

'Ah, that would explain it,' said Lord Paisley. 'And I suppose Mrs Delamer poached you from Lady Hartwood's parents?' he asked Stevens.

'There was no need,' replied the butler with perfect truth. 'When Lady Hartwood's father passed away, Mrs Delamer was kind enough to offer me employment.'

'Why are we lingering outside in the snow?' Lady Hartwood exclaimed all at once. 'Do let us go in and warm ourselves!'

'Of course, my love,' agreed Lord Paisley, a laughing look in his eyes.

While Lord Paisley escorted her ladyship indoors, April offered the butler an apologetic smile.

'She will tell him in her own time. For now, we must do what we can to stop her from tangling herself in her fabrications. She feels her duplicity greatly, poor love, and suffers for it. There was never a person less suited to deception!'

'You can be assured of my discretion, Miss April.'

'Thank you, Stevens. Would you be so good as to see to the unpacking of the second carriage? And also the sleeping arrangements for Lord Paisley's servants? I suspect Keighley will want to sleep in my mother's antechamber again. And, this time, I'm afraid I will have to importune you with my own lady's maid. But if you have assigned me the rose bedchamber as usual, there should be room for a trundle bed to be set up there for her.'

Stevens assured her he would handle all the arrangements and she was left with nothing to do but thank him.

She started towards the house, then stopped and turned back to ask: 'Have the other guests arrived?'

'Yes, Miss April. They arrived earlier and are now changing for dinner.'

'Can you tell me who is to make up our party? I find, from experience, it is best to be armed and prepared before going down to dinner when visiting here,' she said with a wry smile.

197

'You will remember Mrs Bolton, Sir Yarmouth, General Simpson and Mr Oatley from your previous visits. And, this year, we are also honoured to have His Grace, the Duke of Claredon, staying with us, as well as Mrs Starling and her daughter. I believe they are also known to you?'

'Yes, they are. . . and I thought, from something Mrs Delamer said to me, that a Mr Royce was also invited?'

'He was indeed, however, we received a message from him to say he was held up on some business. He is not expected until tomorrow.'

'He means to drive down on Christmas Eve? And with heavy snow forecast? I don't suppose he'll come at all, in that case. The roads will be impassable within a few hours.'

This observation should have pleased her, for she had dreaded having to endure his presence in the intimate setting of a house party. However, she was too disappointed to feel the benefits attached to his absence.

'That may well be the case. I only know his intention is to arrive tomorrow.'

'Of course. Not that it matters to me if he comes or not, you understand! I was only satisfying my curiosity.'

'We do have one more guest who was not expected,' Stevens said conscientiously. 'Mr Kepling, His Grace's cousin. He escorted the Starling ladies from London in Mr Royce's stead and Mrs Delamer thought it only right to invite him to stay.'

'Oh dear, she cannot have liked that,' said April, smiling. 'We know how strictly she likes to adhere to her guest lists! Unless she has perceived some way to make use of the poor man and turn him to good account?'

Since he was speaking to one of the *Family*, Stevens allowed a glimmer of a smile to show in his eyes.

'I couldn't say, Miss April. However, as His Grace was kind enough to condescend to sharing his room with his cousin, there could be no objection.'

April thanked him for the information and retreated into the house to put herself into the capable hands of Mrs Delamer's housekeeper.

Thirty-Two

The evening meal at Marble Hill Manor was customarily served according to country hours, although, on this occasion, it had been put back to allow the late arrivals time to dress for dinner. It was therefore not until just before seven o'clock that April encountered the other guests.

They were all assembled in the music parlour, off the dining room, when the Hartwood ladies and Lord Paisley joined them. Once greetings and introductions had been exchanged, Mrs Delamer assigned everyone their partners for dinner, in an efficient manner that spoke of premeditation, and, taking hold of General Simpson's enthusiastically offered arm, led the way to the dining room.

Adhering to their hostess' wishes, Mrs Starling and Sir Yarmouth were next. The baronet was an amiable roué in his late fifties and had enough good looks remaining to cause Mrs Starling to blush in appreciation as he worked his charm on her.

They were followed by Lady Hartwood and Lord Paisley; Mrs Bolton and Mr Oatley (who were the elders of the group and appeared to be supporting each other in defiance of gravity); Miss Starling and Mr Kepling; and finally April and the duke.

'I am not at all used to being relegated to last place,' bemoaned His Grace. 'It has quite dented my self-importance!'

'I thought nothing could dent your self-importance?' teased April. 'And besides, you should have surmised by now that your purpose in this house is to serve, not to be flattered.'

'My feeble intelligence did allow me to perceive that some plan was afoot to make use of me. But I would never presume to spoil Mrs Delamer's enjoyment by admitting I am conscious of it.'

'You do her too great a kindness! Personally, I think her shameless and *I* have the distinction of being greatly attached to her.'

'Ah, but I am always kindest to those who amuse me the most. Most sins can be forgiven of a person who can make one laugh, don't you agree?'

'Not entirely,' she said with a tolerant smile, 'but I take your meaning.'

'You always do, fair Aphrodite, which is why you never disappoint me! Have I mentioned you look enchantingly ravishing this evening?'

'You haven't, and thank you. However, I cannot claim it was on purpose.'

'I did not suppose it was,' he returned smoothly. 'Your *purpose* has not yet arrived.'

She threw him a circumspect, quizzing look.

'Am I being too obtuse on this occasion? This lamentable tact of mine! I only wish I could be as direct as Mr Royce.' He cast her an impish glance. 'What I should have said is: there is no one about at present to inspire you to *purposefully* look your best. But that time will come.'

'Unlikely. I never dress myself with anything in mind other than my own whims and comfort.'

'Now *that* I believe! And tonight you can have the consolation of knowing that your whims have not misled you. Those high-necked, demur gowns you favour will, for once, serve a proper purpose. . . it is exceedingly cold, is it not?'

A surprised laugh rose to her lips.

'Eustace, surely. . . *surely* you cannot be mocking my clothes?'

'Have I overstepped the line?'

'Overstepped the line? I should think so!' she exclaimed, justifiably incensed. 'When I think of how modish my gowns could have been, were it not for your puritanical leanings in female attire, I could cry!'

'What can you mean?' he asked, genuinely surprised. 'I have no puritanical leanings of any kind, I assure you!'

'But all this. . .' she waved a hand in front of the demure primrose silk that encased her, 'is for *your* benefit!'

'Why ever would you think that I – a true connoisseur of beauty in all its forms – would want such a glorious figure as yours covered up?'

'I was told you preferred a lady to conceal her flesh. . . *oh*, devil take her! She *tricked* me!' spluttered April, furious.

'Did you wish to catch my fancy?' he asked with a chuckle. 'I fear that even you, fair Aphrodite, were doomed to fail.'

'I most certainly never had such a wish! And you need not tell me something I knew almost from the start. I am well aware that your tastes, *Eros*, don't run in my direction – yes, I too know my Greek mythology! I am not as innocent as you seem to think me.'

'Eros?' repeated His Grace, looking delighted. 'Apt indeed! But more so the earlier incarnations, I hope?'

She could not stop an exasperated laugh from bubbling up.

'You vain creature! Yes, certainly the earlier. You might fire your arrows mischievously but I do no picture you as a chubby winged infant.'

'A virile young god of love then? I am immeasurably touched!'

She did not respond, her thoughts elsewhere, and after a moment asked: 'Why would she want to misdirect me in such a way?'

'If we are speaking of Mrs Delamer, I have my suspicions. But I am not certain you are ready to hear them,' he said as they entered the dining room.

Their discussion had to be abandoned at this point and April could not say whether she was pleased or disappointed.

Despite being relegated to last place in the procession to dinner, His Grace was given the place of honour at the foot of the table, with April on his right and Lord Paisley on his left.

April was disconcerted to discover that her other neighbour was none other than Mrs Bolton, and could only hope that the elderly lady (who, as Lady Hartwood had prophesied, was lavishly adorned with jewellery, including a tiara!) would exert herself to control her loose tongue.

'I have not seen you in too long a time, Miss Hartwood! Have you been well?' asked Mrs Bolton in a high-pitched, doddering voice that travelled remarkably well.

'Yes, very well, thank you,' replied April, relieved at this perfectly respectable opening. 'And you too look to be in fine health, Mrs Bolton.'

'Well, at my age, I count myself fortunate if I wake up in the morning, so I cannot complain.' Her wizened features broke into a wide smile that, despite it missing several teeth, was difficult to resist. '*Do* tell me, my dear Miss Hartwood, are you and that fancy young duke going to make a match of it?'

April glanced nervously towards His Grace.

He was conversing with Lord Paisley but she could tell from the quirk of his lips that he had heard the remark.

'We are friends and nothing more,' she said with quiet finality.

'Good, good!' declared Mrs Bolton. After taking a generous gulp of wine, she leant in and continued in a confidential way: 'Charming boy, by all accounts, with a great deal of address. And there's the title to consider, of course. But what you need, dear, is a man in your bed! A title won't keep you warm at night, if you take my meaning?'

A shocked gurgle of laughter escaped April.

She hoped the question had been rhetorical for she found it impossible to conjure up an answer; and was most thankful when Mr Oatley, Mrs Bolton's other neighbour (and, if servants' gossip was to be believed, her lover), claimed their attention with a salacious piece of news concerning the king's brother and a well-known French opera singer.

Part way through the first course, April saw the butler approach her grandmother and speak into her ear. Surprise registered on Mrs Delamer's countenance, followed by amusement; then she gave Stevens some instructions and he hurried out of the room. April wondered what was afoot, but it was another half an hour before her curiosity was to be appeased.

Shortly after the first course was removed, a team of footmen entered, carrying an extra leaf for the dining table and two settings, at which point Mrs Delamer rose majestically to her feet and addressed the table.

'Dear friends, I have been informed that Lord Wulfingston and his grandson, Mr Royce, arrived a short while ago and will be joining us for dinner. I trust you will forgive the disruption while my staff prepare their places.'

Seemingly oblivious to the surprised murmurings around her, Mrs Delamer sat back down and continued her conversation with General Simpson and Sir Yarmouth.

April's hand rose to pat the loose arrangement of curls her maid had worked into her short hair. Becoming aware of the duke's smiling gaze on her, she lowered her hand and threw him an exasperated look (which, if she was being honest, was aimed mostly at herself).

Hugh and his grandfather were shown into the room soon after. While Hugh offered his apologies to Mrs Delamer and the assembled company, Lord Wulfingston, nodded to those of his acquaintance with the confidence of a man assured of his welcome.

Standing side by side, as they were, April thought their resemblance was more marked than usual. Both were tall and imposing in their stature, with similar strong features and an air of command about them.

There was no denying that Lord Wulfingston was the more elegantly dressed of the two. However, as cream satin knee-breeches, a heavily embroidered velvet coat and diamond-buckled shoes would have looked out of place on Hugh, April found nothing to fault in his well-cut olive-green evening coat, dark trousers, and crisp white linen cravat.

She had not seen him for over two weeks and was dismayed to discover that her memory had not deceived her, as she had begun to hope. He was still regrettably attractive.

While Mrs Delamer showed Lord Wulfingston to his seat, Hugh took the opportunity to walk over to his fiancée and her mother and exchange a few terse pleasantries with them; a distinction that appeared to delight neither lady.

Over the last fortnight, ever since it had occurred to him it was not in his best interest to be agreeable, he had made every effort to be surly and aloof in his dealings with them. He knew he was succeeding in unraveling their good opinion of him, however, they had not yet shown him the door and he had come to the realisation that his fortune had the power to overcome their objections to his character.

It was a sobering thought, and as he walked over to take the last remaining seat, beside April, a pronounced scowl marred his features.

April noticed at once that something had put him in a black mood and found herself inclined to try and lift him out of it.

'Good evening, Mr Royce,' she said, offering him a bright smile. 'We heard you were delayed and did not expect you until tomorrow.'

'My grandfather insisted we attempt the journey today,' he replied, his manner too abrupt to be courteous.

'I had not realised Mrs Delamer extended an invitation to Lord Wulfingston?'

'She didn't, as you well know.'

'Yes, I *do* know,' she replied, undaunted, 'but it would have been ill-mannered to admit as much. Instead, I chose to use my tact and pose the information as a question, in the hope you would divulge the reason for his presence.'

'Tact is wasted on me.'

'Unquestionably!'

Hugh cracked a smile and unbent a little.

'My grandfather decided to accompany me as he is engaged to visit Lord Dysart. Ham House is less than a mile away from here and even you must own his excuse is reasonable.'

'Oh, perfectly reasonable! Only, unless my eyes deceive me, he does not appear to have made it to his destination.'

'He wanted to pay his respects to Mrs Delamer.'

'Lord help us!' she laughed.

Hugh's smile widened. 'He has promised to be on his best behaviour. Do you mind if he shows an interest in her?'

'It's no concern of mine. And I can hardly blame him, he is not the first to fall under her spell. . . she may even be flattered,' she said doubtfully.

'*Do* tell me, my dear Miss Hartwood, who your large, strapping friend might be?' interrupted Mrs Bolton, her gap-filled smile on display.

Doing her best to mask her reluctance, April introduced Hugh to her.

'Your name certainly sounds familiar, Mr Royce – have we met before?' asked Mrs Bolton. 'No? Well, I certainly feel as if I *should* remember you. My damned memory. . . oh, pardon me! I hope I have not offended you with my language? I was not raised in these prudish times. . . *ah*, I have it! You, sir, are the nephew of our dear Eleanor's fiancé. Thirty thousand a year – I remember now!'

April's mortification was complete. Hugh must now think they had been discussing his wealth.

She threw him an apologetic look.

'No need to look so, dear Miss Hartwood!' cried Mrs Bolton with a merry laugh, clearly a good deal sharper than her doddery persona would suggest. 'I don't mention his money because I am impressed. Why, I could buy your young man thrice over!'

'He is not *my* young man!' April objected; knowing even as she said the words that it would have been preferable to hold her tongue. 'Perhaps, ma'am, you were unaware that Mr Royce is engaged to Miss Starling?'

'Yes, I'm aware of it,' replied Mrs Bolton, throwing April into confusion.

Hugh smiled. He might not understand why Mrs Bolton showed a tendency to pair him with April, but as his own thoughts had veered in that direction too often for his comfort, he found it impossible to be insulted.

Besides, he found her tactics refreshingly honest.

With a discernable tremor of amusement, he changed the subject by asking the elderly provocateur if she lived in these parts.

'Oh, indeed I do! Twickenham. But my family comes from Newcastle, which is where I'd now be if my papa hadn't made his fortune in coal and made me so perfectly acceptable to my husband – God rest his soul – and his family.'

This was said without the least rancour and with such a jovial twinkle in her rheumy eyes that Hugh laughed, and even April was drawn into a smile.

'I have no doubt Mr Bolton had the better part of the bargain,' he said.

'Well, he certainly came to dote on me, and I on him. Although neither of us had the least pretensions to beauty! And were considered ill-matched from the start. But love is quite blind and does not care for the boundaries we set on it.'

April and Hugh glanced at each other.

'To my mind,' he said, rather brusquely, 'what is commonly referred to as love is nothing more than a natural attraction that does not survive the realities of a long acquaintance. Loyalty and respect are far worthier sentiments. And, when coupled with an affinity between two people, are more likely to lead to a comfortable union.'

'Have you and Miss Starling been rehearsing that rationalisation?' asked April. 'You appear to share exactly the same thoughts on the matter.'

'And you do not?'

'No, certainly not! My dogs give me loyalty; respect can be earned from anyone; and if I want comfort I look to my couch! From my husband I expect rather more.'

After a pause, he asked: 'What do you expect?'

'Why, nothing less than love! But not the primitive, feeble emotion you describe – which you have reduced to simple attraction – but something deeper and richer that will last a lifetime.'

'But surely you can see that loyalty and respect will outlive the more transient emotions that overwhelm us in the beginning?'

'I place a great deal of importance on loyalty and respect. And for some they are enough. . . but, good God, if that is all I can expect from marriage, I want none of it! And if you believe that true love is a transient emotion then you know nothing of the matter! My grandparents were devoted to each other for over thirty years and it was not loyalty and respect alone that sustained them!'

'*Brava!*' cried Mrs Bolton, clapping her hands together.

With a jolt, April realised she had worked herself into such a passion that her chest was heaving as if from great exertion. She stretched out an unsteady hand to her glass of water and took a sip.

'How right you are, dear,' said Mrs Bolton, looking like the cat that got the cream. 'Life is full of mysteries beyond our understanding – love being one of them. You, dear boy, are quite outnumbered on this.'

'I hope I am never so fixed in my views that I can't appreciate the validity of a compelling argument,' replied Hugh, his unwavering gaze on April's face.

If he hoped to earn a response from her with this comment he was to be disappointed.

She refused to say another word, or even to look at him, and gave her attention to serving herself from the platter of venison that had been placed before her.

After what seemed to her like an interminable amount of time, Hugh finally looked away and joined in the duke's and Lord Wulfingston's discussion on the latest horseflesh on offer at Tattersall's.

'Don't let it concern you, dear,' whispered Mrs Bolton. 'They always resist it in the beginning.'

Good manners alone forced April to look up from her plate and smile.

'I assure you, ma'am, I am not in the least concerned.'

From across the table, Miss Starling drew Mrs Bolton's attention by admiring her tiara and April was freed from further embarrassment.

Although she doubted her liberation had been intentional, her gratitude was so great she felt genuine amicability towards Hugh's fiancée for the first time in their acquaintance.

Miss Starling had indeed acted on a benevolent impulse. She had suffered through one of Mrs Bolton's unnerving conversations earlier in the day and found she could not ignore the strained look on April's countenance, which had alerted her that something was wrong.

She was surprised at her own self-sacrifice and, being a well brought up girl who knew she should not speak across the table, was also rather daunted by her boldness.

There was some consolation to be had in the fact that this was not a formal party, and the table was not so wide that she could not address Mrs Bolton easily and without drawing her mother's censorious eye. Even so, she was relieved when Mr Kepling joined in their conversation and made her less conspicuous.

Her fine brown eyes conveyed her appreciation to him; and when he offered her a friendly wink in return she could not bring herself to condemn this familiarity.

After dinner the ladies retired to the reception rooms, while the gentlemen congregated at one end of the dinner table to enjoy their port.

'You did well to make it to Richmond today,' His Grace addressed Hugh. 'I doubt I would have braved all that snow, even for the promise of such stimulating company.'

'It was not my decision to set out today,' replied Hugh.

He nodded his thanks as he accepted a glass of port from his uncle, who had taken on the role of host and was pouring the drinks from the crystal decanter the butler had left on the table.

'Ah, I see!' said His Grace. 'I assumed – forgive the impertinence – that the draw of a certain lady had served as enticement.'

Hugh frowned and responded a little too sharply: 'Your assumption is incorrect.'

'Do not, I beg you, admit as much to her! She is bound to be gravely disappointed.'

Hugh sipped his port in silence.

When he could contain himself no longer, he asked: 'Why the devil do you think she'd be disappointed?'

'I do not presume to be an expert in this area, however, I'm told it is always the case when a woman sets her heart on a man. She becomes exceedingly possessive and wishes to be first in his thoughts, and even to compel his actions.'

Hugh dismissed this with a gesture. 'Any man of sense would find that a difficult wish to fulfil. . . and you would be hard-pressed to convince me her heart is engaged!'

His Grace inclined his head in acceptance of this dictum.

'Has she admitted otherwise to you?' Hugh demanded.

'No, not at all! But that is hardly surprising. We have a *very* slight acquaintance.'

'You have lived in each other's pocket for over two months,' Hugh remarked abrasively. 'Hardly a slight acquaintance.'

'I assure you, I have spoken to your fiancée barely a handful of times!'

'My fiancée? What has. . . ' Hugh pulled himself up short and glowered at the duke. 'You were speaking of Miss Starling?'

'Of course! Who else? Only the marriage contract – or love – can stir such possessiveness.'

'Love!' scoffed Hugh. 'It seems I'm to be plagued by romantics this evening.'

Feeling he had stirred the pot sufficiently, His Grace allowed himself to be drawn into the general conversation and left Hugh to sit in grim silence with his thoughts.

Thirty-Three

April entered the breakfast parlour the following morning expecting to have the room to herself. She was usually the only early riser in residence and was startled to find that, on this occasion, another guest had arrived before her.

Hugh was already sitting down to a hearty breakfast and perusing the last copy of the Morning Post to have been delivered to Marble Hill Manor before the snowstorm had hit.

They had said very little to one another since their uncomfortable exchange over dinner, and she was conscious of a cowardly urge to retreat.

'Good morning,' she spoke up defiantly before she could change her mind.

Hugh looked up in surprise.

'Good morning.'

He glanced at the clock on the mantle. It showed the hour was not much advanced past eight o'clock.

'Couldn't sleep?' he asked.

'I slept very well, thank you. I usually take my breakfast at this time.'

'You do?'

The unwelcome suspicion crossed her mind that he might think she had come down early to catch him alone.

'Yes, I always breakfast early!' she declared, determined to set him straight. 'You may ask anyone who knows me!'

'That won't be necessary,' he replied, amusement creeping into his voice. 'I'm happy to take your word on it.'

She cringed inwardly, for her delivery had been a little too vehement, and walked over to the sideboard where breakfast had been laid out for the guests.

'The truth is,' she continued in a light tone as she began to serve herself, 'I have never liked to waste my mornings in bed. And when I am at home there are usually a hundred and one things to be done on estate business, before my mother compels me to join her on her various social engagements.'

'Would you rather remain at home?'

'Oh, I am very happy to bear her company! And I have my own engagements, of course. But, of the two of us, she is the one most devoted to the social whirl. She has an enviable capacity to enjoy whatever company she finds herself in. And, as you have no doubt observed, she has a talent for making people fall in love with her.'

'She's not the only one,' muttered Hugh.

'Pardon?'

'I was agreeing with you.'

'Everyone must! I am blessed with the best of mothers. If I could possess half her excellent qualities I would be content, but there is more of my father in me than I care to admit.' It struck her suddenly that she was being too revealing. 'Listen to me go on! You must be wishing for some peace and quiet. I know there is nothing more calculated to put a man in a foul mood than idle chatter over breakfast.'

Her back was to Hugh as she spoke and she did not see the raw tenderness that had crept into his eyes as he watched her. Or, on realising he was betraying himself, the quick frown that followed.

April served herself from the dishes spread out before her for some time, until it occurred to her that she was delaying joining Hugh at the table, and, taking herself to task for her foolishness, she stiffened her resolve and walked over to take a seat opposite him.

'Hungry?' he asked, looking at her plate.

'Oh...' She saw that she had served herself enough food to feed three people. 'Yes, very!' she lied.

Heaping her fork with ham and coddled egg, she took a rather large mouthful.

Hugh returned to his newspaper.

April was relieved his attention was no longer on her for she was struggling to chew the unladylike quantity of food in her mouth. Her eyes watered from the effort and several times she feared she would choke.

Hugh poured out a glass of water and leant across the table to place it before her, then went back to his reading.

Grateful despite her embarrassment, she drank deeply and murmured her thanks.

A companionable silence followed.

When she could no longer look upon the food on her plate with anything but aversion, April pushed it to the side and stood to pour herself some coffee from the pot in the centre of the table.

She absentmindedly refilled Hugh's cup as well, before sitting down to drink the dark brew and wrestle with a problem that had plagued her over the last two weeks.

She should have sought Hugh's counsel on the matter sooner but she had no enthusiasm for the task and had been putting it off. Now, however, the perfect opportunity presented itself and could not be ignored.

Clearing her throat, she put down her cup and said: 'It is fortunate we are alone at last. . .'

'I fail to see why?' interjected Hugh, looking up from his paper with an annoyed expression.

April was momentarily surprised into silence.

Recovering quickly, she said with spirit: 'And I fail to see why you expect me to put up with your acerbic charm? Others of your acquaintance might be inclined to do so, but I, strange creature that I am, will not! And, furthermore,' she went on crossly, 'if you could rid yourself of the notion – which you evidently possess – that I desire your company for any reason other than necessity, I would be greatly obliged to you!'

Hugh's mood had deteriorated over the last few minutes. He had found himself re-reading the same few lines on the page in front of him as his attention, well and truly having escaped his control, was centred on the woman opposite. But at this line of attack, a reluctant smile broke through his forbidding countenance.

'I'm never at my best first thing in the morning,' he offered as way of apology.

'Oh no, you do yourself a disservice! I find your behaviour consistent no matter the time of day.'

'Minx.'

April ignored this provocation and returned to her subject.

'As I was saying, I am glad we are alone for I wish to speak to you about a matter we touched upon the last time we met. I fear I may not have reacted in the best possible manner at the time, and I want to return to it with a cooler head.'

Hugh gave no sign of understanding her meaning.

She took a deep breath and made, what she considered to be, a truly heroic effort at self-possession.

'You must know I am speaking of the mortgage on St Mawes, so please spare me your obtuse looks,' she said tartly. 'In particular, I wish to speak about the repayment terms going forward.'

Hugh had known they were bound to return to this subject sooner or later, however, he would have preferred to delay the discussion until he had figured out how to deal with the matter to his liking.

He found himself in something of a conundrum. The thought of making a profit out of April repelled him. And even asking her to repay the principle of the mortgage, when she was clearly in straitened circumstances, did not sit well with him.

He would have liked nothing better than to tear up the mortgage documents, and would have done so by now had he not known he would be wounding her pride in the process. And although this consideration should not have had any bearing on his actions, there was no denying that it did.

For some time now, he had found himself wishing April would follow the example set by his numerous relations, who saw nothing wrong in relying on his charity to settle their monetary embarrassments. At least then it would be in his power to free her from her financial burden. . . and, at the same time, diminish her appeal to him.

'What are the present terms?' he asked in a noncommittal fashion.

'Don't you know?' she said, surprised.

'I have a large number of investments. I can't be expected to know the minutiae of each of their terms. Particularly, if they are of insignificant value,' he added, hoping to spare her any anxiety over repaying him.

'As of last quarter, the principal and interest came to three hundred and seventy pounds.'

'And the rate of interest?'

'Five percent.'

Hugh assumed a surprised expression.

'Five? You were being fleeced. Two is all I expect from the mortgages I hold,' he said, perjuring himself willingly.

'But I was told five is a reasonable rate,' she said, looking troubled. 'Is that not the case?'

Five was indeed reasonable, although Hugh was not about to admit as much.

'In some instances, perhaps. But when an investment is as secure and low in risk as your mortgage, I always offer two percent.'

Her brow wrinkled in thought as she did some quick calculations in her head.

'That would mean, the repayments will now be in the region of one hundred and fifty pounds quarterly.'

'Closer to one hundred.'

'One hundred! You cannot be serious? The numbers do not add up!'

'They do when you take into account the additional loading I use for my safest investments.'

April's expression hardened.

'I fail to see how such a low return could possibly constitute a good investment for you?' she said accusingly.

'And I fail to see what concern it is of yours how I handle my investments?' he countered, changing strategy and going on the attack.

'Do you take me for a simpleton? You are pushing down the repayments on purpose! Probably from some misplaced chivalrous instinct. But I wish you would not!'

'It's my own business if I choose to. . . '

'Please do not make me beholden to you, Hugh!' she cried, the words wrenched from her. 'I could not bear it!'

Hugh remained silent, his eyes locked with hers.

She looked away first, painfully conscious that her colour was heightened.

'I apologise,' she said stiffly. 'I am being unnecessarily emotional.'

'No, the fault is mine,' he said in a mild tone. 'I appear to have given you an incorrect impression of my reasoning. I take a long-term view on all the mortgages I hold and look for continuity and stability. That, in turn, allows me to seek higher yields on the riskier, shorter term investments. So, you see, the only reason I am able to offer you two percent, with preferential loading, is that I believe the St Mawes mortgage to be exceptionally low risk. If, in the future, your circumstances take a turn for the worse, I will of course have to re-evaluate.'

April sipped her coffee as she considered this.

After a long pause, she looked up and offered him a troubled smile. It tugged at his heart and made him fervently wish he had it in his power to relieve her of all her cares.

'Yes, I suppose that makes sense,' she said. 'I have heard Mrs Delamer speak of how a guaranteed income is the foundation of a healthy investment portfolio.'

Hugh regarded her in silence, appearing to debate something with himself, and presently said: 'May I ask you a question about the previous holder of your mortgage?'

'Mr Pimlico? Yes, of course. What would you like to know?'

'How did he come to hold your mortgage?'

'I don't know. I only became aware that he did hold it when my father became ill and I had to take over the management of the estate, some three or four years ago.'

'And did you ever meet him?'

'No. All my dealings with him have always been through our respective men of business. Why do you ask? Surely that is not unusual?'

'I merely wondered,' he said.

'Is he well known to you?'

'I have never met him.'

'Never met him!' she exclaimed. 'But I thought he was your business associate? How did you come to buy all the mortgages he held?'

'Mrs Delamer first alerted me to the opportunity. She explained that an acquaintance of hers was obliged to sell them upon favourable terms.'

Suspicion flared in April's eyes.

'*Mrs Delamer?*'

Hugh nodded.

She opened her mouth to speak. . . then closed it.

Her fingers drummed a staccato rhythm on the table, while her brain worked furiously to put together the pieces of a puzzle that had only just occurred to her.

All of a sudden, her grandmother's words came rushing back to her: *all that is required is a little resolution to create the opportunities that will throw them together and bind them inexorably.*

'When did she approach you with this opportunity?' she asked sharply. 'Was it after the dinner party my mother and I hosted?'

'I believe so, yes.'

'*Oh*, how dare she!' she gasped. 'She was speaking of *us*!'

'Us?' he echoed with new alertness.

She had no wish to explain that Mrs Delamer, and most likely her mother as well, had been making plans to bind them together.

'There never was a Mr Pimlico, was there?' she said instead.

'I suspect not.'

She groaned, and, resting her elbows on the table, dropped her head into her hands.

'I don't know what to say, Hugh. . . I promise you, I had no hand in this! I know you have no reason to believe me. . . '

'Of course I believe you,' he cut in. 'I have little doubt this is all Mrs Delamer's doing.'

'If only I had had your insight,' she said bitterly, sitting back in her chair. 'But perhaps we are wrong. Would she go to such lengths? And, why?'

'I have always thought her perfectly capable of doing anything necessary to achieve her aims, although I know nothing of her reasons.'

'So it was she who held the St Mawes' mortgage all this time! And yet she told me the only money my father ever borrowed from her was for his horses.'

She took a sip of water to calm herself, but it had no beneficial effect.

'Do you know why she might wish to hide the truth from you?' Hugh asked gently.

'My father's pride, most likely,' she replied with a sigh. 'He would not have liked it to be known that he was beholden to her. And after he passed... well, I suppose for a similar reason: my own pride. I have always refused to accept money from her.'

She looked down at her glass and traced the etchings in the crystal with her finger.

'I can forgive her deception with regards to this first part,' she said after some moments. 'She no doubt meant it for the best, however high-handed. But the other part - to use the mortgage to bind us together in some plot to suit her own wishes - *that* is unforgiveable!'

'And what, do you suppose, are her wishes?' Hugh asked, looking at her intently.

She lifted her eyes to his.

'Can you not see?' she said, her anger burning away her embarrassment. 'Mrs Delamer appears to harbour a determined wish to see us end up together - the Lord only knows why! Even if we were both inclined to it, which clearly we are not, how does she expect you to honourably end your engagement to Miss Starling? She must realise you would never do so dishonourably. But it appears her delusion knows no bounds! She sees fit to play with us as if we are nothing more than pawns in her game with no will of our own... *argh*, it is beyond anything!'

The sound of breaking glass penetrated her anger.

She looked down at her hand and saw the delicate crystal water glass had shattered in her grip.

As if from a great distance she watched as the first drops of crimson fell onto the pristine white tablecloth.

In the next instant, her hand was snatched up and Hugh began picking shards of glass from her flesh. She had no recollection of how he had moved to her side.

214

After a silence of some minutes, he said roughly: 'There... that appears to be the last of them.'

He bound up her hand in a clean napkin and pressed down against the small wounds.

'Ouch!' she cried out.

'Let that be a lesson to you to better control that temper of yours!' he snapped, barely in control of his own. 'You're lucky the cuts are not an inch higher on the wrist. If they were, there is little I or anyone else could have done to save you.'

For a reason at present unknown to her, tears welled in her eyes and she turned her face away from him.

'Come, what is this? Don't cry,' he commanded. 'Does it still pain you?'

She shook her head.

Hugh drew her to his chest and put a protective arm around her.

'What then?' he asked in a gentler tone. 'Don't tell me you have allowed my own wretched temper to affect you? You are perfectly capable of putting me in my place when I deserve it.'

'And you so often deserve it,' she replied with a weak chuckle, feeling innumerably better.

'That's more like it!' He released her and went on: 'Now, come with me. We need to clean the wounds before we bandage you up properly.'

'They are hardly wounds. Mere scratches... and look, the bleeding has almost stopped.'

'For God's sake, keep that pressed down! And for once allow someone else to take control of a matter you know nothing about! How many festering wounds have you had to deal with? I can assure you, whatever the number, you have never been in battle and can't better my experience!'

Thinking his reaction was out of all proportion, she was about to tell him as much when she noticed his eyes were conveying their own message. This man, who would never belong to her, cared deeply about her wellbeing.

'You know, you can tell me you are worried about me without shouting at me,' she said with a soft smile, teasing him a little.

'Levity again, Miss Hartwood?' he asked dangerously.

'Forgive me, it is *most* inappropriate,' she replied, constraining her smile. 'And you are right, I did not consider infection.'

Hugh grunted in response, and, still scowling, led her out of the room and up the stairs to her bedchamber. He left her in the care of her maid and went off to find the supplies he needed.

He returned within ten minutes with a bottle of whisky and some bandages.

He picked up the bowl from the washstand and pulled up a chair to sit opposite April, beside the fire. Putting the bowl on his lap, he held her hand over it and proceeded to slowly pour the contents of the bottle over her wounds.

While he was concentrating on his task, April said to her maid: 'Rachel, can you please let the housekeeper know she will need to change the tablecloth in the dining room. I'm afraid it is splattered with blood.'

'Don't leave,' Hugh ordered the girl without looking up. 'You may ring for one of the other staff to relay the message, or wait until I'm finished.'

Annoyed at having her instructions to her own servant countered in such a highhanded manner, April asked him: 'Do you mean to explain yourself?'

'Considering how many times I've had to speak to you on the subject, I would have thought by now my reasoning would be plainly obvious.'

'You cannot mean to keep Rachel in the room as a chaperone? It is not as if we are in public.'

'Worse – we are in your bedchamber!' he retorted, happy to give free rein to his temper and put an end to the harmony that had grown between them. 'And although you may not care about people's opinion of your morals, I have no wish to have mine unduly remarked upon.'

'If your morals are so wounded by your presence in my bedchamber, then I can only wonder as to why you saw fit to bring me here.'

'Had I known you were so indelicate as to prefer me to dress your wounds in a more public setting, I would have obliged you.'

April's eyes flashed as she struggled to swallow the sharp retort on her lips. She did not know why he had suddenly turned antagonistic, she only knew it would be beneath her to continue to engage with him.

And so, she held her tongue and allowed him to continue binding her hand.

The moment he was finished, she thanked him with frosty civility, rose to her feet and exited the room without another word.

Hugh returned his chair to its place by the window and gathered up the bowl and soiled napkin.

'I'll take them, sir,' said Rachel, rushing forward to relieve him of the items.

He thanked her absentmindedly.

The bleak look in his eyes emboldened the maid to say: 'I'm certain Miss is grateful for your assistance, sir.'

'I don't want her gratitude,' he replied grimly, and stalked out of the room.

Thirty-Four

After leaving her bedchamber, April went downstairs to the music parlour and vented her tangled emotions on her grandmother's prized Clementi piano.

With one hand heavily bandaged, it was an indifferent practice, and by the time His Grace and Mr Kepling made an appearance she was happy to be cajoled into joining them in the connecting room while they breakfasted.

She was part way through an edited explanation as to the cause of the injury to her hand when the Starling ladies joined them.

Mother and daughter glided into the room, a picture of femininity, and graciously greeted April and His Grace, who were already seated at the table. They then joined Mr Kepling at the sideboard, where he was serving himself, and proceeded to engage him in what appeared to be a mutually enjoyable conversation.

'When my cousin turns his attention on our companions,' observed His Grace, leaning closer to April, 'they become so agreeable I have never liked them better!'

'It would be difficult to be anything but agreeable in Alfie's company,' she replied. 'He is exceptionally good-natured.'

'True, however, the effect is particularly pronounced in this instance. One can almost warm to Mrs Starling – which is saying a great deal! And as for Miss Starling, we have all suffered from her diligent attempts to be amiable, but it is only with my cousin that she truly achieves her objective. Her practised performance is forgotten and she blossoms into a remarkably charming girl. . . surely you have noticed?'

April had not noticed.

Disconcerted by what he might mean, she turned to observe Miss Starling as she conversed with Mr Kepling.

'I suppose there is an openness to her that is not usually there,' she admitted.

'And note the blushes! It is almost as if she is...oh, but *of course*!' he exclaimed dramatically, a sparkle of mischief in his eye. 'Why did I not think of it before? My cousin and Miss Starling would be an ideal coupling!'

April looked at him sharply, frowning.

'Perhaps it never occurred to you because Miss Starling is betrothed to Mr Royce.'

'No, that's not it,' he replied incorrigibly.

'Eustace! It would be most improper to attempt to break off their engagement!'

'But if Miss Starling were to break it off, surely then there could be no objection?'

'There might be at least *one* objection.'

'You are thinking of Mr Royce? Never fear, *he* won't object. He is as pleasantly indifferent to Miss Starling as she is to him. In fact, I have reason to believe he would be greatly relieved.'

'Unless you are in his confidence, you can know nothing of the sort!'

'Unlike some I could mention – if I did not so lamentably lack the courage – I have never been blind to Mr Royce's feelings on this particular subject.'

'I fail to understand you when you become clever,' she said tetchily.

'Fail or wilfully refuse?'

She threw him a reproving look.

'It is entirely Mr Royce's affair if he has chosen Miss Starling. Whether or not we believe them to be ill-matched is irrelevant.'

'I never said they were ill-matched.'

'Did you not?' she said, looking self-conscious. 'I supposed that was what you meant.'

'Not at all! I do not doubt they would have had a tolerably successful marriage, if fate had not presented them with a more perfect alternative.'

'And I suppose you would be *delighted* to have Mrs Starling in the family?' she rallied, raising an eyebrow at him. 'Can you tell me with all honesty that you would want such a mother-in-law for Alfie?'

'She may not be to our taste, but we cannot deny my cousin is not as fastidious,' he replied regretfully. 'And besides, Mrs Starling's character resembles his mother's, so he is well accustomed to being managed and led. He cannot be content unless he surrenders his will to another.'

'How... *appalling*,' she remarked, taken aback.

'That does not make it untrue.'

'Well, no, but…oh, please don't meddle, Eustace! There are enough people in this house who see fit to meddle in matters that don't concern them. You cannot throw two people together and hope for a foregone conclusion. Love is not so easily conjured up!'

'Perhaps not. But once its tender shoots have sprung forth of their own accord, is it so wrong to offer them a little assistance to grow in a direction better suited to all?'

'You should have become a poet,' she observed dryly.

'But am I wrong?'

April held his gaze for few moments, before looking away and playing with the place setting before her.

'You have failed to take into account that I have no wish to be saddled with that man,' she said crossly, no longer pretending to misunderstand him. 'If you only knew the harsh things he has said to me throughout our acquaintance – including this very morning! – you would not be so hasty to pair us together. Sometimes I can almost believe he dislikes me!'

'Has it not occurred to you, my dear, that knowing himself to be shackled he believes he must do what he can to repel you? For honour's sake, and for his own sanity.'

'That is simply conjecture on your part! I will not allow you to so neatly explain away the defects of his character… and even if, by some miracle, you were correct, you must realise I don't want…he is not what I…' She broke off in frustration.

'It is difficult to lie to yourself, is it not?'

Before April could tell him it was no such thing, Mrs Delamer and Lady Hartwood walked into the dining room.

Her annoyance suddenly found a new outlet and, on the spur of the moment, she decided to teach them both a well-earned lesson.

'Eustace, I want you to make love to me,' she said urgently under her breath.

'Here?' he asked with a good deal of amusement.

'Yes, you provoking creature! You know very well I mean *flirt* with me. It must appear as if we are on the brink of making a connection.'

'And are we?'

'Of course not! Pray don't be difficult, I need your help. There are certain persons present who must be brought to realise their scheming will only produce an outcome they never desired.'

'If you wish to teach Mrs Delamer and your mother a lesson I am at your disposal.' He laughed at her vexed expression. 'Surely you did not expect me to misunderstand you?'

'No, however, I had hoped the discretion on which you pride yourself would have made an appearance.'

His Grace took hold of her unbound hand and kissed it reverentially.

'For you, fair Aphrodite, anything!' he declared.

April offered him a demure smile, happy in the knowledge that all eyes were on them.

After allowing her hand to remain in his for a suitably noteworthy length of time, she removed it and picked up her teacup.

Under cover of taking a sip, she said softly: 'Perfect!'

Thirty-Five

April and His Grace flirted their way through the next few hours in full view of their desired audience; an easy state of affairs to arrange as there was a snowstorm raging outside and everyone was confined to the house.

Their efforts were greeted with a variety of reactions, depending on the predispositions of each spectator.

Mrs Bolton and Mr Oatley welcomed the display with amusement and the occasional gleeful glance in Hugh's direction.

Mrs Starling, when her thoughts were not centred on Sir Yarmouth and his flattering attentions, resigned herself to the notion that an engagement between April and His Grace was imminent, and, apart from some superior looks, took as lenient a view of the matter as could to be expected.

Her daughter, on the other hand, felt compelled to voice her disapproval to Mr Kepling and attempted to draw him into condemning the amorous couple's behaviour. But Mr Kepling's temperament and deep affection for his cousin overrode all self-righteous inclinations, and within a short space of time he had managed to cajole Miss Starling into exercising the compassionate side of her nature.

Lord Wulfingston, Lord Paisley, General Simpson and Sir Yarmouth spent a good part of the day playing whist and faro in one of the reception rooms, and, for the times they were in the couple's presence, April's sense of decorum shied away from any outrageous displays of affection.

So, there were in fact only three people who were unduly affected by April's and the duke's determined flirting.

After recovering from the shock of seeing her daughter making a spectacle of herself with the wrong gentleman, Lady Hartwood attempted to drop a hint in her ear that her behaviour was unbecoming. April's conscience was stung by her mother's evident distress, however, she was reconciled to her course by a deep-seated conviction that she would have been spared her mother's reproaches had her flirting been directed at Hugh.

Mrs Delamer kept her emotions better hidden than her daughter, but it was clear that she too was greatly displeased.

After one of April's particularly coquettish displays of partiality, when the opportunity for a private word presented itself, she told her granddaughter with some astringency: 'If you lean into His Grace any closer when you speak to him, you may as well sit on his lap!'

Lady Hartwood, also present, added: 'Indeed, love, it is *most* unseemly! What in the world has led you to behave in such a way?'

'But I thought this is what you both wanted?' replied April, all innocence.

'Certainly not!' said Lady Hartwood, looking shocked. 'It may have *seemed* as if we had a preference for His Grace...'

'Yes, it certainly *did* seem that way to me,' April could not help interrupting.

Her ladyship coloured faintly but persevered: 'But, love, it has been clear for weeks that you have little interest in *that* direction.'

'I have changed my mind!' declared April.

'Then you should prepare to be a wife in name only!' her grandmother said bitterly, entering the fray. 'The duke, you may as well know, is not interested in your sex. What have you to say to that?'

'Oh, *that* I know already,' April replied with great nonchalance.

Her grandmother's eyes flashed with annoyance.

'Do you? Then you should also know he is unlikely to go to the effort of siring an heir. Are you prepared to sacrifice the prospect of children?'

'Perhaps you should have considered that when you forced me into the position of trying to attach him,' April all but snapped.

'Oh, no, not *forced*, love!' Lady Hartwood cried weakly. 'Perhaps there was some *persuasion*, but it was meant for the best.'

'The best for whom?' asked April indignantly.

'For you, of course!'

'To marry a man who can never love me as I wish, and is unlikely to give me children? That is hardly what I would call the best for me!'

'Yes, *most* unsuitable,' agreed Lady Hartwood, oblivious to her mother's warning look. 'But we never wished for you to marry His Grace.'

Mrs Delamer rolled her eyes in exasperation.

April felt a strong desire to press them further, until they admitted their true purpose was to orchestrate a match between herself and Hugh. However, such a declaration would only bring an early end to the lesson she was intent on teaching them, and so she forced a smile.

'It matters not, Mama,' she said in a more conciliatory tone. 'I'm perfectly content with how matters stand. I have decided I have a fancy to become a duchess.'

'No grandchildren?' wailed Lady Hartwood.

April almost crumbled at this point and confessed all.

Happily for the success of her plan, His Grace approached with her lemonade and begged her to honour him with a game of chess. As they walked away to the other side of the room, where the chessboard had been set up, April thanked him for his timely intervention.

'I am, as always, yours to command,' he said with a dramatic flourish of the hand. 'Only, I fear that in doing my very agreeable duty to you I may have placed myself in great jeopardy. I hold quite firm suspicions that I will not live out the day. You may have noticed, ever since I had the happy notion to sit beside you on the window seat and read you poetry, Mrs Delamer has been staring daggers at me. As for Mr Royce, before he detached his fiancée from my cousin and bore her away, he gave me the cut direct! Honesty compels me to warn you that I am not the bravest of men. If he should try to force a quarrel on me, for the privilege of calling me out, I am likely to betray you and admit the whole to him!'

April laughed perfunctorily at this foolishness and pointed out, somewhat tartly, that it clearly mattered not to Mr Royce to whom she gave her affections, for his attention had been fixed on Miss Starling ever since he had deigned to join them downstairs, and, at the first opportunity offered, he had invented an excuse to be alone with her.

Which was only as it should be, she added with a deflated look in her eyes.

Thirty-Six

Despite April's thoughts to the contrary, Hugh's attention had been fixed on her from the moment he had entered the reception room to find His Grace reading to her in the intimate setting of the window embrasure.

It had taken him several minutes, in fact, to realise that his fiancée was even in the room. And, on perceiving her, he had not gone immediately to her side. Instead, under cover of pouring himself a drink, he had watched her as she sat happily employed in the task of sketching Mr Kepling's likeness, while this gentleman remained as still as he could beside her and kept her amused with his chatter.

An arrested expression had settled over Hugh's countenance as he watched them; and for the first time in many weeks the feeling of being trapped had begun to ease. After finishing his drink, he had walked over to them and asked Miss Starling for a few moments of her time.

She had looked a little startled but declared herself delighted to oblige him, and, excusing herself to Mr Kepling, had allowed herself to be escorted from the room.

But as Hugh now led her across the hall to the library, she was conscious of a feeling of dread. She felt herself to be in the wrong and wondered why that should be the case.

After all, Alfred was simply a friend to her and her mother. . . and so she would inform Mr Royce should he be so impertinent as to question her on the matter.

It was not as if she held him in deep affection. . . at least, not in any *inappropriate* way.

And it was not her fault she had frequently found herself in his company over the last few weeks. It was only natural he sought out her mother to reminisce about his dear departed parent, so no one could wonder at the fact that he could be found at her house on most days.

And even if she had been so foolish as to develop a partiality for him, she thought miserably, she knew where her duty lay.

Hugh read the apprehension in Miss Starling's eyes and made an effort to smile. He had given her cause to be anxious around him of late with his boorish behaviour.

'When we first entered into our engagement, Miss Starling,' he began gently, 'I believe we did so as friends, and were truthful with each other as to our wishes and expectations. I hope we can be as truthful now as we were in the beginning?'

Miss Starling nodded, her nervousness only increased by this speech. Some instinct for self-preservation warned her that the termination of her engagement was imminent, and, until this moment, she had not fully appreciated how truly brilliant a match she had secured for herself and her family.

To lose Mr Royce now would plunge her into public scrutiny (and even ridicule!) and would certainly bring her mother's censure down upon her.

Hugh was aware of the pragmatic nature of her dilemma but he kept his annoyance firmly in check. It would be idiosyncratic of him to expect anything more profound from her; their relationship had always been more in line with a business arrangement than a romantic attachment.

'I have come to suspect,' he said, 'that your feelings may have undergone a change since our betrothal was announced. I want you to know, if you wish to break off our engagement you need only say so and you'll have my complete support.'

'Oh no!' breathed Miss Starling, looking wretched.

'You have nothing to fear, I promise you! I'll make certain I alone bear any recriminations. My temperament is well known and no one will wonder at you for making so sensible a decision. As for any concerns you may have that your mother will be displeased, I'll make generous financial reparations that will preclude her from viewing the matter with anything but indulgence.'

'Mr Royce, I-I am deeply sorry if I have given you the least indication that. . . that I wish to break off our engagement. I assure you, sir, I. . . '

'You need not assure me now!' he cut in, anger creeping into his voice. 'I suggest you give the matter the proper thought it deserves before we speak on it again.'

He might understand her predicament, however, he was not so magnanimous that he could pretend to be content with her hasty disregard for their future happiness in light of more worldly considerations.

Miss Starling nodded glumly and allowed him to escort her back to the reception room.

But when he attempted to return her to her seat beside Mr Kepling she demurred, saying she had been neglecting her mother, and, excusing herself to both gentlemen, left them and went to sit beside Mrs Starling.

As Sir Yarmouth's card game had come to an end, Mrs Starling was once again enjoying his attentions and it was uncertain if she appreciated her daughter's show of filial duty.

From his position at the chess table, His Grace observed the whole with an amused eye.

'Mr Royce appears to have bungled a relatively simple matter,' he remarked to April. 'If only he had stayed in character and ranted and raved at Miss Starling, forbidding her to go near my cousin, he would have better achieved his aim. I suppose it is left to me to mend matters! Really, it is quite exhausting minding other people's business for them.'

'You must be mistaken. I cannot imagine he would be eager for Miss Starling to transfer her affections to your cousin,' she said mildly, resisting an urge to look over her shoulder at Hugh.

'There is nothing to transfer. He never had her affections. In fact, I would not be at all surprised if he took her out of the room just now to convince her to break off their engagement. . . and failed miserably, judging by the look on his face.'

April could resist no longer and her eyes found Hugh across the room. His countenance was set along grim lines; but he was not looking at Miss Starling, he was looking at her.

She quickly lowered her gaze.

'You mistake his thoughts. His black mood appears to be directed at me. He has evidently found something else to disparage about me.'

'For someone of your undeniable intelligence, it often surprises me. . .'

'Checkmate!' she snapped and swiped his king with undue violence. 'And now, I believe I will retire and recoup my strength before dinner.'

'My dear, those stormy looks might stir Mr Royce with unbridled passion but they are quite lost on me,' he said provocatively. 'And they are certainly not in keeping with the little charade we were putting on for everyone's enjoyment – is it at an end?'

She looked torn for a moment; then, shaking her head at him, she recovered her smile and said: 'You are quite maddening on occasion, Eustace, did you know that? However, I am indebted to you for humouring me. . . the charade continues.'

'In that case…'

He took her hand to help her to rise, and, placing it in the crook of his arm, escorted her to the doors leading to the corridor.

'Until tonight, fair Aphrodite!' he announced and kissed her fingers.

Lord Wulfingston, who was standing nearby, turned abruptly and stared at them; his expression oddly arrested.

His gaze then travelled across the room, to where Mrs Delamer was allowing General Simpson to educate her on her porcelain collection, and remained fixed there.

After some minutes, his son drew his notice by tapping him on the shoulder and informing him that Mrs Bolton had just addressed him.

Lord Wulfingston asked her to repeat her remark, but in so abrupt a manner that Lord Paisley was dismayed by his lack of courtesy.

'Father, please,' he objected under his breath.

'Good God, Albert!' snapped Lord Wulfingston. 'You can't think Mrs Bolton cares a jot for flowery manners? Do you, ma'am? I may have only recently made your acquaintance but it doesn't seem to me that you dabble in hypocrisy.'

While Mrs Bolton was cackling with laughter at such an accurate assessment of her character, His Grace was standing in the doorway and making a show of watching April walk up the central staircase.

'Laying it on too thick, Claredon,' Hugh observed dispassionately, coming to stand beside him. 'A little less ardour and you could almost be believable.'

'Not at all!' replied His Grace, smiling. 'Miss Hartwood inspires the utmost of chivalry in one.'

'If by chivalry you mean a desire to throttle her, then yes, I agree! But make no mistake, if whatever game you're playing should end with her feelings being injured, I'll hold you personally responsible.'

And on those sinister words, he quit the room for the sanctuary of the library.

His Grace looked after him, a mischievous smile playing about his lips.

'What do you make of Mr Royce?' asked Mr Kepling, materialising at his side suddenly.

'Why? Has he been uncivil?'

'Oh, no, no! Quite the opposite, actually! He was…well, not friendly exactly, but pleasant. Makes it hard to dislike the fellow. Not that I have cause to dislike him, of course! It just seems a shame someone as sweet and innocent as Miss Starling should be forced into marriage with a man of his stamp.'

'I do not believe she is being forced per se,' said His Grace with wonderful understatement.

'Well, perhaps not forced in the usual sense. But I fear she has been driven by circumstance into an engagement she has come to regret. I know it's none of my business, only it makes a fellow wish there was something he could do to help her.'

'Does it? I cannot say I suffer from any such wish.'

'Yes I know *you* wouldn't, but. . . what I mean is. . . '

'I beg you do not put yourself to the trouble of explaining it to me! I believe I understand you well enough. What has Mr Royce done to make you seek my opinion of him?'

'It was dashed odd. If you can believe it, he's been quizzing me on my prospects. If he had a daughter to marry off I'd be worried he was sizing me up as husband material!'

His Grace chuckled to himself.

Finding his cousin's questioning gaze on him, he said: 'It is always gratifying when one's instincts are proven correct. . . no, do not ask me to enlighten you! It would be quite impossible to explain it all without affecting the outcome. And, if we are to have a happy conclusion to this comedy, the Chorus cannot interact with the actors.'

'Sometimes, Eustace, you say the damnedest things!' objected Mr Kepling.

Thirty-Seven

April attempted to put on the white evening gloves her maid had handed to her, however, her bandaged hand would not fit within the tight silk sheath so she gave up and handed them back. Tonight was Christmas Eve and dinner was to be a formal affair, but it would be ludicrous for her to go downstairs with only one glove on.

She walked over to the mirror and studied her reflection with a critical eye.

The scarlet velvet dress was exquisite and revealed every inch of skin allowed within the bounds of propriety; it was the only one she had managed to save from the demure fate her grandmother had inflicted on the rest of her new wardrobe.

It had small puff sleeves that sat off the shoulder and it moulded itself tightly to her bust, before falling to her feet in graceful folds and pooling in a demi-train behind her.

'It looks magnificent on you, miss!' Rachel exclaimed with breathless admiration. 'What a pleasure it is to dress you in something so *modish*.'

April laughed and threw her maid a twinkling look.

'Modish or indecent? After dressing so modestly for weeks, the experience appears to have left its mark on me. I find the woman in the mirror rather brazen! Are you certain the amount of bosom I have on display is not beyond what is acceptable?'

'It is entirely respectable, miss, I promise you. If you remember, for your dinner party in London, Miss Starling wore a blue gown that was cut just as low across the bust, and no one could accuse *her* of being fast.'

Rachel could have added that Miss Starling was not as shapely and could therefore wear more daringly cut gowns. But this was the first opportunity she had had to show off her mistress to her full advantage and she was not inclined to sabotage it; and certainly not when she was assailed by the pleasant notion that she would now be able to settle a score with Miss Starling's maid, who had directed several snide remarks at her since their arrival yesterday, laying the blame for Miss Hartwood's conservative appearance at her feet.

'Hmm. . . perhaps you are right,' said April, looking herself over one last time before turning away. 'In any case, it will serve its purpose.'

What better way to show her grandmother she would accept no more dictates from her?

And if a certain gentleman was brought to realise what it was he could never have, who was she to quibble?

Such an improper thought may have been unworthy of her but she was a woman first and foremost and a lady second, and Hugh's harsh words from earlier, and his subsequent avoidance of her, rankled more than she cared to admit.

These reflections brought a certain intensity to her countenance and by the time she entered the music parlour, where some of the guests had already gathered before dinner, she was looking magnificent and rather forbidding.

'I say!' exclaimed General Simpson, raising his quizzing-glass for a better view.

Sir Yarmouth noticed his friend's preoccupation and abruptly broke off his conversation with Mrs Starling. On realising who had stolen his attention away from her, the matron was roused to jealousy and muttered 'indecent' for all to hear.

'Oh hush!' Mrs Bolton rebuked her. 'The dear girl looks utterly beautiful!'

'I do not dispute her beauty,' Mrs Starling replied in a superior way. 'But if *my* daughter decided to make a spectacle of herself in such a dress I would be mortified.'

'I should think so! She'd never carry it off,' said Mrs Bolton with a waspish chuckle that made Mrs Starling bristle. 'And you know, dear, there is no point pretending to be prudish *now*. I distinctly remember that at the Wentworth masked ball last year, you wore a Marie Antoinette costume that even I would have blushed to own in my youth!'

Rather startled by the elderly lady's excellent memory, Mrs Starling attempted to explain that her fichu had been lost in the crush.

She was silenced by an all-too-knowing look.

Feeling smug over her victory in this little skirmish, Mrs Bolton turned to Mr Oatley and asked: 'Our Miss Hartwood looks ravishing, don't you agree, sir?'

'Indeed, madam, indeed!' he replied, his eyes twinkling merrily amongst the folds of his numerous wrinkles.

Mrs Starling knew herself to be outnumbered and decided on a different strategy. She clutched Sir Yarmouth's arm and in a weak voice begged him to procure a glass of water for her as she was feeling faint.

The amiable roué was all solicitude and, after gallantly assisting her to sit down, rushed off to do her bidding.

Hugh was in conversation with Lord Wulfingston, a little apart from the others, and did not notice April until his grandfather put up his quizzing-glass and looked past him.

Assailed by a sudden feeling of foreboding, Hugh slowly turned. . . and found himself staring at a defiant goddess.

He wrenched his gaze away, jaw clenched rigid.

Lord Wulfingston dropped his quizzing-glass and, throwing Hugh a look of wicked amusement, walked across the room to April's side.

'Well played,' he told her as he bowed over her hand. 'I'm inclined to think that if my grandson doesn't come up to scratch soon, he doesn't deserve you!'

'You mistake the matter, your lordship,' April replied coolly.

Lord Wulfingston laughed and regarded her with a good deal of cynicism.

'My dear girl, I've been around long enough to recognise female tactics when I see them! May I pour you a glass of Madeira? Or perhaps you prefer some punch? We were told it was made to a special recipe conceived by our hostess.'

'Scotch, if you please.'

Lord Wulfingston's brows rose slightly.

'You are in luck, Miss Hartwood. You appear to share the same tastes as Mrs Delamer. She keeps her liquor trolley well stocked with whisky.'

Peremptorily taking her hand and placing it on his arm, he led her over to his grandson, and, after advising him to refrain from boring her, went off to procure her drink.

'Good evening,' said Hugh, offering her a formal bow.

'Good evening,' she replied, inclining her head regally.

They regarded each other warily.

'How is your hand?' he asked.

Her fingers closed reflexively into her palm and she felt the sting of the wounds. 'Better, thank you.'

'If it should become inflamed tomorrow you must tell m. . . Mrs Delamer, so that she can call a doctor.'

'That won't be necessary. It is not. . .'

'For God's sake!' he snapped, making her start. 'Don't be a fool! You can hardly want to bring about your own demise simply for the pleasure of spiting me?'

She glared at him, then lowered her gaze to get herself under control.

It did not take long. The concern underlying his words was once more plainly evident.

She allowed herself to consider the possibility that Eustace was correct and it was circumstance alone that kept Hugh playing the role of antagonist. It was a possibility that greatly rattled her, and she did not have the luxury of time at present to sort out her jumbled thoughts.

When she looked back up at him, the goddess had disappeared and in her place stood a bewildered young lady.

'I will follow your advice,' she said briefly. 'Now, if you will excuse me...' And she walked off.

Hugh's hand stretched out towards her of its own volition.

He quickly brought it back under control and, gripping both hands behind his back, walked over to the windows to watch the snow as it fell in soft flurries against the glass.

April joined Lord Wulfingston beside the drinks trolley and accepted the glass he held out to her.

She took a healthy sip, and, meeting his probing gaze, raised an eyebrow to challenge his scrutiny.

'You don't greatly resemble the women in your family,' he observed. 'Perhaps only a slight similarity about the eyes.'

'My mother and I are quite different in looks.'

'Did I hear Claredon call you Aphrodite earlier?'

This question was so unexpected she answered with less than her usual calm: 'Oh... why, yes... he did do so... but it is nothing more than a foolish name he invented to tease me.'

'I once knew another called by the name Aphrodite,' he said meditatively. 'She used to wear the most charming bows around her neck! Silk, from memory. We were all in love with her, back in the day – face, figure, spirit, all were perfection! And her wit, when she deigned to turn it on us, was razor sharp. A heady combination for greenhorns, I can tell you.'

'I imagine it would have been,' she said, smiling politely. 'She sounds fascinating. You make me wish I had known her.'

'Perhaps you did.'

'I do not know anyone worthy of such an impressive description! At least, I do not think I do. What was her name?'

'Lucille Nelson.'

'I have never heard of her.'

'Some fifty years ago, she was the most celebrated courtesan in all of Paris!'

April almost dropped her glass.

It took all her self-control to assume the affronted mien of a young lady who had just been confronted with a reference to the demi-monde.

'Naturally, I can have no knowledge of such things,' she said in an indignant tone.

'Did I wound your delicate sensibilities?' he drawled. 'You must allow me to beg your pardon.'

'Lord Wulfingston, I do not understand what you hope to achieve by this deliberate attempt to shock me?'

'I hold, not unfounded, hopes that our conversation will reach the ears of Mrs Delamer... although really it would be more accurate to call her *Madame De La Mer.*'

'Why should the French pronunciation be more...'

She gasped, a hand flying to her mouth.

'Dear Lord,' she murmured, utterly stunned. '*De la mer*... from the sea.'

'Well done, Miss Hartwood!' he said approvingly. 'Yes, Aphrodite was indeed born from the sea, in fully formed perfection. A nice touch, isn't it? You have to give her credit for so cleverly hiding in plain sight.'

'No, it is not possible! It would be ludicrous to suppose she would be so... so...'

'Brazen?' supplied Lord Wulfingston. 'I remember her audacity knew no bounds! It's little wonder she had Paris at her feet.'

April made an effort to gather her scattered wits.

'You do have some fantastical notions, your lordship!' she said with a shaky laugh. 'I have been vastly entertained, but now I must go and...'

'Yes, go,' he interrupted. 'There's not the least need to make up an excuse for my benefit.'

'I can see where your grandson learnt his manners!' she observed tartly.

Putting her glass back down on the drinks trolley, she offered him an inclination of the head and walked quickly out of the room.

Thirty-Eight

April intercepted her grandmother on the stairs as she was making her way down.

Her well-preserved relative was looking particularly attractive in a gown of bronze satin, worn with gloves of the same colour, and with an ornate diamond necklace displayed against her milky white *décolleté*.

'Oh, thank goodness I have found you!' April exclaimed in an urgent whisper.

Giving her grandmother no opportunity to speak, she linked arms with her and led her to the nearest room at the bottom of the staircase, which happened to be the library, and shut the door.

'What are you about, child?' asked Mrs Delamer, none-too-pleased to be manhandled in such a way. 'And why are you wearing that dress?'

'Because I wanted to!' replied April, momentarily sidetracked. 'And there is no point pretending His Grace won't like it, for I know for a fact he will!'

Mrs Delamer looked her over with careful consideration.

'Hmm, perhaps tonight is the perfect night after all. It is certainly an impossible dress to ignore.'

'Forget the dress! I did not bring you in here to talk of my clothing. Lord Wulfingston knows all!'

'I beg you refrain from going into theatrics. Tell me simply what you mean.'

'Lord Wulfingston overheard His Grace call me *Aphrodite*,' said April, clasping her hands together in agitation and then wincing in pain.

'His Grace calls you Aphrodite, does he?' laughed Mrs Delamer. 'Well, well. . . that is certainly ironic!'

'Ironic? Whatever can you mean?' asked April with feigned innocence. 'Lord Wulfingston appeared to find it merely amusing. And he fell into reminiscing of another Aphrodite he knew fifty years ago. . . a courtesan. . . *in Paris!*'

Mrs Delamer's rich laughter filled the air.

April regarded her with exasperation and added wryly: 'So yes, you are quite correct to call it ironic.'

'He has worked it out at last – it took him long enough! Why, he was one of my most determined admirers. He even lost his head one night and asked me to. . . but that is unimportant.'

'God give me strength,' April exhaled. 'Did you actually want him to uncover the truth? After all the years you drummed into Mama and I how we were to keep our relationship a secret – why, it's the outside of enough!'

'Do, I beg you, rein in these tumults of emotion. There's no reason to suppose he knows of our connection.'

'He may not know, but he certainly suspects! He told me I did not resemble the *women* in my family.'

Mrs Delamer smiled and lifted a perfectly shaped eyebrow.

'I am almost flattered by such perception after the passage of five decades.'

'Aren't you concerned?' asked April, quite bewildered.

'No, of course not! I'll say this for Barnaby, he was never a puritan.'

'But that was a long time ago.'

'I have spent some time in his company over the last few weeks and I still hold by my opinion. Still, one cannot help wondering what he'll do next with the information. It's really quite stimulating not knowing what to expect!'

April marvelled at her sang-froid.

'Really, Grandmama, to hear you talk one would suppose this is nothing but a game to you.'

'For the brave, what is life but a game of our own choosing?'

Suddenly remembering another grievance, April asked: 'Why did you never tell me your real name was Lucille Nelson? Or the reason you chose the name *De-la-mer*? I had to find out from Lord Wulfingston, of all people!'

'There was no reason for you to know,' said Mrs Delamer simply.

'I suppose I should have expected that answer,' said April, smiling resignedly. 'I am in awe of your audacity. Still, I can barely believe you would do anything so foolhardy as to call yourself *from the sea* when you were known as Aphrodite. If Lord Wulfingston could decipher the meaning, then surely there was a danger of others doing so?'

'I could not resist,' said her grandmother, the naughty gleam of a much younger woman in her eyes. 'And what you cannot realise, child, is that the fashion of the time lent itself to me creating whatever character I wished, with little chance of discovery. The face paint, wigs, and clothes I wore in Paris as Lucille Nelson, courtesan, were not the same as those I put on as Mrs Delamer, widow of a respectable Northumberland landowner and mistress of the Earl of Windermere. At least, not in public!' she finished with a throaty laugh.

'Thank you for putting such an image in my head!' complained April, smiling despite herself. 'I could have done without knowing that you played the courtesan for my grandfather in private.'

Mrs Delamer laughed again and it struck April that she had seen her laugh more in the last two days than during the whole course of the last year.

This thought was quickly followed by the suspicion that her grandmother was not as indifferent to Lord Wulfingston as she pretended.

'Come, child, enough of this tête-à-tête! We must not to hold up the Christmas Eve festivities.'

'But what are we to do about Lord Wulfingston?' asked April.

'Why nothing! He must be the first to act.'

Thirty-Nine

A short while later, April found herself placed between Hugh and His Grace at one end of the dinner table, while Miss Starling and Mr Kepling were seated together at the other.

This obvious ploy on her grandmother's part embarrassed April to such a degree she found it difficult to meet Hugh's eye when he attempted some mild conversation.

His efforts were perfunctory at best, in any case, and so it fell on His Grace to take up the reins and lead them through a variety of subjects that were as entertaining as they were unexceptionable.

Her friend's only misstep occurred early on, when he attempted to carry on his flirtation with her, thinking it was expected of him. But a subtle shake of her head was all that was needed to put an end to his efforts. It had never been part of her plan to put on such a performance for Hugh's benefit.

Owing to His Grace's skilful handling, April soon recovered her spirits and began to converse with her neighbours more naturally. Although she did suffer a temporary setback when Lord Wulfingston caught her eye and smiled in a manner calculated to throw her into confusion.

Fortunately, Mrs Delamer came to her rescue by drawing his notice with a remark that appeared to simultaneously amuse and put him in his place, and April was left feeling deeply thankful for her grandmother's wide experience of men, which made it possible for her to handle the earl so masterfully.

Catching April's smile as her gaze rested on Mrs Delamer and Lord Wulfingston, Hugh asked her: 'What has put that impish sparkle in your eyes? Have you perhaps noticed how well our hostess has managed to keep my grandfather from insulting the other guests?'

'As a matter of fact, I had noticed,' she replied, laughing a little. 'It is quite an achievement! But perhaps your grandfather's manners improve of their own accord when in company?'

'You're quite out there! We were in company the first time you met him and on that occasion, you'll remember, he barged into your home intent on mischief.'

'How could I forget! Mrs Delamer clearly deserves all the credit for any improvement.'

They shared a look of unholy amusement.

'He made it perfectly clear that night,' she continued, returning her attention to her plate and cutting into her game pie, 'that he was not at all reconciled to the idea of my mother marrying his son.'

'I believe he has since changed his mind.'

She faced him again, knife and fork poised, and asked eagerly: 'Do you really think so? Has he said something to you? Was it after he invited my mother and Lord Paisley to visit him at his house?'

A smile tugged at a corner of Hugh's mouth but he replied with perfect gravity: 'Yes, yes and yes.'

'Please tell me what he said?'

'He didn't go into it at any length. He simply remarked that your mother would make a better wife than my uncle deserved.'

'Oh, but that is a wonderful sign! Is that all he said?'

'Yes, I believe so.' As she turned back to her dinner, he added: 'He seemed more interested to talk of Mrs Delamer, and asked me a great many questions in that direction.'

April stilled for an instant; then raised the fork to her mouth and wrapped her lips around the morsel of pie, before slowly withdrawing the fork and laying down her cutlery with great precision.

Hugh found the whole sequence inexplicably seductive.

He looked down at his glass of burgundy, his countenance so hard and unyielding that to an observer it must have appeared that he found fault with the vintage.

'What did Lord Wulfingston want to know about Mrs Delamer?' April asked casually when she had finished her mouthful.

'Where I had met her; how long ago; that sort of thing,' he replied, keeping his eyes on his wine.

'That was some weeks ago?' she asked, frowning.

'Yes.'

'I wonder. . . could he have changed his mind about her?'

'Mrs Delamer?'

'Oh, no. . . I mean my mother. . . never mind! I spoke without thinking.'

'You believe something may have occurred to change his good opinion of her?' he asked, looking at her again.

'No,' she replied carefully, eyes flicking to Mrs Delamer. 'Nothing of that nature.'

Hugh wondered what mystery lay in Mrs Delamer's past that made it impossible for Lady Hartwood to recognise her as her mother. He doubted his grandfather would care in any case.

He certainly did not. And he was ready to annihilate anyone imprudent enough to give April one moment's pain over the matter.

'Whatever's in that mind of yours, don't let it concern you,' he said. 'Your mother and my uncle are independent of my grandfather and can control their own destiny.'

'You're right. But then, it is difficult for persons of our nature to comprehend my mother's feelings on the matter. She would be exceedingly cast down if Albert's father did not approve of her. And also, he is bound to have some sway over public opinion. Not that there is any reason why he shouldn't approve of her! He does not appear to be moralistic or prudish. . . wouldn't you agree?' she asked with a hopeful expression.

'No, my grandfather could never be accused of being either,' replied Hugh, amused.

The tentative smile she gave him clawed at his heart and he wanted nothing more than to draw her into his arms and kiss away her concerns; but until he could find a way to untangle himself from his engagement all he could do was offer her some advice.

'You know, whether or not my grandfather approves of your mother is, for the most part, irrelevant. At the risk of sounding like a coxcomb, the truth of the matter is, if *I* endorse Lady Hartwood there are few in society who would go against my judgment.'

'Oh. . . I had not considered that,' she said, breaking into a relieved smile. 'Who would have thought I would be grateful to you for puffing up your own consequence!'

Forty

A little later that same evening, when everyone was gathered in the double reception room after dinner, the butler served Mrs Delamer's specially brewed punch to all her guests, and even those who showed little inclination for it found a glass with Christmas-themed etchings thrust into their hands.

'Dear friends!' Mrs Delamer called out, claiming everyone's attention. 'Some of you I have come to know only recently, and count myself fortunate to have done so.'

She inclined her head in the direction of the Starlings; smiled at His Grace and Mr Kepling; and threw a glittering glance at Lord Wulfingston.

'Others of you,' she went on, 'I love as if you were my own family! And the rest of you old scoundrels, I have put up with you for so long – let us agree *never* to count the years! – you have embedded yourselves in my heart and my life would be poorer without you. Whatever the reasons that have brought you here, I thank you for sharing your Christmas with me.' She raised her glass. 'Let the games begin!'

To the sound of resounding cheers, Mrs Delamer finished her punch in one, and then watched with a satisfied smile as her guests followed her example.

The first parlour game of the evening was known to everyone as Cup and Ball. Each player was placed in the centre of the room and given a wooden handle with a shallow cup at the top end, which had a ball attached to it by way of a length of string.

The aim of the game was to throw the ball in the air and catch it in the cup, using only one hand, and whoever managed to do so the most times in one minute was the winner.

However, Mrs Delamer had given this children's game a greater degree of difficulty by insisting that each player was blindfolded with a piece of black silk.

Only Mrs Bolton and Mr Oatley were exempt from playing, since it was considered highly doubtful they could remain upright without the use of their eyesight.

This did not preclude Mrs Bolton from being a vocal observer, and she initiated her droll commentary by remarking in a shrill voice that it was just like Mrs Delamer to have a long piece of silk binding lying about the house.

On hearing this suggestive remark, Mrs Starling, who was already having qualms about this added element to the game, made up her mind to forbid her daughter to participate.

Before she could do so, however, a footman appeared at her elbow and refilled her punch glass. And, at the same time, Sir Yarmouth (in whose ear Mrs Delamer had dropped a quiet word) held up the piece of black silk and begged her to assist him in tying it around his eyes.

Mrs Starling tittered and demurred, but in the end did not deny him.

Finishing off her punch, she handed the empty glass to the footman, took the silk from Sir Yarmouth and proceeded to wrap it around his head with an enthusiasm that surprised her daughter.

Then, while the onlookers voiced their encouragement, she led the blinded Sir Yarmouth to the centre of the room, helpfully redirected his searching hands away from her bosom and wrapped them around the cup and ball.

It quickly became apparent that it was almost impossible to score without the use of sight. To much laughter and shouts of support, Sir Yarmouth managed to catch the ball only once.

Lord Paisley stepped up next and did not fare any better.

It was evident the ladies were holding themselves back, so Mrs Delamer went next to set an example. She succeeded in scoring three, and this amazing feat was greeted with loud cheers and much clapping.

Her competitive instincts stirred, April laughingly begged to be allowed to go next.

'And so you shall!' declared Mrs Delamer, handing over the cup and ball to her. 'Hugh, would you do the honours and tie up Miss Hartwood? I must go and speak with my butler. I can see him trying to catch my attention.'

She held out the piece of silk to him.

After a slight hesitation, Hugh came forward and took it from her. Mrs Delamer smiled her approval and walked off in the direction of Stevens, who was setting up for the next game and was quite unconscious of having done anything to attract his mistress' attention.

April's smile wavered as Hugh came to stand in front of her.

'May I?' he asked, holding up the silk with both hands.

'Of course,' she replied huskily.

He gently pressed the material against her eyes; and heard her soft intake of breath.

'Oh. . . how *extraordinary*,' she murmured and raised her fingertips to touch the silk.

With the disappearance of her sight, her blackened world took on a strangely intimate quality: the exotic feel of the silk on her face; the heat and scent emanating from the man in front of her; and the disconcerting impression that it was only the two of them in the room.

It took an inordinately long time for Hugh to wind the strip of material around her head and tie off the ends. . . or so it seemed to her.

Once he was finished, he lifted her unbandaged hand into position and wrapped it securely around the cup and ball. He then released her, and Lord Paisley, in the role of timekeeper, gave her the go-ahead to begin.

As everyone cheered her on, April threw the ball awkwardly into the air and attempted to catch it. It felt to be a hopeless task, but she was determined and after many groans of frustration, and a few shrieks of triumph, she managed to score four.

Pulling off her blindfold, she asked excitedly: 'Am I winning?'

'You certainly are, my dear!' replied Lord Paisley, smiling proudly at her.

Miss Starling took the next turn, with some urging from April and Mr Kepling, and quite by accident scored one point. She was so happy with her efforts that her pleasure was infectious, and even her mother then condescended to take her turn.

And so the game went on, with Hugh being the last of the group to step forward. Lord Wulfingston, having just completed his turn, and scored three, removed the silk from his head and held it out to Miss Starling.

'Would you care to bind your fiancé?' he asked her baldly.

Miss Starling blushed and declined the offer with a vigorous shake of her head.

'No? Too allegorical for you?' he remarked, a mocking gleam in his eyes.

'Barnaby, don't tease the child!' Mrs Delamer rebuked him.

Lord Wulfingston grinned and offered Miss Starling a trim bow as way of apology. Walking over to his grandson, he bade him to stand still and, in a rough fashion, bound the silk around his head and knotted it tightly.

'I am not your purse, sir!' objected Hugh, making his audience laugh.

He then proceeded to delight them all by surpassing April's score of four and catching his ball six times.

His win was greeted with congratulations and a good deal of banter; and when Mr Kepling pressed him to reveal his secret, he once more drew everyone's laughter by attributing his performance to a misspent youth.

This initiated a few ribald comments from those of the group who had known him before he had joined the army.

Hugh accepted their teasing in good form, but April could see he was uncomfortable with their reminiscing, and she was not at all surprised when he deflected everyone's attention away from himself by offering a toast to their hostess.

Forty-One

Next on Mrs Delamer's agenda was a game of Snapdragon, a Christmas Eve tradition that was popular with most of the guests because of its theatrical qualities.

Once everyone's punch glasses had been topped up, they all congregated around a small circular table, in the middle of which sat a shallow silver dish that contained an inch of heated brandy and a layer of raisins.

At Mrs Delamer nod, the butler and two footmen armed with long-handled snuffers proceeded to extinguish all the candles in the room, until the only light remaining came from a candle in the butler's possession.

'Oh dear me,' Mrs Starling spoke up in a fragile voice. 'How dark it is now.'

'If it will ease your fears,' said Sir Yarmouth, leaning in close to her, 'I would be honoured to place my hand at your disposal.'

'Oh, how kind, thank you, sir. But of course you mean *arm?*' she said, taking hold of his limb.

'As you wish, madam,' he replied promptly. 'I offer up any part of my anatomy to be of service to you!'

Several low chuckles were heard from the older members of the group.

Hugh went to stand beside April in the darkness, feeling protective of her. He was annoyed at Mrs Delamer for subjecting an innocent to such boisterous company.

It had not escaped his notice that their glasses were never allowed to remain empty, and although the punch tasted mild, it was not; the liquor was well masked by syrup, spices, and the juice of different fruits.

April looked up at him with a slightly perplexed expression, her befuddled mind finding it odd that he had suddenly materialised at her side.

She was glad of it, however, for it allowed her to lean into him and share something terribly amusing.

'Sir Yarmouth's attentions towards Mrs Starling are rather *warm*,' she said in a low voice, emphasising her words. 'How funny it would be if he became your father-in-law!'

'Funny is not the word I would use,' replied Hugh.

'What word *would* you use?'

'Unlikely.'

'Ah... you think his intentions are not *honourable*,' she said knowledgeably. 'You could be right. His drinking has loosened his inhibitions and we cannot, in all fairness, *expect* someone of his character to remain decorous under such circumstances.'

'And what do you know of such matters?' he asked, smiling at her in the dim light.

'I'm not *stupid*,' she stressed, swaying a little. 'I can tell when someone is foxed... *and* indelicate. I'll have you know, I have been in the presence of unconventional and *quite* liberally-minded persons my whole life!'

'Your father and mother, perhaps?'

'Well, no... not *them*.'

'Uncles and aunts?'

'I never knew them.'

'Your grandmother?'

'Yes, certainly *her*! And my grandfather, when he was alive. And their friends.'

'Sir Yarmouth and General Simpson?'

'Yes,' she replied, unaware she had been led into an indiscretion.

'Do you mean to tell me your grandparents were such loose-screws as to introduce a young girl to their set?' he asked, feeling a rush of anger.

'They were *not* loose-screws,' she objected, frowning at him. 'Only a few of their most trusted friends were ever introduced to me. And they were *very* sweet and most sincerely *tried* to be on their best behaviour.'

'Well, that's a relief,' he observed sarcastically. 'At least they tried!'

'Now, don't be disagreeable in that *odious* way you have! I don't know where you picked up such a bad habit, but you really should make a push to overcome it. You can hardly blame people for thinking you disagreeable. Why, even *I* find it difficult on occasion to remember I like you.'

'You like me, do you?' he asked, a smile in his voice.

'Of course I like you! What a sing... singu-larly stupid question. You are not quite yourself tonight, are you? Now, *hush*! Here comes Stevens to set the brandy alight and I do so love this part!'

Hugh found his arm clutched with anticipation.

He doubted she was even aware of the action, yet his whole body tensed in response.

In the dark cocoon of the reception room it felt as if they had all entered a different, more informal world; one that allowed them to drop whatever facades the years had impressed upon them. But he knew it would not do.

After an inward battle, common sense grudgingly prevailed. He removed her hand from his sleeve, and, stroking it once, allowed it to drop between them.

April did not notice, her attention on the butler as he lit the brandy with his candle. He then snuffed it out and the room was plunged into darkness, save for the soft blue light that emanated from the centre of the table.

Fourteen faces peered down at the flames licking at the edges of the silver bowl.

'You all know the rules,' said Mrs Delamer. 'And remember, the person who manages to eat the most raisins will marry their true love within one year!'

'But I know *you* have no intention to marry,' Mrs Bolton ribbed her.

'As your hostess, this game need not apply to me.'

'I object!' expostulated Lord Wulfingston beside her. 'If we are to burn ourselves in the pursuit of true love, everyone must participate.'

Mrs Delamer held his gaze for a long moment.

'As you wish, my lord,' she said coyly, raising an eyebrow. 'Far be it for me to deny you when you appear to be in one of your rare domineering moods.'

Everyone laughed at this sally, even Lord Wulfingston; his eyes never leaving her face.

She threw him a saucy look, and continued: 'We shall proceed clockwise. Mr Kepling, would you be so good as to lead us into the game?'

Mr Kepling agreed to it at once and gamely put his hand into the blue fire and plucked out a raisin. The flames appeared to try and follow him as he withdrew his hand, but he escaped unharmed and popped the heated fruit into his mouth.

After suitable applause had been given for this feat of heroism, all eyes turned on Miss Starling, on Mr Kepling's left.

Having never before participated in this game, she was a little afraid and tried to forfeit her go. However, everyone's spirits had been considerably stoked by the free-flowing punch and their cheerful prompting was also rather ruthless.

Miss Starling wished she had chosen to stand on Mr Kepling's other side (or better still, had resisted the tender smile that had beckoned her to him), but when he assured her he would come to her aid, should the need arise, she mustered her courage to please him.

Removing one of her gloves, she snatched a raisin out of the fire. Mr Kepling then surprised her by catching her hand and blowing on the fruit between her bare fingers.

'I think that should do it,' he said in a low voice, embarrassed to have followed his inclinations in front of an audience. 'We wouldn't want you to burn your lips.'

'Thank you,' murmured Miss Starling as their eyes held over their hands.

Observing them from a few feet away, Mrs Starling was struck by what an attractive couple they made; and she could not help regretting that, by all accounts, dear Roberta's son had inherited only a mere competence.

Miss Starling's thoughts were not dissimilar to her mother's as she reluctantly pulled her hand free of Mr Kepling's and, to the sound of universal approval, placed the raisin in her mouth.

The game continued in a rowdy fashion for some time, until most of the players had withdrawn to lick their wounds and only two combatants remained.

Lord Wulfingston and Hugh stared at one another over the bowl of blue fire and took turns to pick out the fruit. There was a playful rivalry in their eyes, but on the part of his lordship also a certain determination.

With only a handful of raisins left in the bowl, Hugh noticed his grandfather wince as he threw his latest catch into his mouth.

Hugh stretched a hand towards the fire, then withdrew it suddenly and said with a groan of defeat: 'No, I'm done! I've burnt myself sufficiently for one night. The game belongs to you, sir.'

Lord Wulfingston let out a shout of victory...

...and before anyone could guess what he was about he pulled Mrs Delamer into his arms and soundly kissed her.

This treatment so startled the lady that for some moments she lay inert against him, her eyes wide with shock.

Then she threw her arms around his neck and kissed him back in full abandon.

Forty-Two

Lord Wulfingston was the first to pull away.

Taking Mrs Delamer's hands into his own, he said in a voice gruff with emotion: 'Lucille, will you do me the honour of finally becoming my countess?'

A profound silence followed.

It was broken by Mrs Starling's whisper: 'Finally? Has he asked her before, then?'

Oblivious to all but the man before her, Mrs Delamer stared into his eyes.

'Marriage?' she asked at last, incredulous.

'Nothing less than marriage will do, m'dear,' replied Lord Wulfingston. 'I'm not going to lose you again to a better offer!'

April alone caught the fleeting look of vulnerability in her grandmother's eyes.

'You old fool! We hardly know each other!'

Lord Wulfingston offered her an arrogant smile.

'Whatever more there is to learn we can learn after the knot is tied! Neither one of us has the luxury of time. We might live another year or another ten, but I'll be damned if I wait another minute to call you mine... are you willing to risk it all, Aphrodite?'

His Grace flicked a surprised glance at April; while everyone else held their breath, conscious they were witnessing a moment of uncommon rarity.

Mrs Delamer laughed softly and shook her head, seemingly unable to believe the turn of events fate had presented her.

'I have always had a weakness for games of risk... but you already know that, don't you?' she remarked in a saucy voice. She scanned Lord Wulfingston's countenance, as if searching for something, then said with sudden vehemence: 'If I should be so foolish as to accept you, be warned, I shan't go easy on you! And if you try my temper there'll be hell to pay!'

'I'm counting on it!'

She smiled and leisurely ran one gloved finger down his profile to his lips.

'You always were a handsome devil,' she mused. 'Yes, Barnaby, I do believe I have a fancy to be your wife.'

A wolfish grin spread across his lordship's face and he pulled her into his arms again.

The room erupted in cheers and a throng of well-wishers surged forward to surround them.

Only Lady Hartwood was looking less than pleased.

Hurrying over to her daughter, she exclaimed: 'Oh, love, what will become of us now! He is bound to discover her past and I shudder to think what will happen then!'

April wiped away an emotional tear with the handkerchief Hugh had kindly put into her hand and gave her mother a reassuring, slightly unfocused, smile.

'Don't fret, Mama. He knows *all*, and clearly cares not!'

'He knows? But how?'

Becoming conscious of the fact that Hugh was still standing beside her, April leaned towards her mother and whispered: 'I shall tell you *later*. But know that you can be *perfectly* comfortable.'

Lady Hartwood seemed happy to accept this, and her spirits, always easily led, brightened considerably.

'Well, if you think so, love, then it must be so. And I believe it would be best if I take that,' she said firmly, removing April's punch glass from her hand. 'Some water would do you a world of good! And you, Hugh-dear, what do you think of their engagement?'

'I think it will allow them to focus their energies on each other and leave their family to stumble through life without their interference.'

'Oh, I had not considered the matter from that perspective!' she said delightedly. 'Let us hope you are correct. . . for their sake, of course.'

'Of course,' he agreed with a slight tremor.

'And to think he has been in love with her all these years! Who would have thought!'

'Years? Only a few weeks, surely?' said Hugh, unable to refrain from teasing her a little.

'Oh, one can easily suppose they have met at some point in the past,' said Lady Hartwood airily. 'They likely moved in the same circles. And, if that is the case, then one cannot help but feel for poor Lord Wulfingston – almost his whole life blighted, pining for her!'

Hugh preserved his countenance with difficulty as he thought of the considerable amusement his grandfather had derived from the last fifty years in the company of a multitude of dashing mistresses, who had kept him entertained even throughout a twenty-year marriage.

'Mama, you are being fanciful,' said April, smiling fondly at her.

'Not at all! If you had been standing as close to them as I was, you too would have been struck by the look in his eyes. It was so romantic! It... it quite overcomes one to think about it... all that time... oh, thank you, Hugh-dear,' she said, sniffing delicately and accepting the handkerchief April had only just returned to him. 'I must go and offer them my felicitations!'

As her mother walked off to join the group surrounding the newly affianced couple, April remarked: 'What an unexpected turn of events! Did *you* have any idea he meant to propose?'

'None at all,' replied Hugh.

'I only hope they don't come to regret such a *shockingly* impulsive decision.'

'I doubt it. They both have well-honed instincts. You must be delighted, of course,' he said with amusement. 'You will now be able to call Mrs Delamer *grandmother* quite freely.'

Alarm registered on her countenance, and, grabbing his arm, she pulled him out of the small circle of blue light and into the darkness beyond.

Unfortunately, she could not see where she was going and tripped over something in her path, almost bringing Hugh down on top of her.

'Are you alright?' he asked, bracing himself against a chair and helping her to stand upright.

'Yes, but it's of no import! Why did you say I could call Mrs Delamer *grandmother*?' she whispered urgently.

'Through a process of deduction I've managed to surmise that Mrs Delamer is set to become your grandmother through marriage. Why are we whispering?'

'Oh, yes, of course! How *stupid* of me... we're not whispering.'

'I shan't contradict you. But I feel I should point out, Miss Hartwood, that it's now safe for you to let go of my coat.'

Becoming aware that both her hands were clutching the lapels of this garment, she loosened her grip, but did not let go.

'I'm sorry, is it crushed? And I *wish* you wouldn't call me *Miss Hartwood*. I know you only do so to annoy me!'

'I don't know if it's crushed, it's somewhat hard to tell in the dark. And I apologise for annoying you by calling you by your name.'

She did not reply and continued to cling to him.

'It's a particularly fine coat, isn't it?' he went on. 'I can understand why you're not quite ready to release it.'

'I hope you do not mind the imposition? I am feeling a little unsteady,' she confided. 'The room keeps spinning around and around in a most *dreadful* manner.'

She swayed to one side and Hugh gently took hold of her shoulders and righted her.

'Steady, my darling girl. How much have you had to drink?'

'I don't know *what* you are implying?' she said, affronted. 'I've only had *one* glass since dinner. . . and I'm most definitely *not* your darling girl!'

'I saw the servants top up your one glass at least three times. And if I say you're my darling girl then you are.'

'Miss Starling won't allow it,' she said somewhat sadly.

'She won't have anything to say in the matter.'

'Silly! *Of course* she will! You don't imagine she'll allow you to go around calling me your darling girl? It's *ludicrous*. . . oh dear. . . the room is spinning again.'

Before she knew what was happening, Hugh had lifted her off her feet and was holding her against him.

'Is that better?' he asked.

'I'm floating,' she said in wonder, close to his ear.

'I'm going to carry you to bed.'

'Oh no, you cannot do *that*,' she said with exaggerated reasonableness. 'It isn't proper! Only a husband is allowed those privileges.'

'I'm carrying you to your own bed, to sleep,' he clarified as he began to navigate his way in the dark. 'But don't put thoughts into my head if you don't want me to. . .' He paused.

'If I don't want you to what?'

'Never mind.'

'It seems grossly unfair,' she sighed.

'What does?'

She did not reply and he assumed she had fallen asleep.

He managed to pass out of the room unseen just as the servants were beginning to relight the candles.

As he crossed the corridor to the staircase, the light from the candles in the wall-sconces showed him that April was wide awake and regarding him thoughtfully.

'I think it unfair,' she continued their conversation as if no time had passed, 'that men are not restricted to the marriage bed. Do *you* intend on taking a mistress after you wed?'

'Good God no! I'll have my hands full with my wife.'

'I suppose Miss Starling will be pleased to know that,' she said, stroking a tuft of hair under his ear.

He turned his head to look at her.

'I doubt she'll care either way,' he said gruffly, his gaze dropping to her lips.

'I would care if my husband had a mistress. In fact, I imagine I would be furious enough to *shoot* him.'

'Thank you for the warning.'

'But I was forgetting. . . I'll never marry,' she said forlornly.

'Don't you want to get married?'

'I do, but I won't,' she explained, thinking herself to be making perfect sense.

'Not even to your duke?'

She yawned and put up a hand to cover her mouth, before replying: 'Eustace? Yes, I suppose if I *had* to marry without love, I would rather marry him than anyone else. But he's my friend and I could not serve him such a trick. He never wants to marry.'

'Just as well. Your husband would have something to say about you having thoughts of marrying another man.'

'You are being particularly obtuse this evening! I've just told you I will *never* marry, so it stands to reason my husband won't exist to object. . . you see?'

'Yes, my darling girl, I see.'

'You mustn't call me that,' she said, yawning again and closing her eyes. 'It makes me feel *very* peculiar.'

Hugh had reached her bedchamber by this time, and, as April's maid was nowhere to be seen, he put her down on the bed and pulled on the bell rope.

He filled a glass with water from the jug left out on the bedside table and, supporting her, forced her to drink the lot. When she was finished, he gently lay her back down.

She curled up on her side and watched him through heavy-lidded eyes, her good hand under her cheek and the bandaged one flung out.

'I wish with all my heart you were unattractive and disagreeable,' she murmured.

Hugh sat down on the bed beside her and stroked her short curls away from her forehead.

'My poor girl, don't delude yourself. I am unattractive, and I can be very disagreeable on occasion.'

'You're not to me,' she said simply.

'Close your eyes. I'll stay with you until your maid comes.'

When Rachel entered the room, a few minutes later, she found Hugh sitting beside the sleeping form of her mistress, carefully re-bandaging her hand.

On catching sight of her, he said quietly: 'Rachel, is it?'

'Miss Hartwood calls me Rachel, sir, but Browning would be more proper,' she replied diffidently.

'Which do you prefer?'

The question seemed to startle her and she hesitated.

'Rachel is my given name, but... but the other servants... they don't always understand...' She drifted off helplessly.

'They've given you grief, have they? Then, Browning it shall be. I'm sure Miss Hartwood will agree once I explain the matter to her.'

Rachel smiled her thanks, her female intuition finding nothing curious about the fact that Hugh was taking it upon himself to sort out a matter her mistress would undoubtedly consider entirely private.

'Miss Hartwood's hand is healing well,' he went on, 'but I'd like you to clean the wounds again in the morning and put on a fresh bandage. And refill the water jug. She's going to have a headache when she wakes up.'

With an easy smile, entirely at odds with the mood in which she had last seen him this morning, Hugh stood and walked out of the room.

Forty-Three

Downstairs in the reception room, the candles had once more been lit, flooding the space with a warm, yellow light, and the guests were preparing to toast the newly affianced couple.

While they waited for the best champagne to be brought up from the cellar, His Grace found an opportunity to approach Mrs Starling. She was sitting alone by the fire, temporarily deprived of Sir Yarmouth's company (while he and General Simpson followed the butler downstairs to the bowels of the house, having drunkenly declared their intention to assist this harassed individual in choosing the correct vintage).

'May I?' asked His Grace at his most charming, indicating to the place beside Mrs Starling.

'Certainly, Your Grace. Please do,' she replied, gratified.

'A remarkable night is it not, ma'am?' he said, slurring his words a little. 'I am quite overcome!'

'Yes, indeed, *most* surprising.'

'It almost makes one wish to enter the marriage state.'

Mrs Starling smiled smugly, thinking herself to have been a spectator over the course of the day to his own courtship.

'I expect your time will come soon, Your Grace.

'Ah, I would give anything were it so! But, alas, I can never marry,' he sighed. 'Whatever happiness I can garner from matrimonial bliss I must do so through observing others.'

'But surely you will marry?' Mrs Starling said with some surprise.

He shook his head and smiled sadly.

'Why ever not?' she asked, unable to keep herself from uttering such an impertinent question.

His Grace hesitated, then looked about them to see if anyone could overhear.

'Can I depend on your discretion, ma'am?' he asked in a lowered voice, leaning towards her.

'Certainly you can,' she breathed, agog with curiosity.

After hiccupping delicately into his hand, he proceeded with a confidential air: 'A most unfortunate accident in my youth – I cannot think about it without shuddering! – resulted in an *impairment*. It is quite impossible for me to sire offspring, however much I might wish to do so. Now can you understand why it would be unpardonably selfish of me to subject any lady to such a childless existence?'

'Oh my, how unfortunate. I had no notion. . . but your thoughts do you credit, Your Grace.'

'Thank you.'

There was a pause while Mrs Starling considered her next words.

His Grace waited patiently; amused by her struggle with the opposing demands of delicacy and curiosity.

'Whoever your heir might be,' she said carefully, 'it is to be hoped he meets with your approval.' The quizzical gleam in her eyes invited him to reveal more.

'Oh, I am perfectly content for my cousin to succeed me.'

'Ah, of course. There must be many cousins in your family. . . am I, perhaps, acquainted with him?'

'Why, yes! It is not widely known as yet, but as of earlier this year the next in line to inherit the dukedom is none other than Mr Kepling.'

Mrs Starling's eyes almost started from her head.

'You cannot mean *Alfred?*'

'But I do.'

'But...but he is not your *first* cousin, surely? I would have known if his mother had married into. . . ' She stopped herself from continuing, feeling she had betrayed too much interest to suit the nicety of her manners.

'Third cousin, to be precise,' said His Grace. 'Sadly, the last of my more closely related heirs passed away in September – a frighteningly pious man, if truth be told, which makes it rather difficult to mourn his passing, but one does one's best.'

Mrs Starling was ready to faint from shock and barely heard this last part. Her eyes travelled to where her daughter was standing (a little unsteadily) beside Mr Kepling and giggling at something he was whispering into her ear.

His Grace leant back in his seat and, lounging at his ease, watched Mrs Starling.

All signs of inebriation had vanished from his demeanour and he wore a peculiarly bland expression. His mother would have recognised this at a glance and dotingly thought to herself that her son would have been better suited to a Machiavellian court in Italy, in centuries past, rather than the more pedestrian times he inhabited.

Some minutes later, Hugh was slowly making his way down the marble staircase, lost in his thoughts, when he caught sight of Mr Kepling supporting a visibly intoxicated Miss Starling. She was leaning heavily on his arm and walking up the stairs in a pronounced meandering motion, her unfocused gaze fixed adoringly on his face as he encouraged her steps.

A sardonic smile curved Hugh's lips.

Meeting them on the landing, he startled them by saying pleasantly: 'I see you have the matter well in-hand, Kepling, and need no assistance from me.'

He offered them a brief nod and continued on his way.

This treatment so disconcerted the pair that it took them several moments to find their voices, at which point they proceeded to address him in unison.

'Mother gave Mr Kepling her permission to assist me...'

'You need not think, sir, anything untoward is going on...'

Amusement lurked in Hugh's eyes as he looked back at them, but he kept himself from laughing outright to spare their feelings.

'You need not think I disapprove,' he said. 'Nothing, in fact, would please me more! Miss Starling, could you spare me a moment of your time tomorrow when you are feeling more yourself, so we can settle this business of our engagement.'

All this was said in a matter-of-fact way but as both Miss Starling and Mr Kepling were suffering from the burden of guilt, and as Hugh's naturally austere countenance often led people to suppose he was scowling at them, they imagined an implied threat in his words.

If their heads had been clearer it may have occurred to them that it was unlike Hugh to threaten.

However, without this clarity of thought, the self-imagined star-crossed lovers watched in turmoil as Hugh descended the stairs and disappeared into the reception room.

'Oh, Alfred! What am I to do?' cried Miss Starling and clung to Mr Kepling.

With her lovely eyes beseeching him with such despair it was impossible for Mr Kepling to keep a proper distance. Nor was he insensate to the heady feeling of being needed by one who appeared to place great value in his judgment.

Gathering her into his arms, he kissed her forehead and told her the first thing that came into his head.

'You must not worry, my sweet – all will be well!'

This singularly meaningless remark seemed to have a soothing effect on Miss Starling, and she succumbed to admiration of his superior reasoning.

Looking down into her upturned face, charmingly lit by the candles in the wall-sconces beside them, Mr Kepling forgot the precepts of honour that should have governed his actions and kissed her.

Miss Starling allowed this impropriety without complaint, and even with some enthusiasm. But when at last they broke apart a tear rolled down her cheek.

'Mother!' she uttered miserably.

Mr Kepling understood her only too well and his brow clouded over. Being a diffident young man, raised to live within the means of his small inheritance, he had not as yet learnt to view himself with the self-satisfaction to be expected of the heir to a wealthy dukedom.

He had, in fact, only vaguely considered the possibility of becoming the next Duke of Claredon. He knew of his cousin's determination never to marry but he placed little importance on it. To his mind, they shared similar odds when it came to who would meet their maker first.

And even if one day, decades from now, he found himself stepping into his cousin's shoes, he did not value his attractions so highly as to believe that Mrs Starling would allow her daughter to live on his modest income for all that time, when she could have the resources of Hugh's large fortune at her disposal in the immediate future.

And so, although he tucked Miss Starling's head under his chin and murmured into her hair that he would find a way for them to be together, he could not but be daunted by how he was to go about achieving such a miracle.

Forty-Four

On the following morning, Miss Starling came down to breakfast late. She had slept very little, having been consumed by her worries, and dark shadows marred the usual excellence of her complexion.

At some point during her sleepless hours she had reached the dismal conclusion that it was her duty to marry Mr Royce, and that she must do all in her power to keep him from breaking their engagement.

And so, when she entered the breakfast parlour and found that it was inhabited by April, the duke, and his cousin, she painstakingly avoided Mr Kepling's eye as he rose and greeted her, and, after offering a general 'good morning, asked April if she knew where Mr Royce could be found.

April had woken up with a splitting headache and a hazy but largely intact memory of what had passed between herself and Hugh on the previous evening, and, mortified by her own behaviour, she answered rather defensively: 'I have not the least idea where Mr Royce could be! His movements are of no interest to me!'

Miss Starling was too absorbed in her own problems to note anything unusual in this sharp response and, excusing herself, went in search of her fiancé.

She found him in the library, skimming through a copy of Shakespeare's Anthony and Cleopatra, which he had come across on the shelves and planned to show to April.

He looked up as she walked in and offered her a sympathetic smile.

'How do you feel this morning, Miss Starling?'

She was quick to note that he had not used his customary 'my dear' and her apprehension grew.

Steeling herself, she walked over to him and tentatively put her hands on his chest.

'Mr Royce, I hope you can forgive me? I had a little too much to drink last night and, although I remember very little, I fear I may have acted in a manner that displeased you.'

Hugh's arms remained impassively at his sides as he looked down into her face. A scowling look, quite intentional on this occasion, had descended over his features.

Noting it, Miss Starling was a little daunted, however, well aware of her natural attractions, she pushed aside her qualms and stood on tip toe to kiss his unresponsive lips.

Hugh was furious.

Her evident desire to keep them entangled in a betrothal that was in neither of their best interests, all for the sake of his fortune, snapped the thread of his control.

Roughly grabbing her shoulders, he kissed her back with punishing force.

Miss Starling uttered an alarmed squeak in the back of her throat and tried to pull away, but he would not allow it and continued to assault her mouth.

'Alfie, you cannot barge in and interrupt their conversation!' said April. 'Miss Starling clearly wishes to speak to Mr Royce in private – look, she has closed the door!'

They were standing in the corridor outside the library, to where April and His Grace had followed Mr Kepling after he had declared he must speak with Miss Starling and had rushed out of the breakfast parlour.

'But did you see her face?' asked Mr Kepling, greatly agitated. 'She means to sacrifice herself!'

Taking exception to this, April said tartly: 'It is hardly a sacrifice! If anything, she should be elated to have managed to secure Mr Royce's affection.'

'*Affection* is not the most accurate word one could use under the circumstances,' observed His Grace.

'Eustace, don't *you* start!' she warned him.

'You don't understand!' exclaimed Mr Kepling. 'She doesn't *want* to marry him.'

'Well, if she doesn't want to marry him, she need only say so and she'll have her wish!' retorted April.

'*That* is why I must speak to her!' And before anyone could raise any more objections, Mr Kepling threw open the library door and burst into the room.

He was greeted by the sight of Miss Starling in Hugh's arms, being roughly kissed.

'Unhand her at once!' he cried angrily and moved towards them.

Hugh released Miss Starling so abruptly she stumbled backwards into Mr Kepling.

'I cannot do it!' she sobbed and turned to bury her face in his conveniently placed chest.

'No one will make you do anything you don't want to do, my sweet,' he said soothingly, looking over her head at Hugh with deep reproach.

Hugh ignored them both.

His eyes were locked with April's, willing her not to jump to obvious conclusions. Her shock were so great, however, she was insensate to the message he was attempting to relay.

For a long moment she stood frozen in the doorway, her face an expressionless mask, and then, without a word, she turned and disappeared.

Hugh went to follow her but found his arm seized by Mr Kepling.

'Name your seconds, sir!'

Hugh would have liked nothing better than to shake him off and go after April. But he needed to strike the final deathblow to his engagement.

'You wish to call me out, do you?' he said with exaggerated derision. 'What is your reason? Until she tells me otherwise, Miss Starling is my fiancée, and I'll continue to treat her as my property!'

'Y-your property!' spluttered Mr Kepling, becoming even more incensed. 'If you think I'll allow you to use her in such a fashion...'

'How do you plan to stop me? I have the law on my side.'

'Not if I marry her first!' Looking down at Miss Starling, Mr Kepling said urgently: 'I know I've no fortune to offer you, my sweet, but if you chose me I would cherish you every day of my life!'

'Oh, Alfred, I would love it above all things!' she replied through her tears. 'Only, you must know, Mother is unlikely to approve.'

His Grace, sensing his moment had come, stepped forward.

'If you think your mother would object to you marrying the heir to the dukedom of Claredon,' he said in a dry voice, 'I think you have done her an injustice, Miss Starling.'

She regarded him in a dumbfounded way.

'But... you cannot mean *Alfred* is your heir?'

'He is. As of three months ago, if one were to be precise. And apart from our ancestral home in Yorkshire and a mansion in Berkley Square – in which, I hasten to add, I do not reside as it is too large for my bachelor tastes – you will also have three other estates at your disposal should you wish to set up house in them.'

'Regardless of my cousin's generosity,' Mr Kepling put in conscientiously, 'you should know my personal fortune is not large.'

'It is, however, more than sufficient,' said His Grace, 'when you consider most of your living costs will be paid for by the Claredon estate.'

'But I've no ambition to step into Eustace's shoes,' insisted Mr Kepling, 'and may well die before him!'

'Be that as it may, your son, Miss Starling, if not your husband, is destined to become the next Duke of Claredon,' countered His Grace.

While Miss Starling's gaze travelled in a dazed fashion from one cousin to the other, Hugh saw his chance of escape.

On his way out of the room, he cast the duke a heartfelt look of gratitude; which was accepted with the briefest of nods and a faint smile.

Forty-Five

After searching the downstairs rooms, Hugh made his way to April's bedchamber and knocked firmly on the door.

He was about to knock a second time when Rachel opened it.

'Is you mistress inside?' he asked without preamble.

'No, sir,' she replied with a troubled expression. 'She left!'

'Left?'

The girl nodded vigorously.

'Yes, sir. She came in all in a flutter, put on her boots and cloak, and, before I'd time to do more than blink, she told me she was going to Christmas mass in the village and left!'

'She's walking to the village in this weather?'

'Yes, sir. I did my best to dissuade her but she... she seemed determined.'

'I take it she was in a temper? Nothing else could explain such idiocy!' he declared savagely.

'Not in a temper exactly. But so agitated I could barely coax a handful of words from her.'

'In high dudgeon then. Either way, she's a fool! Stoke up the fire. I'm going to bring her back before she catches her death of cold.'

Wasting no more time on words, he quickly made his way to the bedchamber he was sharing with his grandfather, and, bursting into the room, surprised the personage who looked after his grandfather's wardrobe (and who had temporarily condescended to look after his own) with a hasty order to prepare his riding clothes.

'You wish to go riding *now*, sir?' the valet asked with marked disbelief as he glanced out the window at the deep snow on the ground.

'Yes, and at once!' replied Hugh as he began to strip off his clothing.

In less than fifteen minutes, he was entering the stables and ordering the stablehands to saddle up a horse best suited to the current conditions.

The boys exchanged looks of surprise but rushed to do his bidding, and within a short space of time Hugh was riding down the driveway, following the deeply imprinted trail April had left behind her.

It took only a few minutes of trudging through snow that came to her knees for April to realise she had acted in a singularly foolish fashion. Her temper often led her down paths she later came to regret, but in this instance, she ruthlessly told herself, she had outdone herself with her stupidity.

Had she been dressed like a man, in breeches and top boots, she may well have enjoyed the walk. However, as her skirts made it difficult to traverse the snow and her half-boots had become sodden almost immediately, she found it impossible to appreciate the frosted beauty around her.

And neither did it help that her mind was in turmoil, flitting from one memory to the next, yet never fully landing on any to rest for fear her pain would intensify.

When she reached the road she found the snow there was not as heavy on the ground, for the high banks on either side and the thick canopy of denuded trees formed a partial barrier against it.

As she proceeded along this natural tunnel an all-encompassing stillness surrounded her; only occasionally disturbed by the snapping of a twig in the underbrush or a falling clump of snow from the branches.

She was halfway to the village when another sound reached her ears; a soft thumping of hooves behind her that seemed to be getting louder. She wondered who in the world had chosen to go riding today of all days and stepped to the side of the road to let the rider pass.

The instant a tall, familiar figure rode around the bend, she let out an infuriated gasp, and, turning swiftly about, continued on her way.

Hugh slowed and followed her, making certain to keep far enough away so that his horse would not make her uncomfortable.

Now that he could see she was safe (and in a temper, if the tilt of her head was anything to go by) his anxiety faded away and an irrepressible chuckle rose to his lips.

April whirled around.

'How dare you laugh at me?'

He reined in the horse, a rather large animal, a few feet away from her.

'I'm not laughing at you,' he replied.

'Well, you are not laughing *with* me!'

'No, I can see I'm not. But I am laughing at the absurdity of the situation we find ourselves in.'

'There is no *we* in this situation, Mr Royce,' she retorted. "There is *me*, on my way to the village, minding my own business, and there is *you*, minding your own.'

'You are my business.'

Indignation swelled within her.

'Oh, is *that* how it is to be? It is not enough for you to have one woman, you must also have another waiting in the wings? How I pity Miss Starling! If she doesn't yet know it, she will soon discover you are the most appallingly behaved man alive!'

'I hope to God she has discovered it. I've certainly been at great pains to point it out to her over the last few weeks.'

'How charming! And the wedding band not yet even on her finger.'

'Whatever wedding band she may agree to wear in future, I'm happy to say, it won't be mine.'

She advanced towards him, momentarily forgetting the horse.

'Do you mean to tell me,' she said in appalled accents, 'that after kissing the poor girl in what I can only describe as an *impassioned* manner, you are now withdrawing your offer to marry her?'

Hugh's own temper flared at this unflattering reading of his character.

'I don't mean to tell you anything of the sort! But I can see you're only too ready to believe me lost to all sense of honour. What sort of a loose-screw do you think I am?'

His anger gave her pause.

'I don't think you're a loose-screw,' she replied carefully, an uncertain look entering her eyes. 'I would never have thought you capable of such conduct.'

'I'm not! My only wish in subjecting Miss Starling to a kiss I knew she would find distasteful was to convince her to break off our engagement – an engagement I've been regretting for near enough two months!'

April's heart leapt with sudden joy.

Although she had a poor opinion of his tactics. It was inconceivable to her how any woman not yet in her dotage could be anything but thrilled to be kissed by him in such a manner.

'You thought to drive her away by kissing her?' she said with incredulity. 'That is *absurd*. . . not that it is any concern of mine!' she hastened to add, retreating from her point before she could betray herself.

'Isn't it?' he asked, a half-smile on his lips.

'Certainly not! I am of course very sorry to hear that you are regretting your engagement. . . but what is to be done? Oh, for goodness sake, do come down off that colossal animal! I'll soon have a crick in my neck if I'm forced to continue looking up at you,' she said irritably, not enjoying the feeling of vulnerability that had come over her.

A warmth entered Hugh's eyes as he surveyed her upturned countenance.

'Of course, forgive me.'

He transferred the reins into one hand and was on the point of dismounting when a loud cracking noise startled the horse and it reared in fright.

As Hugh struggled to get the animal back under control, a large branch that had snapped under a load of snow fell from above and landed with a sickening thud on his head, before crashing to the ground and narrowly missing April.

Hugh lurched sideways off his saddle and landed face down in the snow in an inanimate heap.

It all happened so quickly that for several moments all April could do was to stare down at him in horror.

'Hugh!' she cried, falling on her knees beside him. 'Are you alright? Say something!'

With a growing sense of dread she managed to push him onto his back, and saw at once that he had an ugly gash in the hairline above his forehead that was bleeding profusely.

Her stomach lurched uncomfortably, but as she had been raised in the country, and had seen her fair share of injured animals, she did not experience the least desire to faint.

Picking up a handful of snow, she compacted it between her fur mittens and pressed it against the wound. She held it there until it had melted and repeated the procedure.

After several minutes, the bleeding had slowed until it merely oozed sluggishly.

Satisfied that he was no longer in danger of blood loss, she took off her mittens and unwrapped the new bandage her maid had used to dress her hand that morning, then wound it as tightly as she dared around Hugh's head.

When she was finished, she sat back on her heels and studied him with a worried expression. He had not moved a muscle throughout her ministrations; he was so still, in fact, that had it not been for the faint puffs of steam created by his breath she would have feared the worst.

'Why won't you wake up?' she asked in a small voice, overly loud in the dense silence.

She may have managed to stop the bleeding but she knew if he remained in the snow for much longer he would succumb to frostbite, or worse.

The cold had already seeped through her own clothing and her extremities had started to go numb. She stood up and began to stomp her feet and rub her hands together, while her anxious gaze swept up and down the road in the hope of seeing someone approach.

However, she knew it was a vain hope; no sane person would be out in these conditions on Christmas Day.

She let out a rather hysterical laugh for, by that reasoning, Hugh and herself were evidently not sane.

A gentle neigh interrupted these dismal thoughts and she looked across at the horse whose presence she had forgotten. He appeared to be none the worse from his fright and was standing a few feet away, watching her.

'Oh, dear God, no. . . must it be you?' she asked the creature wretchedly.

No response was forthcoming.

With a loud groan that was half battle-cry and half despair, she threw off her fur-lined cloak and, dropping down beside Hugh again, wrapped it tightly around him.

Then, without giving herself time to consider the biting cold or her fears, she marched over to the horse.

'Now look here,' she told it in what she hoped was a firm yet soothing voice, 'we may not know each other but I can promise you that I will not hurt you. And you, sir, must promise to give me the same courtesy – do we understand one another?'

The horse twitched one ear and continued to regard her in a placid manner.

'I suppose I must take that for a yes!'

Continuing to talk nonsense to the animal, she led it to the bank of the road, where a prominent tree root had grown beyond the manmade boundary, and, clambering up onto it, attempted to place her foot in the stirrup.

It was an awkward business but mercifully the horse remained still; until she managed it at last and pulled herself up onto the saddle.

She had never before ridden astride and discovered it was horribly uncomfortable. In addition to the strange sensation of having the saddle between her legs, she also had to contend with her skirts riding up and exposing her shins. But at least the cold numbed her fear, as well as her body.

Giving the horse a tap with her heels, they set off at an easy trot in the direction of the village.

Forty-Six

After what felt like a frighteningly long time, but was in fact no more than a quarter of an hour, April saw smoke over the next hill. With a sob of relief she spurred on her large companion and they were soon entering the yard of a small, picturesque inn with age-blackened timbers and a thatched roof.

'*Hello!*' she called out, riding up to the front door. '*Hello!* Is anyone there?'

She did not have long to wait before she heard a bolt being scraped back; then the door was swung open and a man of wide girth and short stature, sporting a bountiful red beard, peered out at her in astonishment.

'Can I help you, m'lady?' he asked, taking note of her expensive attire.

She was shivering violently from the cold but did her best to explain what had transpired, before adding through chattering teeth: 'P-please send t-two or three men. The gentleman is quite l-large. And they m-must go at once. He has been in the s-snow too long.'

She was immensely thankful to see that the landlord grasped the urgency of the situation.

Quickly turning to speak to some persons within the inn, he told them to go and prepare the farm cart, then head down the road towards Mrs Delamer's place and bring back a gent who'd fallen off his horse.

'Hobb is my name,' he said, looking back at April. 'It's my place you've come to, m'lady. Never you fear, my lads work quick and they'll bring back your gentleman in no time! Let me help you down so you can come inside before you catch your death,' he said kindly, holding up his hands to assist her.

However, with all the good will in the world, April could not see how someone of his size could help her down from such a large horse.

'I d-don't think I can d-dismount,' she said apologetically. 'I can-not m-move my legs.'

A woman in an apron, at least a head taller than Mr Hobb, appeared in the doorway.

Taking in the situation at a glance, she hollered over her shoulder: 'Sam, get yourself over here!' And when a tall and strapping young man, who held a strong resemblance to her, presently appeared she told him: 'Help your Pa lift the lady out of the saddle and carry her to the private parlour. And be quick about it! I'll go heat up some rum.'

While the woman disappeared back inside, the young man plucked April from the horse (with some vocal assistance from his father) and was soon depositing her in front of a cosy fire in a small parlour at the back of the inn.

'Here you go, m'lady,' said Mrs Hobb bustling into the room with a steaming mug of some concoction. 'You drink this now and let it warm you through! But slowly mind! Slow and steady is what I've always found to be best when warming a body that's been chilled to the bone.'

April managed a weary smile but had no strength left to correct the landlady's form of address.

Mrs Hobb shooed her husband and son out of the room by telling them to go and see to the horse, then turned back to April and clucked her tongue.

'We'll have to get you out of those wet clothes as soon as can be! But there's no point me taking you up to the guest bedrooms. Being Christmas and all, we've no one staying with us and it'll take time to heat a room for you. We'll just have to get you changed in here!' And on those daunting words she left the room.

When she returned, a few minutes later, she was holding slippers and a voluminous dressing gown in a rather garish green and white check pattern.

'I've told my husband to keep everyone out, never you fear!' she said cheerily, and, before her dazed guest could object, she pulled off her hat and mittens and started undoing the laces of her half-boots.

April watched with a strange sense of detachment as her boots, stockings and pelisse were removed with ruthless efficiency. But when Mrs Hobb began to unbutton her dress, she felt moved to offer a protest.

'God bless you, there's no need for modesty around me!' Mrs Hobb scolded her good-naturedly. 'I've reared two daughters, both of them married now and with little ones on the way, and I've my four boys as well to try my patience. Not to mention I'm the only midwife around these parts and have done my fair share of nursing when the need arises!'

'I beg your pardon, it is merely habit,' April said shakily. 'I don't feel modest... or anything at all, for that matter.'

'We'll soon have you right again! There's nothing wrong with you that a good fire and a bit of warmed rum can't fix. Now, take another sip, like a good girl.'

April obeyed her, and felt a reminiscent pang for her childhood nurse, who had had just such a forceful yet caring manner.

Once she had drunk enough of the warm liquid to satisfy Mrs Hobb, the landlady took the cup out of her hands and continued to remove her clothing, until she was standing only in her chemise.

Mrs Hobb then wrapped her in the overly-large dressing gown, saying proudly it had been a present from her husband and had cost him a pretty penny, and finished by thrusting the slippers onto April's feet as if she were no more than a child.

Directing her to sit down and drink her spiced rum, she picked up the wet clothing and boots and once more left the room.

After a few minutes of sitting in front of the fire the cold began to recede from April's bones. Unfortunately, this allowed her fears to rise to the surface and she began to keep an anxious eye on the clock on the mantle.

Her mind had just begun to torment her with images of Hugh's lifeless body when the landlady returned.

'Now don't you be getting yourself into a pucker! said Mrs Hobb, taking note of her beautiful guest's worried expression. 'I've come to tell you they've just carried in your gentleman and he's more than alive, he is!'

April jumped to her feet and took a few unsteady steps towards her.

'He is? Oh, thank God! But I did not hear anyone come in?'

'They brought him in the back way and are taking him up to my best bedchamber now.'

'Please, take me to him!'

'I will, never you fear. Just you stay where you are for now and give me and the boys a little time to get him cleaned up. He's got a nice bump on his head, which looks a sight worse than it is because of all the dried blood. Head wounds always bleed freely at first, so you needn't put yourself in a worry. Why, he even woke up for a minute or two and said a few words, and that's always a good sign!'

Tears sprung into April's eyes and she took hold of the kindly woman's hands.

'I don't know how to thank you, Mrs Hobb. . . you and your family. . .' She became choked up with emotion and could not continue.

Mrs Hobb patted her hand in a motherly fashion.

'There, there. . . we're only doing what any good Christian would do! Now, I'm thinking it be best to send a message up to Mrs Delamer's place to let them know where you are?'

'Oh, yes! Thank you! I expect they have already begun to worry.'

'I'll get my son to ride over right away. You wait here just a few more minutes and I'll come get you when we're ready for you.'

Forty-Seven

In the end it was an hour before Mrs Hobb returned, and April had been pacing the room for most of that time.

The landlady reassured her once again and then took her up the stairs to a small bedchamber, neatly but sparsely decorated with some necessary items of furniture and blue and white dimity curtains.

A rough-hewn timber bed was pushed up against one wall and on it lay Hugh's inert form, propped up with pillows and covered with several blankets.

A fire had been lit in the grate but the room felt cold to April and, with a frown, she walked to Hugh's side and placed her hand against his cheek.

'He is so very cold,' she said, turning an anxious face to Mrs Hobb.

'And it's no wonder, seeing he was in the snow a fair time,' she replied, clearly untroubled. 'He'll warm through soon enough! I've put a bed-warmer pan under the covers so there's no need to be worrying yourself. I'll leave you now and reheat some of the chicken soup we had for dinner last night. I know from my Ma it's just the thing to put a person on the road to recovery when they've been brought low.'

Mrs Hobb bustled out of the room and discreetly closed the door behind her.

April sat down on top of the blankets beside the large, prostrate figure that took up most of the bed. Every inch of his body had been covered, apart from his head, and it occurred to her that he might be naked inside his cocoon.

Heat rushed into her cheeks and her eyes travelled cautiously over him; but then she saw the collar of a night-shirt peeking above the blankets and, a little disappointed, had to quell her unruly imagination.

Forcing her mind onto more pertinent matters, she noticed that his makeshift bandage had been removed and the ugly gash in his hairline had been cleaned. The wound appeared to have closed up of its own accord and did not need stiches, but a large lump had formed beside it.

What worried her most, however, was that Hugh's skin had taken on a bluish tinge. Unable to think of anything else to do, she rubbed her hands together until they were warm and placed them on his cheeks.

She studied him closely as she leant over him.

The harsh planes of his face had softened in repose and he looked younger, and disconcertingly vulnerable. A strong feeling of protectiveness came over her... and possessiveness. The ferocity of the emotion alarmed her and she shied away from examining it too closely.

She warmed her hands again and placed them on his forehead. His colour was beginning to return.

Hugh opened his eyes to find an angel hovering over him.

She was a dark-haired angel, which surprised him for he thought they were alleged to be fair, with shimmering eyes that were tinted every shade of the sea.

'Hello,' said the angel, smiling down at him.

'Hello.'

'How do you feel?'

'Your front tooth is crooked.'

'How like you to point out my faults!' laughed April, relief shining in her eyes as she dropped her hands from his face and sat back.

'No... it's charming. But not perfect.'

'As you already know, I'm far from perfect! But, by all means, if it will make you feel better, I give you leave to catalogue each of my imperfections.'

Hugh tried to reach up and touch her face to satisfy himself that she was real but his hands felt strangely unresponsive. He looked down at himself and, wincing from a sharp pain in his head, saw that he was covered by a mountain of blankets.

'I take it I'm not in heaven,' he remarked with enough of his customary dryness to make April laugh again.

'I should hope not after all the effort I went to! We are at an inn not far from the village.' Picking up a glass of water that had been left on the bedside table by some thoughtful individual, she said coaxingly: 'Drink a little water, Hugh. You'll feel better for it, I promise.'

She carefully supported his head and helped him to take a few sips.

274

'Thank you. . . which village?'

'Why, Richmond, of course!'

Hugh's eyes roamed over her face, seeming to absorb every detail. After a long pause, he asked: 'Who are you?'

'I. . . I'm April,' she blurted out, too startled to expand further.

He frowned faintly.

'And, I am?'

'*Oh*. . . I see. . .' Greatly shaken, she forced a smile on her lips. 'Your name is Hugh Royce. It would appear you have lost your memory. . . which is not at all surprising when you consider that a rather large branch fell on your head. But you must not worry! You are going to be perfectly all right. . . now, if you'll excuse me for just a few minutes, I must go and speak with our landlady.'

More worried than she cared to admit, she hurried out of the room to seek Mrs Hobb's counsel, her gaudy dressing gown sweeping the floor behind her.

A few minutes after her departure, the landlord entered to find Hugh had managed to pull himself up into a sitting position against the pillows and was looking about him with a thoughtful and remarkably clear-eyed expression, considering the state he had been in an hour earlier.

'Ah, it's good to see you properly awake now, sir,' said Mr Hobb. 'How are you feeling, if I may ask?'

'Better,' replied Hugh. 'I don't yet perfectly remember what happened, but am I right in thinking I'm in your debt, Mr. . . ?'

'Joe Hobb is my name, sir, but everyone calls me Hobb. And there's no need for you to be talking of debts! It was my boys that fetched you out of the snow but it was your wife's quick thinking that saved you. If she hadn't wrapped you up in her cloak, I figure it would've been touch and go with you!'

'My wife?'

'Yes, sir. Mrs Hobb tells me the poor lady's been worrying herself witless over you.'

'I see. . . I had not realised,' Hugh said meditatively.

'All's well that ends well, as the saying goes! Is there anything you need, sir?'

'Hmm? Oh. . . yes. If I'm to face any more revelations, some French brandy wouldn't go amiss. I don't suppose you have any?'

'I may be able to lay my hands on a bottle,' Mr Hobb replied discreetly, thinking of a certain smuggled consignment he had hidden in his cellar.

April came back at that moment carrying a bowl of soup and a spoon.

'Oh, you look so much better already!' she exclaimed.

Giving Mr Hobb a nod of thanks as he passed her on his way out of the room, she went to sit on the bed beside Hugh.

'Have you managed to remember anything?'

'Not as yet. I'm sorry,' he said with a rueful smile.

April reacted to his smile as she always did; only on this occasion she could not prevent her eyes from betraying her.

'There's no need to apologise to me! You'll be yourself soon enough. Mrs Hobb – our excellent landlady, and a nurse besides – assures me it could take a few hours or a few days but you will eventually regain your memory. Does your head still pain you?'

She looked so concerned that Hugh refrained from telling her his head hurt like the devil.

'Only a little,' he replied.

'I can tell you are being untruthful! To make it up to me you must finish the lovely chicken broth that Mrs Hobb prepared for you.'

She dipped the spoon in the bowl and held it to his lips.

Hugh's eyes travelled over her face in an attempt to ignite some spark of memory. Nothing solid came to him, only a deep-seated feeling that this woman belonged to him. There was something infinitely dear and familiar about her.

'Please,' she said coaxingly, thinking he did not want the broth.

Watching her through half-closed eyes, Hugh opened his mouth and allowed her to feed him.

She maintained her concentration on her task until all the soup was finished, and then raised her eyes to his and smiled.

'There! That wasn't as horrid as you thought, was it?'

Hugh realised he did in fact feel better for having something warm inside him. While April was putting down the bowl on the bedside table, he freed his hands from the blankets and explored the bump on his head.

'What are you doing?' she said sternly and put a stop to his examination by taking hold of his hand. 'That lump won't go down if you insist on prodding it. I kept the area covered with snow for a good while but it's still the size of an egg! Although the snow did seem to help with the bleeding – you cannot imagine what a fright you gave me at first, there was so much blood! Thankfully, by the time I had to leave you and get help it had all but stopped.'

His gaze dropped to where her hand held his.

She instantly let go of him; but before she could move away he grabbed her hand and raised it to his lips.

'You *are* an angel,' he said with rough tenderness and kissed her fingers.

April laughed uncertainly.

'Good God, Hugh, that branch must have hit you harder than I supposed! When you regain your memory you will remember I'm nothing of the sort!'

'A heroine, then. But it must be one or the other. I can only imagine how cold the walk in the snow must have been without your cloak.'

'Oh, I did not walk – it would have taken too long! I took your horse. Thank goodness the poor animal did not take fright and run away when the branch fell.'

Hugh looked at her a little strangely.

'Horse...' he murmured.

She grimaced expressively.

'It was awful! But what else could I do? I could not risk leaving you in the cold for an instant longer than I had to.'

He studied her for such a long time that she began to feel self-conscious.

'Why are you looking at me like that? Have I grown horns?' she asked with a wobbly smile.

'You got onto a horse?' he asked in a wondering way; then thought to add: 'It would've been near impossible without anyone there to help you to mount.'

'Yes, it was a little difficult, but I managed it in the end. I had to! You were lying in the sno...'

Hugh suddenly grabbed the back of her head and crushed his lips against hers.

She let out a muffled protest.

He responded by deepening the kiss.

After a minute of really quite futile and half-hearted struggles, her resistance deserted her altogether and, melting against him, she kissed him back.

A disgracefully improper amount of time later, she pulled out of his arms with a dazed expression, looking thoroughly disheveled and adorable to Hugh's eyes; and also rather annoyed.

'You shouldn't have done that!' she said, frowning at him. 'What would Miss Starling say?'

'I don't know and I don't care,' he replied with an untroubled grin. 'It's no one's business if I decide to kiss my own wife.'

'Your wife!' she exclaimed. 'But why on earth would you think...'

Tugging her roughly onto his chest again, he kissed her with a determination that put to flight all her rational thoughts.

Forty-Eight

'Well!' said a sarcastic voice from the doorway. 'If I'd known all it would take was a knock on the head to make you come to your senses, I'd have hit you myself weeks ago!'

'Grandmama!' cried April, pulling away from Hugh with a start and almost sliding off the bed. On noticing Lord Wulfingston beside her relative, she added guiltily: 'Oh. . . I mean, Mrs Delamer!'

'You're as bad as your mother,' sighed Mrs Delamer. 'It's fortunate Barnaby has guessed the truth otherwise I'd be in a devil of a fix with the two of you calling me *mama* and *grandmama* at the drop of a hat!'

'I trust you don't make a habit of bursting into a man's bedchamber without first knocking?' Hugh grumbled, annoyed at having his kiss interrupted.

'There was nothing to knock on,' Lord Wulfingston informed him. 'If you mean to ravage a girl at least have the decency to close the damn door!'

Hugh's lips twitched but he managed to say: 'Who the devil are you?'

'Oho! So that's the way of it, is it? Let me enlighten you, young man – I am your grandfather! And if I'm to have my breakfast interrupted by a note from some person who goes by the bourgeois name of Hobb, giving me to understand you've been gravely injured, the least I expect after rushing to your bedside – and with a snowstorm on the way – is to see you at death's door and not enacting some badly scripted love scene!'

'I beg pardon, sir,' replied Hugh, a reprehensible twinkle in his eyes. 'I didn't know you'd been inconvenienced. You'd best be off with all possible speed before the storm hits. As you can see, my wife is here to provide all the nursing I require.'

'Your wife? Oh, this gets better and better!' laughed Mrs Delamer. 'I could not have planned it more perfectly myself!'

'There is not the least cause for amusement in any of this,' said April tartly. 'And am I to take from your words, Grandmama, that your plan all along was to throw me together with Hugh, and not the Duke of Claredon, as you led me to suppose?'

Her grandmother smiled at her in a manner she found utterly provoking.

'Of course, you foolish child! I needed *some* decoy to distract you so you would not guess the truth and put up your barriers. And His Grace was perfect for the task as there was never any danger of him falling in love with you.'

'How convenient!' retorted April. 'When I think of all the times I allowed you to manipulate and. . . ' She momentarily lost the power of speech, so great was her annoyance. But on recalling a particularly galling incident, she exclaimed: 'That ludicrous list! All those prerequisites the duke supposedly expected of his bride must have been fictitious! But why, for goodness sake, did I have to cut my hair?'

'I thought it would suit you better,' Mrs Delamer replied quite brazenly.

'I suppose simply offering me your opinion on the matter was out of the question? And why did all those lovely new dresses have to be altered until they were absurdly demure?'

'It occurred to me, although unfortunately only after our first visit to the modiste, that the more reserved your style of dress – and the more contained your temper! – the less likely Hugh would be to compare you to his Jezebel of a mother. You must have guessed how assiduously he has steered himself away from choosing a wife who resembles her? That was also the reason I invited the beautiful Miss Beechcroft to your dinner party. She served as a perfect contrast! When placed in the same room together, any fool could see your character in no way resembled hers. . . Hugh, I know I need not beg your pardon for speaking so freely. You like circumlocution no more than do I! Although, I suppose at present you cannot remember either way?'

'No, ma'am,' he replied, smiling. 'But that in no way diminishes my appreciation of your strategy.'

'And the horse riding?' asked April, unimpressed by how easily her grandmother had won Hugh over. 'What possible reason could you have to force me onto a horse?'

'Why, a very good one, of course!' replied Mrs Delamer. 'Hugh's nutty on horseflesh – he owns two stud farms, did you know? – so clearly it would be advantageous for his wife to conquer her irrational fear of horses.'

April's eyes glittered with indignation.

Preempting her eruption, Hugh said in a self-deprecating way: 'Surely you must be out there, ma'am? I'd be an unpardonably self-absorbed numbskull to expect my wife to share my eccentricities. And I hope to God I'm not that!'

'No, my boy, you're not,' agreed Mrs Delamer. 'It was worth a try, nonetheless!'

'Well then, now that you have explained yourself to Hugh's satisfaction, if not my own,' April remarked loftily, 'I will leave you to continue this fascinating conversation without me.'

She tried to walk away from her position by the bed, but Hugh's hand shot out and pulled her down onto the mattress beside him.

'What do you think you're doing?' she protested. 'You cannot manhandle me whenever you wish! I'm not your. . .'

'Oh, love, we came as soon as we heard!' cried Lady Hartwood, walking into the room, closely followed by Lord Paisley.

'Hello, Mama,' April greeted her in a stoic voice.

'Are you unharmed?'

April tried to rise from the bed but Hugh's hand held her in place. She had no wish to engage in a vulgar tussle with him in front of an audience so allowed him to have his way; much to the amusement of Mrs Delamer and Lord Wulfingston, who had moved to stand by the window to make room for the new arrivals.

'Yes, Mama, I am unharmed. Hugh was the only one to be hit on the head. . . and what a tiresome injury it's proving to be!' said April, throwing him an exasperated look.

'Oh, your poor head!' exclaimed her ladyship, walking over to the bed. 'What a nasty bump you have, Hugh-dear – does it pain you?'

'Yes, ma'am,' he admitted docilely.

Lady Hartwood put a hand on his forehead.

'You are a *little* colder than I would like, but certainly nothing as serious as I feared from that terrible note we received. To be knocked on the head and left in the snow for near enough an hour –I shudder every time I think about it!'

'Did you come in the carriage?' asked April. 'I think it would be prudent to take Hugh back to the house as soon as possible.'

'No, too much snow, my dear,' Lord Paisley answered her. 'We rode over.'

April noticed for the first time that they were all in their riding clothes.

'But how will we get him back?' she asked, looking from one to the other. 'He won't be able to ride for days.'

'I suppose he must remain here until then,' said Lord Paisley, his unconcerned manner putting April a little out of charity with him.

'And who, pray, is to nurse him?' she asked.

'Don't you worry, my dear, the boy was a soldier and can take care of himself! And I expect the landlady here will look in on him now and then. How are you feeling, Hugh?' he asked, coming forwards to take a good look at his nephew.

'Lord Paisley is your uncle,' April informed Hugh helpfully. 'Albert, I must tell you, he has lost his memory and although Mrs Hobb does not believe there is any permanent damage, I cannot feel comfortable leaving him here alone. One of us must stay behind with him.'

'That bourgeois name again,' grumbled Lord Wulfingston. 'I tell you, I won't allow my grandson to be doctored by anyone who goes by the name of *Hobb*. A proper physician must be sent for and at once!'

'In this weather?' said Mrs Delamer mildly. 'You may have an aversion to their name, Barnaby – although for the life of me I cannot imagine why! – but, I assure you, the Hobbs are excellent people and I wouldn't cavil to leave Hugh in their care. My physician must certainly be called, but it would be unreasonable to expect him to ride over until the storm has passed.'

'It seems to me,' put in Hugh, 'that you should all be hurrying off before the storm hits.'

'Perhaps you are right, Hugh-dear,' agreed Lady Hartwood. 'We would not want to be stranded here without so much as an overnight bag between... us... good gracious, love, what in the world are you wearing?' she expostulated suddenly, distracted by the garish garment swathing her daughter. 'It really is quite *hideous*.'

'It's a dressing gown, Mama, and I'm most thankful for it! My clothing was wet and Mrs Hobb was kind enough to lend it to me.'

'Oh! Well, in that case, I perfectly understand... only, one cannot help but wish those green and white checks were not *quite* so bold.' Lowering her voice, she added: 'And also, love, if you must wear a dressing gown in public, perhaps it is not quite the thing to be sitting on a gentleman's bed and holding his hand while you do so. *I* may not mind in this instance – in fact, nothing pleases me more! – but we cannot expect others to take so lenient a view of the matter.'

April rolled her eyes expressively and said with a good deal of annoyance: 'He will not allow me to move from this spot! And don't you lie there laughing at me, you devil! You should be defending me to my mother since you know very well I speak nothing but the truth!'

Hugh turned a soulful expression on her ladyship and said: 'Ma'am, my head is hurting something fierce and it does me a great deal of good to have my wife by my side.'

'Your *wife*!' exclaimed Lady Hartwood and looked from him to her daughter with blank astonishment. 'But. . . *already*? How is this possible?'

April instantly bristled.

'It is not possible! But I'd like to know, Mama, what you mean when you say *already*?'

Before her ladyship was forced to answer this home question, three more persons walked into the already crowded bedchamber.

Mrs Starling, her daughter and Mr Kepling came to a halt just inside the threshold, unable to progress further. While her young companions remained silent and looked decidedly ill at ease, Mrs Starling boldly scanned the room until her eyes settled on Hugh.

'Oh, thank the Lord, he is alive,' she uttered with profound relief.

'Of course, he's alive!' retorted Mrs Delamer, looking down her nose at the matron as if a particularly unpleasant odour was emanating from her. 'I distinctly remember telling you there was no reason to think otherwise.'

April attempted to pull her hand from Hugh's grip and rise but he simply winked at her and would not allow it.

'Welcome!' he addressed the new arrivals in a cheerful voice. 'And who might you be?'

All three gaped at him with stunned expressions.

'The poor boy has lost his memory,' Lady Hartwood explained, taking pity on them. 'You must not mind if he does not recognise you at present.'

'It's not their place to mind!' said Mrs Delamer. 'I believe I made it quite clear there was no need for them to ride over.'

Miss Starling and Mr Kepling quailed a little at this attack.

Mrs Starling, despite her assumed frailty, was made from a firmer mould and would not allow a few barbed remarks to sway her from her course.

'With all due respect, Mrs Delamer,' she said in her superior voice, 'my daughter is currently Mr Royce's fiancée, and as such has as much right as anyone else in this room to be here.'

'But she won't be his fiancée for long!' Mr Kepling spoke up, placing a protective arm around Miss Starling's shoulders.

'Alfred, please,' Mrs Starling checked him gently. 'It is quite true, however. My daughter has decided that she and Mr Royce will not suit. And that being the case, I counselled her it was her duty to advise Mr Royce at the earliest opportunity.'

Lord Wulfingston eyed her with a satirical twist of his mouth.

'In case my grandson should be so inconsiderate as to die from his injuries whilst still engaged,' he observed blandly. 'Thus plunging your daughter into an inconvenient period of mourning, just when she should be announcing her engagement to Claredon's heir. . . I believe that is what you mean to say, is it not, madam?'

This ruthlessly correct summation of the matter disconcerted Mrs Starling sufficiently to cause her to lose some of her tranquility.

'Why, nothing of the sort. . . I do assure you.'

His lordship uttered a rude 'Ha!' in response.

Mustering her reserves, Mrs Starling looked pointedly at the bed, where Hugh's hand gripped April's on top of the covers.

'Whatever my daughter's reasons may be, I can see with my own eyes that she has made the right decision,' she said waspishly.

'I am a loose-screw after all,' Hugh remarked. 'I appear to have a wife *and* a fiancée.'

April turned to stare at him, a slight crease between her brows.

Something about his remark prodded at her memory. Her suspicion was further aroused by the fact that he had the look of a man enjoying a good joke.

'Wife!' cried Mrs Starling, startled. 'Are you telling me, Mr Royce, that you are so lost to all sense of propriety as to have married Miss Hartwood whilst being engaged to my daughter?'

'That is certainly not the case,' April assured her, casting a warning glance at Hugh. 'Without his memory, Mr Royce has simply drawn an incorrect conclusion and at present his mind is enfeebled and cannot comprehend the truth.'

'Then, you are not my wife?' asked the shameless invalid, looking shaken. 'But you kissed me so soundly, what was I to think?'

April could have easily given him another whack on the head at this point. She no longer doubted he was amusing himself at their expense.

'That is only his injury speaking,' she insisted. 'I trust you'll pay no heed to the bizarre things he may say! We do not expect him to make a full recovery for quite some time.'

In some nebulous way Mrs Starling sensed she was being misled and, thinking herself to be the butt of some joke, her bosom swelled with indignation.

'I see it is useless to expect rational conversation in this room,' she uttered in accents of grave displeasure. 'Mr Royce, I cannot tell you how relieved I am that my daughter will not be aligning herself with your family. I have said all I have to say on the subject. Come, Luella, come, Alfred.'

On that valedictory note, she swept out of the room with her nose in the air and the long skirt of her riding habit swishing behind her.

Miss Starling, however, did not follow her immediately. She glanced at Mr Kepling for support, and, seeming to take comfort from his smile, approached the bed.

'Thank you, Mr Royce,' she said, taking off her engagement ring and giving it back to him. 'I am conscious of the honour you did me by asking for my hand. And I believe I owe you an apology, sir. . . for. . . kissing you,' she forced out, blushing. 'It was badly done of me. I hope you will be able to forgive me when you regain your memory?'

'I don't believe that will be a problem,' said Hugh, smiling at her kindly.

She visibly relaxed and smiled back.

'And I hope you will both be very happy,' she said, looking across at April.

'Oh, you need not think. . . ' began April.

'And you too, Miss Starling,' Hugh said over the top of his captive. 'Kepling, you are to be congratulated! The best man won in this instance.'

'I see you have remembered their names,' April muttered darkly.

'Did I?' he responded with a look of great innocence. 'Someone must have mentioned them.'

'No, they did not!'

Oblivious to this exchange, Mr Kepling stepped forward to shake hands with his former rival with the utmost of good will, his natural affability having reasserted itself as soon as he had secured his prize.

Next, he embarrassed April by wishing her all the happiness in the world with touching sincerity; and, after taking punctilious leave of the remaining occupants of the room, he placed a hand on Miss Starling's back and led her out of the room.

Forty-Nine

'Good riddance!' declared Lord Wulfingston. 'I don't know what windmills you had in your head, Lucille, when you invited them to stay with you?'

'Whatever windmills they were, they were most effective!' replied Mrs Delamer. 'Did you think I invited them for my own enjoyment? I'll have you know, Barnaby, they served my purpose admirably! Although I admit, as it turned out, the final part of my plan for them was superfluous. Mr Kepling's timely stumbling onto the scene made it unnecessary for me to orchestrate Miss Starling's denouement.'

'Good God, I shudder to think what you had in mind for the poor girl!' exclaimed April.

'Oh, nothing too drastic! I was only going to add a little something to her punch, and the duke's, and put them together in his bed to be discovered by a group of us. Hugh would then have been perfectly justified in breaking off his ridiculous engagement.'

April stiffened at this casual recounting of such a reprehensible plot. And even Hugh, who had been enjoying himself until this point, was looking stern.

Lord Wulfingston, however, was all admiration.

'Lucille, you always had a genius for intrigue!' he said, taking hold of her gloved hand and kissing it passionately. 'I can see life with you will never be dull.'

'Well, I for one think it appalling,' April cut in on this touching interlude.

'And I know I risk sounding like a dull-dog,' said Hugh, 'but I almost wish you had not been so busy on my account, ma'am, and had trusted me to take care of my own business.'

'Poof!' expostulated Mrs Delamer. 'If I had waited until you bestirred yourself, you would have woken up one day to find yourself riveted to a tediously starched-up girl. She would have bored you within a month of your wedding vows!'

Having come to much the same conclusion over the last few weeks, Hugh had no reply to make to this masterful put-down.

'How can you give in to her so meekly?' April reproached him. 'You will only be encouraging her to be even more outrageous in future! And you, Grandmama, did you consider that His Grace – an innocent party in all this – would have been put in the unconscionable position of having to marry Miss Starling had your plan succeeded?'

'I would have hushed up the matter and he would have escaped unscathed – nothing to get on your high ropes about, child!'

'He would not have escaped if Miss Starling's mother had anything to say in the matter! She would have liked nothing better than to have secured a duke for her daughter.'

Mrs Delamer's smile took on a sly quality.

'Not if she thought the duke had suffered a delicate injury in his youth that made it impossible for him to sire children.'

'And did he suffer such an injury?' asked April, fascinated despite herself.

'Once I dropped a word in his ear, His Grace immediately perceived the benefit of adopting the story. That young man does not lack imagination! Which cannot be said for most of the people one meets in these sadly puritan times.'

The clearing of a throat focused everyone's attention on the landlord as he walked in carrying a bottle of brandy and one glass.

'Begging pardon for the interruption. I've got what you asked for, sir,' he told Hugh, putting the bottle and glass on the bedside table.

Lord Paisley's interest was piqued and he asked: 'Nantes brandy, is it?'

'Yes, sir,' replied the landlord. 'The best I've had for quite some time, if I do say so!'

'Well then, man, what do you mean by bringing up only one glass?' said his lordship in affronted accents.

'I'll fetch some more right away,' said Mr Hobb, bowing and hurrying out of the room.

'I wouldn't want you all to think that I don't appreciate this vigil by my bedside,' Hugh addressed his elders with an ironic expression, 'but the sky has darkened considerably over the last few minutes. I expect you only have a short time left before the snow arrives.'

'I think the boy's trying to get rid of us,' chuckled Lord Paisley. 'Can't for the life of me think why!'

'Wants to be alone with his *wife*, no doubt,' Lord Wulfingston joined in the ribbing.

Father and son, for once in harmony, laughed heartily at this joke.

'But we do not even know if he has proposed to her,' Lady Hartwood pointed out.

'If he hasn't, he will soon enough,' remarked Mrs Delamer.

'I'd greatly appreciate it,' said Hugh in a lethally dry voice, 'if you would all leave me to take care of my own proposal.'

'You're taking your time about it!' said his grandfather.

'It may have escaped your notice, sir, but I was an engaged man until a few minutes ago.'

'I wish you would all stop talking in this ridiculous way,' April said crossly, her colour greatly heightened. 'If any of you think I want a proposal from a man not in his right mind, who may or may not have lost his memory...'

'How can you doubt it?' interjected Hugh, looking hurt.

'...then you are all as insane as he is!'

'Perhaps we *should* leave now,' said Lady Hartwood, noting the signs of her daughter's rising temper. 'Only, love, you will have to come with us. I cannot leave you here without a chaperone, even if you are staying with your fiancé.'

'He is not my fiancé!' April all but shouted.

'Of course not,' agreed her ladyship soothingly. 'I simply misspoke.'

'Forgive me, Mama, I did not mean to raise my voice,' said April contritely, rubbing a hand across her brow. 'It has been a most trying day. I will be only too happy to walk back to the house as soon as the storm has passed, but *nothing* will induce me to ride. So until I can escape this den of iniquity, we must hope Hugh is sufficiently incapacitated and will be incapable of losing control of his baser urges.'

'*Baser urges?*' Hugh murmured, lifting an eyebrow.

An inappropriate giggle threatened to erupt, but she suppressed and whispered: 'Shh, you wretch!'

'Really, love, such an *indelicate* turn of phrase,' objected Lady Hartwood. 'But I know you are merely jesting. No one could ever think dear Hugh would act in such a manner! Still, if anyone were to find out that you had stayed here alone with him, your reputation would be in shreds.'

'No one will find out. And quite frankly, if it will spare me from getting back onto a horse, I don't care if they do.'

Just then Mr Hobb returned with the additional glasses, as well as the intelligence that the snow storm had hit at last and it did not look as if anyone would be leaving the inn for some time.

'Did the gentleman and two ladies who were here earlier ride out?' Mrs Delamer asked him.

'No need for you to worry over them, ma'am. I'm happy to say I managed to convince them not to set out. I could see there'd be no time for them to make it back before the snow arrived. I've settled them downstairs in the parlour with some refreshments.'

'How diligent of you,' observed Lord Wulfingston without appreciation. 'We're now trapped here with *that woman*.' He turned a jaundiced eye on his grandson. 'The fact that you were willing to accept her as your mother-in-law, Hugh, gives me a very poor opinion of your intellect.'

'It was his intellect that got him into trouble in the first place,' said Mrs Delamer. 'One cannot rely solely on logic when choosing a partner. If he had used his instincts we could have avoided the farce of the last few months... although, had that been the case, I suppose we would have missed out a great deal of entertainment!'

'I'm delighted to have provided you with so much amusement,' said Hugh.

Mrs Delamer laughed unrepentantly, and, turning to the landlord, asked: 'Do you have room to put us all up, Hobb? The storm may well continue into the night.'

'Certainly, Mrs Delamer,' he replied, happy to be able to satisfy her on this point. 'And you need not worry that we won't be able to make you all comfortable. I've already set my boys to getting the guest rooms ready. And Mrs Hobb bade me tell you, you're welcome to share our Christmas dinner. She was in a bit of a twitter at first, thinking there'd not be enough to go round,' he imparted loquaciously, 'but she discovered some nice pig trotters in the larder, and plans to kill more chickens besides, so while it won't be a grand meal you need not fear it'll be a meagre one.'

'I detest pig trotters!' announced Lord Wulfingston.

April and her mother, both equally appalled at such poor manners, rushed to reassure the landlord.

'Please tell Mrs Hobb we would be *most* grateful for whatever food she can find for us!' said Lady Hartwood.

'And let her know how sorry we are to be such a bother to her,' added April.

'I say, this brandy is uncommonly good!' Lord Paisley informed his companions, and took another sip from the glass he had poured out for himself. 'You must try some, sir. Here, take mine!'

Lord Wulfingston accepted his glass and, taking a healthy slug, closed his eyes and swilled the brandy around his mouth before swallowing.

'Not bad at all!' he agreed. 'The brandy may be the only thing to make our stay here tolerable.'

'Why don't you take the bottle downstairs with you?' suggested Hugh.

'I refuse to share a parlour with that rabbit-faced woman! What other room can you offer us?' Lord Wulfingston asked the landlord.

'I suppose I could place your lordship in the public room,' Mr Hobb said uncertainly. 'I can't say it'll be as comfortable as the parlour, mind, but we've no other guests staying so it'll be entirely at your disposal.'

'It will have to do!' Turning to Mrs Delamer, Lord Wulfingston said in quite a different voice: 'Will you join me, m'dear? We can resurrect that drinking game with the lit brandy that you invented in Paris – if these old bones allow me!'

'Our will alone can overcome whatever limitations time has imposed on us,' she replied with an intimate smile, sliding a hand up his well-muscled shoulder.

'So it shall, m'dear, so it shall.' Something unspoken passed between them as he held her gaze. After a few moments, he went on: 'And if we find ourselves in need of further amusement, we can attempt to teach the game to your daughter and my stolid son – now *that* would be a sight to see!'

'Whatever can you mean?' Lady Hartwood laughed nervously. 'I am not Mrs Delamer's *daughter.*'

'He is entirely in my confidence, Eleanor,' her mother informed her in a nonchalant manner.

'Oh. . . h-he is?' stammered her ladyship, thrown into acute discomfort. Her eyes travelled slowly to Lord Paisley. 'Oh, Albert, I *wanted* to tell you!' she said wretchedly. 'Truly, I did! I hope you can forgive me, dearest?'

Lord Paisley took her fluttering hands into his own.

'My love, you need not be so distressed. Will you think me unpardonably sly if I admit I've suspected it for some time? I did hope you would trust me with the truth one day, but it was not for me to rush you when you were clearly not ready to explain it all to me.'

Tears glistened in Lady Hartwood's eyes and she said in a constricted way: 'I must be the luckiest woman alive!'

And then, discarding all the proper constraint expected of her, she flung her arms around Lord Paisley's neck and kissed him with no thought for their audience.

'Yes, yes, very touching,' Lord Wulfingston uttered impatiently, 'but that's quite enough! Come Albert, and bring the brandy.' Taking Mrs Delamer's arm, he steered her out of the room, saying on a chuckle: 'Who'd have thought our children would make a match of it, eh? Two generations at that!'

'I've had my eye on Hugh for some time, if you must know,' she replied. 'But he's a Royce. Your son was a different matter, and quite unforeseen! I was not at all reconciled to it at first – as you can well imagine! If only they knew what happened in Paris all those years ago. . .'

As their voices faded away, Lady Hartwood pulled out of Lord Paisley's arms and said excitedly: 'Dearest, I have only just realised that *three* generations of our families will soon be bound in matrimony! How delightful it will be! Do you think that perhaps we should plan a triple wedding?'

'Mama, I beg you, *stop*,' groaned April and buried her face in her hands.

'Of course, love, you are quite right. It is too soon to speak of such things. Perhaps over dinner?'

She offered Hugh an incorrigible, twinkling look and, linking arms with Lord Paisley, exited the room.

Fifty

April was painfully conscious of the fact that she had been left alone with Hugh, and, lowering her hands from her face, discovered a sudden fascination with the pattern of her dressing gown.

Hugh seemed content with the silence that followed, and when at last she ventured to look at him she saw that he was watching her with a smile in his eyes.

'When did your memory return?' she asked reproachfully. 'Or was it all a sham?'

'It wasn't a sham in the beginning, I can promise you that!' he replied. 'I woke up not knowing who I was, or anything about my life – it was a devil of a state to find myself in!'

'At what point did you remember?'

He hesitated.

'When you told me you had ridden the horse,' he admitted with a rueful look. 'My memories came flooding back. . . and then, all I could think about was, how in God's name did you manage to go near a horse, let alone mount one?'

'But that was *before* you kissed me! The part where you thought I was your wife, was that all pretence?'

'No. . . well, not entirely,' he amended. 'Our landlord referred to you as my wife and as I had no memory at that point I had no reason to doubt him. And when my memory returned, I realised it was just the excuse I needed to cast aside all the damned inconvenient reasons that have held me back for weeks.'

'For weeks? How can that be?' she asked, colouring. 'I never realised.'

'You must have?' he said, raising a hand to stroke her cheek.

'But I did not! On a couple of occasions I did think you *might* have a slight preference for me, but there were plenty of other times when I thought you disapproved of me quite amazingly!'

'My darling girl, I've been in love with you from the very first night I met you!'

April laughed uncertainly.

'You mean you fell in love with my face,' she remarked, turning away.

Hugh took a firm hold of her shoulders and compelled her to look at him.

'I didn't say *from the first moment* so you can acquit me of that! It has never been about your face – never! Do you understand?'

She nodded mutely, unable to break free from the force his gaze exerted on her.

'I had some suspicion I was in danger when we were first introduced,' he went on. 'You gave me leave to call you *Hugh* – do you remember? – and then offered me the sweetest smile I'd ever seen! But I was certain of it by the time you tried to convince me of your frivolous and mercenary nature over dinner. And all the while your hairpins were losing their battle and a knot of hair was sliding down your head, until it sat charmingly over one ear... *that* was the moment I knew I was lost.'

'Do you mean to say,' she said in an incredulous voice, 'that you fell in love with me when I was acting mercenary and frivolous and my hair was in a mess? You must be out of your mind!'

He offered her a lopsided smile.

'I thought so too.'

She continued to regard him in an amazed way.

'But I was so certain – especially over dinner! – that you disapproved of me.'

'If that was the impression I gave you, forgive me! It didn't take me long to see through your act and realise it was an attempt to antagonise me.'

'It was,' she conceded, smiling. 'But, in my defence, you were acting odiously cool and judgmental.'

'I was trying my hardest to remain detached and in control of my reaction to you – although a lot of good that did me! After weeks of doing my best to keep you at a proper distance, it has become abundantly clear that it's a pointless endeavour. And I'm damn-well sick of fighting it! So if you don't agree to marry me, I'll probably end up following you about like a lovelorn fool until I wear you down. It would be easier on you in the long run to simply say yes to me now.'

Her eyes widened with a sense of the magnitude of the moment.

'Hugh, are you proposing to me?'

'Clearly I didn't do it properly if you must ask,' he said with a sudden grin. 'But I've never been one for making flowery speeches. The only way to make you understand is to show you.'

'No, please don't!' she said agitatedly, putting her hands on his chest to stop him from pulling her towards him.

'What is it?' he asked, sobering.

She looked torn for a moment, and then sighed.

'How can you be certain I won't be marrying you simply to rid myself of the mortgage on St Mawes? That is what people will think. And I could not bear it if one day you began to doubt me... it would break me.'

'They're more likely to say I bought a title for my son and got a better deal than you,' he said pragmatically.

She regarded him with an arrested expression.

'Yes, that is true! My son will be the next Baron Hartwood. I had not considered that.'

'These nameless hordes that have you worried will certainly consider it, and we'll both be seen to be making a prudent connection – if you care for that nonsense, which I don't!'

'And you won't mind if we spend part of the year in Cornwall? The estate will require my ongoing attention and I cannot...'

'I look forward to it!'

She was momentarily nonplussed and could only stare at him.

'Oh, but I forgot!' she exclaimed, looking dejected all of a sudden. 'Everyone will know you do not covet a mere barony for your son when you are set to inherit the Marquisate of Talbott one day.'

'That may be, however, they will also know that I've always had an abiding wish to own a castle,' Hugh rallied.

A tremulous smile hovered about her lips.

'That is simply not true, is it?'

'Sweetheart, I'll come up with whatever story you want to satisfy the hordes, as long as *you* understand I could never doubt you. What you don't seem to realise is that I know you're not indifferent to me.'

'You do?'

'Unequivocally.' He stroked away a curl that had fallen over her eye. 'I've never been more certain of anything in my life.'

'That is terribly immodest of you... but, as it happens, you are correct,' she informed his shoulder. 'I am as far away removed from being indifferent to you as is humanly possible.'

'Why, Miss Hartwood, are you trying to tell me that you love me?'

She lifted her eyes to his, accepting her fate at last.

'I believe I am.'

The intensity in Hugh's gaze returned and he pulled her towards him... but once again she resisted.

'No, please wait! There is one more thing you must know about me!'

Hugh was strongly inclined to tell her that nothing she could say could keep him away from her, but he held his tongue for he could see she needed to unburden herself.

'You think me a mere girl of three and twenty.' She paused and looked down to where her hands were braced against his chest. 'But what you cannot know is that Mrs Delamer...'

'Your grandmother,' he corrected.

'Hmm?' She looked back up at him. 'Oh...yes, my grandmother. But that is an entirely different story so please don't interrupt!'

'Yes, ma'am,' he replied meekly.

'And you accuse *me* of levity!' she grumbled. 'As I was saying, Mrs Delamer thought it necessary that I assume a younger age, and I, fool that I am, allowed her to convince me.' She took a deep breath, and then continued in a rush: 'I know it will come as something of a shock to you but the truth is I am almost *nine and twenty*!'

'Well, thank God for that,' he returned instantly. 'You don't know how many sleepless nights I've had thinking I was too old for you.'

'Fibber,' she said, her lovely smile blooming. 'How can you say such a thing when Miss Starling is younger still and you clearly had no concerns in her case?'

'And see what an error of judgment that turned out to be? But I've learnt my lesson. Only a mature woman of nine and twenty will do for me.'

'*Almost* nine and twenty.'

'Sweetheart, I wouldn't care if you were nine and forty,' he said, suddenly serious. Taking her right hand, he moved it a few inches until it lay over his heart. 'We are meant to be together. I can feel it here.'

This time, when Hugh drew her towards him, she had no more resistance left to offer.

'*Ahem*...I hope I am not intruding?' the Duke of Claredon's voice asked from the doorway.

April lifted her head and smiled at her friend in welcome.

Hugh was not so complacent.

'What the devil are *you* doing here?' he demanded in a voice pushed beyond endurance.

'I thought it preferable to ride over, risking life and limb, than to spend an afternoon in the company of Mrs Bolton without reinforcements – delightful though she is! Had I been forced to hear the words '*My dear duke, do tell me...*' one more time, I fear I would have been driven to do her bodily harm – and you must agree that would not have been at all the thing! But there is only so much impertinent interest in my love life that I can be expected to tolerate with an assumption of docility. And so, here I am!'

'In other words, you ran away,' said Hugh, patently unsympathetic.

'If we must shine such an uncompromising light on it, then, yes,' agreed His Grace.

'Well, I for one am glad to see you, Eustace,' said April. 'I know it will come as no great surprise to you but I am to be married!'

'Did I propose after all? My shocking memory! I have no recollection of it.'

'Fiend! You know very well you did not.'

'Ah, you relieve my mind! Then, may I take it that this is not a scene of ravishment, as I had supposed, but a formal proposal?'

'Yes, you may,' she replied, smiling radiantly from within the circle of Hugh's arms.

'I cannot tell you how happy I am to hear you say so! Had it been otherwise I would have been obliged to challenge Mr Royce to a duel,' he said prosaically. 'And although I have a deep aversion to the sight of blood, for your sake, fair Aphrodite, I would have exerted myself and muddled through the affair.'

'Would you really have fought a duel for my honour?' she asked, surprised and rather touched.

He offered her a frank smile, his affectations momentarily stripped away.

'Of course, my dear. Can you doubt it?'

Hugh had listened to this exchange with what he considered to be a good deal of patience, however, this was now at an end.

'I'm gratified to know you've reached the conclusion that April is in no danger of being ravished – if you and my grandfather are to be believed, I seem to have earned myself a reputation of which I was not aware! And now, I'd be obliged to you if you'd be so good as to close the door on your way out. And tell anyone else who fancies bursting into my room that they'll have me to answer to!'

'Of course, I perfectly understand you,' said His Grace. 'Only, before I go, I must confess I was sent upstairs by Lady Hartwood to tell you that she expects her daughter downstairs within the next fifteen minutes.' His lips curved in amusement as he added: 'There was some discussion between your elders on whether ten or fifteen minutes should be fixed upon as the limit. They finally reached agreement that fifteen minutes is unlikely to prove. . . *ruinous.*'

'I don't know whether to take that as a compliment or not?' remarked Hugh, doing his best to keep a straight face.

'Allow me to clarify,' said His Grace obligingly. 'It was generally thought that the time would have had to be reduced to five minutes had you been in full health.'

Hugh let out a shout of laughter and winced as pain shot through his head.

'Please tell my mother I will be down directly,' April said in a choked voice. 'Thank you, Eustace.'

His Grace bowed gracefully and, still grinning, quit the room.

'Not *directly*,' said Hugh. 'We have fifteen minutes and I intend to use every last second!'

'I suppose I should be heartened to know your family is just as likely to put me to blush as my own,' she said, smiling. 'How appalling of them to discuss us in such a way! I'm tempted to stay in your room indefinitely to teach them a lesson.'

'Is that the only reason you're tempted?'

April's smile faded a little.

'No,' she admitted shyly.

Placing his hands on either side of her face, Hugh drew her nearer.

'This better be a short engagement, sweetheart,' he murmured against her lips. 'If my patience is tried too far I'll be forced to abduct you and to hell with them all!'

'But are we not going to wait for the triple wedding my mother has set her heart on?' she teased.

'Good God, no!' he replied with a grimace. 'You know how fond I am of your mother, but I'll be damned if I'll share our wedding with anyone.'

'Abduction it is then,' she sighed contentedly.

Hugh grunted his approval, and then seized her lips in a kiss that spoke of love, desire, and possession. . . enough to fill a whole lifetime.

THE END

Dear Reader

I hope you had as much fun reading APHRODITE as I had writing it! I would be very grateful if you would share the love and leave a rating and/or a review on Amazon and Goodreads so that other readers can find my books. Thank you!

xDG

DGRampton.com
Facebook.com/DGRampton
Instagram.com/fortheloveofjaneausten

The Regency Goddesses Series

The novels in the Regency Goddesses series are standalone and can be enjoyed in any order. They share only one minor character (have you spotted them yet?).

Chronological order:

Artemisia – Book 1 (1812)
Aphrodite – Book 2 (1820)
Aurora – Book 3 (1821)

"Delightful, funny and filled with clever conversation. Two thumbs up!"
A. Sockwell

"There are so few Regency novels that are this well-written, with such strong characters, a good plot and sexy, but clean relationships."
C. Sparks

"An enthralling Regency romp full of endearing and meddlesome characters, a stubborn hero and heroine, and hilariously entertaining mix-ups and tangles!"
Austenesque Reviews

"Truly witty, delightful characters .... the author has mastered the art of satire with a heart."
Dragonlady

ARTEMISIA

#1 Amazon Best Seller, British Historical Literature

'You forget yourself, your lordship. You have no rights to allow or disallow anything I may choose to do. You have, in fact, no claim over me whatsoever – a circumstance for which I thank the Lord on a daily basis! I am not your ward, or your dependent, and I will not allow you to speak to me in that odiously overbearing fashion!'

High-spirited Artemisia Grantley, niece to the Duke of Wentworth, has never made any attempt to conform to the feminine ideal expected of a lady of quality; nor has she ever had the benefit of an unfavourable opinion formed against her. But when the Marquess of Chysm enters her life, it seems to her that his lordship is always at hand to witness her shortcomings and bring them to her attention.

As she reluctantly embarks upon her first London Season, a scandalous family secret and a conspiracy that stretches all the way to Napoleonic France threaten to entangle her with the one person she could happily throttle.

AURORA

#2 Amazon Hot New Release (Australia)

"I think the women of your acquaintance have done you a great disservice by allowing you to continue in your deceit. Perhaps next time you meet a lady you will not be so quick to think she is only interested in fortune and matrimony!"

Miss Aurora Wesley is a lady who never allows a seemingly insurmountable problem to overwhelm her. Blessed with irrepressible optimism and ingenuity, she knows how to set about achieving her goals without the burden of excessive scruples. Whether it is establishing a brother to his rightful place in society, rescuing a young heiress from the clutches of her guardian, or match-making for a reticent spinster, Aurora has her hands full sorting out other people's lives, with little thought for her own.

Until, after one extraordinary encounter, she discovers an overmastering desire to amuse herself by provoking the formidable Duke of Rothworth and turning his well-ordered, respectable existence on its head.

An Adaptation of North and South

ELIZABETH GASKELL

NORTH AND SOUTH – A Victorian Romance (exclusive to Kindle)

Brought to you by Manor House Books, this classic novel has been adapted for a modern readership by bestselling historical romance author D.G. Rampton.

Set in Victorian England, North and South by Elizabeth Gaskell was first published in 1854. This adaptation stays true to the dramatic social commentary of the original, while bringing into greater prominence the love story at its core, which is reminiscent of Jane Austen's Pride and Prejudice.

Uprooted from her idyllic existence in the South of England, Margaret Hale moves with her family to an industrial town in the North, where she develops a passionate sense of social justice upon witnessing the hardships suffered by the local mill workers. Her views often bring her into conflict with wealthy mill-owner John Thornton, who befriends her family. But their turbulent relationship masks a deep attraction that cannot be subdued, and a bond that only strengthens when tested by the vagaries of fate.

Made in the USA
Las Vegas, NV
16 November 2024

11949436R00177